# PAUL IS DEAD

## ALSO BY C.C. BENISON

*Death at Buckingham Palace*

*Death at Sandringham House*

*Death at Windsor Castle*

*Death in Cold Type*

*Twelve Drummers Drumming*

*Eleven Pipers Piping*

*Ten Lords A-Leaping*

# PAUL IS DEAD

A NOVEL

C.C. BENISON

Signature EDITIONS

Cover design by Doowah Design.
Photo of author by Cynthia Bettencourt.

This book was printed on Ancient Forest Friendly paper.
Printed and bound in Canada by Hignell Book Printing Inc.

We acknowledge the support of the Canada Council for the Arts and the Manitoba Arts Council for our publishing program.

Library and Archives Canada Cataloguing in Publication

Benison, C. C., author

Paul is dead / C.C. Benison.

Issued in print and electronic formats.

ISBN 978-1-77324-031-2 (softcover).--ISBN 978-1-77324-032-9 (EPUB)

I. Title.

PS8553.E5135P38 2018 C813'.54 C2018-905152-3
C2018-905153-1

Signature Editions
P.O. Box 206, RPO Corydon, Winnipeg, Manitoba, R3M 3S7
www.signature-editions.com

Nov 20/18 12.97

# 1

Later, when Lydia makes her living as an editor, she'll think about Briony's words as if they were set in a novel she might be revising. She will add an ellipsis.

" ... Paul is dead," she will have the character Briony say, which is correct.

But now, on this waning Friday afternoon, October 31, 1969, in this unimaginary world, Lydia is paying little attention to the real Briony's patter. Her thoughts are interned elsewhere and so her ears dial into Briony's three words as a simple declarative sentence. It terrifies her. She would italicize it, embolden it.

***"PAUL IS DEAD."***

And she cuts herself.

She's been peeling carrots over the sink under the kitchen window where the light is dying. The peeler twists, burying a razor edge into the side of her index finger, a hairbreadth from a fresh scar formed two months ago. The pain is instant. Shock shimmers along her skin. The peeler drops to the sink bottom among the vegetable peelings. Her knees buckle—feeling faint has lately been a new sensation—and she grips the side of the countertop with her other hand. She sees the thin line of bloody ooze bubbling along the cut and suppresses a scream.

Briony's been bent into the refrigerator, pushing beer bottles along the metal shelves, her conversation partly muffled by the rattling of glass and by the barrier of the door itself. Lydia's been peeling carrots, making crudités from assorted vegetables. Pigs-in-blankets cool in the refrigerator, as do celery sticks filled with blue cheese, and mushroom caps filled with bacon and crab. Though her stomach's queasy, she's readying a party for her friends as her mother would for hers. This is what she knows to do. She's never hosted her own party before. Didn't want to host this one, in fact. And in a few hours, she'll think her diligence absurd and pointless.

Lydia's parents are away for a few days, in Toronto, for a medical convention. Lydia's father is a surgeon. Lydia is an only child and she has the house to herself. They apply the usual caution—*no wild parties*—though they can't imagine she would have one. And Lydia very much wanted *not* to host a Halloween party—which is putting it mildly. But her friends knew Dr. and Mrs. Eadon would be absent. And Lydia realizes she needs to nip in the bud any notion that something is wrong.

As best she can, she's avoided her friends—Briony, Alanna and Alan, and, most particularly, Dorian—since those August days they were together at the Eadons' lake cottage. Her excuse? Fewer college courses, hence fewer seminars. Less need to be on campus. (Though she *was* cornered about Halloween in her single foray into the University College lounge.) She can get more work accomplished at home than in the gossipy library carrels, she explains. She slips into classrooms and slips out again. She's not carpooling this year. She takes the bus. She's a surgeon's daughter. She might have her own car, but her father doesn't indulge her with one.

But now Briony is poking her head above the refrigerator door. She's aware Lydia's offered little more than a greeting since she stepped into the kitchen five minutes ago. She's excused the silence because Lydia is absorbed in a task and her back is to her and the water is running. But Lydia's silences and absences have been part of a worrying pattern for many weeks, and now the water is roaring.

"Are you all right?" Briony sees Lydia's finger splitting the column of water. "Oh! You've cut yourself!"

"It's nothing," says Lydia. The water is frigid along her finger, pain upon pain, but it steels her for the question she must ask: "How do you know?"

"Know what? That Paul is dead?" Briony stares at Lydia's back, at the curtain of dark hair. "Where have you been, Lydia? I just told you. It's all over the news. It's silly anyway."

The cold water is not working. Lydia can feel the sick rising from her stomach, much as it did this morning, much as it has many mornings these last weeks. "Have they found the body?"

"The ... ?" Briony begins. She frowns and shuts the fridge door. As Lydia nurses her finger in the running water, she repeats the story—with some exasperation: Paul McCartney is dead, victim of a horrific car crash three years earlier, replaced by a doppelgänger, and mourned—but surreptitiously—by his bandmates. The clues are everywhere: encrypted in song lyrics and concealed in album cover art.

It's a hoax, of course, born on the fringe of some college campus, but it captures a zeitgeist and spreads with a peculiar power. Briony was debating it with Alan and Alanna this very morning at school. Briony had been reading an article in *Time*, until Alan, who thinks *Time* a house organ of U.S. imperialism, snatched it and threw it in the trash.

This time Lydia is all ears to Briony. Relief washes over her. Briony notes the effect. It's like watching the beach raft they had at the Eadons' cottage deflate at a puncture along the rock.

"What did you *think* I was talking about?" Briony asks. "Do we know another Paul?" She pauses. "You didn't think I was talking about that Paul Godwin, did you?"

Of course, that's exactly who Lydia thought Briony was talking about. The name has haunted her waking hours for two months. Paul Godwin—the stranger Dorian brought to Eadon Lodge.

"I don't know what I was thinking." She says this to her reflection, clear now in the darkening window glass.

"I'm getting you a bandage." Briony moves toward the hall off the kitchen. As she pushes through the door she glances back at the figure by the sink and has the funniest feeling: a sudden, unexpected, almost brutal, sense of doom that snatches her breath away before vanishing in swift release. She hesitates, shaken, but moves on.

Lydia sees Briony's reflection in the window glass, notes the shifts in her expression, watches as she passes through the door, her red hair swinging over the back of her buckskin jacket. Briony's wearing the same cinched-top jeans she'd had on that second-last day at Eadon

Lodge, that cool evening at the end of August when Lydia had agreed to drive her back to the city.

If only, Lydia thinks, as she will think again and again and again, she had driven Briony *into* the city and not pulled into Winnipeg Beach to put her on the bus. If only Briony's migraine, her excuse to leave Eadon Lodge, had been full-blown, then she would have broken the speed limit to get her to the darkness and solitude of her bedroom at home in the city. But it wasn't full-blown. Lydia knew her friend too well. She could recognize the signs, the glaze in Briony's grey-blue eyes, the pinprick pupils, the stiffening of her facial muscles, which had manifested themselves at puberty and would usher in days of agony. That last evening at Eadon Lodge Briony's eyes sparkled, for some reason, which Lydia couldn't interpret, and her face burned, not from the sun on her fair skin, but from some indeterminate cause, which Lydia—in that hour—didn't want to know. So she felt only a snippet of guilt stopping by the restaurant where the Greyhound waited and telling Briony the first of many lies.

It's a morning in early July, almost four decades later. The bedside phone is ringing, much too early, yanking Lydia from a disturbing, recurring dream, of frantic, hopeless searchings through shadowed corridors of some nameless decaying hospital.

Lydia lives in a different country now, in a different city, where outward reminders of her youth in Winnipeg are few. She and her parents travelled to San Francisco in mid-December 1969, to spend Christmas with her mother's cousin, Helen. But her parents, as planned, returned in the New Year. Lydia—and this was not planned—never came back, at least never to stay longer than a dutiful week or ten days.

Helen Clifford stood halfway in age between Lydia and her mother, but in attitude and outward appearance was closer to Lydia and her generation. Twelve years earlier, she, too, had fled town, after her graduation.

Helen told Lydia she could stay as long as she liked—forever, if she wished. She didn't know—and would never know—that but for the incident at Eadon Lodge Lydia's stay in San Francisco would have been the half-year hiatus Bibs and Marion Eadon expected it would be. Lydia would have returned home to finish her undergraduate degree and have her life move along an entirely other trajectory.

Lydia contrives never to visit Winnipeg in the summer when she might be obligated to visit Eadon Lodge. She finds excuses to avoid hometown weddings or class reunions, her chief claim—and it's true—that the fall publishing season means busy summers, so she can't get away from San Francisco. Even her father had the grace to die in February, but her mother dies in July, this July, for that's why Lydia's phone is ringing so early in the morning, a Saturday morning. Her mother's neighbour, troubled by the lack of activity at 350 Oxford Street, took her spare key, given for such emergencies, and let herself in. She found Marion cold in bed. In a moment, Lydia will receive that especially poignant piece of news, the death of one's mother, far away. Though she and her mother were not Hallmark close, Lydia will be shocked. Stunned, really. Only later will grief come over her with force. She will replace the receiver, turn in the bed to seek her husband's comfort, and whimper, remembering he was called to the other side of the world only a week ago. Then she will think, with a guilty twinge, that she inherits. Money and the house on Oxford Street. The timing is a mercy.

And then she will remember Eadon Lodge. She inherits that, too.

"If Ray can't get back from Japan, I'll come with you," Helen volunteers a few hours later, when a more composed Lydia reaches her preparing food for the Fourth of July barbeque. In the intervening years, Helen has grown sentimental about her birthplace. "Do you remember the wonderful beaches?" she once enthused after a return trip.

Lydia does remember, but doesn't say, as her only wish is to avoid the subject of cottages and cabins and beaches. She recalls going up on the train, once, when she was four or five years old, in the last days of train travel to the beach. Her father couldn't take them in the car for some reason, a medical emergency with one of his patients, likely, so she and her mother had taken the train to Gimli.

All Lydia remembers is a drenching rain when they disembarked, the sky and the land flat and grey. Somehow they found a cab, which took them east through the drab townscape, then north through a sodden curtain of trees shrouding tiny cottages until they reached a muddy rutted track. The route afforded no glimpse of the great prairie lake, Lake Winnipeg. Her mother sat in the gloom of the cab's interior, her face drawn, her lips pinched, her silence warning Lydia to keep hers. It's her first memory of Gimli, though her mother assured her in later years that her first visit was in the late summer of 1949, as a two-month-old, and that caring for a baby where running water doesn't exist is pure hell. All Lydia's life her mother calls the town "*Grim*li".

As a little girl, Lydia found Gimli dull. The cottage was isolated; her father, little communicative anyway, turned melancholic and remote, almost as if the annual two-week stay were a test of perseverance. Her mother grew frazzled and tetchy. There was never anyone to play with, unless Briony joined them, which she did—for one of the two weeks. Why, she asked her mother once after school, when she was about ten and realized her schoolmates spent their summers in places much more fun, did Grandpa Eadon build his cottage at *Grim*li?

"Well," her mother responded, lifting her eyelash curler and leaning into her vanity mirror, part of her *toilette* in anticipation of Bibs's suppertime arrival, "your grandfather was a bit of a character."

Lydia had heard this before, though no examples were ever proffered. At any rate, it was no explanation.

"But why?" she pressed.

Marion thought Henry Eadon, her father-in-law, a horrible, bitter man. Before marrying his son, worried that he might become a chip-off, she had a moment of cold feet. She was not unhappy when he dropped dead—straining on the toilet, it was surmised—soon after Lydia was born. She said none of this to her daughter, never did. Instead, she replied in time-honoured fashion: "Wait until your father comes home. You can ask him."

And, of course, Lydia was in bed asleep by the time her father returned late from the hospital, the question forgotten.

# 2

Dorian's outside, in the backyard, taking a long drag on a cigarette.

Smoking is the last of his vices, and he craves the rush of nicotine only in moments when a certain tension twitches along his nerves. He's out in the yard thinking about a choice he must make, though, really, it's a Hobson's choice.

He's quit smoking several times over the past forty years, without complete success. A pack and lighter are usually tucked in the junk drawer in the kitchen, which is where he headed while talking on the phone with his agent. He was in the act of pulling a ciggy from the pack—*indoors*—the phone cocked on his shoulder, when Mark came through, home early. Mark's eyes went straight to Dorian's hand.

Like Lydia in her parents' kitchen that October afternoon nearly four decades earlier, Dorian looks at the view—toward the tips of Vancouver's North Shore Mountains—but does not see. It might as easily be a scrim on stage or a set decoration. It's Charmaine's phone call: her news has set his life flickering through his mind, like the clicketty clack of old film stock or like the fade-to-black of a drowning man. He can't believe that life has brought him to this big house, this leafy neighbourhood, these comfortable, safe surroundings, this façade of respectability. "Bourgeois," Alan Rayner would have said—with a straight face. Dorian remembers Alan with no fondness.

He remembers Briony Telfer, too, and her hippie chatter. And the self-possessed Alanna Roth. And Lydia, of course, who became his co-conspirator.

And Paul.

He resists thinking about the five of them, but some association will snap him back. "I Am The Walrus" comes on the radio and his mind races to that sickening Halloween party at Lydia's—the last time he saw her.

He's learned—the hard way—to push them away. But he can never expel them from his dreams.

He returns his mind to the Vancouver garden, takes a last drag and flicks the butt over the fence into the neighbouring yard. A few moments later, Mark steps through the sliding doors onto the patio holding a martini glass in one hand and a tall tumbler in the other. Dorian catches a whiff of gin as Mark hands him his Pellegrino with ice and a slice of lime. His nostrils quiver. Dorian has been sober for fifteen years.

"Have you decided?" Mark asks.

There's really nothing to decide. If Mark hadn't arrived unexpectedly the moment he did, Dorian might have told his agent "no, thanks," or told her he would think about it and call back later with the same response. No one would have been the wiser. Once, almost four decades ago, an unexpected arrival violently changed the course of his life.

Why hadn't he lied when Mark asked, "Who was that?" Telling lies was what actors did on stage. And he had learned to lie convincingly. But he was the one who insisted on maintaining a landline. The landline has call display. Erasing the call in Mark's full view would only excite suspicion.

"Charmaine."

"Your agent?"

"Do we know any other Charmaines?"

The snap in the voice, the sarcastic tone, the flush of red along Dorian's neck, alerts Mark to Dorian's agitation. He knows Dorian. Or he thinks he does. Mark is in his second year as an attending psychiatrist in the inpatient unit of Vancouver General Hospital, a brisk walk away from their home, and pegged Dorian earlier in their relationship as "cluster B" (dramatic, emotional, erratic) with a tendency to histrionic personality—not untypical of professional actors. Dorian has heard this analysis before. Saying it amuses Mark.

But Dorian dislikes it. It feels like pinning a butterfly to a corkboard. He received some benefit from a psychiatrist, once, long ago, in an episode he's never confided to Mark. Never will.

Charmaine called about a job. The terms are acceptable. It's a season of TV, with the promise of a second season, possibly a third. It's hardly Shakespeare, but it's steady work with adequate remuneration. He should be pleased. He's been "resting," as actors do, since *It's a Wonderful Life* closed at the Arts Club after Christmas.

"Well?" Mark finishes his sip and folds his lips primly.

"As I said earlier, it means I'll be away much of the summer."

"I can come and visit." Mark reaches for a deck chair. "Where exactly is this place they're filming?"

"Winnipeg Beach." Dorian takes the chair opposite. "A little north of Winnipeg."

"You've been there before, I presume."

A lie perches on Dorian's tongue, but he chooses vagueness instead: "A few times." He takes a swig of the gassy water and glances at Mark's martini, craving its juniper bitterness.

"Is there something off-putting about the role? What is the role, anyway?"

"I would play the owner of a marina, a widower, with a daughter and a grandson. The series is called *Morningstar Cove*. It's about a bunch of teenagers summering at some lake town. Manitoba masquerading as Minnesota or Michigan. It's been sold to Global, and to ABC in the States, I think."

"Sounds all right, I guess. No audition?"

"Someone else was cast, but had to withdraw suddenly, so no audition. No time."

"Then your 'grandson'"—Mark's fingers wiggle quotation marks—"in this show is a teenager or something."

"And your point?"

"You'll have to let your hair go … for one thing."

"Not necessarily."

"Oh, I think so." Mark grins, revealing a set of perfect teeth. "Owner of a marina in some rural backwater? I'm thinking 'crusty' and 'curmudgeonly.' No Nice'n Easy in *his* bathroom cabinet." He takes another sip. "Or you could go bald. Shave it all off, like you did in high school."

Dorian is at times disturbed by Mark's retentive memory—which must have got him through all those years of medical school. Had he really told him that story? And what other stories has he told and forgotten he told?

When he was in grade twelve, the principal issued an edict forbidding long hair on boys—long hair, in the definition of the day, meaning hair creeping over your ears or your shirt collar. Dorian shaved his head in protest. Hardly worth notice today. But then? A shock wave surged through the student body. Crowds gathered outside the school to stare.

"Maybe you should shave *yours* off," Dorian counters. "You'll be a cue ball in ten years anyway."

Tit for tat. It's Mark's turn not to rise to the bait. But it's true. Mark's hair, black, but shot with a little grey that he tries to contain with the very Nice'n Easy he dissed Dorian for, is thinning. Dorian sees the pinkish crown turned away from him in bed. If Mark is top dog in the salary sweepstakes, Dorian is top dog in looks. He is, Mark admits, but not out loud, handsome, even as he approaches sixty, even with a history of smoking. Though the lips have thinned, the jaw-line remains firm, the skin smooth, the few wrinkles charming, the blue eyes—which can flicker with a frightening madness at times—clear, and the hair remarkably thick and full—and, in this instance, sort of—what would you call it?—medium chestnut? He pulled off George Bailey in *It's a Wonderful Life,* didn't he? Jimmy Stewart couldn't have been forty in the movie.

Dorian is running his hand through that hair now. *Will* he have to let the colour go? Or will he let them dye it white, the colour of an old man—which, in fact, is his natural colour? The dark blond leached swiftly from his hair in his early twenties. He searched for a familial cause; couldn't find one. His father looked to have white hair, too, at an early age. But Jim Grant was blond blond.

It's this call from Charmaine. It's this talk of the beach that stirs a particular memory: Dorian arriving at Eadon Lodge that last year of college, entering through the screen door on its shrieking hinges, his eyes travelling to his father's name and a date in pencil on the wooden slats of the wall nearest the door. It was the thing to do if you were a guest at Eadon Lodge—write your name somewhere on one of the walls rather than in a guest book.

*Jim Grant, July 12, 1952.* There it was, under a frayed pennant of Niagara Falls. And just below, his mother's—*Lillian Grant, July 13, 1952.* Jim had gone back to the city Saturday afternoon, alone, less than twenty-four hours after he'd arrived. Dorian's mother stayed on. She continued the holiday with Bibs and Marion Eadon and Lydia, who was a few months younger than he. Neither he nor Lydia could remember being three years old, of course. Thus Dorian can't remember going home with his mother—Dr. Eadon drove them, he was told much later. Jim had taken their car. He remembers nothing of that Monday afternoon. He really doesn't remember having a father—who left Eadon Lodge that Saturday, July 12, 1952 and—he was told—died in a car accident on the way home.

You were supposed to sign Eadon Lodge's wall when you left, perhaps with a jaunty "had wonderful time" or "great weather." But Dorian, to be contrary, signed his name upon his arrival: *Dorian Grant, August 21, 1969.* Bad luck if I sign it when we leave, he said to Lydia, who understood his meaning (but knew the truth of Jim's death where Dorian did not) and watched as he attached his grand looping signature below those of his parents.

How wrong he had been about the luck. It was from those days at Eadon Lodge that Dorian marked the beginning of his hair's swift journey to a freakish, albino white.

Paul stole the camera, brazenly lifted it with a raptor's swoop from a blanket on the public beach at Gimli—their one excursion together into town from Eadon Lodge those ten days in August in 1969, their turn to buy groceries. Dorian remembers the sand pulsing with bodies clinging to the last of the summer sun, and for a long time he thought this impulse of Paul's, this foolish impulse, which made him laugh and his heart soar with wicked glee, would spell his doom. There *had* to be some witness to the theft, someone who noticed, despite not giving a shit if someone lost a crappy Instamatic, someone who would come forward later, when it was important, and say that he or she recognized Paul.

Dorian flung the camera into a ditch along the highway as he sped—fled, alone—past harvested fields back to Winnipeg the morning after that last full day at Eadon Lodge, somehow finding the presence of mind to first remove the film cartridge. He secreted it at the back of the desk drawer in his bedroom at his grandparents' where he lived after his mother remarried, but at night when he couldn't sleep he sensed it there glowing, beating like Poe's telltale heart.

He should have thrown it in the river, dropped it in the neighbour's trash, buried it in the park, smashed it to smithereens and exposed the film to light, but in those months reason slipped its moorings.

He transferred it to his shaving kit, bought the year before for his first summer scrounging movie-related work in New York, where it sank below the jumble of toiletries. The kit was always with him—in a cupboard or drawer wherever he was living or in his luggage when he travelled to this or that locale for work. But his fingers would sometimes brush it when he was rooting through his kit, for a buried emery board, say. The fanciful telltale heart beat no more, but a touch of the cartridge was electric along his skin.

And it was evidence.

Dorian had the film developed in Toronto on February 26, 1993—which he counts as his sobriety date, though when he put that empty scotch glass down on the bar of the King Eddy that Friday afternoon he didn't know it would be his last drink. He said goodbye to some actor friends and passed from the hotel's clubby glow into the silver damp of King Street. He wasn't drunk. He was certain of that. He would later describe himself in AA as a "high-functioning alcoholic." So when he looked into the face of a man about his own age emerge out of the drizzle at the Yonge Street crossing he was certain he wasn't hallucinating. The man glanced at him as they waited for the light to turn, but with no surprise—or shock—of recognition. Dorian drank in his features, parsed the triangulations of chin, nose, cheekbones (forceful, straight, wide, respectively) resolved now into a mature, faintly coarsened, edition of the youth he'd once known. The Bacchus curls were traded for short-back-and-sides, the eyebrows were thicker, but the eyes—their essential Paulness—were unchanged, only in this instance they brimmed with a hostility Dorian had never witnessed in Paul's. "Fuck off," the man snarled at Dorian, shouldering past him as the walk sign flashed green.

Dorian remained rooted to the pavement. Was he watching a pink elephant vanishing into the grey of sodden humanity?

He couldn't take it anymore. His heart was racing. His mouth was sucked of moisture. Nearly a quarter century had passed. No one—no teenaged drone in those photo shops—paid an iota of attention to the dull work of processing people's dumb pictures. Surely that was true. He had long avoided having the film developed because one image on the cartridge—depending on how he'd angled the camera—might arouse curiosity or concern, might be considered by some prude to be pornographic. But now he cared less. Something else was at stake: Only the developed photos of those days at Eadon Lodge could tell him he wasn't losing his mind. Again.

He returned to the Spruce Street house he co-owned with his ex-wife, fetched the cartridge from his kit, took it into a Japan Camera on Bloor, and paid the extra for one-hour processing.

Dorian looks at the pictures. He slipped out of bed earlier, careful not to wake Mark. It's 3:40, according to an old digital clock stored in the fourth bedroom—the "box room," Mark calls it, which houses their luggage, orphan tables and lamps, one of which he switches on, and, yes, boxes, too—for computers, kitchen appliances, and so on. In the third of a Russian-doll set of suitcases is where Dorian keeps his travelling shaving kit. And in the kit, where once he hid the film cartridge, he keeps two photographs. Three by five inches, they fit into a slim silver cigarette case that belonged to Dey, his grandfather.

His fingers fumble along the case's rim. He feels edgy. Fifteen years ago, a sickness filled him as he peeled the seal back and lifted the photographs from the packet's inner pocket. He craved a drink badly then. He could use one now. A ghost scent of Mark's martini teases his nostrils.

Fifteen or sixteen pictures were on the cartridge, the first four or five of a chubby, frowning little girl sashed in a Band-Aid pink bikini, which he threw away.

The first picture past Band-Aid Girl—startling, heartbreaking—was of his own face, younger, of course—impossibly younger, impossibly leaner, hair flying past the frame of the Volkswagen, eyes crossed and crazed, as he mugged for Paul. It was taken as they drove up the gravel road through Loney Beach north to Eadon Lodge. Paul had been greedy with the camera, immune to sharing, maniacally snapping away at Dorian, until he grew bored with the thing and tossed it onto the back seat.

All the pictures, which shared the fate of the Band-Air Girl photos, were poorly lit close-ups of him driving, but for the last two. Dorian retrieved the camera from the back seat with the groceries, hid it in his knapsack and forgot about it for a few days, then thought to bring it to the Eadons' stretch of beach their last day together.

He'd snapped one of Paul, he remembered, as Paul emerged from the lake. He groaned as he came upon it. It was unexpectedly beautiful—the composition all golden ratio, a chance of the moment, the pattern all shapes and shadows, a trick of the light. And there was Paul in his unguarded moment, skinny boy's chest gleaming, with wet, tanned face angled into the distance in a way that seemed stylized, like a figure in an Avedon photograph. The photo might have, but didn't, catch anything below Paul's waist.

How long did Dorian stand with it in his hand, staring, stunned, before crumpling to the rug by his bed? Who knows? How long do you remain stricken after that late-night phone call? How long before the grief surges from your belly and the hot tears squeeze out of your eyes and you howl an animal howl? How long?

Dorian studies the photo now with less torment. In the fifteen years that have passed since that night in Toronto he's learned some things that have blunted the anguish—a little—though not the fear. Even now he can feel a hot bubble of grief swelling in his chest. He suppresses it before it bursts in his throat. He doesn't want to alert Mark even if Mark does sleep like fallen timber.

But look at the glistening cap of black hair, sleek as an otter's, unruly curls tamed by the weight of water streaming to rivulets down his slim neck. And the eyes—large, black-black, and glisteny. There's a slight shadow under them, an effect of the angled sun, that sets his face to Cubist planes.

Dorian twists the picture into the light. There's something of Paul's precociousness there, in the set of his eyes, the strange knowing in one so young, which confounded and excited and, finally, terrified him—though by then he was too lost in the spell to stop what they were doing. And there's something else as well, he's sure, something heavy in those taut features, though perhaps, he thinks, he's reading into Paul's expression what he knows now. What Paul didn't tell him.

Dorian turns to the second picture, the only one of the two of them—Paul and him—together. Briony snapped it.

She was so clueless, Briony. Lydia always knew at some level, but didn't name it. Alanna Roth, always sharp, guessed and didn't care. Alanna told Alan. Dorian could pinpoint the hour, the minute, when he realized she had. Alan was straight, entitled, oblivious—typical. He was too unimaginative to discern it on his own. But Alan was cool with contempt once enlightened.

Briony was blinded by her own wishful thinking. Dorian was to have arrived at Eadon Lodge with Blair Connon, an extra he'd befriended on the set of the student film *And No Birds Sing* the year before. It was a set-up—Blair paired to the slightly chubby, slightly gauche, freckle-peppered Briony. (Blair, a little heavyset himself, was no prize.) But Blair had met some woman over the summer and that was the end of that. So Dorian arrived with Paul, who, he told everyone, was his cousin—or second cousin once removed or something—from Toronto.

Dorian set the camera on the wooden stairs up to the cottage when they returned from the beach. They slung their wet towels over the clothesline that stretched between the front porch and an old elm and together shook the sand from the old blanket they'd used at the beach, draping it over the line next to the towels.

A rustle along the grass in the seconds before the camera clicked alerted them to a presence slipping by the blanket barrier. Enough time for Paul and him to pull apart, but not enough to assume some unaffected posture. Dorian can see the discomfit in his own face in the photograph, his mouth and eyes three little O's. But Paul's expression conveys challenge, calculation, and disdain. He remembers Briony lowering the camera from her eye, her face gone scarlet. Before long she would leave Eadon Lodge claiming a migraine.

And before long Paul would be dead.

Dorian returns the photographs to their little archive. He walks to the window. He's naked, light streaming behind him, but no one is on the street at this time of night and the window frame is decently above his crotch. There's pallid lemon streetlight on the pavement. It looks like it's rained a little. Someone has left a full garbage bag on the sidewalk. How did it get there? Tossed from a car? Body parts within? There's something sinister about suburban emptiness. Farther off, past the cars lining the street, the houses retreat into shadow. He almost wishes some fellow insomniac would come and set a window aglow and wave to him. *You know I can't sleep, I can't stop my brain.* What's that from? *The White Album*?

Dorian isn't given to the mystical. Not like Briony. *Could she be, still? Didn't she go into social work? And surely Alan dropped all that Communist crap.* But he feels again, as he felt in the garden earlier, a shiver travel along his nerves, a chill of premonition. The feeling's not entirely new. Beginnings of new projects often jangle with uncertainty: it all looks good on paper, then it all turns sour in the execution.

But this has a different shading. It isn't the job, the silly YA TV program. That doesn't matter. It will end—well or badly—after a season or two or three. He can take the money—which he could use—and run. His "career arc" doesn't trouble him much any more.

No, quite simply, it's the setting that sends cold fingers along his spine. The horror at Eadon Lodge—not so many miles from fictional Morningstar Cove—sent his life hurtling down an unimagined path. He can't pretend he isn't the man he is because of it. He can't pretend he doesn't act in the world the way he does because of it. When memory of it intrudes, he pulls his mind away violently. He suppresses it. It's much easier to do in Toronto or New York or Los Angeles.

Or in Vancouver.

All is dark. But two time zones away the sun is advancing over the curve of the earth, pouring a pitiless light over prairie lakes barely emerging from the weight of winter ice and over frozen shores with buried secrets. Dorian can see the great orb in his mind's eye as he leans out the casement window for an eastward view. No glimmer separates the mountains from the sky. Yet. All *is* dark. But light—a terrible, ruthless light, colder than the sun's—is fast approaching, he's convinced.

He's taking the job. Hobson's choice.

# 3

To include her stepdaughter and step-granddaughter in the obituary or not?

Lydia glances at the samples she culled from the *Free Press*'s online obits section. The funeral director offered to compose it but she turned him down, vaguely affronted. Of course, how could he know anything of her professional background? She's worked in one editorial capacity or other, freelance or staffer, for several Bay Area publishers in thirty-five years and has been, for the last eleven, editor-in-chief of the esteemed independent (well, *formerly* independent) Berkeley-based publisher, Countervail Press.

Writing the obituary for her mother gives Lydia a funny feeling, as if the very act were drawing her somehow closer to her own inevitable death. She shifts her attention to Helen audible in the hall on the telephone in yet another recitation. *Quite suddenly, yes. A neighbour found her. Yes, a good age.* Lydia drops her fingers to the keyboard:

> It is with great sadness we announce the passing of Marion Patricia Eadon (née Clifford) on July 4, 2008 at the age of 84. She will be remembered
>
> *lovingly* remembered by daughter Lydia

Lydia pauses again. Should she incorporate Ray's last name? Technically, she is Mrs. Ray Beddoes, which is how her mother addressed birthday cards to her, but she never really relinquished the surname she was born with, and Ray never insisted she did. She types in "Beddoes" anyway. She's missing him terribly.

She chews at the skin along her thumb and thinks again about whether to include Ray's daughter, Erin, and his granddaughter, Misaki.

Marion met Erin—what? twice?—in San Francisco. When Ray moved with Lydia into the house on Lincoln Way, Erin was a spikey, peevish teenager living with her mother in San Mateo and visiting her father once in a blue moon. Erin removed herself to Japan in her twenties to teach English, wedded a Japanese boy, and softened in the wake of motherhood. There have been trans-Pacific visits. There is Skype. Lydia is in love with Misaki, eight years old and cute as pie, grateful in a way she can't bear to acknowledge to herself that Erin gave birth to a girl, not a boy. She's eager for their patriation to the States, which is why Ray is in Japan. He's helping Erin extricate herself from a failed marriage and fraught custody battle. It makes no sense for him to leave for Canada for a funeral, then circle back to Asia. They're counting pennies these days.

Lydia wonders how her mother handled the spectre of grandchildren, never able to match or trump her friends in a showdown of wallet photos. Marion couldn't say that, yes, she had a grandchild, because that would lay bare the lie forty years ago that Lydia had decided to stay in San Francisco to finish her education. Marion had a grandson, born May 26, 1970, who disappeared into the arms of strangers hours after he was born. Name? As the child swelled in her womb, Lydia tried to resist this dreamy rumination, but couldn't: Jennifer or Elizabeth or Michelle, if it was a girl; Andrew or Matthew or David, if it was a boy. Matthew it became. Lydia's only glimpse of Matthew was a little shred of blue blanket visible over the nurse's white shoulder as he vanished through the door, vanished from her life, vanished from conversation.

Lydia handles grandmotherhood—as a number of her contemporaries have lately slid into the state—by doing what she did when her contemporaries became mothers—forcing herself to imagine all these little parcels of vanilla or chocolate flesh as kittens or puppies, something lovely she can coo over without feeling her heart shatter. For a long time, she couldn't bear to have another child because she couldn't bear to think about the stages she's missed with her first—first words, first steps, first teeth, first day at school. And when she thought she could bear it, she remained childless. Secondary infertility, the doctor confided to her. Ray hid his disappointment. But he had one child at least. *They* had one. Erin. And a grandchild.

Marion never ever alluded to her absent grandson. And never asked her why she never had another child. Emerging from childhood to view her parents in a colder light, Lydia came to see that her mother's values lay in externals: in how she looked and how the house looked. Marion might have elected to remain childless herself if her times had permitted. She had the one, perhaps for presentation sake. Some children crave a sibling. Every baby boomer seemed to have one. Lydia didn't. Dorian didn't either. She recalls this now. Being only children was among the things that bound them at first, in grade four, though Dorian gained a half-sister, later, when he was too old for it to matter.

She moves the cursor and reluctantly removes mention of Erin and Misaki from the screen. She imagines the funeral reception. There will be enough questions to answer.

Lydia is sitting at the old Georgian bureau desk in her father's den. Bibs disappeared here every day after work if he wasn't working late. DO NOT DISTURB. Here he kept his own cache of liquor. Here Marion placed a bowl of fresh ice daily. Here he reclined on a red leather sofa and listened to jazz on his own Webcor phonograph. An hour later he would emerge in a fug of cigarette smoke and smoky rye. (The daddy smell. It lingers still in this office.) He took his place at the head of the table and withheld his thoughts from his wife and daughter.

Bibs's den is the only room in the house—other than her childhood bedroom—untouched by her mother's decorating cravings, and it's remarkable, given that Bibs died ten years ago, that Marion with her mania for renovation didn't sweep in and turn it into a guest room or a little conservatory. When Lydia arrived yesterday, it looked as if the room hadn't been swept at all, or dusted, in some time, as if the cleaning lady—the faithful Mrs. C.—were barred from entering. Lydia twists her head and looks around at the couch, its leather worn in predictable places, at the wooden filing cabinets, the '70s-vintage record player that replaced the Webcor, and the shelves of dull-covered medical texts and Louis L'Amour novels—all of which *she,* helpless to stop herself, dusted and wiped, even though she knew most of it would be carted away. Did her mother grow fond of Bibs's old things in his absence? She's not sure. The room felt sealed off when she arrived. Entombed.

The word "entombed" sends a chill down her spine. She twists her head back to the task at hand and finds instant comfort in the pleasing Georgian symmetry of small drawers and aligned slots in the desk interior. It was here she found a copy of her mother's will, folded now next to her elbow.

There were no nasty surprises, thank god. Her mother named Lydia executor and, but for some small bequests, the sole beneficiary. But how much money is there? Bibs left his widow sufficiently provided for in *his* will, but he left a sizable sum to the Society for Manitobans with Disabilities that surprised Marion and Lydia by its munificence, though not by its inclusion.

Bibs had a brother younger by fourteen months. They were "Irish twins." They do look like brothers, at a glance. Lydia can see this in the picture of the two, aged twelve and almost-eleven, that sits with a few other others on the desk: A snap of Marion and Bibs, confetti-covered, on their wedding day, a formal sepia portrait of Bibs's mother and her sister, Nell and May, in their best little-girl dresses, haunting uncertainty in their round little faces, and a formal black-and-white high school portrait of herself, her expression as stiff as the mortar board on her head, but it's the one of her father and uncle she lifts for closer examination. She knows it best. A copy sat on the old sideboard at Eadon Lodge. Bibs and Lits. Malcolm and Wallace. Wallace is "Lits"—little. Malcolm is "Bibs"—big. It's a studio portrait, black and white. Lits's face appears vaguely apprehensive. Bibs is holding his hand. In childhood this troubled Lydia. Boys don't hold hands! *Why are you holding Uncle Lits's hand, Daddy?* Bibs was a man of few words. These few weren't illuminating: *Because he was my brother.*

The gesture, the hand drawn to the other, is protective. Lydia sees that now. Protective against what or whom? And there's a wariness behind Bibs's squint. Yes, there is. Wary of what? Who wielded the camera?

She studies the boys' features, the narrow, high bridge of the nose, which she shares, the large eyes, the generous forehead. But Lits's face is longer. His ears protrude. There's no subtext in that squint. Lits has an intellectual disability.

Lydia's grandfather, Henry—made a widower by the birth of his second son—took his two boys overseas in the 1930s. Lydia has thought it remarkable of her grandfather, in those days when people with intellectual disabilities were hidden away, institutionalized, god help us, lobotomized, to take Lits on such a long journey—train, boat, train. And perhaps it wasn't wise. Lits caught influenza and died at Narborough, in Norfolk, where the Eadons originated, from where Henry Eadon emigrated in 1903. Lits was buried there, in the churchyard.

Lydia travelled to England once, in 1987, for the London Book Fair. On impulse, on a spare day, she took the train to King's Lynn, then found a cab to take her to Narborough. She couldn't find Lits's stone in the graveyard at All Saints Church. There was a helpful directory to the burials pinned to a board inside the church, but though there were several Eadons, there was only one listing for a *Wallace* Eadon (1843–1899). The elderly sexton who happened to be trimming the churchyard grass had no recollection of another Wallace Eadon. She reported this absence to her father in a phone call after she returned to San Francisco. *You had the wrong church then.* She didn't argue. Bibs was beginning his slide into dementia then. He was furious, as furious as he had been seventeen years earlier when she broke the key to Eadon Lodge sneaking in with her then boyfriend, Ross.

Lydia looks up from the framed photograph as Helen pokes her head through the door, coffee in one hand, phone in the other.

"How goes it?" Helen's sympathetic, of course, but she's enjoying this, the busy-ness. She's almost done phoning various relatives.

"Fine," Lydia replies, glancing at what little she's written. "Thanks for making the calls."

"Who are those two sweet boys?"

Lydia is still holding the picture. "Bibs and Lits," she answers, replacing the frame atop the desk.

"Ah, yes, of course." Helen knows the story. "Is there anything else I can do?" she adds, moving to the couch. Lydia nudges something behind her laptop, a gesture Helen notes from the corner of her eye as she turns to sit. The will, she guesses, and here's Lydia being silly secretive about it—observing proprieties, Marion-like. And thinking of Marion, she hopes her cousin wasn't a fool with the money. She knows about Lydia's housing dilemma, though Lydia's breezed over the details, affecting unconcern. She and Ray have rented the house on Lincoln for decades, in a sweet deal, from a couple who moved to Bolinas. But the couple's children recently inherited the property and they share nothing of their parents' hippie qualms about ownership. They want to sell it. Lydia has first refusal. House prices have collapsed in many cities, but not in San Francisco. The two little Gen-Xers want a hair under a million dollars for the 3-bed, 2-bath, 1,800 square-foot Outer Sunset house. Lydia and Ray are scrambling, Helen is certain. And there's trouble brewing at Lydia's workplace on top of it.

Lydia doesn't immediately respond to Helen's offer of help. Her thoughts are snagged on Lits and where he might be interred.

Thank god her mother changed her mind about burial. Bibs—before his mind turned to jelly—left instructions that he be cremated, with the proviso that his ashes not be interred like *his* father's, that they be scattered at Eadon Lodge. But Lydia and Marion, each for her own reasons, decided to ignore his wishes. Together, they scattered Bibs's ashes over Assiniboine Park, in the middle of bitter February, quickly, furtively, two black figures in a stark white landscape.

Lydia can tolerate a religious service, but never graveside—the lowering of casket into cavity fills her with atavistic horror. Marion thought scattering Bibs's ashes in a public park in the dead of winter undignified. She remained po-faced as confetti of her late husband caught the sun and glittered in the air before descent to the snow along the riverbank. What changed Marion's mind about burial? She didn't want to be alone through eternity. At least this is what Lydia presumes.

"Lunch, perhaps?" Lydia at last responds to Helen's solicitation.

"How about pigs-in-blankets? You know, sausage rolls?"

Lydia looks at Helen sharply.

"I saw them in the freezer. Can't think of the last time I ate one. But a bit greasy and heavy, I think, for ... now." Helen slows. She studies Lydia's frown.

The frown is staunching nausea. "Let's go out somewhere," Lydia says. "I shouldn't be much longer with this."

Helen rises. "Then I'll leave you to finish."

Halloween 1969: Lydia is at the kitchen island tonging sizzling pigs-in-blankets from the oven tray onto a platter and battling a sudden wave of queasiness, when she sees Dorian emerge from the darkness of the back stairwell. A whiff of the outdoors curls off him. So does a whiff of something sour. She didn't hear the back door open, the clomp of shoes on the steps. Her ears were pitched to the rising decibels in the living room. She's beginning to realize parsley-lined platters are a mistake.

"I didn't think you would come," she says, striving for an even tone as her heart lurches. Two months have passed since she last saw him, at Eadon Lodge, and no day has gone by without images of the last twenty-four hours there ripping into her thoughts. Her eyes travel from the beige trench coat Dorian's wearing—*is that new?*—to his face, cheeks pale as breath, summer tan vanished. New beard—blondish-red, straggly, Rasputin-y. Hair brushes shoulders now. He's wearing a fedora, of all things. His eyes are bruised. The full impact of him fills her with dismay and breaks her heart at the same time.

"Didn't you want me here?" Dorian manoeuvres the linoleum and reaches for a sausage roll with a kind of studied nonchalance, but the pastry sears his fingers and he drops it with a quacking *fuck*. The smell of booze on his breath invades Lydia's nostrils. There's a rankness around him. Briony's told her that he's been cutting most classes;

she says he passes the days in one of the off-campus bars, plastered, stoned, whatever.

"Did you drive?" Lydia lets her eyes drop to the broken pastry roll, its flakes scattered over the counter.

"Walked. I asked you, didn't you want me to come?"

"You're shouting, Dorian. Look, I didn't mail engraved invitations. I haven't seen you since—"

Lydia stops herself and scrapes violently at a sausage roll. Some of them have burned on the bottom. The greasy smell is turning her stomach. Her mornings lately have been punctuated with nausea. She flicks a glance at Dorian. *What costume is this? What's he supposed to be? The tie, the shirt collar, the coat, the hat, the beard, the hair. Jesus in business dress?* She doesn't want to look at his face, but she can feel his eyes boring into her.

"Your parents closed up the cottage, yes?" Dorian's speech is over articulated. He's drunk trying to sound sober.

"Yes. Of course they closed the cottage. Well, Bibs went up and closed it. Before Thanksgiving."

"Did he say anything?"

"No, he didn't *say* anything. What's there to say?"

"I mean, did he *notice* anything?"

"Like what, Dorian?"

"Like ... the signature on the wall."

"Paul's signature? I washed it off."

"The missing blanket."

"My father doesn't notice things like that."

"Your mother does."

"There are half a dozen old blankets in that cupboard. She doesn't count them every time she goes up."

"But it was that Coronation blanket—"

"Steed," Lydia finds her nerve, reverts to a pet name. (He is Steed. She is Mrs. Peel. They loved *The Avengers*.) She lifts her eyes to meet his, which are bleary. "I've told you before—Marion only puts up with Eadon Lodge for my father's sake. She hates the place and the stuff in it.

She won't notice. She won't care. And if she does, I'll make something up. It's only a blanket. Please don't worry."

"They'll come looking for him, Lydia."

"We have our story, remember? *Remember*?" She lowers her voice to a crisp whisper. "You've got to stop this ... this ... look at you! Dorian, you look like hell."

"Maybe that's because I *feel* like hell. I am *in* hell! Aren't *you* in hell, Mrs. Peel?"

The words feel like a slap in her face, and they sting. A sob clutches her throat. She battles it, thinks: if only she could slap *his* face, slap him hard, Dorian, the author of this misery, of her own misery, of her own double hell. Zen-slap them back to their former world of innocent obedience. She swallows hard, gestures with the spatula toward the door to the front rooms. Pastry flakes float to the floor. "You're the one who wants to be an actor. So start acting. Get out there and act. Act normal."

"What the fuck do you think I've been doing all my life?"

"And what is this costume?" Lydia redirects the spatula down toward Dorian's calves. She's noticed them bare and hairy below the hem of the trench coat and above the black socks and shoes. "What are you dressed as? What are you supposed to be?" But the truth swiftly dawns. Incredulous, she asks: "Did you learn that from Paul, too?"

*Too?*

"No, I did not learn this from Paul, *too*."

He fiddles the coat buttons with the speed of a sober man and flings open the flaps. She assumes he'll be wearing short pants or, at least, underwear. He is not.

The white dress shirt is tucked up around the pale abdomen. The necktie points to a pink snake in a garden of red-blond thatch. Lydia averts her eyes. Up they race, to Dorian's face, wreathed in provocation and glee and triumph, and higher still, as if drawn by an irresistible force, to the ceiling lamp, a simple white ellipse—nothing like the electrolier suspended from Eadon Lodge's high ceiling—its cool efficient glow nothing like the rich golden radiance that two months ago in the gloom of a damp August evening burnished that abdomen, those thighs, that *thing*, then rod not snake.

Dorian slurs the words, pushes the hat back on his head: "I'm *Dick* Tracy. Get it?"

Lydia's breath comes in short spurts. She can't make words. Years later, when a man flashes her at City College, she better articulates—to herself, to one or two others—her shock and outrage. But not this night. She can't sort feelings from thoughts. She pulls one strand from the skein, however: She's growing sick of masculine bravado. That head-shaving incident in high school? Driving down the Trans-Canada at night with the headlights off? (He told her about that once.) This get-up? All show, so much show. In the heat, Dorian dissolves. She's seen it.

And one more strand, the most important: she must keep her cool, and keep Dorian's. He can't be let off half-cocked to speak of their crime.

Lydia senses the night arcing dangerously out of her control. The jungle throb in the next room shivers the dividing wall and passes along her skin. Someone makes a madhouse shriek, then another, and another. The Westminster chimes of the front door bong bong bong bong again and again and again. And this boy, her old friend Steed, in this ridiculous, stupid flasher costume, is about to pour himself through that door there—yes, over there—into the swelling tide. She wants to really lose her cool, *really* lose it, this once, this time. She wants it all—*everything*—to stop. Now.

But it's much too late.

# 4

Dorian is driving west along the Trans-Canada Highway from West Hawk Lake. The radio, not the landscape, has his attention—or at least half of it: It's the day after Woodstock and CKRC is full of its muddy glories. The other half of his attention dwells on his fucking family. He's coming off three days with his mother, his half-sister and his stepfather—which was all he could take. He told his mother that he would spend a week, but his stepfather, Bob, is an ex-military bully with a mouthful of *you should*: get off your ass, cut the lawn, get a haircut, get a job, respect your mother, turn off that crap music, and finally, this morning, about eleven o'clock—get out of bed. Dorian gave the departing figure the finger.

The summer had not tripped along groovily. The summer before, on a quest to find film work, any film work, maybe snatch at a little fame, he'd travelled to New York and after knocking on a lot of doors landed a gofer job at a production house on 44th, which led to a production-assistant job on a Norman Mailer film, which climaxed in a debauched weekend of shooting at Sag Harbor—which, with judicious editing, he had been regaling everyone at home with through the fall and winter. Hungry for more, he returned to New York days after his last exam, in early June. Nothing. No work. The summer of 1968 he felt his whole world blossom. The summer of 1969 he felt adrift in the city's ghastly heat, a stranger among strangers. Out of money, he retreated home in July.

Visiting his mother had been duty call anyway. He left before she set out lunch, threw his backpack into the Beetle's back seat, and heedless of his empty stomach or his near-empty gas tank or his near-full bladder, drove off without a goodbye. He should have stopped at the West Hawk Esso for gas, but so pissed off was he that he didn't think to look at the gauge until many miles along the highway. He rolled into a Shell station on fumes and rolled into his destiny. Afterwards, often, he thinks about that ribbon of chance—how untransformed life would have been, for him, for others, if he had not flounced off that day, that hour, that minute. If he had left Lillian and Bob's at twelve-ten, say, instead of noon, Paul would not have stepped out of the washroom at the back of the Shell station in those very moments he was ready and anxious to step in.

"Some creep truck driver might have picked you up instead," Dorian said to him a couple of days later at his grandparents' when they were watching a report on TV about some unsolved murders of a starlet and a middle-aged couple in Los Angeles. "Fucked you, strangled you, and left your body in the woods."

"What makes you think some creep truck driver didn't?"

"Because here you are. With me."

"Well, I wasn't strangled and left in the woods."

Dorian noted the telling absences and the puckish smile linger on Paul's lips. Vaguely shocked, he said nothing. His next thoughts—they were in Dey's bedroom, which had a TV—were jealous ones, tinged with a kind of febrile excitement at the imagined scene: Those big trucks, their back compartments, those beefy truckers, their stripped flesh. Two weeks later those thoughts would turn to fear and dread: Who along the highway out of Toronto saw Paul with his thumb out? Who picked him up? Who would remember him?

The door opens. Finally! Dorian has been standing, arms folded across his chest, the very model of impatience, jingling his car keys, hearing not a quick whoosh of a urinal flushing but a protracted sequence of water splashing, paper towel dispenser slamming, water splashing again—a *toilette* of some nature. Dorian is glancing past the side of the filling station for a concealing bush or a tree when a face framed by dark curls and sunglasses pushed to the forehead emerges from the grey half-light of the men's washroom. The facial expression is set to preoccupation.

Long strong fingers pushing a paper towel across a tanned forehead bright with damp are curling to ball the paper and send it to join the other rubbish in the scrub when the eyes find Dorian's.

A split-second lingering. A burrowing down into the psyche, an electric sensation of connection. But Dorian pushes past—he has to pee! now!—but as he does his arm brushes the other man's hand. The paper towel, balled up now, begins its descent. Their eyes rise from the ball's falling arc to meet again. An ironic smile flickers along the other's cheeks, freshly shaven, Dorian can see now, as he can see the top of the backpack behind his neck. He catches a whiff of cheap soap and musk.

In the dimly lit men's room he struggles at first to release urine against the countervailing rush of blood to his hardening penis. He is quick as can be. Painfully shoves the thing back in. Zips up. Flushes. Runs the tap a second, a nod to the rituals of cleanliness and, with galloping heartbeat, pulls the door open. Surprise! Paul is there. Bovver boots, frayed jeans, a clean white T-shirt with a red star in the middle. He has replicated Dorian's earlier stance, arms crossed below chest, backpack straps straining shirt fabric, tracing nipples. But the posture, unlike Dorian's foot-tapping impatient pose, is louche, sinuously curved. His head is cocked to one side like a robin's and his thumb is pointed in the air. "Which way you going, man?" he says in a smiling voice, eyeing the keys in Dorian's hand.

"West."

"I'm going west, too."

In 1998, Dorian went west again. This time to escape a woman, his "hag," in the parlance of some of his bitchier friends. Dixie-May Lang: She's society blue book, old money, terribly discreet, well known within a very tight circle, but largely unknown to the knucklehead on the street—even though she has that silly Dogpatch first name, a momentary lapse in taste by her very Old Ontario mother.

Dixie-May's pedigree didn't come from the Langs, pickle producers who, in the scheme of things, are relative parvenus. A descendant of the Family Compact family Godwin, she *married* a Lang. Gerhard Lang

(1919–1995) was Dixie-May's third husband, as she (1926–) was his second wife. She married him in 1973. Husband #1 (William Radcliffe) and #2 (Rorie Bryce) died young, much too young.

All this Dorian gleaned from Dixie-May herself in dribs and drabs or from friends of hers they might run into at the theatre or at dinner parties. Among other biographical tidbits: Dixie-May Lang was on the board of Gardiner Museum, is a trustee of the ROM, and is chair of Neurological Heath Charities Ontario.

Which is how Dorian met Dix, as her close friends call her.

Every year, Neurological Health Charities Ontario puts on a fundraiser, Date With A Star! Dorian was a Star!, one of about twenty that early November evening at the downtown Hilton. He had been lately visible in *Riverdale,* an evening TV drama with little future. Like others of his ilk, he had cast his net to Hollywood, which had led to a part or two in *Law & Order* and *NYPD Blue.* His small turn in David Cronenberg's *Crash* had garnered favorable notice. And his run at the Tarragon in *The Designated Mourner* has just finished to good reviews. That's where Dix noticed him. She's been lately on the Tarragon Theatre's board, too.

This was the arrangement: Punters paid $500 for a ticket to Date With A Star!—the money usually coming out of some corporate coffer. They gathered at the Hilton for drinks, then in groups of eight or ten travelled to a surprise restaurant destination where they were to nosh and bask in the glory of their designated star.

The lucky eight who joined Dorian atop the TD Bank Tower at Canoe were not very much entertained by the handsome man at least a few of them vaguely recalled seeing on TV. And that's because he was monopolized by an older woman named Dix Lang.

And it's true. Dix did monopolize Dorian. It turned out she had a lively interest in theatre. She had been on the board of governors of the Stratford Festival (Ah! *Now* the name was familiar!) and knew all sorts of people and had all sorts of gossip. But something else drew Dorian to her. Something about the face? That, in part. Or the eyes. Large, lively—renegade? It was a Harlequin Romance word, but it was there, flecked in their black-blackness. And a gesture. A certain way she inclined her head when she voiced a question.

Dix, for her part, because she was chair of the NHCO board, had engineered Dorian as the Star! of her table. At the Tarragon performance, she was taken with his beauty—he reminded her a little of her first husband, William, with his slim hips and eyes of the piercing blue variety. She made a few calls, asked a few questions, and got the answer she wanted. Dix was shopping around for what they used to call a "walker." She had buried three husbands and wasn't interested in a fourth. What she wanted was something fetching on her arm from time to time, for opening nights at the ballet, the opera, the symphony—the occasional dinner party. She couldn't depend on her son to fill in on such occasions. He was married, busy, and barely tolerated the arts. Dorian fit the bill. He was easy on the eyes, gay as a goose (but passing straight), and had an uncertain relationship with a steady income. She wasn't going to pay him, for god's sake. But she would pick up the tickets and the lunch tabs.

So their encounter wasn't some sort of Dickens coincidence. You couldn't hear scenery moving or trapdoors opening. The real coincidence was to manifest itself later.

Dorian wasn't surprised when Dix called. They had clicked at Canoe; she suggested lunch sometime soon. Dorian had actually been flirted with by older women along these lines in the past. One he could remember was quite forthright about wanting sex, and he might have accommodated, but he detected a whiff of bunny boiler about her. No such whiff came off Dix. He became her Rosenkavalier.

In December Dix invites him to her Christmas party.

The house is typical Rosedale—a massing of grey stone on a cul de sac at the edge of a ravine approached through a labyrinth of heavily treed streets. It has an ivy-softened portico and a turret—dusted with new snow—and expansive curved windows that on a dark December evening, from the candle-lit interior, seem more like cave walls flickering with silhouettes. The interior is all clubby dark wood and gorgeous rugs and soft furniture with a winter scene by Krieghoff over the fireplace. The house smells spicy, piney, Christmassy, a little like his grandparents' in the same holiday season. He sips his cranberry juice and soda. Not only is the fire roaring, so is the conversation. Dix's Christmas parties are legendary and so the rooms hum with merriment, rather like a full house on opening night before the curtain goes up.

Which is a fine thing. Dorian loves the stage. It's where he feels most at home in the world. There's a little tickle of excitement in the pit of his stomach, an anticipation (like when he knows he's going to get laid) that this is going to be a fun evening. And what better? He is a Figure of Fascination. Not because he's As Seen on TV. But because he's rumoured as Dix's new "friend." How nice she's recovering from Gerhard's death. (*Meow!*) Dorian takes a position by the fireplace where the backlighting is flattering. He's talking to a friend of Dix's—Nicola somebody. He can sense some eye candy moving about the room, the frame of a man with linebacker shoulders, but he's learned to keep his eyes trained on his interlocutor, to keep the delighted smile twitching around his lips.

Dix interrupts. She fingers her ropes of pearls with one hand and lays the other on Dorian's arm, giving it a proprietary little squeeze. She has someone she wants Dorian to meet and has nothing to do with wanting two men to become fast friends. Or anything. She's simply feeling mischievous, full of a wicked kind of Christmas cheer. Peter is such a dull boy.

"Excuse me, Nicola, I have someone I want Dorian to meet."

Dorian looks to the half-turned figure behind Dix's head. Nice, he thinks, noticing a certain heft in the upper body, then takes in the man's face as it pivots toward him. He blinks. It's the eye candy he thought worth a cruising earlier—when he could get way from chittychatty Nicola—but now the planes and angles of the man's face, sharpened by the firelight, fuse into a familiarity. He can't place him. He *can* place him. Lifted from memory come those lips, now restraining a scowl, those eyes—Dix's eyes, but more deeply set—now flickering balefully. He is at King and Yonge four years ago, staring at a man who tells him to fuck off, whose dark good looks set him on the path to sobriety. He doesn't need an introduction. He knows who this must be and he knows who Dix must be. He feels the blood drain from his face.

"Dorian." Dix parts to allow the men room to shake hands. "This is my son, Peter. Peter Radcliff."

Peter's frown softens a little at the sight of Dorian's discomfort as he stretches forth his hand. The little faggot knows his cards are marked, he's sure. He'd worried his mother might get up to something like this, now that his stepfather was dead—pick up some toy boy, fiddle the will, embarrass the family somehow. When he gets Dorian alone—and he will—he will read him the riot act, run him out on a rail, make sure he never works in this town again. Peter thinks in clichés, but he's completely misinterpreted Dorian's reaction.

So has Dix. She opens her lips to speak, but hesitates. She wants to enjoy Peter's disapproval, but Dorian looks so odd, so pale. Eyes fixed and burning. Might he have met Peter before? She feels a fillip of fear and immediately dismisses it. She never, ever, had a qualm about *this* son's deviance, sexual or otherwise. She looks down. Dorian's hand fails to meet her son's.

# 5

"Welcome to the cliff's edge." Briony breaks into Lydia's thoughts, handing her a cup of milky tea.

Lydia glances past the other funeral guests and smiles. She understands Briony's meaning instantly and is a little surprised at the gallows humour. Briony, minister's daughter, has always been so earnest, humourless in a way, never quite getting *it* (whatever *it* was), into the fashion just when the fashion was passing. Briony's parents died years ago. Her husband has multiple sclerosis and one of her two sons somehow landed himself in jail, in California, no less, which accounted for Briony's intermittent visits to San Francisco for a couple of years in the nineties.

Lydia accompanied her to the prison in Sacramento once and met Jason. She struggled to disguise her dislike of the supercilious boy-man, who got himself caught in some scheme to defraud the elderly. He slouched and smirked and spoke to his mother in such a patronizing fashion she could only wonder how he'd sprung from Briony the Good's loins. He had committed a crime and showed no remorse. Dorian and she had committed a crime at Eadon Lodge, but they had been driven by shame and fear and dread and lived the days after imprisoned by the days before. How different their lives—hers and Dorian's—might have been if their transgressions had happened in 1999 not 1969, a year touched still by the tendrils of Victorianism curling down the generations.

"I hadn't really thought about it that way," Lydia responds to the cliff's-edge remark. "But my mother is the last of her sisters, and my dad's brother died before the war, so, yes, that generation is gone ... at least for me."

"I wonder if we're the last generation to say 'the war' and mean World War Two?"

"What about your kids?"

"They seem to have no interest in politics or history. I don't think any of their friends do, either. Remember how Alan would go on?" Briony lifts her teacup and takes a smiling sip. She clings to these old days, Lydia thinks, with a pang of pity for her friend, who has grown old and disappointed and frazzled in the intervening years, whose dark blouse shows evidence of an old stain.

"About the revolution, remember?" Briony returns the cup to its matching saucer.

"How is Alan, I wonder?"

"Oh, Alan's gone to the dark side. Some Marxist he ever was. Big into real estate and you know how corrupt that world is." Briony's face darkens, subsuming her freckles. "I'd love all those quotes of his in the student paper about overthrowing the capitalist system to come back to spook him."

Briony works for Child and Family Services and sees the spreading taint of the city's poverty. "Oh! You probably wouldn't know this, but Alan's company is having some fight in Winnipeg Beach—or is it Gimli?—over condo development. But there's a group that wants to give heritage designation to—"

"Wait. What? Heritage designation? In *Gimli*?"

"There's some old stuff there, Lydia." Briony responds defensively. "How about Eadon Lodge—that's old. Didn't your grandfather build it in something like the 1920s?"

"About then."

"You know, I'll bet you haven't been back to the cottage since that week we were all there, have you? When was it? '69?" Briony knows the year perfectly well. "That strange week." She says the words brightly, as if it were all a frothy memory, but the events, stained by the shooting—and by something else—remain emblazoned. "Do you ever think about it?"

"No," Lydia replies, scraping her cup along its saucer. Did her denial sound too sharp? "No, not really," she amends, adding quickly, "Tell me about the heritage designation."

"Some old fishing shack or something near the docks—I'm not sure what exactly—that's important to the old Icelanders, Alan's firm wants to raze it to build condos. There's lots of construction going on up that side of the lake now. Retiring boomers, you know. Summers at the beach in Gimli. Winters in Mexico or Florida. Never have to put up with another Winnipeg winter. If you can afford it," she adds glumly.

Heritage designation. Lydia's mind grips this. How serious could some little lake town be about preserving historic properties? What force of law would such designation have? Is *this* the answer?

Eadon Lodge was surely one of the oldest cottages in the area. Not simply old, but untouched. Her father resisted change, adamant all his life the cottage remain as he'd known it as a boy. Still, this and that changed. Marion won a protracted battle over indoor plumbing, installed—Lydia remembers with cruel clarity as the place of the outdoor privy turned site of her very hell—in early August 1969.

After Bibs died in 1998, Lydia expected what she had dreaded, that Marion would turn to her and announce that she was going to sell the bloody cottage, that she was too old to keep it up and—of course—she always hated it anyway. Lydia was prepared to counterargue for sentimentality, for family memory, for efficacy—she and Ray would come up to Canada and spend summers at Gimli, they would enjoy it in retirement—all of it a lie, anything to stave off a reckoning she knew one day would come. Then, nine years ago, when financial burden was not set to crush her, she was prepared to *buy* Eadon Lodge, if she had to.

But her mother surprised her, astonished her. Marion not only kept the cottage, she kept it *intact*—unlike her home on Oxford Street—down to the last knickknack. All she added was a deck. She mailed Lydia a picture—several pictures, inside and out Eadon Lodge, as if to prove she wasn't kidding. Lydia remembers looking at the pictures—her first views of the cottage in thirty years—and then setting them afire on the gas stove.

Now, that day had come.

Could she cede Eadon Lodge to the town of Gimli in some fashion, so that it would remain as it is into perpetuity—or at least until her death? And yet it seems so farcical. What would they do? Have guided tours?

*Could* a heritage designation preserve the status quo?

"What *are* you going to do with the cottage?" Briony asks.

Lydia affects a shrug. "Sell it." She glances at her friend; a sudden thought grips her. "Why? Would you like to buy it?"

"Oh, no. I mean ..." In truth she and her husband could ill afford a second property. She envies Lydia the windfall that two properties will give her, along with money her father surely socked away. She has no idea how urgently Lydia needs the cash.

But Lydia is weighing that very need against the equally desperate need to keep Eadon Lodge and its grounds intact. She makes a swift decision: "Briony, why don't you just ... have it. Take the cottage. A gift. I'll have the lawyer—"

"Oh, Lydia." Briony puts her free hand on her friend's arm. She is touched yet somehow freaked by the extravagant offer. "It's too much. I'm—"

"You'd be doing me a favour, really. My only condition would be that you keep the cottage as it is."

"Oh, Lydia." Briony continues to gush, but feels somehow that some penny has dropped. There's a flicker of urgency in Lydia's eyes. "It's unbelievable, but I couldn't. Tim, you know ... I mean ... the cottage isn't accessible, is it?"

"You could put in a ramp."

"But the bathroom. I would need to ..." Briony is caught between bewilderment and horror. She doesn't wish to sound churlish. But she doesn't want the cottage, not with the peculiar condition attached. Her last memory of Eadon Lodge is one of distaste, of anger and confusion and embarrassment. And Tim's health is worsening. He will have to be institutionalized before long. This she hasn't told Lydia. Briony has no energy for any of this. She would do with Eadon Lodge what Lydia must do: sell it. She needs money, too. They all need money.

"Well, it's a thought." Lydia says, lifting her teacup. She can see from Briony's troubled expression that the offer has been a mistake.

Helen breaks away from a clump of cousins, old women and a few old men whom Lydia had earlier smiled and clucked with in half remembrance, and joins them.

"Lydia, eat something, dear," she says, proffering her plate. "The salmon ones are quite good.

"I'm not very hungry."

"Have you ever been to Eadon Lodge, Helen?" Briony interrupts, Lydia's offer clinging.

"Oh!" The question startles Helen. Of course, the cottage is part of the estate, too. Funny Lydia hasn't mentioned it. "Once, in the fifties," she replies after searching her memory, "before I moved away. I went up with my parents. Why?" She glances sideways at Briony, sensing some subtext to the question.

"We were just talking about it. I used to go up with Lydia when we were small."

"What I remember most is the high ceiling." Helen says. "I know cathedral ceilings are common now, but then, particularly in a summer cottage, it seemed ... almost outlandish. Oh, and that peculiar lamp hanging from a long chain from the ceiling. That sticks in my mind, too. Not really a chandelier, more like a ..."

"An upside-down crown," Briony supplies.

"Yes! Very good. All the light bulbs like jewels. Is it still there, I wonder, Lydia?"

Lydia's heart gallops. She steadies the teacup with her other hand and tries to purge her mind of an obscene memory. "I don't know. It's been years for me, too. It's probably still there. My father didn't like anything to change at the cottage. You know, I really should go over and say a word to—"

"... it seemed so remote, the cottage." Helen pops a pinwheel sandwich into her mouth. "Not now, I suppose?" She glances at both women for confirmation.

"Lots of new building going on now," Briony replies.

"Funny your grandfather building it there, well north of the town," Helen turns to Lydia.

"I wondered that, too. Years ago." A vague memory arises of asking her mother, after school, and being told to ask her father, which she never did. Lydia pieced it together later from overheard conversation and her own speculations on her family's psychology. "My grandfather was a snob, I think, and misanthrope."

Helen and Briony exchange glances.

"Your grandfather coped with a challenged child, though, didn't he?" Briony says soothingly. "That would have been hard in the twenties and thirties."

Lydia, troubled by her spurt of vehemence, makes murmuring agreement. Grandpa Eadon coped because a woman stepped in, as women do. Henry's spinster sister-in-law, May, gave up her life in Renfrew, Ontario, to manage the Winnipeg household and the two motherless little boys and left abruptly fifteen or so years later. Lydia recalls only the outlines of this ancient history, from some dinner table conversation. The idea of not having a mother disturbed her as a child. *So who brought you up then, Daddy? Why did she go, Daddy?* Bibs supplied only an outline. Marion attempted context "when she was old enough to understand," as they say: May likely "set her cap" for Henry and had been rebuffed or dismissed or something. Even Marion had never been able to pull the full story from her husband. The child Lydia soon lost interest. But the teenaged Lydia speculated that her father must surely have thought of May as his mother. And the middle-aged Lydia realized it with force when, in one of her Christmas stays, she first visited her now-frail father in his last residence, a nursing home, and found him confusing her with May in a storm of childish tears that left her shattered and exhausted.

As troubling was her father's confusing an aide in the nursing home, one of the petit Filipinos who seemed to populate the place, as his long-dead brother, Lits. "I'm sorry," he would repeat over and over to the young man who looked past his head to Lydia with a smiling forbearance. "I'm sorry, I'm sorry, I'm sorry."

# 6

Dorian glances at the date at the top of the page: July 8, 2008.

Today is July 11.

He tosses the *Free Press* onto the table. He'd like a cigarette, but the PA's arrival is imminent, and there's no smoking in the trailer, even if it's *his* bloody assigned trailer. In the scene they're set to shoot, he, as Bert Hammell, owner of the Morningstar Cove Marina, will extend to his teenaged fatherless grandson, Adam, some pithy advice about women's hearts. Adam, the troubled blond studmuffin with the heart of gold, is played by Ethan Elias, for whom Dorian stands *in loco parentis* on the set and off. Ethan peppers him with questions about his roles and his goals, which Dorian neatly elides, sidesteps, dissembles, grandiosifies—because he can. He's an *actor*! If you can lie, you can act, baby!

*Who said that? Brando?*

He can almost prophesy Ethan's career arc, because its foundation is much like his own: a modicum of talent married to a certain genetic happenstance: being a good-looking white guy. Ethan will do okay. He'll almost always have work. He might even hit the heights. But for that, talent and looks aren't enough. You need luck.

Dorian remembers fucking up a chance to play a lead in a revival in the late '70s of *Rope*. Where might his career have gone if Bruce Greenwood hadn't replaced him? He's beginning to fantasize. It's true, acting is mostly a lot of waiting around. He's bored. The role is unchallenging, much of it him projecting some variation of gruff love. Most of the cast, and crew, is very young. His only contemporary is Sara Hindle, with whom he's shared stage and screen in Toronto productions. She has a role parallel to his, the grandmother of Ethan's character's love interest. Sara's a laugh, but she's a dyke who likes a drink. She *really* likes a drink, and Dorian, teetotal for fifteen years now, itches for the velvety, oily feel of vodka on the tip of his tongue and the back of his throat whenever he joins her after the day's shoot. Itches for it more than he does at home, in Vancouver, craves the rush along his veins, sometimes thinks—against all wisdom—maybe one. Just one. I can handle one.

He's ambushed by memory in this place. He imagined he would be, but never anticipated the ferocity. Is it the light, the unsparing prairie light? Is it the aroma, the scent of sage in the heated breeze? Or is it the lake, the great grey sea of a lake? He can glimpse it if he turns his head just so outside his trailer window. Those hot August afternoons of sunbathing forty years ago at Eadon Lodge, made vaguely restive by the tedium of his book or the delicious plane of Paul's thigh, he would lift his eyes and send them roving over its characterless surface—darker grey through sunglasses—to the shimmering mirage of the distant shore.

Dorian's eyes fall back on the newspaper. The *Free Press* has a daily obituary summary on the front page, boxed, above the fold. He hadn't noticed this before. The list is alphabetical; the second name is Eadon, Marion. His attention sharpens. Wasn't Lydia's mother's first name Marion? Of course it was. He knows this perfectly well.

A production assistant pokes her head in, ready to take him to the dock where the scene is set. Dorian holds up a warning hand. He scrambles though the disarray of newsprint for the correct section and finds the full obituary. With picture. Marion Patricia Eadon (née Clifford), 1924 to 2008. A picture forty years old. When Dorian last saw her. Marion, crisply coiffed. His heart jolts. He begins reading the words Lydia composed a week ago.

But the production assistant is quivering with annoyance. Time is money. Dorian rises. He doesn't need the details. Knowing Marion is dead is enough. Why had he put off thinking this day would come? All the parents are gone. They had to be. He knew Bibs was. Briony told him. She'd announced herself backstage at the Manitoba Theatre Centre—when was it? 2004?—when he had appeared in *Night of the*

*Iguana.* But Marion was going strong. Dorian thought her an eternally skinny clotheshorse, like the Duchess of Windsor. Did he really think she would live on and on? Lydia must be in the city. The funeral was when? He makes a quick last glance at the paper. July 9—two days ago. There would be the house on Oxford Street to deal with.

And Eadon Lodge.

*What if your parents sell it?* he hissed at her at the Halloween party. This was in the kitchen at Oxford Street, before the evening descended into chaos. *What if somebody else buys it? What then?*

It won't happen, Lydia assured him.

*But your mother* hates *the cottage. Grimli, she calls it, remember?* Grim-*li.*

Marion reigns, but Bibs rules, Dorian. Bibs loves the cottage.

*Your father's older than your mother. Men die younger. What will the widow Eadon do, Mrs. Peel?*

He remembers Lydia faltering. It was hard at twenty to imagine your life at sixty, seventy, parents gone, children grown. If, Lydia told him, my mother tries to sell, I will stop her, of course.

*And if you can't?*

I will.

*And if you can't?*

I'll call you. Don't worry.

*Promise.*

Promise.

Would she remember after ... what was it? Thirty-nine years? She was the only one sober at that party. She should remember. But to what length would she go to find him? Their ties were cut that Halloween.

Dorian follows the PA to the set, composing himself, bringing his lines to mind, pushing away thoughts of Eadon Lodge. But they seep back in. Two days earlier, they were filming on Lake Winnipeg, north of Winnipeg Beach, in a sailboat. The scene, three minutes in the finished work, was hours in the capturing, the morning's filming filled with take after take, the camera buggering up at one point, a second assistant falling into the water, the weather turning abruptly, Dorian himself flubbing a line, then again, and again. It all felt unlucky, and actors, Dorian included, are a superstitious tribe. To auditions, Dorian wears his father's watch on his right wrist, for example.

Dorian sensed something off that morning, some nascent *atmosphere* as they sped northward in the speedboat to where the sailboat and the camera boat were waiting for them. He thought of it later as Paul's flickering shadow over shadowless waters, stirring them in death as he had in life. They shot across the lake's murky surface, engine roar obliterating all conversation, Dorian scanning the scallops of beach along the shore as they drew closer to Gimli, then past Gimli, until they stopped across from a spit of land half curtained by trees. He kept his focus on the work, but boats are fickle things in moving water and in some turn of the bow, his eyes found it over Ethan's shoulder: a white box trimmed with green, small and neat as a doll's house, catching the sun, catching his breath. Eadon Lodge. Still there.

For now.

Whenever Dorian thinks of Halloween 1969 at the Eadons' house he thinks of one of those mazy trees in films set in India dripping with chattering monkeys. Monkeys on the china cabinet and sofa backs, monkeys up the banister, monkeys swinging from the chandelier.

Nominally a Halloween party, it's really a party at Halloween. Few are invited. Few are costumed, and none so provocatively as Dorian. Of the *invited* guests, Briony is still wearing her buckskin jacket, but she's added a headband with a feather and rouged her cheeks into an Indian princess effect, the memory of which will make her cringe in later years. Alanna chose an elaborate—and gauzy—harem costume from Mallabar's, which has ignited Alan's censure and his lust. In a concession to the frippery of the event—and to Alanna—Alan is wearing a walrus half-mask. From the outside, he looks like a wizened, bearded (the beard is new) old brown man with obscenely long canine teeth. From the inside, the mask stinks of rubber atomized by the heat of his own breath. He gets a lot of *goo-goo-ga-joob* from the others as he passes into the kitchen to get another beer. "Are you the walrus?" several ask.

The walrus was the bad guy in the story, man, someone says to provoke Alan. He was the *capitalist,* man. Dorian is at the edge of this clutch of young men, uncomfortably damp in the cocoon of his trench coat. "Capitalist! You should see this guy play Monopoly." He slurs the words. "Ruthless. Fucking ruthless."

A thunderstorm rose over the lake and enveloped Eadon Lodge one afternoon when the six of them were finishing lunch. Who suggested a game of Monopoly? Mother Briony probably. Lydia, for one, was content to read in the bedroom, rain on the roof being so cozy, but the game was dragged out of the shelf at the bottom of the Victrola anyway. Paul dozed on one of the two old fold-out couches that anchored the living room. The rest gathered around a card table erected under the harsh light of the electrolier and played the game where, rather like life, luck was misinterpreted as virtue. Alan *was* ruthless, extending into this silly game all the aggression at his command. Immune to mockery, he soured everyone, even his girlfriend, until finally Paul rose from the couch and tipped the board onto the floor.

Dorian realizes too late it was unwise to mention Monopoly. Alan pushes the mask to the top of his head and shoots him a look that he interprets, his eyes swimming, as *knowing*. The vodka doesn't dull the jangle of fright along his nerves. Here's why: Alan came back, unexpectedly, to Eadon Lodge the morning of that last day, from the hotel where he and Alanna had repaired after the shotgun incident. He showed up to help—as he'd promised earlier he would—the boys lift the wooden covering from the old outhouse hole and fill it with the tarpaulined pile of dirt that had been sitting around for several days along with some sod. But he arrived about eleven to find most of the task done and the cottage closed and locked and silent and Lydia appearing—finally—at the door, pale as a wraith.

Another smartass in passing says to Alan, "Hey, man, are you the walrus?" and Alan, his eyes still on that fuck Dorian Grant for lampooning his righteous politics, quotes:

"'Here's another clue for you all: the walrus was Paul.'"

Dorian's stomach lurches. Lydia may have been unaware of Paul McCartney's rumoured death, but Dorian, in a drunken haze at the Montcalm, has heard it all from the other class-cutting reprobates. The word "walrus" is supposedly Greek for "corpse."

Oh, Jesus, *does* Alan know something?

Is he suspicious?

At least Lydia had kept her cool about Paul's whereabouts that morning. Dorian caught snatches of her conversation with Alan through Eadon Lodge's thin walls. They're asleep, Lydia said. But Alan's skeptical tone—"Yeah, I'm sure they are"—will pierce his consciousness in later years if ever "Glass Onion" is played. He will remember all the stoned earnestness about who the walrus was or wasn't. John or Paul. He'll recall that Halloween party from another angle because a few feet away others are poring over the cover of *Abbey Road* for the most sinister of the Paul-is-dead clues, the dirge of "She's So Heavy" pounding from the hi-fi muffling their words.

Dorian watches in silent stoned misery various guys yanking one Beatles record off the turntable and slapping on another, each jockeying to expose some profound death clue or other. A song, part of a song, part of a part of a song, is played over and over. The needle skips. The speakers pop. The tone arm lifts and the sudden absence of sound sets heads swivelling, voices groaning, frowns forming. People take turns pressing their ears to the fabric of the hi-fi's speakers as the most arcane of the clues are buried within the fadeouts. One guy with a black beard forces the record groove against the needle *backwards*. "Listen! Can you hear it? Lennon's saying, 'turn me on, dead man.'" The guy turns, his face beatific, his eyes glittering.

But the revellers are growing weary of this fucking around with the music. The Paul-is-dead controversy is a couple of weeks old and wearing thin. Music's background. Foreground is drinking, smoking weed, flirting ... more.

The *White Album* comes off, bringing a new silence and a new burst of groans. The bearded guy—whoever he is—reaches for *Magical Mystery Tour*, pulling the disk from the cover. "Fucking cut it out, man," a male voice slices through the air, but Mister Beardy, smiling stupidly, is oblivious. Click, clunk, pop and the tone arm is bouncing in another vinyl groove and the trippy swirl of Mellotron fills the absence. Dorian recognizes it instantly as the coda, the last thirty seconds, of "Strawberry Fields Forever." *Here's another clue for you all.* Dorian knows which one *this* is. He can't bear it. He stumbles to his feet. He's tall—six, one—and in trench coat and dress shoes he projects, even with naked calves, enough adultlike authority to elbow Mr. Beardy out of the way and snatch the tone arm, catching it before Lennon intones a terrifying confession. The needle rips across the vinyl like a nail on a chalkboard and he feels his gorge loosen. He could spew the contents of his guts into the hi-fi's cavity right now.

"Zeppelin!" someone shouts.

Dorian's hand reaches blindly into the pile. *Meet The Beatles!* An album from the age of innocence—his own, and the Beatles, before they discovered acid and Stockhausen and Yoko. Only six years gone, it's already an oldie. But it's rock'n'roll. Dorian wants to dance. He grabs Alanna's hand as Paul (McCartney—or his doppelgänger) does the count: *One! Two! Three! Four!* Alanna's nearest. She smiles. She's instantly game. Alan has been a drag all evening. They fought over coming to the party, over her costume, over his wearing any costume at all. You can't get Alan to dance anyway except under extreme duress. Screw him.

*Well, she was just seventeen, you know what I mean.*

Dorian remembers dancing with Alanna to this song at a sock hop in grade ten. Or maybe it was Lydia. He's not sure now. He may have a partner—he and Alanna are doing a sloppy jive, hands slipping and gripping in the small space where the coffee table once stood—but he feels he's dancing by himself, on the threshold of a kind of animal joy he hasn't felt in many months, since long before the catastrophe at Eadon Lodge. Okay, he's pretty drunk, but Alanna knows the moves and steers his. In her harem outfit, her breasts jiggle, and her ass, when she turns, is a fetching thing, too. Dorian can see through the blur of movement and drink, the eyes of several men stray to her and he almost cackles with glee, knowing how this will provoke her territorial boyfriend. Someone is sufficiently taken with the little show before them to move the tone arm to "It Won't Be Long," another little rocker on the A side. Dorian and Alanna continue, as if there had been no break in the music. The faces turned to them are a little blurry now. That's good. He feels the pure pleasure of the moment washing over him. At a turn, he glimpses Alan push through to the front of the growing knot of onlookers. At the next turn, he glimpses Alan cross his arms over his chest, his beer tucked into the crook of his arm. Alan's frowning. *Aw, too bad, asshole.* Dorian lets his smile widen at Alan's displeasure. Dorian's fedora falls off his head. The belt of his trench slips. Alanna comes out of a swinging turn, her astonished laugh rising above the song's busy bass line as the coat flies open like cupboard door. The others watching, all University College compatriots, laugh, too. Dorian swings near Alan. Alan leans in, his lips brushing Dorian's ear, a prelude to a kiss that will never happen.

"Faggot," he hisses.

# 7

The weather in August 1969 was gloriously hot and sunny. Perhaps if it had been a filthy rainy day when Briony stepped out onto the street, her social work field placement at the Family Bureau having come to an end, her mind wouldn't have lit on the notion of a beach idyll at Eadon Lodge. A seed had been planted earlier—Lydia had told her that her parents were spending the last two weeks of the month, not at Gimli as Bibs insisted they do each year, but in Europe, on a tour. Marion's cudgel had been their wedding anniversary, August 26, which she was *not* spending at "that goddamn cottage *again.*"

Lydia, rarely given to impulse, needed little persuading in this instance. This was her third summer as a fill-in receptionist at a downtown clinic and she was weary of being all young-lady smiles for impatient doctors and apprehensive patients, and unsettled by unseen germs, washing her hands a dozen times a day. She had enough money saved for tuition anyway. But would Bibs let them have the cottage all to themselves? She had to ask his permission. Last summer, Ross—her now ex-boyfriend—cajoled her into sneaking the keys to Eadon Lodge and having a day of *privacy,* but one of the two keys to the side door, an antique skeleton variety, somehow, maddeningly, *infuriatingly,* stuck in the lock, then snapped in two. Lydia's shame before her father was complete. This time, no deceit.

There were really so many ifs, so many variables, so many possible outcomes—though Lydia entertained these thoughts only afterwards. The issue of a transportation for instance. How were they to get to the cottage? Briony only had a learner's permit and didn't have her own car anyway. Bibs had a Buick that he wouldn't be using while he and Marion were away, but Bibs brought the Spanish Inquisition to Lydia whenever she asked to borrow the car. So Lydia tried car-owning friends.

Dorian and his black Beetle first: But Dorian, returned early from New York, groaned that after several boring weeks of enforced incarceration with his grandparents at Lake of the Woods, he now had to turn around and visit his mother and stepfather at West Hawk. How long he'd be gone, he didn't know.

Alanna and her white Mustang convertible next: Alanna might be more flexible. She was nominally employed at Rhondaco, her father's company, but spent most of her time at the stables. She was horse mad.

Here Lydia hesitated: She knew Briony, despite her minister's-daughter best, didn't warm to Alanna. So, she argued to Briony, she couldn't ask Alanna to just drop them off at Eadon Lodge. She would have to invite her to *stay* with them and hope that maybe the lure of the horses—and Alan—would send her back to town.

Alanna detected the insincerity in Lydia's invitation, but it gave her the upper hand. She used it: she insisted on a departure date convenient to *her* and said Alan, laid off from his construction job, would join them. Briony uttered a rare expletive, plus—*how come she gets to have a boyfriend come up?*—but there was nothing to be done. They were going to have to take the—*ick!*—bus if they were to hone to *their* schedule. Alanna would drive them back to town later.

Resigned to the Greyhound, Lydia went to her father for permission to use the cottage. *Why don't you use my car?* he said. She remembers being stunned by this unusual bout of expansiveness and groped for its source. Was her father actually looking forward to his European trip? He hated travel, another of her mother's complaints as all her smart friends seemed to be jetting all over the place. Perhaps the war had leached the desire from him. Or that trip he took with his father and brother to England before the war, where Lits died of influenza. Whatever the case, Lydia recovered from her surprise quickly and said, Great, yes, thanks, we'll use your car, thanks again, Dad.

So the seeds of disaster were planted. If Lydia had asked her father for the car in the first place, she and Briony would have spent two weeks at Eadon Lodge most likely without company. Briony had no boyfriend to drive up and be useful. Lydia had ended her relationship with Ross—for the second time—the previous Valentine's Day.

On August 15, an ordinary Friday, Lydia and Briony stuffed their luggage into the trunk of Bibs's Buick and drove off to the lake. Alanna would arrive, with Alan, in a few days. Bibs said at the last minute that they had to take delivery, unconscionably delayed, of some soil and sod and fill in the old outhouse pit. "Get the boy—or boys—to do it," he said, countering her blush with a knowing glance. It was his only proviso, a crimp in their plans for pure indolence, an imperfect start to an otherwise perfect day, the temperature a perfect 77, the sky a perfect blue, perfectly cloudless. Lydia would remember vividly—however hard she tried to push it from her mind—the terrible return journey two weeks later, when the August heat wave had spent itself, when the skies had greyed, the wind risen, and the rain spattered the windshield, but most details of the journey north that late morning eluded her powers of recall.

What had Briony and she talked about in the car, two young women on the brink of blooming adulthood, their bright lives rolling out in front of them? Books and boys? Jobs and plans? Shops and shoes and whatever was on the news? A song, yes, one—"Lay Lady Lay." Dylan's words saturated the car, stirring a longing in Lydia that she gave no utterance of to Briony, who shifted in the passenger seat, turning to study the ripening fields outside the window. Her spurning of other romantic chances in the wake of her break-up with Ross at Valentine's now seemed foolish, and Lydia's mind travelled to the iron bedstead at Eadon Lodge, proxy for Dylan's big brass bed, single billet these coming days. *Why wait any longer for the world to begin?* the singer sang.

"Grammatically, shouldn't it be 'lie lady lie'?" Briony broke in, plucking at the frayed edge of her cutoffs. "Otherwise it sounds like he's bossing around some poor chicken." Feeling cold water on heated thought—this detail Lydia remembers; she uses it later in editorial seminars—she agreed that it should. "Yes," she repeated with a small sigh, "it should be 'lie lady lie.'"

# 8

Dorian twists around Alanna to the final notes of "It Won't Be Long" in the Eadons' living room, a red mist descending, adrenalin rushing to his fists. The last time he heard the word "faggot" directed at him flashes in his mind diamond bright. He is once again among the multiple thousands amassed up and down Fifth Avenue across from St. Patrick's Cathedral the second Saturday in June 1968. Unable to penetrate the thick cords of Robert Kennedy's humble, mostly silent, mourners at the West 50th corner, he finds himself stood against a shop window, his eyes first caught by the glint of sunshine on the cathedral's soaring spires, then by a glint in the eye of a man a few feet away who appears a few years older and a few pounds bulkier than Dorian, with visible tennis-ball biceps. His dress, like Dorian's, is too casual for this solemn assembly: jeans, a T-shirt, sunglasses perched on his head. But Dorian arrived in the city only two days before, on a half-baked quest for a job, any job, in New York's film industry—and though he brought a tie, he never thought to put it on before leaving his hotel room, drawn, like half the city, through the humid heat to this place of mute grief. But it won't be this prince's funeral that sticks in Dorian's memory. He is gone by the time the flag-draped casket is carried out of the cathedral. The bicepy guy smiles a smile Dorian already knows, but has never responded to before in the way he will. He feels the hollow burn of attraction in his stomach and reads the message in the other's cool grey-eyed gaze.

The other is Ric (*sans* "k," he explains as they move in lockstep west through thinning crowds). He's also a Canadian, from Toronto, in New York, finishing his degree in journalism at Columbia. He shares a Hell's Kitchen apartment, his roommate, an American, more stricken by

Kennedy's death, is lost somewhere in the multitude on Fifth Avenue. Dorian and Ric go back to Ric's room, which is the last-stop room of a railroad flat. It is here, in the hallelujah moments, that Dorian hears the f-word—the six-letter one—bawled, not in scorn, as it was a few seconds ago, but in the sticky throes of pure desire.

But now Dorian's fist has found the hard bone beneath Alan's bearded cheek. Alan's head snaps back, blood spurts from his nose. The walrus mask twists away. The beer bottle he's been nestling to his chest slips to the hardwood, not breaking but bouncing, sending an arc of amber fizz over pant legs and socks, and rattling along the floor—noisily, for in the very same moment someone lifts the tone arm and music and conversation halt at once. Bloodlust, like a kind of electricity, surges and soars along the living room with its sectional sofa and pole lamps and step tables that Marion has so tastefully assembled and these children have so quickly disassembled. The nearest noncombatants draw back. A woman screams. Dorian is numbed, dazed by drink and fury. If it wasn't so, he'd drop to the hardwood from the pain in the balled hand that connected with Alan's face, but instead, he raises it again, tighter, more conscious now of his task: to beat the living shit out of Alan Rayner, shut his fucking mouth. But Alan is no tyro. He is shorter than Dorian, but those construction jobs over the past two summers have added a layer of hardened muscle to his upper body. Having two brothers, he's been in more fights than Dorian. He knows where to hit back. Somewhere soft and vulnerable. Dorian's pale torso, exposed in the frame of the flapping trench coat, for instance. Or Dorian's flopping genitals, equally exposed. Alan can end Dorian's attack with a precise blow to the solar plexus or a swift knee to the testicles.

Alanna's face rises past Dorian's shoulder like a new moon. Indignation swiftly replaces shock but Alan's twisted expression, the blood, his animal verve, thrums along her nerves. Something passes from her to Alan in his adrenalin cloud—consent, though he doesn't need it. He's goaded by that shrieking female, too, though he's in no need of that, either. He senses fandom from the males in the room, though, really, they're only keen for a fight to continue at interesting length. He doesn't know half of them would be happy to see his sanctimonious ass creamed.

Alan jerks his knee upward. Dorian gasps, collapses in slo-mo shock, clutches his genitals, groans. Sympathy, there is little. Alanna rushes to Alan, leads him to the bathroom to wash away the blood. Dorian has no champion, and no one, each for his or her own reason, wants to lend succor to a naked man in an open trench coat in some sort of thrall to his bits. The shunning deepens when Dorian, suddenly ashen, flips onto his stomach and scrambles crablike to Marion's potted aspidistra and vomits, a torrent of spew splashing onto the soil and dead leaves, spitting onto the rolled carpet and the couch edge. It's like he's gagging up all the fear and anxiety and nightmare of the last two months, exorcising it in one rainbow arc of liquors. His head sags over the acrid fumes, one hand clutching the rim of the planter, almost tipping it over with his sweating head. Briony and Lydia zip past each other through the kitchen door, Briony to wet a towel to clean the upholstery, Lydia to seek and destroy the source of this latest disturbance. She passes into the dining room, more crowded and noisy and frowsty than the kitchen.

She elbows her way into the living room, record player blasting again, to find Dorian's blond head in a pool of sick and everyone else a measured distance away, oblivious. As some complete stranger leers at her through a scrim of marijuana smoke, Lydia experiences a rising tide of disgust joined with apprehension. She knows Dorian's weakness for the overblown gesture. She's seen him drunk before. She's seen him sick before. She's seen him gauche before. But now he hoards a secret with her that, let loose, would bring their world to an end. It's all too much.

She doesn't know if she can bear to be in his presence any more. The realization hits her like cold rain, but it's only her conscious mind acknowledging a truth burrowing *sub terra* for two months. She is falling away from affection. She and he were introduced to each other as babies—so her mother told her, at Eadon Lodge in the summer of 1950—but Lydia's first memory of him is in Miss Strath's kindergarten classroom, a blond boy with pale eyelashes filtered through a halo of September sunshine, tripping with a tray of watercolours, rainbowing her little dress, bursting into tears. But some presentiment of love stopped her shrieking before the wet seeped to her skin, even though fastidiousness was already invested in her with her mother's milk. Where was young Miss Strath? Nipped out. Lydia comforted Dorian, cleaned herself as best she could, cleaned the floor as best she could. It's a tiny but telling scene, an augury, the start of a trajectory that has all the inevitability of fate.

Lydia weathered the hormonal storms beginning eight years later by recasting Dorian as some romantic figure out of book or film, Gilbert Blythe in *Anne of Green Gables,* say, or Ashley Wilkes in *Gone with the Wind.* He is safe. Smoke abounds, but no fire erupts. And Dorian's response, though she doesn't really sense it, is confused and unanchored. "My life will be in your keeping, waking, sleeping, laughing, weeping." His eyes stray to hers in choir rehearsal, where their teacher has introduced a new song, from some new film they're too young to see, *Mondo Cane,* her old spinsterish self tearing at such words of promise in such young voices. Passionate and pure, Lydia waits. Dorian hovers. He phones her and hangs up. She knows it's him. He bicycles down Oxford. She sees it's him. And yet something stays him, at friend's length.

The apple doesn't fall far from the tree, her father remarks one June evening as they both watch from the porch Dorian ride off on his bike into the shadows of the street's towering elms. The saying, trite as it is, is new to her, even at fourteen, though its implication eludes her even as her understanding grows that Dorian is somehow, permanently, unfixably different than other boys. They remain friends through high school, part of a brainy, artsy clique. They are Steed and Mrs. Peel, their relationship as mysterious and ambiguous as that of the leads in *The Avengers,* their comportment stylish and witty and ironic. Meanwhile, on the sidelines, there's Ross Stubbs to fill another bill. He's not really someone you can hang much imagination on. He's practical, rough and ready (he's on the high school football team), lacks the rounder depths of soul of someone like, well, Dorian, but he's ardent. Give him that. Lydia accepts his attentions, though she and Dorian look so much better together, prom king and queen material, and wishes sometimes, as high school passes to college, it were Dorian making love to her. Ross shows little curiosity about Dorian. *Gosh, Ross is thick,* she thinks at times. But then Dorian never, as they say, flaunts it.

And then, at Eadon Lodge, at the very end, he flaunted it.

Lydia ignores Briony, who is fluttering around Dorian with a tea towel, and seeks out Alanna. "I'm taking him home," she shouts over the music into her ear. No need to say who "he" is. Alanna nods. She's to mind the fort in Lydia's absence. Car keys fetched, Lydia abandons her parents' home to god-knows-who-half-these-people-are, affecting indifference, though she's on the verge of panic, trusting that Alanna, officious even in a harem dress, is insurance against disaster.

Briony is the more solicitous, taking the towel from Dorian's trembling hand and gingerly retying the trench coat belt, staring away lest her eyes burn. Coatless, as neither girl can find her coat in the jumble in the front closet, they steer Dorian across the porchful of mildly curious dope smokers to Bibs's Buick. Thank god no one's blocked the driveway. Getting Dorian into the passenger seat is like folding an ironing board into a box, but finally they can push the heavy door shut. The rich chunking sound is almost satisfying, like a lock turned on a prison door. Then Briony flicks the lock on the back door and scrambles into the blackness of the interior before Lydia can stop her. Lydia dreads having her with them, but can't find a reason to order her out of the car. Crossing the lawn to the driveway, Dorian began to babble, not a word unslurred, but Lydia fears the moment of clarity, the unguarded utterance. And Briony with ears alert.

The drive to the Grant home on Dromore Avenue is not far—walkable, in other circumstances. The car starting with its throaty rasp triggers some shift in Dorian's consciousness. As Lydia backs the car into the dark street, he lets go a damp sob that bubblebursts into a keening howl. Lydia's hands grip the cold steering wheel. Her nerves, taut, pull her along an arc of recent memory. She is back at Eadon Lodge, the night of the abomination, her eyes unbelieving, her world spinning.

*Don't speak, don't speak, don't speak, for Christ's sake, don't speak,* her mind shouts at him as she crosses Kingsway, her teeth grinding. Briony pushes herself into the soft cushion of the back seat, transfixed by the dramatics, groping for comprehension. This ... *agony* of Dorian's. His elusiveness all fall. His abandonment of the car pool. His no-shows for lunch at University College cafeteria. His afternoons at the Montcalm's bar. His class cutting. Lydia's, too. She looks at the back of Lydia's head, at the dark hair disappearing behind the headrest. She is rigid. Driving like a drunk, overcautious. But Lydia had no drink. None at all, that Briony could see. *Odd.* Meanwhile, Dorian's unrelenting sobs wrench at her heart, but there seems no comforting gesture she can make from the restraint of a back seat and his pickled breath, off-putting, is filling the claustrophobic space. She rolls down the back window a crack.

And now they are outside the Grant house. Windows like blackened eyes. No front light on. Lawn streetlit greygreen with greyer mottlings of dead leaves. Lydia brakes, but keeps the car in gear. The motor purrs richly. Dorian slumps, oblivious, gasping sobs, wheezing to catch his breath to begin again. Lydia's knuckles whiten along the steering wheel. *Get out, get out, get out. For Christ's sake, get out of the car.* Briony is pinned by indecision. Should she help Dorian to his door? But there comes a break in the extravagant storm. Lydia sees Dorian's hand grope for the door handle. *Thank god.* He pulls out of his slump, turns his head to her, his eyes blurred with tears, his lips begin to part. The eyes focus now. It is beseeching she sees. In later years, that is what she will think of it. He pushes against the handle, the door swings open heavily. He says, Briony hears, Lydia shudders:

"I loved him."

*Loved him?*

"Alan?" Briony is foggy with confusion.

Lydia's eyes flick from the figure of Dorian stumbling through the shadows of the Grants' front yard to Briony's disembodied head in the car's rear-view mirror. She wants to weep, but can't, doesn't dare. She manages to croak: "No, of course not."

Briony is schooled in an instant. Of course. Not Alan. *Paul.*

Love*d.*

Dorian love*d* Paul. The fatal past tense, how curious. She sensed all the girls found Paul ... diverting in one way or another. Alanna seemed more to study him, coolly, in that way of hers. Lydia—*umph,* well ... Lydia, she could have anyone she wanted, if she set her mind to it. She herself, little Briony, could wish upon a star and anything her heart desired would *not* come true. (It *does* make a difference who you are.) Paul was well out of her league. And then, it seems, there was Dorian. His attraction to Paul she realized too suddenly, too late, and acted very silly about—making Lydia drive her back to the city, then switching to the bus at Winnipeg Beach, never mind, too late for regrets now.

But Dorian love*d* Paul. The love ended. Briony will mull this state—or statelessness—for a little while to come. Dorian's misery actually gives her some small satisfaction, which isn't very nice. Her reverend daddy wouldn't approve. And there's karma to think of. She daren't ask Lydia for details (love*d*?) as she got short shrift the one and only time she nerved herself to ask Lydia the whatever-happened-to question about Paul Godwin. *Weren't Dorian and Paul going together to Los Angeles to seek fame and fortune?* Apparently not, said Lydia. This was on their first day back in classes in early September. *So what happened?* I suppose Dorian came to his senses. *Then ... ?* Continuing west, I guess, Lydia shrugged. I think Dorian dropped him off on the Trans-Canada somewhere. *Has Dorian heard from him?* I don't know.

Love*d*?

Briony won't fall in love until her first-born is placed in her arms.

# 9

Dorian struggles to keep his breath steady, to control the muscles of his mouth and throat as, finally, he extends his hand and feels Peter Radcliff's dry palm along his dampening one and a grip more aggressive than polite. He murmurs "pleasure to meet you," almost inaudible amid the merry Christmas party chatter in Dixie-May's living room. He smiles with all the thespian facility at his command and continues a semblance of conversation with Peter and Dix and the others in the little grouping by the fireplace, all the while feeling his ears pulsing with blood and his brain afire like the first time he dropped acid, conversation now turned jabbering glossolalia. Finally comes a moment when he can excuse himself—*flee!* He threads his way through the revellers, cranberry punch in hand, to the downstairs powder room, ablaze with scented candles. As he lets his mask of bonhomie drop, a tremor flies along his nerves and the drink glass slips from his hand into the sink, shattering, the cascade of cranberry red—near black in this light—joined by spurts of blood red—more viscously black—from his scrabbling fingers. *Fuck, fuck, fucking Christ.* Dorian stuffs the bleeding fingers of his right hand into his mouth, his eyes grazing his image in the mirror. Candles uplighting his face, hollowing his cheeks, fevering his eyes. He would let no lighting director do this. His left hand finds the light switch. The bathroom blazes as bathrooms should.

Peter Radcliff is Paul's brother. There is no mistake. He may be Lennon's bullet-headed Saxon mother's son grown up now, coarsened, thickened, but beneath the skin is the skull: nose, chin, brow sculpted and aligned so unmistakably in imitation of someone he once knew, that flame in his heart and weight on his soul, Paul Godwin.

And Dixie-May Lang is Paul's mother.

No doubt.

But the names, the *names*?

The next day he will visit the library and pull *Canadian Who's Who* from the reference room shelf.

Dorian and Paul are in Dorian's little black Bug. It's a 1967 model Volkswagen that Dorian bought used from a neighbour for high school graduation. Neither speaks as the car rattles down the Trans-Canada. It's not because the windows are open and the summer air an unrelenting whoosh past their ears. It's not the radio blasting. Dorian switched it off before he rolled into the Shell station, the song, "Hot Fun in the Summertime," inescapable that season, reminding him of his failures—unlike the summer before—to find any film work or romance in New York. No, it's because conversation feels beside the point. The air is freighted with a certain expectation. But an expectation fulfilled so soon? Dorian glances from the road to his passenger's scuffed boots, to the frayed jeans, which he sees now mended here and there with red embroidery stars that match the T-shirt star, to the tantalizing line of exposed flesh peeking above the belt line. The stranger catches his eye. A dirty angel smirk creases his cheeks—a smile to smite Dorian again and again in the days ahead. His eyes seem to sparkle with shared complicity.

They drive a short distance.

A hand rounds the top of Dorian's thigh. Dorian is wearing shorts. Fingers silk their way under the hem. Dorian doesn't flinch, but his heart beats a mad tattoo, blood rushing and surging. When the fingers seek a new destination along the zipper, Dorian gasps, suppresses a yelp. What happens next is unsurprising, though it's useful to know that a mouth, not a hand, is the instrument of pleasure. Such a shenanigan hardly seems novel now, but then Dorian was lost in enchantment. What was the protocol? Brake to the side of the road. Pull off onto a byway? Keep driving? The takeaway here is the risk. Two docked bodies careening at sixty miles an hour down a single lane. No seatbelts. Cars speeding toward you, mere feet on their side of the white line. The blinding moment of release. The point is, our stranger—Paul—very much liked to take a risk. And Dorian's desire for a larger world was feverish.

New York had been a sour place that summer. Dorian couldn't explain why, and no one else, the others he met scrounging—and not finding—film work among the offices on 45th and 46th Streets seemed able to put a finger on it. It was as if a pall had been cast over the city, a harbinger of the decade to come when New York descended into grunginess, danger, and bankruptcy. Dorian found a place in a rooming house at West 72nd and Broadway and spent the empty hours visiting the art galleries and museums and nervously skirting the edges of the West Village.

The summer before, Robert Kennedy's funeral notwithstanding, the city had shimmered for Dorian. He found work at the offices of Leacock-Pennebaker where—*wow!*—Dylan's *Dont Look Back* film had been produced. Okay, he toiled for many weeks as a sort of messenger and doing some tedious gruntwork, re-ordering film footage, but a floor above Norman Mailer established a film office for his vainglorious experiments in *cinéma vérité* and through the Pennebaker connection, Dorian became a sound assistant on Mailer's *Maidstone.*

So radical! No script. No one had any idea what they were doing. Something about political assassination or male prostitutes or both. Topless starlets all over the lawns of East Hampton. Negro militants, Warhol hangers-on, rich socialites, Mailer strutting around shirtless barking orders, Mailer breaking some actor's jaw, Mailer bashed over the head with a hammer by Rip Torn, crates of booze, bags of drugs, and the sex, Jesus, everywhere. *Get any?* Maybe. Not telling. (Nothing to tell. The atmosphere of excess grew so freaky his appetite moved swiftly from fascination to flight.) The experience is reputation burnishing, though, and partly on the strength of it, he lands his first film role—a speaking part (five lines!) in *And No Birds Sing,* an hour-long feature produced by the university students' union.

Dorian lets this information tumble out as he drives along the highway, able now to drive without distraction. Particulars have been forthcoming: names, dates, places. Paul. His name is Paul. Paul Godwin.

He's from Toronto. Headed for Los Angeles—the long way, at a right angle, the vertex being Vancouver. See the country. He's never been through western Canada. He's in no rush. He was hitching through Europe most of the past year, Barcelona, Berlin, Mykonos. Which is why Dorian, who has yet to travel to Europe, brings up New York and his adventures there, eager not to appear uncooler than thou.

"Far out," says Paul, reaching into a leather bag attached to his belt. "So you're into acting?" He pulls out a joint and beams at Dorian. There's a kind of wonder and enthusiasm and approval in his voice that makes Dorian an instant ally. The beat of the sentence falls on "acting."

"A cousin of mine's a big producer out there." Paul wets the joint with his mouth.

"*Really*?"

Paul pulls a lighter from the bag. "Yeah," he says as he flicks at the recalcitrant thing. "Edgar Z. Rusoff, King of the B's. *Swamp Monster*? Heard of it? Fuck this *fucking* lighter."

"Try that," Dorian gestures to the car's cigarette lighter, ignoring the explosion of pique, his mind roiling with several confused thoughts: "bees"? and "Rusoff"? Is Paul Jewish?

"I'm going to be staying with him while I'm there."

"Far out."

"You should come with me."

"To L.A.?"

"Why not?"

"School in September?"

Paul makes dismissive gesture as he reaches for the car lighter. "Edgar could set you up in something, get you an audition. Is going to school how you become an actor?"

"Is that why you're going to L.A.? To become an actor?"

"Me? Maybe. What do you think?" Paul positions the joint between his fingers like one of those bitch-goddess actresses, Joan Crawford or Bette Davis, and takes a campy drag. Dorian explodes with laughter. Paul explodes, too, the smoke exiting his nose in jagged plumes.

"I think you just want me to drive you to Los Angeles."

Paul gasps for breath and hands him the joint. He rubs Dorian's thigh. "Wouldn't you enjoy my company?"

A cousin who's a Hollywood producer? Sounds like bullshit. What are the chances that the ambitions of one young man could so neatly align with the opportunities afforded by another? But Paul does have a familial connection in Hollywood, no lie, though "cousin" is shorthand, stretching it a bit. With some prompting, Paul explains that the "cousin" is the husband of a cousin of his mother's—a second cousin, then?—anyway, a girl from Ottawa, Alice, who went to Los Angeles before the war, or during the war, to meet an agent or a producer, and become a star. Instead she became a wife. And the "bees"? That's "B's," as in "B" movies. Edgar Z. produced tons of them—monster movies, horror movies, beach blanket bingo bikini à go go movies. Dorian remembers going with Lydia once, around 1963, to see *Gidget Goes Bananas* or some such crap at the Gaiety. Did Edgar Z. produce Gidget movies?

"Probably," Paul shrugs. "Alice and my mother are pretty close," he adds, stuffing the roach into the car's ashtray. "You'll like Alice. She was in one of Edgar Z.'s films—an early one, *Attack of the Ant People* or something."

"Mmm," Dorian murmurs. Not exactly Fellini or Antonioni or Polanski, but, still, a foot in the door is a foot in the door. The summer had been so goddamn unpromising—New York a bust, his grandparents at their cottage on Coney Island reproving, his mother at West Hawk distant and his stepfather a bastard—and the next school year looked pretty T.S. Eliotsville. He had a notion to apply for admission to one of the theatre schools in the country when he graduated from the University of Manitoba, but, what the hell, he could cut out the educational middleman, couldn't he? Was there any practicality in having a BA in English? The future, like the sun-drenched road ahead, suddenly dazzled.

# 10

"'Monday, July 27, 2008,'" Briony reads from her dream diary as she nibbles a cube of cheese. "'At the beginning I am in a small Italian grocery store and I meet a boy there, whom I had met before, probably in a previous dream. He invites me to dinner at his place. The next setting is along the lines of Eadon Lodge ...'"

Lydia yearns for the conversation to go anywhere but to the cottage and lets her attention drift to Briony's untidy dining room and living room beyond. Briony's dream is the usual surreal grab bag of images anyway.

She notes the middens of photographs (Ted, her husband, was a professional photographer before MS struck), the plastic dog bone resting on the floor by the baseboard, the clutter of magazines and books. Every fibre of Lydia's being screams to wipe and clean, tidy and sort. Her heart goes out to her old friend, whose life seems devoted to keeping chaos at bay.

"Blackbird?" She interrupts Briony, drawn by the word.

"Yes," Briony beams up from the page, where a drop of perspiration has fallen from her forehead. "The boy starts to sing the lines. From the song, you know, from the *White Album*."

Briony's been keeping a dream diary since January 1, 1968 after a brief infatuation with Eckankar and soul travel and some guy who thought Eckankar and soul travel was where it was at. Lately, after dinner, she's been bringing it out and reading bits to entertain Ted, who more and more has withdrawn into himself as his MS has worsened, his volubility shrinking as hers has grown. She's quite used now to voicing the ramblings from the cavern of her dreams.

"I wrote 'boy.'" Briony's attention returns again to the page. "I seem to be my teenaged self in the dream. I remember that. You know, I think the boy is … Paul. Do you remember him? Dorian's … cousin, or whatever he was. Who came to the cottage that time?"

Lydia stirs in her chair. She reaches for a pear slice. Dessert is fruit and cheese. She can't lie. She can feel Briony's eyes resting on her. She wonders sometimes if Briony guessed why she moved to San Francisco. "Yes, I remember him."

"I wonder whatever became of him? He was hitching to Vancouver. Or California. And wasn't Dorian going to go with him?"

"So long ago. Hard to remember."

"And then there's the blackbird."

"Baked in a pie," Ted contributes.

"Actually, blackbirds in dreams are portents of death."

"Oh, honestly, Briony." Lydia sinks her teeth into the pear.

"They are, too."

"Well, the two of us will turn sixty next year."

"I'm sixty-three," Ted says.

"Oh, sweetie, it's not about you." Lydia notes a guilty blush cross Briony's face. "Or us." Briony gestures toward her. "Do you remember, Lydia, that blackbird flying into the cottage? Crow, whatever it was."

"No."

"Oh, you must!"

"Oh … yes, all right," Lydia concedes. "I do remember now." She remembers perfectly well. Afterwards, after the events at Eadon Lodge, she thought of it, the bird, exactly as Briony described, as a portent. "I remember you shrieking. But then you shrieked every time a moth came near you."

"True." Briony looks at Ted. "I couldn't go to sleep until every moth in the cottage was killed. But a bird! It was horrible. The thing was panicked, flying blindly around the room, crashing into things."

"You ran out of the cottage, I remember."

"I couldn't bear it. I thought it would come at me."

"And it got out?" Ted stirs himself.

"Well, no, the poor thing died inside." Briony closes the scribbler. "Shock, I guess."

For Lydia, the memory rushes back: Paul lithe, Paul cool, Paul in an electric blue Jantzen stepping off a ladder, swinging from the rafters with one hand, nabbing the bird with the other, landing neatly on the floor. The bird had collapsed, exhausted, on a supporting beam from which the electrolier was suspended. Another memory, suppressed then, awakened now: Had the bird been dead? What had Paul done, turned away from her for those few seconds? Her attention had been occupied by his backside. They wrapped the bird in a small Union Jack flag found in a drawer and buried it in a far corner of the yard.

"Do you ever dream of Eadon Lodge?" Briony asks, tilting her head, taking a biscuit. She remains troubled by Lydia's peculiar offer of the cottage to her and Ted as a gift. That, she thinks, may be behind her dream, so faithfully recorded.

"I don't dream." The lie slips from her tongue.

"Lydia, don't be silly, everyone dreams."

"Well, I don't remember them then."

Another lie. But she's eager to end conversation of Eadon Lodge, eager to go home. Of course she dreams. But their function, she would say, is practical: to tell us enthralling stories so that we're tricked into getting the sleep we need, then vanish before they become a weight upon our waking thoughts. But what of nightmares? What of dreams so harrowing they set you twisting and thrashing, breaking your sleep, leaving you staring with terror into empty darkness until your heart ceases crashing? What is their function? She remembers nightmares menacing her sleep all that autumn 1969.

But now, these last weeks, though she should collapse, exhausted, into deep sleep from all the work preparing to sell the house on Oxford Street, the nightmares have returned with their shifting inventory of mad, gabbling images. She jolts awake and reaches for Ray but he's not there, of course; he's 5,000 miles away in Toyonaka, Japan. She huddles in her childhood bed—such an alien place now—chasing away the memories the dream lets swim into her mind. She falls back asleep only when the dawn light, so early in summer at Canadian latitudes, begins to flame the bedroom curtains.

There is one particular dream, and it starts the same way. She is walking down Oxford Street. She is a little girl, hand in hand with her father, whose grip, unaccountably, is crushing hers. Overhead soars the vaulted cathedral ceiling of elms, so inescapably the enchanted forest of her childhood, but contracting now quickly, oppressively into a dark tunnel, the tree branches turned roots, exposed and twisted, stretching toward a distance ever falling away, stoppered by a bright disk of sunlight. As they walk, the light intensifies, draws nearer, and in terror she sees it's a head, disembodied: the head is wreathed in a crown of candles, like a Swedish girl's at Christmas, only the candles, imprisoning bars, fall upside-down over the face—a man's—blazing and burning, uncommanded by gravity. Her father crushes her hand, won't let her tear away to safety. He is furious with her for breaking the key to Eadon Lodge. She is being punished. Her terror dilates as the candles turn fiery snakes, the head a flaming Medusa head, a ball of writhing, hissing, glowing tendrils that somehow intertwine and fuse with the tree roots. She breaks free of her father and starts to run, the snakes in furious pursuit, curling and twisting around her body, the tunnel stretching impossibly further and further, growing darker and darker, narrower and narrower, the snakes vanishing, until she and black void merge in what can only be the moment of death, a scream building in her throat only to melt from her lips as she bolts awake—bursts into consciousness, really—to find herself stone cold still in bed, exhausted, the inky threads of the dream dissolving in the air.

Lydia's taken to afternoon napping lately. Mercifully, at that time of day, with the sun high and hot, her sleep is unvisited by ghosts.

# 11

Lydia runs her fingers over the silky wood of the Georgian desk. Along with the good china, the silver, and the crystal, this she will have sent to San Francisco—and that's it! The desk was shipped from England, in the 1920s, a bequest to her grandfather when *his* father died. Bibs kept his personal papers in the old desk, but Lydia's decided to leave them there. She can deal with them at home. She's growing weary. She and Helen have been in Bibs's den all morning. It's the last room in the house to be sorted.

When they came into Bib's office, Helen targeted the room's closet for inspection, always a place of treasure. It is crammed. From a top shelf, she pulled down an old briefcase—or perhaps luggage, something small enough for a child to carry, she wasn't sure. She pushed at the locks each side, but the hinge wouldn't spring. Locked, no key. She held it up for Lydia's inspection. Lydia frowned, shrugged, and indicated a box for shipping to San Francisco she'd felt-penned *Oxford Street Stuff*.

Helen would have been more disappointed to have her curiosity unslaked if her attention hadn't travelled to the rows of LPs filed shelf upon shelf. She remembered Bibs as a lover of jazz. He'd even afforded a small combo at his wedding. A record player with a smoked plastic cover sat with patina of dust on a stand by a wall. Tilting her head to read the record sleeves, her eyes went to an irregularity—a photo album, not a record album. Odd, for a drawer in the dining room credenza seemed to be the official photo repository. Helen pulled at it—string bound its pages and a strand hung loosely over the shelf—and out fell a packet of photos, some spilling onto the hardwood. The top one, she noted when she bent to pick them up, was date-stamped

December 1969. But the scene—girded in greenery—was clearly high summer. July? August?

"Oh! The outhouse at Eadon Lodge." Helen recognized the crescent moon door.

Lydia strained to appear amused. There it was, half-remembered, the old biffy. How she loathed and feared it as a child—the stink, the flies, the cobwebs. It was gone by August 1969 when she and Briony arrived, only a board-covered, lime-lined hole waiting to be filled and sodded over.

Bibs, at long last, had installed a proper bathroom in the cottage, and that's what some of these pictures in the packet recorded. In the last one, Marion is wearing a yellow paper crown, sprung from a Christmas cracker, scissors in hand, about to bite into a red ribbon strung across the door to what was once was the tiniest of Eadon Lodge's three bedrooms, now a three-piece bathroom. Her mother's lips twist in that peculiar resigned smile she affected whenever Bibs unleashed his aggressive humour, but her eyes telegraph annoyance. Above her head, on the wall over the door, is the plaque embossed with the words, THIS TOILET OPENED AUGUST 8, 1969, BY HM THE QUEEN.

They turn to the album. It's old. Most of the photos predate Lydia's birth, all of them are of Eadon Lodge. All of them are black and white. A few, from the '20s or '30s, feature Lits. Lydia studies his long face and big ears, known to her only through the studio photograph of her father and uncle, age twelve and eleven, holding hands. Here, they're about eight and seven, perched bony-kneed on the cottage steps, squinting into the sun, into the camera. Lits is smiling, animated, pixieish. Curious, she's not seen these pictures before.

In the '40s, Marion makes an appearance. In a single snapshot from the early Æ50s Dorian's mother and father, Lillian and Jim Grant, are sunk into Adirondack chairs on the lawn. Is this the weekend when Jim went home, alone, and killed himself? Lydia closes the album before Helen can get any more tucked-in memories. Time is a'wasting. The image—imagined—of Dorian's father taking his own life—it was in an attic, wasn't it?—gives Lydia a sudden chill.

Why, Lydia thinks, is this photo album not with the others, in the drawer in the dining room? Why is it half-hidden among record albums? Maybe it was intended for that old briefcase-suitcase thing Helen dropped in the *Oxford Street Stuff* box, only Bibs in his growing dementia had lost the key.

Lydia's unease is not allayed when something else slips from between the pages as she prepares to fit the album into the Georgian desk. It's a half sheet of white paper, bottom frayed as if torn along a ruler's edge. WINNIPEG GENERAL HOSPITAL, the lettering reads in *arte moderne* typeface along the top. The stationery's old, the hospital's name was changed to Health Sciences Centre—what? thirty years ago?—but the markings on it are fresher. Lydia recognizes her father's characteristic hand, but the result's shaky, sabotaged by senility. It's a sketch, a quick, crude, hurried series of shapes and lines—a bird's-eye view of the Eadon Lodge property, Lydia realizes quickly before tucking it back into the album, out of Helen's curious sight. The shapes and their juxtaposition adhere to her memory like photoflash afterimages. There's the rectangle of the cottage itself and the square of the sleeping cottage and bars for the caragana bushes that framed the property and circles for stands of trees.

But what arrests her eye and sets her hand fluttering as she hurriedly stuffs the album into the desk drawer is a simple X, as in, "marks the spot."

Good god, had Bibs somehow known all along? Impossible.

She must look at that paper again.

She can't bear it. She won't look at it.

These moments only add to Lydia's unease. The estate matters move at the pace of an Ottoman court. The lawyer at Pitblado, a craggy, slow-talking fellow, tells her probate could take four or five months. It's maddening. She and Ray will have to seek a bridging loan from their bank to purchase their house on Lincoln Way, with the expectation of an initial disbursement of funds early in 2009, with the estate settled not too much longer after that. A mortgage at fifty-nine? Ray is sixty-two. They talk about this on the phone when they can navigate the fourteen-hour time difference between Toyonaka and Winnipeg. Though he affects optimism, she can hear another strain in his voice, speaking of Ottoman courts: the *saiban rikon,* Erin's court of last resort, is as fatuous as anything out of *Alice*. He and Erin are thinking of *abducting* Misaki, he whispers, and bringing her to the States. Japan, amazingly, never signed any international convention against parents spiriting their children away. *Oh, god* is all Lydia can say. They are, all of them, not at a cliff's edge, but at a rabbit-hole's.

After ten days Helen flies back to San Francisco. Relief contends with guilt as Lydia waves off her mother's cousin—who became more of a mother to her than her own mother—and watches the cab dissolve into a little yellow dot headed down the canyon of elms. Like Garbo, Lydia really does want to be alone. Yes, she can display her grief to Helen, to Briony. They're delighted to offer their womanly comfort. But her agitation she must disguise and it is draining. After Helen went to bed the other night, Lydia battled her dread and looked again at her father's scribbled diagram of the Eadon Lodge property. The "X." Surely, the placement is wrong. But then, by the time he drew it, his mind was moving into darkness. Or at least that's what Lydia tells herself.

On her first visit to San Francisco, in 1967, Lydia fell, almost like one in love, for Helen and her unsentimental ways, her sophistication, her unwillingness to give a damn about crabbed hometown sensibilities that seemed to hedge Lydia's teenaged life. It was to Helen two years later that she turned when she could no longer quell the rising dread as her body succumbed to the new life growing inside her. With Helen, she devised a plan. But first: A girl might confide in her mother, but while her mother was out shopping in stores transitioning from Halloween to Christmas, Lydia made the long walk down the stairs from her bedroom to the den to face her father. She remembers Sinatra singing "Here's That Rainy Day" on the record player when she pushed through the door. She remembers her hand shaking when she lifted the tone arm because her misery didn't need a soundtrack. She remembers

Bibs, being Bibs, saying little when she croaked out her shame in the three classic words "I'm in trouble", but his body language—the tense shoulders, the downturned mouth, the drooping eyes—showed his dismay. *Who's the boy?* he did ask and Lydia was prepared with a lie. She couldn't say *I don't know* and turn her father's dismay to disgust. But she could read the disbelief in her father's eyes when she offered her answer.

Bibs's disbelief swelled to astonishment when Lydia spurned a termination. She was lucky: the law legalizing abortion in Canada had passed five months earlier. But, moreover, she was privileged: No, his hospital had not yet established a *de jure* therapeutic abortion committee, but surgeons at big-city hospitals had always banded together and approved abortions if a pregnancy was deemed dangerous to a woman's health or—and let's be frank—a colleague's daughter or mistress found herself in a tricky situation. And that was Lydia's remonstrance: She knew a couple of these privileged girls. They went to her high school. She could name them. There were no secrets in this little town. This wouldn't be kept secret. And she wanted, desperately, secrecy. Bibs, of course, misunderstood. He thought his daughter strangely out of step for the times, for even he dimly recognized the world of women was changing rapidly. But what Lydia wanted, but could not say, was that no one—*no one!*—turn a thought to those August days at Eadon Lodge.

And more, her plan: she would go to San Francisco, stay with Helen, have the child there, give it up for adoption, and resume her young, promising life. Lydia sensed her mother would seize upon any solution that preserved the veneer of respectability, but her father? She watched him in agony as he worked his way through her reasoning and wept with relief when he acceded, taking her in his arms. She remembers his single editorial whispered in her ear as he hugged her. He'd murmured it when she stopped piano lessons. *You may be sorry one day.* She never regretted finishing with piano; she had no musical aptitude. But his words would burn like a comet across her memory whenever she took a baby—someone's else baby—in her arms.

Helen welcomed and supported Lydia, asked few questions, kept her doubts to herself. Lydia's unbreakable approach to her delicate state (as they used to say) kept her in awe. A termination in the illiberal U.S. was out of the question—Helen didn't even broach it, and why would she when Lydia spurned it in progressive Canada? But she did suggest to Lydia, after Bibs and Marion had departed, that they raise the child, together, she and Lydia. It was a flight of fancy, really, born of her own sense of loss, for she, never revealed to anyone, had had a termination in London, in 1959, a year that seemed like another country from Lydia's 1970, but so botched that she could never have another child. But Lydia wouldn't entertain the notion. Helen witnessed her surrender nothing to the forces of a society predisposed to stigmatize. Her arranging everything to do with the adoption was, Helen could only think, the difference between an intelligent, educated twenty-year-old and a confused, frightened fourteen-year-old, but she worried at Lydia's fierce self-control. She saw her break down only once, after delivery, head propped against pillows, her face streaked with tears. She had told Helen earlier that she would not take the baby in her arms, because she knew she would never be the same. But she had glimpsed her baby son and wept. How could you carry a child for nine months and not bond?

Helen orders a glass of white wine on the plane, closes her eyes and allows her mind to play over the days she's just spent in Lydia's company. In the early seventies, they'd shared the Jackson Street flat in San Francisco while Lydia found her feet, finishing her degree, finding work—compensating, Helen thought, by overachieving. They had rubbed along well enough in those few years. Helen adjusted to Lydia's newfound fastidiousness then, a quirk she guessed was some small way to reassert control over her life. She fell in with it. What else was there to do? Helen's the first to admit she's an indifferent housekeeper. She would much rather read a book than tidy a coffee table.

But they haven't lived at close quarters for decades, so she hadn't quite taken in the escalation in Lydia's fastidiousness: the hand sanitizer pulled from her purse in the restaurant, the spoon for the nut bowl, the cellphone kept in—good heavens!—a ziplock bag.

Had she been doing these things long? She can't remember. She takes another sip of wine and wonders if any of this bothers Ray. Lydia has never told Ray about the child she bore all those years ago, and no rumours have reached him. Helen knows this to be true. She has kept Lydia's secret—even from Joe, her own partner of umpteen years. But Lydia grows quiet every May, as she did that first anniversary of her son's birth. If Ray worries, he doesn't say.

A rubber band, a thin one, tethers Helen to her old hometown. She can sense it stretching as the plane arcs southwestward to her new hometown, her concern for Lydia pulling along its length. Still pretty controlled, that girl. That philosophical telephone call when Marion died. Those efficient arrangements with funeral home and with the rector. That simple scattering of ashes at Assiniboine Park, just the two of them, Lydia's face marked with only a few tears as she tipped the box. Well—Helen glances out the airplane window at the cold blanket of clouds—Marion had good innings, Lydia had lived away for so many decades, visited infrequently, and a kind of disenchantment existed between the two, mother and daughter. Was it because Lydia bore a child out of wedlock?

Dear cousin Marion, pretty, vivacious, ambitious, self-absorbed. Marion was always so *obvious,* she would overhear her older cousins say. But it worked, the *obvious*ness. She did well in the ancient bargain: Tender oaths of devotion in exchange for sex, sex in exchange for social position. However, Marion didn't quite get down to the fine print. Helen's mind wanders wonderfully; a kind of boozy mirth seeps over her as she recalls Marion's thwarted ambitions for a bigger home, grander cottage, newer car, and lots of lovely travel. Helen recalls hearing about Marion putting her foot down over a wedding anniversary trip to Europe, but that was it, outside the occasional medical convention. Bibs honed to his two weeks in August and a few weekends at that isolated, ramshackle cottage on muddy Lake Winnipeg doing who knows what—puttering, probably. Like he was doing penance, Lydia remarked when the two of them were in Bibs's den, sorting through his paraphernalia.

The wine is doing a splendid job. Helen settles her head back in the seat, glances at her seatmate, at his movie selection, and closes her eyes. Her mind soon slips into the delirium of images at the edge of sleep, but a selection contends for attention: she is at a wedding reception—Bibs's and Marion's. She is in a back garden. It is late in the afternoon of August 26, 1948, searing hot. Helen has comported herself decently as flower girl. She loves her dress. She is eleven and the only child present. Kings and Cliffords fill the ranks of guests; Eadons are few. One of them is a looming square-jawed giant of a man, huge to her, anyway, when he steps near, remembered for the pocket watch he draws from a slit in his waistcoat and for shouting at an old woman. The child Helen recognizes domestic conflict. She sees this at home from time to time, though in this instance she's too enchanted with her frock to pay much attention. She lifts the skirt by its hem and waves the satiny fabric back and forth, Cinderella, watching the sunlight dapple on the leaves of the crabapple tree.

The big man, she later learns, is Henry Eadon, Bibs's father. He's a foreman at the CNR Fort Rouge Yards, where her father and most of her uncles work. The woman is May Askwith, Henry's sister-in-law, who has travelled from Renfrew, Ontario, for Bibs's wedding. She sacrificed her life—*sacrificed her life,* in Helen's mother's indignant words—raising Henry's sons after his wife died, and then Henry sending her packing. Tried to reel him in, she did, according to Helen's mother. Something happened. Didn't work out. Those poor boys, losing another mother, and one of those boys, long gone, never right in the head. No wonder Bibs is so cold to his father, and Bibs himself often taciturn.

But today, late on this wedding day, Bibs is coming out of the house resplendent in a navy double-breasted, followed by Marion, triumphant in her going-away outfit, a tailored suit of dusky rose gabardine with navy blue accessories and a corsage of pink roses. The wedding cake has been razed and the car awaits to take them on their honeymoon to Banff. Soon there will be a bouquet to catch. But that is not what Helen remembers well in her boozy airplane reverie. Henry and May blunt their argument, but two of Helen's uncles keep muttering, forgetting that little pitchers have big ears. Later, at home, Helen will voice a new word to her mother and will find herself with a bar of soap in her mouth.

"Henry Eadon, that arrogant fuck," Uncle Fred sidemouths to Uncle Stan.

It's the first time Helen hears the word "fuck."

The rubber band snaps. Helen wakes and smiles to herself as the old wedding memories skitter away. Joe is picking her up at the airport. She's missed him very much.

# 12

"I went to see the film. At the old Imperial. I must have been the oldest person in the audience."

"Alone?"

"Yes, alone. Anyone else would have thought I was clinging at straws." Dix releases a small sigh and glances down at the menu. "And I suppose I was."

Dorian and Dix are at Pastis having lunch. Dix flies to Palm Beach in a few days to spend the next six weeks avoiding the worst of Toronto's grey, damp winter. She thought to ask Dorian to join her, if only for a week or ten days, but he's travelling soon to Edmonton to start rehearsals at the Citadel for *Twelfth Night*, which will then run for three weeks. Their schedules, like their stars, don't align, though Dix wishes she were a few decades younger and Dorian wasn't, well, you know, *that way*. He looks so austerely handsome in the cold light coming off Yonge Street and imagines how fetching he would look across a sunny table at, say, Café L'Europe in Palm Beach. She breathes another small sigh—of regret, this instance—for her vanished youth and for a certain pleasure denied—that of seeing the expression on her son's face when she told him who her travelling companion would be. Not for the first time, she asks herself why she takes an unmotherly pleasure in needling her only child—her only *surviving* child (she presumes, though three decades later she still holds onto a thread of hope), but Peter can be so hidebound, so judgmental. It's true, parents do favour one child over another. Dix favoured her eldest, her firstborn, Paul, though he was, to be sure, a handful. Reckless, the school counsellor told her, but Dix preferred vivacious, and she's never countenanced for a minute Peter's—or anyone else's—insinuations about him.

As for Dorian, since Dix's Christmas party he has lived in a state so febrile Duke Orsino's lines won't adhere to memory. The coincidence is electric; it seems implausible, but it is plausible in this cosmopolitan world where art meets money, where degrees of separation shrink from six to three: Here he is, on January 2, 1998, sitting across from the mother of the boy he once loved, intensely, too briefly, all too aware that a few words from him, only a few, would shatter her and ruin him. (It's no mistake; Paul's name is included in Dix's entry in *Canadian Who's Who.*) The menu items he has barely noticed. His hunger is for detail. *What can she possibly know?* It's easy to extract the details. It's early days in his and Dix's friendship. He met her son Peter at the party. What questions hadn't he asked before? One is, "Do you have other children?"

"I have another son." Dix looked away, a brief frown pinching her lips. "I always say, 'have', still, after all these years, thirty years—this year," she added. "He may still be out there, somewhere in the world."

Dorian rolled through practised actorly expressions—perplexity, concern, surprise. But his heart beat a tattoo, as it still does in the seconds before he walks on stage.

"I don't understand."

"He vanished."

"Vanished?"

"He went to Woodstock, that music festival, you remember, of course you do, you would be about Paul's age ... then. Now. He never returned."

Which is how the conversation travelled to the Imperial, a movie house on Yonge Street, itself vanished. Dix had gone there to see the film version of Woodstock, shot in August 1969, released to theatres the following year. She brought with her the slim hope of glimpsing her son somewhere in the enormous crowd panned by the cameras. Clinging at straws, yes. Dorian turns his head to the restaurant window, sees a ghost. He starts. Paul. No, his own pale reflection.

"Are you okay?" Dix asks, closing her menu.

"Fine. I was just ... imagining your anguish."

Summers Dix spends at a family cottage on Lake Rousseau in Muskoka. Did then. Does now. She was there—she explains, after they order, that summer of Chappaquiddick and the moon landing with Peter while her husband—the boys' stepfather and a corporate lawyer—remained in town working, though due to join them shortly for the last two weeks of August. Paul spent a little time with her that summer, but he had soon grown restless and bored and returned to Toronto. Her last words with him had been about Woodstock. She'd called. It had been a Wednesday. She remembered because of what happened the next day. He said he was driving with some friends to some concert or other in upstate New York. What friends these were she didn't ask. If only she had asked. She never found out who they were. And she asked everyone she knew to be Paul's friend.

"I wanted him home. His father—his stepfather, Rory, my second husband—had died, you see. The day after Paul left for Woodstock. There was just no way to reach him. The news was full of reports of hordes of kids converging on this farm. I was able to delay Rory's funeral a few days, but ..."

Dix sees herself once again in the living room of their house—they lived on Douglas Drive then—gazing in consternation at the old Philco and its images of the music festival turned mayhem, the phone in her hand, talking with the mother of one of Paul's friends, one friend who *did* go to Woodstock, but hitchhiked, not drove. *If your son phones and he's happened to see Paul,* please *tell him to have Paul call me.*

Terrible days: The earlier call at the cottage that alerted her something was wrong came from Rory's secretary: *Is he with you? He's missed several appointments and no one answers at home.* That first flutter of anxiety. *It's not like Rory to miss an appointment.* Then, in quick sequence, Florence, their domestic, finds his body. The ambulance. The police. Dix races back to town. It appears Rory slipped in the bathroom and hit his head on the rim of the porcelain tub. He was fifty-four. And if he wasn't exactly the love of her life (her first husband, William, was), he was a decent man, if a little hard on the boys, a disciplinarian. He was a lieutenant-colonel in the Tor

Scots in the war. Peter thrived under authority; Paul did not. These latter details she spares Dorian, not because she doesn't want to appear forthcoming but because Dorian is regarding her with such peculiar intensity. Her hand reaches blindly for her glass of Chablis and nearly knocks it over.

"Anyway," she continues, deciding this time *not* to ask Dorian if he is okay, "I waited. That concert was extended, I think, an extra day, but it was a nightmare for all those kids to get out. It seemed to create a national emergency in the States. By the Wednesday or Thursday after, I began to wonder a little. But he was that age, you know, when you don't communicate with your parents, and he'd spent the previous school year travelling around Europe and we barely heard from him. But as he was starting his next year at U of T in September I expected him home before long ... Dorian?"

She slips her hand across the linen tablecloth and delicately slides it over his.

The touch, unexpected, is electric. Dorian recoils. "Sorry," he says, returning his hand to hers to allay the suspicion that an old woman's touch is repulsive to him. "I was thinking how awful all this must have been for you."

Dix removes her hand to her wineglass and lifts it to her lips. She regards Dorian speculatively as she does so. He *is* peculiarly intense this afternoon, though his words are meant to soothe, the sort of thing she's heard through the funerals of three husbands. In fact, a friend once suggested a memorial service for her missing son, a way to acknowledge, though it wasn't voiced, that Paul must be dead. Dix refused. She clings to the possibility of her son's vibrant presence somewhere in the world, with all the vigour of mother love. Of course she does. What mother wouldn't? Every scenario has been entertained in her time, from accident to amnesia to abduction. What would keep him away? Had she *driven* him away? Had Rory? Someone else? Had he fallen into terrible trouble? He was her wild child, a *terrible* terrible two, a little demon at nine, a tearaway in adolescence. And Rory's unexpectedly dying at home led inevitably to a report to the coroner. The police sought to question Paul, who was most likely the last person to see him alive—after all, there was no one else inhabiting the Douglas Drive house those weeks—but it was only routine, they were just doing their jobs. In part because Jack Cook, the chief coroner, was an old family friend, a potentially embarrassing inquest was ruled unnecessary. The truth was, apparently (Jack told her this with some discomfiture), Rory had been, *ahem*, pleasuring himself at the bathroom sink and had somehow lost his moorings in the intensity of the moment with a freakishly fatal result.

Dix doesn't respond to Dorian's remarks. Paul rarely enters her conversation with anyone now, but then, in the late 1960s and early 1970s when he failed to return home or communicate with her in any way, his name slipped into speculation (*funny he vanished the same time Rory had his accident*), whispers of which eventually reached Dix's ears—and which she refused to dignify with a response. Dorian, oddly enough, is the first person she's told about going to see the Woodstock film. She sat through it twice, and in the mid-eighties, when a VHS version was released, she made good use of the VCR pause button, looking, looking at the faces.

"I even got in touch with a cousin in Hollywood," Dix continues. "Have you ever heard of Edgar Rusoff? Gone now, I'm afraid."

Dorian nods. Edgar Z. Rusoff, the King of the B's, he remembers well. Rusoff was at the heart of his and Paul's plans to drive to L.A. This—what seemed almost too good to be true at the time—*is* true. Paul did have a relative in Hollywood. But Paul never mentioned he'd intended to go to Woodstock. Not once. Never mentioned it, even when they were lying in Dey's bed watching the TV coverage of it. He said—and later told the others at Eadon Lodge—that he'd set out for the Maritimes but changed his mind on a whim.

"A cousin of mine married him," Dix continues, as the waiter arrives with their meals. "I thought she might have an 'in'. They always talk about a cutting-room floor, don't they? I thought there might be miles of unused film footage sitting somewhere that I might look at. I'm afraid she wasn't much help."

Dorian glances at the steak he ordered as the waiter places it in front of him. The aroma of the meat suddenly sickens him. He can't bear to think of Paul in this moment. He says, "I'm sorry about your husband. He can't have been very old. How did he die, if you don't mind my asking?"

Dix lies. "Heart attack."

"*Comme* Jean Paul Belmondo in *Breathless*," says Dorian, placing his grandfather's fedora on Paul's head.

Paul pushes a single eyebrow into the shadow of the brim and tilts his head toward Dorian.

"You know the film?"

"*Non*."

"French New Wave." Dorian readjusts the hat on Paul's head for raffish effect, though it doesn't quite work with Paul's pagan curls. "Belmondo plays this guy who kills someone—a policeman, I think, a pig, *un cochon*." Dorian burrows his head into Paul's naked armpit and makes a snuffling noise. "He spends the rest of the film on the lam, but he's just so cool about it."

Dorian withdraws his head and matches Paul's smile with one of his own. They are in Dorian's grandfather's bed in Dorian's grandfather's bedroom. Interestingly, Dorian's grandparents have separate bedrooms. (Dorian thinks it has something to do with Nan's drinking.) Dey's room smells of tobacco and lemon-oil polish and something indefinably fuggy and masculine. It, with its adjoining dressing room, is his sanctum sanctorum, a place Dorian is never invited and rarely penetrates. But it has a television, which is the salient point. Paul pushed him over the threshold, laughing. Dorian resisted, at first. *Jesus, what about the sheets! What if ... ?* Such worries tug him from the edge of total abandon. His ear is half-cocked for the key in the door, his lips ready with excuses for the mess in the kitchen, for the presence of Paul, his mind rehearsed with all the great reasons he must go to Los Angeles. But he is much too besotted not to fall into every little adventure that Paul, so clearly more experienced than he, suggests. They have been trailing lust all over the house. It is day three of this. That Dorian wouldn't bring Paul home was never a question. After their little debauchery along the highway, steering car and Paul and knapsack into the city, to the house on Dromore, took on the force of inevitability. Car parked, front door shut, up the stairs they piled with hands and mouth all over each other.

Dorian pushes around the silver ring on the fourth finger of his right hand with his thumb. He does it unconsciously; it's a habit, but it's soothing. He and Paul are sitting shoulder to shoulder, glistening skin to glistening skin, smoking a joint, gorging on ice cream, talking about the high school play Dorian wrote with his English teacher, *Death in Life*, about music, about travel.

"Cool ring," Paul says, taking Dorian's hand and splaying the fingers.

"A friend brought it back for me from San Francisco a couple of years ago. See? It shows the parts of the peace symbol—the semaphore signals for 'N' and 'D', nuclear disarmament—and then how they were merged together."

Paul slips the ring off easily and slides it over one of his own, his third, his fingers being slimmer than Dorian's. "Who's the friend?"

"Lydia. We've known each other since kindergarten."

Dorian wants to hold on to this moment, somehow solemnized by the transfer of the ring—to bottle it, preserve it, keep it forever—all that, all of it, this feeling of fraternity, of oh-so-rightness, of a connection so natural and right and true. His encounter in New York the year before had been brief, anonymous, furtive, fleeting, revelatory, but empty—all that. Ric from Toronto had no conversation, dismissed him with haste, almost disgust, once the deed was done. Another opportunity never seemed to present itself that summer, not even in the midst of Norman Mailer's film-set debauch in East Hampton, not even in the midst of evening circlings of downtown, along the labyrinth of streets in the West Village where he felt prairie-shy and paralyzed. The next summer, *this* summer, no better. No film work, trip truncated by diminished funds (both Dey and his mother refused to forward money this time), his second-last full day there spent drawn, like thousands of others in the fierce heat, to another celebrity funeral—Judy Garland's—on the East Side.

Paul replaces the ring on Dorian's finger, and Dorian lets that hand roam Paul's thigh. He wants to try something he's not done before—and there's a lot he's not done before, as Paul makes evident from his own adventures—what seems like a phantasmagoria of forbidden pleasures that Dorian can barely credit, has not even entered his imagination, makes him almost faint with desire and longing, shock and envy. Paul inventories them: permutations and combinations involving all manner of fauna and flotsam and flux. Far out, far out, and *far out*! The farthest out is something he calls breath play. *Huh*? Paul explains it. He did it with a guy in Barcelona.

"It was incredible—intense. The intense-est. We could try it?"

Dorian's eyes follow Paul's upward, through the barrier of the ceiling, to his own attic bedroom. He's intrigued, more than intrigued, he's young, he's reckless, he's ready for any novelty—now, he's ready, under Paul's guidance, but he's not sure he's ready for this. Shoulder to shoulder on the bed they talk of many things, other things; they talk small talk, big talk, sex talk, family talk. Paul's mother is a housewife. He has one brother, younger. He doesn't remember his father, who died when he was a baby from some illness, and now has a hated stepfather. Likewise, says Dorian, who marvels at the parallels, though his father didn't get sick and die. Jim Grant perished in a car accident, he says (for this is what he believes).

"I'm sorry," Paul responds, stroking Dorian's neck and pulling him into a kiss.

Dorian doesn't want to talk about it, too, because he doesn't want the mood corrupted, the momentum of desire slowed. The marijuana makes him feel loose, wanton, fabulous. He moves down Paul's body, readies his tongue—it's cold from the ice cream. Paul curls around, rolls over, moans at the tender invasion. Later, much later, they will shower together, gobble delivered pizza from Tubby's together, but Dorian feels no urge to go beyond the house's confines and Paul evinces no curiosity for a city he's never before visited. They might be under house arrest; indoors they are two live wires, sparking each other with every passing touch.

Dorian saw *Breathless* at the Playhouse Theatre, a relic of vaudeville days, slowly crumbling along with the rest of the downtown, with Lydia and her father who, strangely, enjoyed foreign films. The Winnipeg Film Society rented the theatre Sunday evenings to show works more *avant-garde* than Hollywood ever produced. Dorian, at fifteen, was intoxicated by the film—or, more precisely, by Belmondo, with his battered *jolie laide* face, his lopsided smile, insouciant cigarette, and—to be even more precise—his naked torso. And the hat, the hat in bed: somehow it caught Belmondo's free spirit, his wild *joie de vivre.* Odd his grandfather should possess much the same hat. It caught nothing of Dey's spirit, which was unreconstructed Scots Presbyterian.

"Are you serious about getting into acting?" Paul passes his thumb across his lips. Dorian stares helplessly. Belmondo uses the same gesture in *Breathless.* Paul can't possibly know that.

They've been half-watching the eleven o'clock news on Dey's TV—surreal programming when you're stoned. Another report on the unsolved L.A. murders the week before focused their attention. Neither had heard of Sharon Tate before.

"Yeah," Dorian replies slowly. "Or something related maybe. Directing, script writing. I think I'm going to apply to the National."

"In Montreal?"

"Mmm. Or York University.

Paul pushes the hat back on his head. "Why?"

"Why what?"

"Why keep on going to school?"

"Well ..." Dorian half shrugs. "Because ..."

"You're majoring in English, you said."

"Yeah."

"And what's that going to do for you?"

"Well, you know, Shakespeare ..."

"Look, Dorian, come with me to L.A. Seriously. I can introduce you to my cousin."

"I have to finish my undergrad degree this year."

"Fuck it."

"Seriously? You sort of mentioned that in the car." In truth, Dorian has been fantasizing about the idea ever since. It's wild. *On the Road,* Kerouac, Cassady, Ginsberg, *Catcher in the Rye.* Holden Caulfield. *The Electric Kool-Aid Acid Test.* Merry Pranksters. *You're either on the bus or off the bus.* Yeah, fuck it! Get the fuck out of here. Blow this town. Be *on* the bus. Hollywood! *Hooray for Hollywood, Where you're terrific if you're even good.* Dorian suddenly can't breath. He's breathless, his heart races. Yes, he should do this! He's been offered a choice. This is his choice. This is how his life shall be from this moment on. *Two roads diverged in a wood, and I—I took the one less travelled by, And that has made all the difference. All* the difference.

He breathes again. Yes! He will go to California. With Paul.

But Dorian is wrong. Going to California with Paul is not the choice that will shape his life. That choice comes with a phone call and the phone is ringing now.

# 13

The ancient skeleton key misses the hole, scraping along the metal plate. Tremors fumble Lydia's fingers. The last time she turned this key she turned it counterclockwise, the final act in the ritual of closing Eadon Lodge and the ritual end of one kind of life. She has a sense memory of doing so, even after thirty-nine years. She needs to turn the key clockwise now, once she steadies her hand. The sun, hot, high, beats down on her back. One foot holds the screen door ajar.

The key finds the hole, turns (awkwardly, trickily; she remembers this, too), and the heavy wooden door, its varnish cracked by weather and age, swings away from the frame into the shadows of the kitchen. Lydia remains rooted on the stoop as the aroma of warmed dust and warmed wood—the cottage smell—assails her nostrils and sets crashing around her wave upon wave of memories.

She takes a breath and steps over the threshold. The screen door slaps shut behind her. Musty heat pours along the exposed skin of her face and arms and legs. No window has been opened in more than a month. No blind. To now dark-adapted eyes, the kitchen seems to simmer in a grey light, everything is a grey shape, the counter a grey surface onto which she drops her bag. She reaches for the blind over the window—again the sense memory; it's like reaching for it in a dream—and pulls. The blind flies up with a vicious bang. Lydia jumps, though she knows every damn blind in the place snaps like a firecracker when it's opened. Light floods into the galley space. Her galloping heart slows as she looks around—in astonishment, though she doesn't know why should be astonished. She didn't expect anything to have changed, and so it hasn't. *Nothing* has changed. It's still the same. Okay, there's a microwave, sitting atop the old wood stove, but everything else—*everything else*—is as she left it August 31, 1969. Her eyes run to the Depression glass butter dish, to the spoon cradle, to the yellow Art Deco dinnerwear. *God!*

She moves quickly into the dining room—yes, unchanged—through the double doors into the living room—snap snap snap of more blinds—stopping to yank at the sliding windows either side of the old desk. Wood against wood, they squeak in their frames, slightly warped, resisting, but they do open. Fresh air sweeps through the screens, flutters a *Chatelaine* magazine on the desk. She glimpses the date—June 2008. Her mother's final visit, she realizes with a pang.

A quick glance around tells her nothing has changed in the living room either, but here memories are sharpest and she doesn't linger, though it will be the logical place to meet with Carol Guttormson, the real estate agent, scheduled to arrive shortly. She goes into the second bedroom, steps onto an old wooden tool chest, reaches up, as if it were yesterday, as if her movements were the most natural in the world, and pulls at a lever on a fuse box high on the wall. There's another snap, a metallic one. The cottage seems to shudder to life as electricity cascades along the ancient wiring, though it's only the old Monitor refrigerator trembling in the kitchen giving the floor a shake. Lydia's ears prick to something nearer, though—the faint pop of light bulbs switching on. The wall in front of her flushes gold. Her mother must have left the electrolier in the living room on when she shut off the electricity. Why? Why did she have *that* lamp on? Both of them always hated the stark, cruel light it cast over the living room, but Lydia hates the lamp and its light more, much more. It stalks her dreams. She steps off the chest, backs out of the bedroom, and feels for the switch on the near wall. The room behind her returns to natural light and the high ceiling retreats into shadow, as does the electrolier.

Lydia returns to the kitchen, turns the tap, and watches the water spurt and thrash into the sink, another cottage sound as familiar as the screen door's slap. She takes the same skeleton key, opens the front door from the inside, unlatches the screen door and looks to the lawn, which appears to have been recently cut. Marion must have some arrangement with someone—a lawn service, a teenager—to keep at least the grass kempt. Perhaps this Carol person will know so she can settle the bill.

Has the lawn shrunk? The property seems rearranged, like a familiar room with new furniture. A thicket of scrubby poplar trees has overtaken the southeast lawn where two big spruce trees stood in stately glory. Her grandfather planted them—one for each son at his birth. There was the Bibs tree. And there was the Lits tree. This is where the hammock once stretched, strung between the two trees. One is gone. (Which one? Which was which?) A spring storm twenty years before—she recalls this now, her mother told her on the phone: Eadon Lodge narrowly missed in the fall. The surviving spruce, towering above the newer poplar, leans a bit precariously. Impacted by that storm? Maybe. Funny Bibs not attending to it, to that picturesque corner, where he'd wanted his ashes strewn.

The caragana hedge between the property and the lake is intact, she notes, pushing through the screen door onto what used to be a stoop, now part of a deck that Marion had wrapped around the south and east sides of the cottage. She turns, walks down the deck and looks northeast, toward the sleeping cottage–tool shed. It appears unchanged, almost a child's version of Eadon Lodge. Northwest of the cottage, at a little distance, is the site of the old outhouse. Lydia hesitates. She didn't—willfully didn't—turn her head to look in that direction when she walked from the car, parked southwestish of the cottage, but now she finds herself helplessly drawn there. She must see, for surely it's all changed, surely roots and branches have overtaken the sod Alan laid nearly four decades ago, as they have elsewhere on the property, encroaching, subsuming, transforming, disguising—doing what nature does when it's left untrammelled.

What brought Alan back here that grey morning, their final one at Eadon Lodge? Why did he *bother*? He—like Dorian, like Paul—had avoided the task set them, to shovel soil delivered earlier and piled under a tarpaulin into the cavity where the outhouse had been. She remembers her simmering annoyance: the boys found common cause only over one thing—not breaking a sweat anywhere but on the beach.

"We'll get to it," Alan said in his hectoring way, but they never did, the three of them.

What impressions did Alan take away with him that last morning when he departed? He arrived unannounced because Eadon Lodge had no phone. Lydia, wakeful, memory of the evening just passed fresh, beating along her nerves, heard some vehicle pull onto the gravel west of the cottage, heard the chunk of a car door's closing, heard advancing footsteps—a man's footsteps—and felt that her heart leaping into her mouth was the only thing keeping her from screaming.

*Police!*

Though this afternoon is hot, Lydia shivers in memory of that morning. Dorian is next to her in the bed, dead to the world. Her eyes dart to his slack features as her ears strain to the sounds outside. The screen door pulled from its hinge. The door handle rattling. A pause. A knock. Dorian stirs in the tangled sheets. *God, how it comes back to her!* She remembers her inability to move, her desperation to suppress her ragged breathing, as if it could be heard through the walls. Only when she realizes her father's Buick and Dorian's Volkswagen declare their presence does she slip from the bed, reach for her dressing gown draped over the iron bedstead, and tiptoe across the cold linoleum toward the front door, unnerved at the floor's every creaking protest.

A second knock, a pause filled by the skittering of some small animal on the roof, a scrape of shoes along the steps. Lydia holds her breath. A shadow flicks past the window over the dining room table. Who's there? She can't tell.

She prays for whoever it is to go away. She hovers in the shadow of the door in indecision, her ears attuned to the sounds of the creature's movements—in her feverish state she thinks of it as a creature—the swish along the grass, the crunch along a few dried leaves, the snap of low-hanging branches. The footfalls fade, dopplerish, but not in the direction from which they came.

And then Lydia hears it. The ugly scrape of metal on metal. *The shovels!* She and Dorian had left the blade of one cupped in the blade of the other on the grass and someone is pulling them apart. Sick with fright, Lydia tiptoes back through the living room, to one of the two small windows on the north wall, and peers through a slit in the curtains.

Alan.

The relief that almost makes her faint lasts but a second. Alan is lifting the shovel. As she did last night, she realizes she must steel her nerves. She tightens the belt of the dressing gown, crosses the floor once again, slides back the bolt of the inner door—slowly, cautiously, so as not to wake Dorian—and slips out, closing it behind her gently. She navigates the stairs, gripping the wobbly balustrade, suddenly conscious of being lightheaded, her feet plunging into the cool damp of the lawn. She follows the trail through the dew already forged by Alan.

"Good morning." Lydia lets her intonation rise, as if her greeting's a question, a matter of debate.

"You did the deed, I see." Alan turns to her. She must have started, for he frowns and adds, as if for clarification, "You filled in the hole."

Lydia feels his eyes searching her face. His frown deepens. She wonders what he's drawing from her appearance. She must look strained; she senses her hair a tangle, and later, when she can look in the bathroom mirror she sees, yes, what he saw, a bruising around the eyes, a raw scraping over her forehead, a pallor below the tan.

"Yes ... well, it ... had to be done, didn't it? Is that why you came this morning?"

Alan grunts, takes another assessing glance at her face, but he makes no response. Alanna's sent him, Lydia thinks. She's the one feeling contrite about the misadventure with the shotgun. He's annoyed it's a wasted trip. "They could have done a better job."

"We don't have your great working-class experience," she says, smiling thinly.

"We?"

"I helped. Dorian did most of the work."

"What? No Paul?"

Lydia inhales sharply. "Yes, he helped. Of course he helped."

"Yeah, right." Alan's mouth twists. His eyes slip past Lydia's shoulders to the sleeping cottage.

"They're asleep."

"Yeah, I'm sure they are. Did you tamp the soil?"

"Tamp?"

"You know, pack it down with something—the back of the shovel, *something*?—as you filled the hole." Alan jabs the shovel end into the soil; Lydia blanches. "You didn't, did you. You know that soil settles? No? Well, it will and you're going to have a hollow. You'll get a hollow anyway, but not so bad a one if you'd done the job properly."

*Go away, Alan.* Lydia remembers wanting to slap his smug face then. She'd ignored his sanctimony through two years of university. A week in closer quarters was more than she could bear.

"Look, I can try and fix it, dig some of the soil out and tamp the rest down."

"*No!*" The word explodes from lips with such force that Alan's head jerks back. "No. If ... if you could just lay the sod."

"Okay, all right." He raises his palms in supplication. Lydia remembers him looking around the property, brow furrowed, nose crinkled, as if he smelled something rotten. "Your funeral. With your father, I mean."

She has to get rid of him. "It's kind of early, Alan ..."

"Yeah?"

"I wouldn't mind going back to bed."

"How about some coffee?"

Alan's eyes travel to her chest. She draws the dressing gown tighter around her. "We're fresh out."

"I can take a hint."

He laid the sod. It only took twenty minutes to cover four square feet. Had Dorian heard them talking, heard Alan working, then his retreating footfalls along the gravel path, heard him starting his car? He never said when he awoke and Lydia never told him. Alan was the only witness to their handiwork. But for the rest of that school year, the few times Lydia ran into Alan, she sensed him appraising her in some altered fashion. Was she being paranoid? She had to be. How could he possibly know anything of the truth? He couldn't.

Lydia can hear the crunch of car wheels on gravel now, the same sound echoing down the decades. It's Carol, the agent from Interlake Realty, she's certain, but still, a chill travels her veins. She passed not a few Interlake Realty signs by the roadside as she drove north through Loney Beach to Eadon Lodge. Has the financial crisis pushed tentacles into even this inconsequential place? Buyer's market here? Or seller's? There are so many more summer homes now. All her childhood—even to her final visit to Eadon Lodge—acres of scrubby woods lay between the cluster of cottages that was Loney Beach and the solitary property that was Eadon Lodge. No more. The woods are almost vanished, a phalanx of new cottages—second homes, really; winterized, suburban, characterless—is pressing northward. She can almost make out, if she peers through the trees, another phalanx pressing south. It feels like a slow strangulation.

Carol will assure her no housing bubble is bursting in this neck of the woods, but then real estate agents say that sort of thing, don't they? Demand is high—well, highish. Those properties for sale along North Lake Street usually go quickly. No, Lydia should have no trouble selling the property. It's large, it's beachfront, it's well-serviced. Carol won't tell her that her cousin Ívar, who teaches English at the University of Manitoba, mentioned a young colleague looking for an affordable ("cheap" was Ívar's exact word) cottage retreat. He's sort of a last resort. But Carol will tell her she knows folk will be much more interested in the land, be willing to pay more, a couple of developers, for instance. It's the *land* that's desirable. Who would want that peculiar old cottage?

Lydia sees Carol coming down the path now. She notes a woman in her forties, with a frosted flip and a beige suit and suede briefcase, looking much like the conventional idea of a real estate agent. She looks up, spots Lydia, and smiles. There's a cast of vague surprise on her face, Lydia thinks, which isn't reassuring, until she realizes Carol has redrawn her eyebrows high on her forehead. This is the woman who must sell Eadon Lodge for her. Lydia has backtracked several times with Ray over the phone in Toyonaka about the fate of the cottage. Keep it? Rent it? Use it? But Ray is firm. He's not being stubborn and mean, he's being logical, and Lydia has no argument against it. They will never use it themselves and they can only rent it, *if* they can rent it—what?—ten weeks a year? There's taxes and maintenance ... even if Lydia were deeply sentimental about the cottage, they would still need to sell it. Ray has a new idea and it's good; it will make Lydia hopeful: they will convert the garage in the Lincoln Way home into a flat for Erin and Misaki. Erin's plan is to go to law school when (*if?*) they get back to the States. Money's now even more the thing.

# 14

Dorian's in a little Roman Catholic church off the highway at Winnipeg Beach. It's Thursday evening—hot, muggy; a fan barely moves the air in the room. The August long weekend is nigh. Does this explain the AA meeting's sparse attendance? Or is there only a handful of struggling alcoholics at a beach town in summer? Dorian wishes the meeting were better attended. More people would make his unwillingness to share less conspicuous. He doesn't want to talk. He barely wants to listen. He only wants to sit in silence and share a space for a time with his fellow-travellers.

*We will not regret the past nor wish to shut the door on it.* AA Promise #3. Someone has tacked the list on a corkboard, covering various church notices. Does Dorian regret the past? Who doesn't regret *something* in the past? Dorian has a regret or two. Or three. One in particular, though "regret" is a feeble little word. Does he wish to shut a door on it? God, yes. Could he do that? Is there a way? Once he thought booze would shut a door on it.

His first drink as a teenager—*lemon gin! yuck!*—gave him wings, brought him insight, made him bold. He became a more brilliant edition of his already brilliant self. Funny, such transformation never seemed to happened to others under the influence. Funny, he paid no attention to the familial link: his grandmother's peppermint breath concealing years of pickledness. At least alcohol never seriously harmed his career. He never missed a rehearsal or a performance because of drink. It was almost as if its effects were something to act *against,* a heroic stand again the invading hangover that somehow sharpened his performance, the way Hemingway and Fitzgerald's writing was sharpened by drink. Or something.

He was drawn to acting as a teenager because he craved to be seen, to be admired, okay, yes, to become famous—he admitted that years ago to a therapist; he admits it to himself now, not for the first time, half listening to a woman moan on about her relationship with her mother. But later—sometime during his six years completing his three-year theatre degree at York—he understood that acting had become an escape from overpowering guilt and despair. Inside a character he was someone else: he knew precisely who he was, he could control his circumstances, and he could expect the unexpected not to happen. On stage he could forget about the past, much less regret it.

But it's a strain here, where the past seems to haunt the present. This dry heat, this flat landscape, that big grey lake, those rustling poplars, this dusty breeze: *in my ears and in my eyes, there beneath the blue da-da-da skies.* What's the missing word? He can't think of it. He's lost touch with everyone in Winnipeg. His mother and grandparents died decades ago. His stepfather's alive, but he feels no obligation to maintain any sort of relationship. If they hadn't argued that August day in 1969, he wouldn't have left West Hawk abruptly, would never have encountered Paul at that gas station, would have seen his life twist in another direction. Bob never accompanied Dorian's mother when she visited him in hospital that December 1969. His old friends didn't visit him. Not Lydia, whom he'd last seen as he stumbled from her car at Halloween. (Her dad came, though. Somehow Dr. Eadon learned of his presence in the psych ward.) Briony didn't visit. Ditto Alanna. That party killed him; he was shunned. New friends didn't visit either: Those from the university drama club and from *And No Birds Sing,* a whole cadre of wannabe thespians. Except for Blair Connon, who was supposed to join him at Eadon Lodge that August, 1969. Blair brought him to emergency one December Saturday—the 13th, as it turned out. Hard to forget the date.

"He's freaking out," big Blair told the battleax charge nurse as he struggled to hold on to a wriggling, thrashing Dorian. "No, he isn't on *fucking* acid. He's had a few drinks."

They'd been at a Christmas party at an old downtown house with a whole lot of people Dorian barely knew. He'd had a few drinks all right and smoked a few joints. But he wasn't drunk or stoned. He was raving.

He woke in a hospital room in a Valium haze in a blaze of shame and disgust. He would be there for a week. The psychiatrist—name since forgotten—was a tiny and very young-looking Jewish woman. They talked. Or, rather, he talked. She blank-screened him, giving no advice nor making any judgment. But before long, they hit a wall. Dorian skirted the trauma of what brought him here, the inciting incident, as it were. Round and round the mulberry bush they went, in a stately Freudian way. Vaguely aware of physician-patient privilege, he asked, in a mulberrybushish way, about confidentiality. Could he tell her anything, *anything*? Anything, she replied. He didn't believe her—or wouldn't believe her, because he couldn't do it, couldn't bring himself to speak the words about the thing that he had done—that he and Lydia had done together. They sat in silence. By their last session, Dorian found the silence so excruciating he broke it by reciting every A.A. Milne poem from his childhood, hoping to shatter her poker face. They parted, he with a prescription for more Valium, she breaking her professional approach not to admonish by saying, rabbinically: guilt will find its own punishment.

*Christ, it is* fucking *hot.* When the meeting ends, when the Lord's Prayer is done, when he can decently leave, he is going to bypass the bad coffee and head for the door, avoid any chat. The meeting will have served its purpose: to reground him, to remind him of the value of sobriety, to reconnect him to a Higher Power, whatever he conceives it to be, and to help him keep his mind off the one thing that's been creeping along the edge of his consciousness these last weeks—Eadon Lodge:

Marion cannot have sold it, because surely to god anyone buying lakefront property like that would have torn it down and replaced it. No one builds little cottages in the style of Eadon Lodge anymore.

Lydia told him all those years ago she would stop her mother selling the cottage if she tried. She must have succeeded. Or else

Marion had a change of heart about *Grim*li after Bibs's death. At any rate, Marion is dead and Eadon Lodge surely passes to Lydia. It must. And just as surely Lydia will keep the cottage and pay the taxes, even if she never ever uses it. They will be safe for as long as she lives (and as a woman, surely she will outlive him). He will never have to face Dix with the truth, for she is still alive and *compos mentis* in Toronto and Palm Beach, and still in touch with Dorian. He had a chatty email from her this very morning.

Dorian stares at the ringing telephone on Dey's bedside table.

"Are you going to answer that?" Paul asks after the sixth ring.

Dorian picks up on the tenth ring, panicked that it's his grandfather, calling from the Kenora docks, and he knows what Dorian is up to. Between rings eight and ten he shuts off the TV. Or is it his mother calling to chew him out for his behaviour toward his stepfather? Is there an emergency? Has something awful happened? *Who, who, who can it be!*

It's Lydia.

"Oh, it's you, Mrs. Peel."

"You sound odd."

"*You* sound odd. Where are you? What's that noise?"

"Traffic. I'm in a phone booth. In Gimli."

"How nice for you. How did you know I was home?"

"I didn't. I guessed. I figured you wouldn't last long with your stepfather. Anyway, why don't you drive up?"

"I don't think so."

"You said you would."

"I said I *might*."

"You've got to come, Steed. I need you. *We* need you. We've got Alanna and Alan with us."

"So? Didn't you invite them?"

"Well, yes, but you know what they're like."

"Alan's such a prick, Lydia." Dorian looks at Paul. The word "prick" seems to catch his attention. Paul's eyebrows nicely graze the fringe of curls over his forehead. Dorian mouths code and makes gestures: "friend" "me" "go" "Gimli" "beach town" "north of here."

"This might be our last summer together, Dorian. Who knows where we'll all be next summer. And bring that friend of yours, Blair—"

"Why?"

"For Briony." Lydia's voice drops to a murmur. Dorian understands that Briony's within earshot.

"He's probably working. And I think he's interested in someone."

"Find out."

"No."

"Well, then, come up on your own. It'll be fun. You haven't been to Eadon Lodge since you were a baby."

"And look what happened then."

"Oh? Oh, sorry, Dorian, I forgot about your father. Oh, god, sorry."

"It's all right. Never mind. Look—"

"Then you're coming."

"Lydia ... I've got ... a guest here."

Dorian's acutely aware of the freighted pause, then the new tone, one of curiosity restrained. "Really," he hears her drawl. But before she can probe, he feels Paul tug at his arm. He says to Lydia, "Just a sec."

Dorian puts his hand over the receiver. He's about to give voice to his earlier mouthings, but Paul telegraphs something to him with his eyes. "Tell her I'm your cousin," he says *sotto voce*.

"What?"

"Your cousin. I'm your cousin. Some kind of relative. I've been hitchhiking. I've shown up at your door, you know. Make it up. Improvise. You're an actor, remember?"

Dorian takes a breath, chest swelling with the challenge. He take his hand off the receiver, hesitates, returns the hand to mask their conversation, and frowns. "You mean you want to go to the beach?"

"Sure, why not?"

"What about L.A?"

"It can wait a while."

Paul's eyes are so beguiling. Dorian is so biddable.

"Sorry," he says to Lydia, returning to the phone. "I've been consulting with my cousin."

"Cousin? What cousin?"

"He's from Toronto, travelling through."

"I didn't know you had cousins in Toronto."

"He's kind of a second cousin. Or third."

"Oh, okay. So ... ?"

"So ... I guess, we'll come up then."

"Oh, good. When?"

"I don't know. Soon." Dorian flashes Paul a look of annoyance. *Women!*

"What does your cousin look like? I'm asking ..." Lydia's voice falls again "... for Briony."

"Are you sure you aren't asking for you?"

"Shut up, Steed. Does your cousin have a name?"

"Yes, he has a name. Paul. His name is Paul."

# 15

Lydia examines the spot on the dining room wall, runs a finger over the painted surface. The ink vanished in the application of soap and water—her last act before closing up Eadon Lodge, August 31, 1969—but the impression of the ballpoint pen did not. It's faint, very faint, but in the right light—bright light—and at the right angle—she can still make out the phantom signature below Dorian's—*Paul Godwin, August 21, 1969.*

Did her parents ever notice the impression in the paint? Did they frown, wondering? Neither asked her about it. The Hudson's Bay blanket's absence was noted, though—the blanket Lydia assured Dorian at that Halloween party her mother would never notice missing. It was *Bibs* who noticed. Had a little bee in his bonnet about it the next summer, 1970. He was indignant that Lydia was staying on in San Francisco, that she intended to make her life in the States, but sublimated his displeasure, among other things over the phone, by ragging on at her about this missing blanket at the cottage. Her grandfather had bought three that Coronation year, 1937. Did she know? They were expensive! One of the blankets was missing.

One missing? Lydia only remembers there ever being two purple blankets, but never mind. She knew exactly where one of them was, then. As she knows where it is now. Unretrievable.

*I have no idea what you're talking about,* she told her father.

Carol prides herself on understanding her clients' psychology. She's had 'em all—the hoarders and the alcoholics and the pervs and the freaks, and she can sum them up in a sec. Nothing, for instance, says depressive like a potential client who greets you in sweatpants. She can see in an instant that Lydia is none of the above. The woman is a model of understatement: an Eileen Fisher white linen shirt over black chinos, small gold hoops in her ears, a vintage tank watch, Ray-Ban tortoise-shell sunglasses perched on hair long and straight, parted in the middle. Only Ms Lydia Eadon's hair is grey. It's abundant, though, and as Carol steps closer and peers through her sunglasses she can see it isn't some aging hippie affectation. More than abundant, it's expensively cut and coloured to a fine and foxy silver framing a city-pale face.

Carol unconsciously pats her own coif and sizes her potential client up: composed, educated, entitled, has a bit of money, wants a bit more. Oh, she'll get it, too. This property should sell easily. She removes her sunglasses, puts out her hand in greeting, and immediately senses the woman's tautness: stiff back, strained eyes, not so composed underneath, really. The hand in hers feels rough; she notes the chewed skin along the thumb as she withdraws.

Condolences, chit-chat, the weather (hot, my yes!), yes, my grandfather built it in 1923 or 1925—one of those years—yes, spent summer here as a little girl, come inside, have you been inside before?

No, Carol lies. *Selling with Soul,* the bible of her profession, would have no truck with this. Carol can't think why the lie tripped so easily off her tongue. (She tagged along for a viewing with the heritage committee in May, before Marion Eadon died.) She's suddenly feeling a little off-kilter.

Lydia gives her the tour—kitchen, dining room, two bedrooms, bathroom, unwinterized. Explains the systems—the well, the septic tank, the electricity. Points out the little design gems, the paned windows, the French doors, the vaulted ceiling. Mentions the separate sleeping cottage–tool shed building on the property.

It dawns on Carol that her client—her *potential* client—thinks that the cottage, this old building full of old junk—is the selling point, that someone will be eager to buy it and maintain it in all its eccentricity. Carol's had these sorts before, people deluded about the charms of their homes or properties. Funny, though, Ms Eadon doesn't seem the deluded type.

"It's adorable," Carol murmurs, glancing at a cobweb joining a lamp to a wall, which Lydia missed. "The market for a cottage of this ... vintage may not be all that large, though. The property, certainly, is attractive—well, very attractive. The beachfront, the size. I think I'll have no trouble finding a buyer. It could get ..."

She mentions a sum. It's about what Lydia thought it might be. Enough to ensure the house on Lincoln is hers and Ray's without a crippling mortgage. However ...

"I'd prefer to sell it as is," Lydia says, studying Carol's face. "To someone who would love it as much as we do."

"As is?" *Good grief.*

"Well, at least the building as is," Lydia continues. "I suppose what people do with the contents is their business, but I would hope they would want to keep some of these antiques."

*Antiques?* "Wouldn't you be taking most of these ... family pieces with you?"

"No, none. I've got no room at home for anything more."

"Well, you know, the trend seems to be for larger cottages—second homes, really—winterized, with basements and garages and the like."

"You mean a tear-down. Someone would buy this, tear it down, and build some huge thing like the ones down the road."

"Well, yes."

"I understand there's a heritage committee ..."

"Yes, but a heritage designation has ..." Carol gropes for the right expression "... no force of law."

Lydia knows this already. The woman is hardly adept at hiding her dismay. Lydia is more adept at hiding hers. She's *acting* the cool customer as much as she can. She imagines Carol has buyers in mind, developers, possibly; certainly no one interested in maintaining a rickety old cottage. She imagines Carol is expecting to make a quick sale, and she realizes she's been avoiding the truth all these weeks: her options for Eadon Lodge are really very narrow.

"Finding someone who wants the cottage as is may take time, if you're prepared to wait," Carol continues to Lydia's silence, though she would like to add: *till hell freezes over.*

"I can't wait too long, I'm afraid. I ... need to be getting home, to San Francisco.

"It's a little late in the season. It's already August."

"I really do need a quick sale."

Carol pauses. There is that colleague of cousin Ívar's. The location is not ideal. The guy seemed keen on something farther south along the lake, near Ívar's little summer arts colony, where there's currently nothing available, but maybe, if Eadon Lodge was more ... affordable. "Do you think you could be flexible on price?" she asks Lydia.

"You mean, go lower."

"Well, yes."

"Do you have someone in mind?"

"You never know," Carol demurs, patting her hair, "a lower price widens the field." And lessens the commission. "Let me see what I can do."

Lydia is slightly more reassured. They do some paperwork, discuss cleaning and "staging," a word her Winnipeg real estate agent irritated her with.

"I thought I'd stay at the hotel while I'm sorting through a few things here," Lydia says.

"Did you book?"

"At the hotel?"

"No."

"I don't think you'll have any luck finding accommodation. It's Islendingadagurinn this weekend."

"Islend ... ?"

"The Icelandic Festival."

"Oh."

"When was the last time—?"

"It's been almost forty years."

"The town fills to the brim. Every room in town is taken, I'm sure. You could phone around, I guess, but why bother? You have this place."

Lydia's eyes sweep the living room. They are seated either side of the old desk under the east window. The light catches their whites and Carol catches a glimpse of something in them—dread? horror? revulsion?

Weird, given she wants *someone else* to live in this ... curiosity. She notes the unhappy tone of Lydia's reply:

"Yes, I do, don't I?"

Was there ever a comfortable seat in Eadon Lodge? Those two Shaker rocking chairs? The bench at the dining room table? This old fold-out couch she's lying on? The place seems designed for self-mortification.

Time has stood still in it. Would that it hadn't. Would that Marion had changed her mind about the interior design, the way she did so frequently with the Oxford Street house. Refurnishing the cottage wouldn't alter the past, of course, but at least the past wouldn't be so cruelly present.

The Victrola. There it is, in the corner, by the cupboard storing old clothes, bedsheets, and blankets. Surely the cache of 78s is still intact behind those cunning little bottom doors, because why would they be chucked, when the ancient books and china and furniture haven't been?

Briony flipped a record on the turntable one evening and suggested everyone dance. Briony was mother, trying, but mostly failing, to organize them, keep them to a schedule of meals, introduce activities, as if she were still a fifteen-year-old counsellor at church camp. She got up early to meditate according to the principles of Maharishi Mahesh Yogi. She made breakfast, though few rose before eleven and couldn't be bothered even with cereal. She did most of the cooking for them. She swept the sand from the floors and tidied the bathroom and kept a shopping list and drove into town for groceries (despite having only a learner's permit) and suggested card games and Monopoly games and so on. It was not nice—Lydia thinks this now—how they took advantage, when it suited, of her essential decency. It was summer, it was hot, the lake was close and cool. They could hardly be bothered to lend her a hand or participate in her "extracurricular activities." They just wanted to lie in the sun, swim, drink, and smoke dope—and in Alanna and Alan's case spend time alone together, in their tent, in the cottage, if no one else was around. It was, Lydia thinks now, the aura of sex that hung over the cottage those days that summer—the doing it of which excluded her—that sent Briony into a spasm of domestic activity. Alan and Alanna's secret smiles and lazy grins were burden enough, but it was Paul who brought sex with him.

She suggested for sleeping arrangements that the boys each take a couch in the cottage. She imagined the electric presence of Paul a dozen feet away, but Dorian had espied the sleeping cottage *cum* gardening shed—the Petit Trianon, he christened it. Might be a bit cramped in the cottage, the four of them, he said. You girls need your privacy, he said. Paul and I don't mind sharing a room—we're cousins, after all, he said. And so the matter was settled. The cousins would sleep in the Petit Trianon. Their cousinship no one questioned in those days of indolence until, one by one, she last, the scales fell from their eyes.

One of the days after Dorian and Paul arrived Briony bought kerosene in town at Golko's Hardware and set herself the task of cleaning and filling Eadon Lodge's oil lamps. Lydia can see one of them across the room now, on its own little stand above the library table, its pretty glass fount scintillating in the sun's rays in low slant through a bedroom window. She doesn't remember the lamps ever lit as a child, but Briony lit them that evening before the six of them sat down to dinner—their third evening? their fourth?—switching off the electric lights. The cottage interior glowed and flickered like an ancient cave.

Lydia knows why Briony put the record on. Some of them had drifted into the living room after a spaghetti dinner, mellowed by drink and carbs, cossetted by the muffled lapping of waves along the shore and the warm golden sunset, feeling no need to continue the conversation. No one had yet lit a joint. If someone had, Paul most likely, as he was the one who brought the dope with him, their enjoyment of the summer evening would have turned from languor to stupor. Dancing? *I can't get up.*

Lydia remembers someone—Dorian?—shouting to Briony over the clatter of plates in the sink to leave the dish-washing to them but recalls more her annoyance when Briony, wiping her hands on a tea towel, joined them in the living room and beelined for the Victrola, as if she'd been planning an evening of music all along. For Lydia, the novelty of the gramophone had long since faded. Most of the records were ancient and brittle, the sound scratchy and tinny, the music quaint and corny.

Lydia realizes she's muddling her thoughts, deliberately—maybe. Or maybe it's the wine she had with the supper she bought in town. The atmosphere that evening, she recalls, wasn't really languid. There was silence, yes, but the silence was partly the hangover of a heated dinner-table argument (Chairman Mao: great helmsman or nasty dictator; Alan vs. Briony) and partly expectation, which Briony precipitated by opening the top of the Victrola, winding its side crank tighter and tighter, and saying brightly *let's dance*. The machine rumbled and shook the floor like a dog too long indoors eager for release. Briony dropped the needle on Jane Froman singing "Embraceable You." Lydia studied her friend's eager face: from among the mostly novelty records and Sousa marches and boogie-woogie, Briony had chosen a slow-dance song. Deliberately. At the ready on the turntable, waiting for the right moment.

Alan was out in the yard, ungracious in defeat (five of the six thought Mao uncool), though just as likely peeing in the bushes. Alanna, on one of the rocking chairs, followed a moth with her eyes as it flitted from oil lamp to oil lamp, battering its soft head against the glare. Like Briony, she was made anxious by their erratic flight.

Who invited Lydia to dance? Not Dorian, as Briony had wished. After all, Lydia and Dorian were seated side by side on the couch, this very one, with its burgundy cover, that she was lying on now, and the two were regular partners at parties and such, Ross Stubbs, her old boyfriend, never much of a dancer. No, it was Paul who came over to her, rising from the other rocking chair, stepping over, bowing deeply and solemnly taking her hand.

Lydia remembers looking up to see his face break into a smile, a sly tuck in one corner of his mouth making a dimple. She remembers, too, Dorian's reaction. She could see from the corner of her eye *his* face founder, which she couldn't interpret, not then.

Her attraction to Paul on his arrival at Eadon Lodge had been immediate—visceral in a way that was new to her. They were on the lawn—she, Briony, Alanna, and Alan—playing, of all things, croquet, when Dorian rounded the corner of the cottage, Paul in tow, and said, as he was given to do when he arrived anywhere, "ta-dah!" Something about Paul's eyes, large, glittering black, intoxicating, even at a distance? She felt herself like one of those ingénues in the Harlequins she devoured when she was thirteen—still water stirred or spring ice freed—the sorts of allusions that would have her tossing the offending book against the wall a year or two later. He smiled his greeting to her, his mouth twisting in a way that suggested more than pleasant invitation—conspiracy, perhaps, a secret alliance, a telegraphing that only they two recognized the absurd theatricality of Dorian's entrance. She smiled back, felt the gravitational pull. He looked little like Dorian (dark vs. blond, brown vs. blue) but then their cousinship was remote. Was it on the Grant side? Or the other side? (What was Dorian's mother's maiden name?) Dorian delineated, seemed unnecessarily eager to do so. But other people's family trees are thickets. Their eyes glazed over. It didn't matter.

Lydia slipped easily into the rhythm of Paul's body, excited to feel the heat of another's flesh and the weight of another's hand along her waist. She can see herself now over there by the gramophone, in a peasant top, midriff bare, in frayed cutoffs, barefoot on the old oriental runner rug. Paul is wearing cutoffs, too, and a T-shirt, this one tie-dyed, an exploding orange mandala that glows in the lamplight. The floor creaks beneath their feet as they sway. She feels his erection stabbing at her. She's unsurprised. She wonders if the others can see the tenting. Perhaps not. The light is low and Dorian is up from the couch inviting Alanna, not Briony, to dance. Briony, left wallflower, replaces "Embraceable You"—a 78 spins for barely three minutes—with Kay Starr's "Everybody's Somebody's Fool" and flashes, uncharacteristically for her, an acid smile.

Perhaps Alan will return and ask her to dance and nicely fill out three couples—however—in Briony's eyes—wrongly matched. Alan does return after a few moments. Lydia hears the screen door squeak (Alan will fix that later to devastating effect), but the next thing she hears, over the final warbles of Kay Starr, is something beating the air. It's Alan dispatching the dreaded moth with a rolled-up *Chatelaine* magazine. He doesn't dance. He doesn't ask poor Briony. But he doesn't have to. The record ends. Before Briony can lift it from the turntable, Alan beats her to the punch with a suggestion, a surprising one, since Lydia finds Marxists much like Victorian aunts: a moonlight dip in the lake.

Yeah! Why not? The cottage is warm from the day's sun. But more: the idea's kind of sexy. Alan's outdone Briony, but Paul does him one better. Scrambles to bedrooms and tent and Petit Trianon for swim suits are aborted as he pushes through the screen door, doffs T-shirt and drops shorts on the steps—almost in a single fluid motion—and vanishes into the darkness, the last of him his tight rounded ass, a dimpled apricot in the yellow porch light.

What? Chicken out? No way. At least not the boys. Dorian and Alan whoop in a holler of mutual goading and race after Paul, dropping their clothes on the lawn, disappearing in a volume of noise. Lydia senses Briony and Alanna hesitating. But she's felt herself since Paul's arrival, since his eyes burrowed into hers, as a woman famished. She's next. She throws open the screen door, races down the steps, tugging at buttons and zips, heedless of Briony's cries. Careless in her excitement, she drops top, shorts, bra and panties, the cooling air on her breasts startling, darts though the gate onto the silhouetted beach, flies along the cold sand and bursts onto the lake, gasping as the chilly water sears her hot skin. Overhead the sky clings to the last of the day's light, a deep navy dome shot with the dying wisps of pink. The boys, shadowy shapes in the rising moon, are well advanced into the waves, splashing and shouting, thrashing about in some horseplay. She pushes herself around against the weight of the water, conscious of her nakedness, her eye catching the twinkle of cottage light through gaps in the foliage, and the shapes, she is sure, of Briony and Alanna. They remind her of anxious wives.

The boys see her approach through the waves, swarm her. She feels unravelled, loosened, naughty—all her qualms and rigidities falling away. She's only a body now, a vessel, a being. A hand brushes her thigh—not Dorian's, not Alan's—and she shivers, anticipating. It's Paul swimming beneath her, touching her, teasing her, grazing places he shouldn't. He bursts through the surface of the waves, water cascading from his hair and face, with a volley of laughter, and though the others don't know quite why, they join in out of the sheer animal joy of the moment. Dorian and Alan mimic him, diving and twisting around her, but they don't touch, each pulled back by some veneer of restraint. But a heightened tension crackles along the churning surface of the water and Lydia is conscious of slipping past moorings set down in childhood. Arousal makes her weak. She lifts her eyes to Paul's, drawn into the depth of their irises caught in the moon's glow, and reads their message.

And then—in a moment—the spell is broken. Alanna is calling from the shore. They hear her now, conscious she has been shouting for a while, her words incomprehensible over the sound of the churning water, but the tone is unmistakably peevish. With a muttered oath, Alan turns away. Dorian glances at Paul, then at Lydia. She sees his bemusement. She wants him gone. "I'm getting cold," he announces and follows after Alan. Two pale backs ply the waves and disappear. Lydia feels a hand on each breast, hot breath nuzzling her neck, the sudden wet warmth of another's skin along her back. And something else. She knows of the effect of cold water on the male organ. It came as a revelation to her in Alanna's parents' pool when she was first dating Ross. But Paul, miraculously, is rampant and is rubbing his hardness against her.

And then he is inside her. This time she does gasp. Some instinct urges her to resist. It's an assault. There is a flash of pain. And yet, helpless in lust, she yields to the rhythm of Paul's body in her and, quickly, to sweet convulsion. Unbidden, this scene will intrude into her mind for the rest of her life—as it does now, as she lies on the old couch nearly four decades later. It was obscene, outrageous, thrilling—a carnal act over as quickly as it began, over before Alan and Dorian climbed onto the beach, the groan of their climax drowned in the turbulence of the waves.

Briony brought four towels down to the beach. Of course, she would think to do such a thing. She was at the water's edge, one towel at the ready in one outstretched hand the moment Lydia, hand where Botticelli placed Venus's, emerged from the lake. She looked past Dorian, shivering in his towel, to see a white phosphorescence—Alan in a white towel—following a shadow—Alanna—back up the path to the cottage limned by the very last rays of the setting sun. She couldn't look at Dorian and thanked god for the masking darkness. Neither did she speak, let her voice betray some new emotion. No one else spoke anyway. It was as if something—and not just lust—had been sated. Did Dorian suspect? Did Briony or Alanna? The two women were facing the lake, but perhaps they had been too concentrated on the returning boys. Briony said nothing as she led Lydia back up the path, kindly picking up Lydia's clothes along the lawn. Paul was still out in the water when they retreated from the shore, a dark shape moving in darkness. They left Dorian waiting for him.

Lydia sleeps fitfully. The day's heat lingers well into the evening and though the windows are open, little breeze passes through the screens of the second bedroom, now a hot box. Lydia's selective memory is of heavenly cool nights at Eadon Lodge, and she prepared the bed just so, topping a duvet with an old blanket—almost impossibly, she's looking forward to a moment at Eadon Lodge, a moment of sleep. And sleep, rare for her, came swiftly. (The wine!) But now, too soon, she's awake, suddenly, startled from a dream—was she screaming in the dream? Her head is heavy, her mouth thick. She feels as if a wet, hot cloth had been pressed down on her face. She finds the sheet pushed to her waist, the duvet and the blanket pushed to one side, and a feeble blush of light in the window. She is discombobulated. Can it be dawn? No, no, the window looks west. West is where the sun sets, yes, but it sets late, freakishly late in Canada's high latitude. The dream—if it's a dream; so early for REM sleep—leaves a ragtag trail end of images. In the dream, she was screaming. She remembers this now. Ray tells her she screams in her sleep from time to time. But if she wakes him in her agitated sleep, he is more likely to find her mouth an Edvard Munch gap with noise only a rattle in her throat, a scream desperate for release. And what do I say when I scream, if I scream, she asks Ray anxiously. You just scream, he shrugs. Perhaps he's lying. She hopes he isn't.

She glances at her watch. It's only a little past eleven. In this eleventh hour she was—once again—with her father, moving through the dark tunnel, terrorized by the flaming Medusa head, fleeing, fleeing into a void, a scream rising in her throat. She wakes up, gasping for breath as the images flitter away on blackened wings. The dream is hateful. If dreams exist to protect sleep, why, she wonders, do some destroy it?

Lydia rises, pads into the dark living room, pushes through the double doors into the dining room, and into the kitchen, a route implanted in memory. She fetches some water, drinks it, goes back to bed and falls into fitful sleep.

When the early morning sun streams through the east window into the living room—before six, a crazy hour—Lydia opens the old trunk in the second bedroom where she knows her father, like his father, kept the tools. She removes pliers and shears—ancient but functional. The old stepladder behind the kitchen door sends a shiver of memory through her; she can barely stand to touch it, but she drags it into the living room, opening it under the rafters. What she's about to do feels mad. Is mad. But so be it.

She pulls the big switch in the second bedroom to turn off the electricity. Tools in hand, she climbs the ladder, which wobbles, the rungs seeming to crack under her weight. A sudden lightheadedness threatens to overwhelm her. It's not the height, it's something more visceral. Terror. She is looking down on the electrolier that once, thirty-nine years ago, she once looked up at with disbelief. It is peculiar and ugly, a Victorian confection, a brass crab with five glass pincer feet—the light bulbs, which she should have removed first. Feverishly now, perspiring though the cottage is morning cool, she hacks and pulls at the electrolier's wires and fastenings and soon—sooner than she imagined—she is done. The reviled lamp crashes to the floor in a glassy explosion.

# 16

Sometimes, most often on sleepless nights, at the turn of the millennium when the Internet was fresh and new, Dorian would enter Paul's name into a search engine, heart in mouth, to see if his name or face would emerge on screen. Of course none did, not *his* Paul Godwin. His Paul Godwin lived only in memory well out of reach of AskJeeves and Dogpile and Google.

He hardly knew what he was expecting to find. A death notice? A missing person's report?

And then, during one search, on a rainy Vancouver night in 2003 when he was living with Mark, his Paul Godwin materialized in an anecdote contained within an oral history of Upper Canada College: Paul ran away from school in grade eleven and went missing for six weeks. He wound up in Mexico and lived with a prostitute. Yes, a prostitute, a woman—as described in the book—with a parrot and superb collection of knives. He travelled by thumb and had no trouble in those more innocent days getting through U.S. customs. And he had no trouble getting back through U.S. customs on his way to Los Angeles where his adventure ended at a relative's in Brentwood with a phone call made to his anxious mother.

By the time he read this online, Dorian knew Paul had attended Upper Canada College. But Paul never said. At Eadon Lodge, after Dorian introduced "cousin" Paul, the usual getting-to-know-you conversations ensued, incorporating the question, *where did you go to school?* Some unextraordinary Toronto high school, the name of which Dorian's long since forgotten. Why did Paul not tell the truth? Was it because the fashion of the day was to present yourself as a proletarian? It was only later that Dorian reckoned that Paul was running away—again—and this time probably didn't want to be found.

Dorian considers this as he checks the flight tracker widget on his laptop. Mark is flying in for the week. The plane is halfway to Alberta, scheduled to land in Winnipeg on time, 4:33 this afternoon. Lovely. Dorian's been a good boy these last many weeks—well, good*ish*—but he has to admit to himself he is missing more the domesticity of life with Mark than he is having his pipes cleaned regularly. But what else will they do together—or apart—while he is here?

He has forgotten how destinationless this corner of the world can be. No *chic boîtes* at the end of the road. Gimli has some weekend festival thingy. Mark might want to attend that, Dorian not at all. He's avoided the town, though he's shopped across the highway at the Sobey's. A deep distaste fills him when he foots it across the parking lot and glimpses the town shimmering in the summer heat like some poisonous prairie Brigadoon. But he can hardly tell Mark why he wants to keep his distance.

Something happened on the fifth day. Or maybe it was the sixth. It doesn't matter. And it wouldn't have mattered, would have been forgotten, but for what happened later.

Where were the others? At the beach, probably. The cottage was unoccupied when he and Paul straggled in from the Petit Trianon to root around for something to eat. It was past noon, the heat of the day dissolving the cool of the interior. Dorian remembers his head pounding with hangover, his annoyance with Briony for tidying up the kitchen, for putting away the bread and jam and cereal and the instant coffee, his need for an aspirin. With the others nowhere in sight, Paul eased his hands past the band of Dorian's shorts, nuzzled his neck and murmured an invitation to shower together. Tenting, he found Paul leading him by his third leg toward the bathroom—this new bathroom that Bibs had installed only a few weeks earlier.

It was another one of the dreaded what-ifs that would flutter along his consciousness long afterwards. What if he had stepped into the shower with Paul? What if they had been together in the cubicle, oblivious to all but themselves, the noise of beating water their shield?

But it was the only time Dorian refused Paul's invitation. He didn't say why, but he and Paul each knew the reason for his resistance. *Someone might come in and find us together.*

"You shower," he said, pushing away Paul's busy fingers. "I'll make us something to eat."

Dorian was allaying his hangover with a very large glass of Tang and a piece of toast, sitting at the dining room table, when his ears pricked to heavy footfalls on the front steps outside. Perhaps it was his being lost in a hazy reverie of sex, his attention resting on Paul over the wall singing in the thrashing water, that a heavy rap on the side of the door sent a shock down his spine. Through the screen, he could glimpse sunlight glancing off a figure in T-shirt and jeans on the stoop. But outside looking in, the figure, Dorian knew, would see only darkness, unless he pressed his face into the screen—which he did. Dorian, who had frozen, hoping the guy would go away, was forced to acknowledge his presence. Somewhere in those few seconds, the shower stopped and Paul stopped singing. As Dorian called out to the stranger, "the door's open," he heard Paul behind him open the door from the bathroom and water drip drip drip along the floor.

But for the events that would later overtake them, Dorian would have recalled the scene as provocative, porn-ish. The guy who stepped into the cottage was about their age, maybe a year or two older, with dark lengths of spaniel hair touching his shoulders and a Sgt. Pepper moustache. He was brawny in an effortless-looking sort of way, Marlon Brando muscles straining below the stained T-shirt, but it wasn't those raw charms that caught Dorian's attention. It was the smell wafting off him—earthy, sweaty, feral. His skin, where it was exposed, glistened with sweat. Dorian saw his small dark eyes light in a strange way as they travelled over his shoulder to a place above and behind him. Dorian turned his head slightly and realized

Paul was at his side, naked, towelling himself off, indifferent to the stranger's presence. *Jesus!* It was over in a moment, but in that moment the guy had their measure, his eyes darting between them, a scowl twisting his lips.

"I've got a delivery, bulk soil and sod," he grunted. "Where do you want it?"

"Have you got the right address?" Dorian asked.

"Yeah, man."

"It's probably for that hole where the outhouse used to be," Paul remarked.

"Right, of course, Lydia mentioned something about it. I guess ... dump it next to ... you'll see a sheet of plywood on the north side of here, covering the hole," Dorian addressed who he'd forever after think of as the Dirt Guy. "You should be able to get the truck in, I think. You'll have to manoeuvre around those three big rocks, though. You brought it in a truck?"

"No, I brought it by bicycle." Dirt Guy yanked a paper from his back pocket and thrust it at him. "I need a signature."

"We're not the ..." Dorian began, a prim response halted by an impatient glare.

"If you've got a pen, man, I'll sign it," Paul said, wrapping the towel around his waist.

Dirt Guy had a pen.

"You know Lydia's going to want us to fill that hole—some deal with her father," Dorian said when Dirt Guy departed and they could hear the sound of a truck backing into the yard.

"Maybe," Paul said, shrugging as Dorian dropped another piece of bread into the toaster, "we can get out of it somehow."

The Dirt Guy was one of only two outside witnesses to Paul's stay at Eadon Lodge. He remembers saying to Lydia later that day, when she remarked on the appearance of a pile of soil, that it had been delivered earlier. The details didn't matter and Lydia didn't ask. None of it was worth thinking about at the time.

But later the Dirt Guy became, for Dorian, a figure of feverish paranoid speculation. He would be their nemesis. The man's hard eyes and deprecating glance haunted Dorian's imaginings for years afterward; he grew into a figure of almost occult prescience and lordly judgment. That night, that horrible night at Eadon Lodge, when Paul was a cooling corpse and he, Dorian, was sick with grief and fear, he told her about Dirt Guy. She worked reason on him. She had taken control. Why would this Dirt Guy have any reason to go to the police? *Why, Dorian, why*? But it didn't matter. He grew possessed by the thought that he would, that he must, given that Paul's disappearance was now the sole preoccupation of the nation. That everywhere in 1969 and 1970 they were looking for Paul. What had become of Paul? *Where is Paul?*

Back in Rosedale, at Pastis, in early 1998, when Dix is dining with Dorian in advance of her trip to Palm Beach, the Internet is still largely a novelty to most. The conversation that began with Dorian's seemingly innocent question about Dix's children has turned to the early days of her search for her missing son. Dorian is by turns frightened and sickened and relieved by what he learns. Dix is stirred by half-buried memories and the interest of the handsome man across the table. The void left behind by her son's disappearance never completely closed. Of course, it wouldn't. She's a mother. Dix, for a short while, didn't find Paul's absence worrying. It was the '60s, hitchhiking was the vogue—until the Tate-LaBianca murders created a distrust of vagabond youths. But by early days of autumn 1969, when Paul didn't return to Toronto to resume his studies as he promised he would—and he didn't phone—she grew increasingly anxious. She went, of course, to the police.

Or did the police come to her first? She can't quite remember. The police found the conjunction of Rory's death and Paul's absence interesting and would have liked to have brought him in for questioning. They had no proof of foul play and the coroner ruled Rory's death an accident, but a whiff of suspicion lingered in some quarters.

None of this Dix tells Dorian, and Dorian only learns of it later from a friend who was a UCC old boy. What he wants to know, even though he can barely stand to know, is what Dix did about her missing child. As in the movies, what happened next?

"Well, the police were no help. They didn't judge someone Paul's age, of sound mind and good health, to be missing. They presumed he went off of his own accord. So, after I got in touch with his friends and relatives, anyone I could think of who might know his whereabouts, I hired a private detective. Someone in Rory's firm recommended him. He had a good reputation, apparently. But he had little success in finding my son." Dix's mouth forms a grim line. "In fact, he ... I can't recall his name now ... believed Paul never crossed the border into the U.S."

Dorian asks sharply, "Why?"

"No record, for one thing."

"But, Dix, in those days, to cross into the U.S., all you needed was—"

"Yes, but they still took note of your coming and going. I argued with him, the detective. I was certain he went to Woodstock. That's where he said he was going and I ... I had no reason to think that wasn't true. I wasn't convinced U.S. border security was very diligent."

"And the second thing?"

Dix looks blank.

"You said you had another reason your son might not have crossed into the U.S."

"Ah." Dix sips her Chablis. "The detective—Tony, that was his name. I just remembered—found a truck driver who made an identification. This driver picked him up somewhere around Vaughan and dropped him off in Barrie."

"Barrie," Dorian repeats dully. He can feel a flush of perspiration along his skin. Barrie is sixty miles north of Toronto.

"There was no reason for Paul to go to Barrie or stay in Barrie. I knew of nothing connecting him—or us, our family—to Barrie."

"Maybe he was coming back to see you. Didn't you say you had a cottage in Muskoka? You can hardly avoid going through Barrie."

"But he'd only just left me to come back here, to Toronto. And if he were going to our cottage, he didn't arrive. If he got as far as Barrie, he must have continued on to somewhere else. He had taken his backpack, the one he had used in Europe earlier. He was hitchhiking, as you kids did in those days. So where did he go from Barrie, if Tony is at all right about Paul not going to the U.S.?" A kind of raw grief breaks through her voice, startling Dorian. "Not east. If you were going to Montreal or Ottawa, you wouldn't go by Barrie, would you?"

"You might," Dorian responds hesitantly. "Sometimes you take the ride that's available and make compromises."

"Did you hitchhike in those days?"

The question catches Dorian off-guard. No. *No!* The idea is grotesque. Paul had hitchhiked and look what happened. "No," he says, "I never did."

The trail vanished there. No one came forward to say they saw Paul anywhere between Barrie, Ontario, and the Shell station west of West Hawk Lake where Dorian picked him up. But someone, or some few, had. Did Dorian ask him about those rides? Who picked him up? What had they talked about? He only remembers asking Paul if anything, you know, like, *happened*—did anybody try anything? And Paul smiled and said no, though afterward, Dorian wondered if someone as unrestrained as Paul didn't have an adventure en route and that someone along the Trans-Canada Highway remembered him and would come forward. The notion that some man—or some woman—out there in the vast hinterland of northern Ontario might recall Paul jabbed his waking thoughts for years until, finally, it seemed there was no one to come forward, there was no investigation.

Only Dirt Guy—and one other guy—resolved into an identifiable witness. And where was Dirt Guy now, today?

# 17

Lydia runs the cloth over the shotgun and watches the dust fall in lumps to the floor next to the Victrola. Whoever cleaned the cottage for her mother in June missed that item. Fear of guns? Afraid it might go off? Perhaps. It did before, once. But the rack in which the gun (COOEY MODEL 84 MADE IN CANADA, she reads on the side of the receiver) rests is difficult to reach if you're woman, and though Lydia is five feet, seven inches, she uses a kitchen stepstool to reach it. She wants badly to clean the tops of the frames of the portraits of her great-grandfather and great-grandmother farther along the wall—assuming they're as neglected by Marion's cleaner as the shotgun—but she would have to climb onto the old sideboard to do so. The urge to clean is like a virus in the blood. She will end up doing it. But first, she steps off the stool, wipes her brow with the back of her hand, and studies the shine.

It was Paul who observed that the shotgun seemed to be pointing at Great-grandfather Eadon and made one of those Freud-would-have-a-field-day remarks, which raised Alan's hackles—Freud's pseudoscience violating some dialectical materialist canon, apparently—a harbinger of unpleasantness to come. This came soon after Paul and Dorian arrived at Eadon Lodge with Paul asking for a cottage tour. She remembers something playful and charged in those early exchanges with Paul. She felt immediately drawn to him, but not unaccountably: He was beautiful. And he conveyed such a lively curiosity about the artifacts his eye happened upon in this museum of a cottage.

The shotgun, for instance. This gun that so shattered their summer idyll. Lydia never saw it off the wall, never saw her father carry it or oil it, though she mightn't have paid attention to him doing so. She never saw him shoot with it, though a box of shells rested at the back of the old desk drawer. She had an idea her father once hunted with his father, but he hadn't since boyhood, had he? She must have asked her father about it, when she was very small, with a child's curiosity, but she couldn't remember his reply then. She can't remember it now. The shotgun by the time of Paul's visit was simply another expression of the masculine taste that governed Eadon Lodge. Deer antlers projected from one wall. A First World War helmet and a regimental sword decorated another. Boy's-bedroom pennants of places visited left few spots blank. There were flags, many flags: the Red Ensign, Union Jacks, a Stars-and-Stripes with forty-eight stars.

"Do you shoot?" Paul asked her, his dark eyes a dizzying thing.

"No," Lydia replied. She was charmed that he asked, her, a woman, without seeming to condescend. She remembers this—the charm. Not silky, it felt. Sincere. She remembers, too, Alan snickering, as if the notion of women with guns were absurd.

"Do you shoot?" Dorian asked Paul, surprise evident in his voice.

"Me? No. My stepfather did ... does. He keeps guns at our cottage."

"Where's that?" Alan asked.

"North of Toronto."

Lydia studies the shotgun now. Dispose of it, too? Earlier, at dawn, in her dressing gown, she dragged the cut-down electrolier, heavy as a severed head, across the wet grass, past the gate, over the cold sand, and dropped it into the turbid waters of the lake—with a madwoman's madness, she thinks now in the strong, clear light of mid-morning. Somewhere nearby a dog had barked at the splash. Had there been human witnesses, too? What would he or she have seen? With the sun a hot pink dot on the far shore and the sky a blue-grey wash of cloud, there was more dark than light—perhaps only a figure silhouetted.

But the shotgun. She despises guns. Would it float if she threw it in the lake? It *is* pointed at her great-grandfather. Or is valuable, collectible, saleable?

That is Ray's notion. She reported her conversation with the real estate agent in an email what the property might fetch. He's delighted. Is there anything in that cottage worth anything? he writes back.

Clutching the dust cloth, she turns to look again around the living room. Is there *any* treasure here? The Victorian mantel clock, the brass flask, the 1930s chinaware? Not really, she messages back.

What about the books? Two opposing walls were lined with hardcover books, shelf upon shelf of faded spines. Most, she remembers from childhood, were stamped inside, DISCARD. All came from the Cornish Street branch of the Winnipeg Public Library.

Unread and unloved, Lydia thinks, passing her eyes over the titles, none of which looks to have been shifted in the years since she last looked at them. Could there be one that is rare, desirable, and valuable? Her cleaning forgotten, she goes from spine to spine, title to title. Nothing. No author, no title, few publishers ring a bell. Near the end of one shelf, next to a small lamp she switched on earlier, one title stirs a memory. *Dead Men Tell No Tales* by E.W. Hornung.

Had she read this one? Unlikely.

And then it comes back to her. This was the book she thought Dorian had desecrated. What possessed him? she thought at the time, though why she didn't blame Paul is a question she only entertained later, when she was no longer under his spell. But then she focused her fury on Dorian.

It was an old book. It was an unread book. It was an unloved book. But it was still a book—somehow a valuable, precious thing.

There was a crude square hole cut into the pages of *Dead Men Tell No Tales*. She came upon Dorian holding the book open and pushing a small bag into the cavity.

"*Why*?"

"I'm hiding our stash in it, Mrs. Peel."

"You ruined this book for *that*? As if the RCMP would be interested in us."

"I didn't do this."

"You didn't cut this book up?"

"*No.* I found it this way."

"Then someone else has done this. Bibs will have a fit."

"Well, it wasn't me. Look, Nancy Drew"—he put the open book under her eyes—"those cuts aren't very fresh. This was done before. It's the 'Mystery of the Hollowed-out Book' by Franklin W. Dixon."

"I think you mean Carolyn Keene."

"There's this." Dorian handed her a piece of folded paper tucked between two pages. "It fell out of the hole when I opened the book."

Lydia unfolded it. The paper was yellowed and contained nothing but numbers: 9 13 8-9-4-9-14-7 21-14-4-5-18 20-8-5 12-9-20-19 20-18-5-5. "A child's hand, but it looks like my father's."

"Then your father did this."

"Code."

"Pretty simple. Look, it's just numbers standing for letters. Nine—'I.' Thirteen—'M': I'M. See? You work out the rest. I'm too stoned."

Dorian was buzzed. They were all buzzed at one time or another, toking up in the evenings, more often then not; Paul the provider of these treats. Did Dorian ever use the book for *our* stash—*our* stash? She can't remember. She does remember deciphering the code: I'M HIDING UNDER THE LITS TREE. Some boyish game between brothers, the cryptogram simple enough for Bibs's mentally challenged little brother. And she does remember checking it before closing up the cottage that late August day. There was no trace of marijuana. She returned the cryptogram to the cavity.

Lydia removes the book, which comes off the shelf in a cloud of dust. Perhaps she should take this one, for Ray. He would be amused. He has tales of his own druggy adolescence in Modesto. She blows more dust off the top, leafs through the first few pages, and comes to the cavity, its edges as crude as she remembers.

But it is not empty.

Puzzled, her heart fluttering a little—why, she's not quite sure; anticipation?—she plucks from the hollow a yellowed piece of paper. The same, after forty years? She unfolds it. Yes, the same, but for one change. A stroke through the first two numbers and a new set of numbers inked above. She recognizes her father's hand, but not as it once was, strong, masculine, cursive, but all of a jitter, as it was in his decline.

25-15-21 18-5
~~9-13~~ 8-9-4-9-14-7 21-14-4-5-18 20-8-5 12-9-20-19 20-18-5-5

# 18

“Gimli’s north of here, isn’t it?” Mark says.

Dorian looks up from his crossword, a distraction born of waiting on set, in dressing rooms, as he places his coffee cup on the patio table. “A short drive, fifteen minutes.”

“Well, it seems someone there’s been murdered.”

Dorian allows a beat to pass. “Really,” he says, returning his attention to the crossword.

“It was on the radio in the kitchen. Some guy, late twenties, beaten to death right on the main street in the middle of the night. They have two teenagers in custody. Kids apparently swarming around when they should be in bed. That sort of thing.” Mark sits, lifts the front section of the *Free Press,* drops it back on the table. “What kind of place is this Gimli? You told me yesterday it meant ‘paradise’ in Icelandic.”

“Do I need to point out that the same people named Greenland ‘*Green*land’?”

“Should we go?”

“Do you want to?”

“Well ...” Mark contemplates the view from the back porch of Dorian’s cottage. “When will I ever have the chance to visit *Gimli* again?”

“We could sunbathe instead.”

“The beach here isn’t much. A thin strip.”

“Well, the lake’s been high this season. The beach at Gimli is much larger.”

“How about this then: we go to Gimli and take our bathing suits. They must have a change house or something on the beach.”

“I can’t remember if they do.”

"Can't remember? You told me in Vancouver you'd never been here before, or to Gimli."

"I was wrong. Once I got here, I realized I *had* been here before. *Okay*?"

"Okay."

Mark looks at Dorian returned to his crossword. He thinks: Dorian is fifty-nine. The mind isn't a keen blade forever. Perhaps a test for cognitive impairment?

The thought passes. Dorian is fine. It's just that after almost a two-month absence, Dorian looks to him to have, well, aged. Or is it just that he's allowed his hair to go back to its natural colourlessness? He hoped he suppressed his little jolt of confusion when he exited his rental car, momentarily taken aback by this trim white-haired figure advancing across the lawn. Dorian was always old enough to be his father. Now he looks the part. *What if, god forbid, he ever let himself go—below the hairline?* They joked about it. The *Morningstar Cove* costume supervisor, he says, has him in these dad jeans and plaid shirts, which, thank god, Dorian has shucked today for black dress Bermudas and a white linen shirt. But Mark thinks of someone he's met recently in Vancouver, Hugh, an environmental lawyer. He's older, though much younger than Dorian, and he's even talked about adopting, wow. Mark would like a child. He can't have one with Dorian. Dorian's even resisted getting a *dog*. Mark's weighing some new options.

Dorian truly doesn't remember if there was a change house at Gimli beach and doesn't know if there is one now. He was only ever on the public beach once, with Paul when he swiped that camera. But he does remember that if you're on the public beach in the summer and look north though the heat haze, you can see shimmering in the distance, the beach narrowing, curving to a point of rocky land. It might be the edge of the world, but, Dorian knows and doesn't like to remind himself, that past the rocky barrier is a scallop of sand, a private enclave, the setting of his revels and his unravelling all those years ago.

Mark settles into his chair, between sips of coffee reading something off this new iPhone he bought before he left Vancouver. Dorian returns to his crossword. Ten across. *All About Eve* actress. Easy. Must include an 'X'. ANNEBAXTER. He pencils it in, but images crowd his mind. He is drifting along that private enclave with Paul, both of them with their eyes to the sand, as a distraction picking up things as they go along, shells and stones—the stones to skip along the water, the shells to pile into a mound—a *shiva lingam,* Briony will call it, blushing for some unaccountable reason.

They had wandered off from the cozy cluster of them sprawled over the Eadon Lodge beachfront, Dorian first, sickened and frightened at having his lie—*their* lie, his and Paul's—exposed, unable to look at Alanna, though her eyes were covered by dark glasses. Paul followed a little later.

"I spoke with Alanna," he said, rounding his arm over Dorian's shoulder.

*Alanna.* Dorian looks up from the crossword again, at Mark preoccupied with his iGizmo. Addison deWitt's sleek baritone slips neatly into his head. *Alanna, the golden girl, the cover girl, the girl next door, the girl on the moon. Has time been good to Alanna?*

Ridiculous, Dorian thinks. Alanna was not golden, not a cover girl, not a girl next door. She was nothing like Machiavellian, manipulative slippery, silky, purring Eve Harrington in *All About Eve.* Alanna had a feline prettiness, it was true—lots of small, upturned features—but no feline temperament Dorian could discern. The girls in high school were mean about her, *bitches,* probably because she knew what she wanted and got what she wanted—including boys of choice—and didn't connive to get them. Alanna kept her counsel, held her tongue, maintained her cool, moved through the halls of Kelvin High and University College in a cocoon of self-possession. Dorian felt sometimes—from a look in her eye, a twist to her lips—that she found them all faintly ridiculous, like they were the amusing denizens of another tribe, but rarely broached an offending comment. Perhaps she was the girl on the moon.

Alanna came upon them, as it happened. Alan was on Eadon Lodge's steps, waiting for Alanna to get out of the bathroom. Lydia and Briony, separately, had exited through the screen door (*squeeeeak!*) not once, but twice, each having forgotten some item necessary for beach lounging—sunglasses, tanning oil, a magazine. *Women!* The fifth squeak was Alanna, by which time Alan had had it up to *here* with that *fucking* squeaky door. A little fed up herself, as Alan was always cranky when she took her time in the bathroom, she paraphrased Marx: "The philosophers, *Alan*, have only complained about the world in various ways. The point, however, is to *change* it"—and marched across the grass to the Petit Trianon where she reasoned some lubricating oil would be stored.

Alan was shouting, "It's *interpreted*! The philosophers have only *interpreted* the world in various goddamn ways" when she crossed the lawn and opened the unsqueaky door of the sleeping cottage and came upon Dorian and Paul in an embrace. For some few seconds they were oblivious to her presence, to the shift of light caused by the open door, to the swell of leaf-rustle and birdsong. It was enough time for Alanna to study them. They were standing. They were wearing their bathing suits, the fabric of which was straining in front. She noted that. But, she thought, together, entwined, they looked rather lovely, Hellenic—or was it Hellenistic?—vaguely like figures on some vase in the slides her professor showed them in art history, which was her minor. She was unbothered, untroubled, unshocked by the scene, though it was something she had never seen before. No gasp did she make. Homosexuality was but a thread in life's rich tapestry, she thought airily, with the new wisdom of her major—psychology. She even accounted herself mildly aroused. The confined space smelled of maleness, of sex. What had they been doing before she arrived?

"Kissing cousins?" she said dryly when the two snapped to her presence. The wit—she thought her words witty—lightened nothing. Dorian gaped at her with wild eyes, his face turned ghost-white, and he shoved Paul away.

"Sorry to disturb you," she said quickly. Her eyes went to Paul. "I'm looking for an oil can or something like that."

"You need the door on the other side." It was Paul who responded. "But it's locked. I think there's a key in the kitchen, near the sink."

Alanna retreated to the cottage and found the key. By the time she returned, Dorian had left for the beach. She saw him cross the lawn unaccompanied as she exited Eadon Lodge's side door.

"Who are you?" she asked as she stepped around the lawnmower and glanced at the rank of shelves on the storage shed side of the Petit Trianon. Only a thin plywood partition wall separated her from Paul in the sleeping cottage side. She could hear him moving.

"The playboy of the western world," came the reply.

Alanna frowned as her eyes searched the shelves. One word, not the phrase (she didn't know it was an allusion to a play) resonated. "I thought you were interested in Lydia."

"I am interested in Lydia."

"I've seen the way she looks at you. And the two of you were up to something in the lake the other night."

"It was dark."

"It wasn't *completely* dark. Does Dorian know?"

"Know what? That Lydia and I ... No, he doesn't know. Why? Are you going to tell him? Or tell Lydia about what you saw here earlier?"

Alanna's eyes landed on a can of Texaco Home Lubrication Oil. She had a glimmering, a recall of lectures in her Psyc 210: Psychology of Personality class last spring, talk of traits married in one type, of confidence, charm, dishonesty, callousness, of those amused by trouble. She could almost sense his eyes burning through the plywood. She no longer smelled oil. She smelled sulphur. "Somehow," she replied evenly, reaching for the can, "I think that you might like it if I did tell."

"Like what?" Alan's voice, sudden, clear, near.

"Oil, Alan." Alanna was always a fast thinker. "Here's the can. Now fix the squeak."

"Alanna's cool," Paul said to him when he joined Dorian up the beach. "She won't tell, if that's what you're worried about."

"You know this how?"

Paul shrugged. "There's something about her." Dorian remembers him as struggling to contain his mirth. Face wreathed in smiles—that sort of thing. "What does it matter, anyway?" he laughed. It mattered. Duck's back for Paul. So cool, so untroubled. The year he'd spent in Europe, the things he'd done: Dorian envied him, envied it all. He felt like Paul's pupil sometimes, struggling to keep up, lying to appear worldly. Jesus, he even said he'd slept with Lydia, inventing a lurid high-school-graduation-night scenario, corny and small as *that* was, after Paul described an encounter with a woman in some club in Berlin who …

How the mind roils when you're having a facsimile of fun. Dorian realizes he is staring at his crossword puzzle at the same time he realizes Mark is puzzled by his unmoving pencil.

"Tough one?" Mark cranes his neck.

"Mm."

"Need help?"

"No." Dorian pulls the newspaper to his chest. "Go back to your pretty little machine."

Another breakfast, another year—1998. Well, brunch—with a few old Toronto pals. Dorian's new hag, Dixie-May Lang, has percolated through the conversation, and it turns out one of them went to UCC during Paul's era. A certain story rolls out: one about Paul and a nurse—a male nurse. Paul, fourteen, the nurse, thirty. The nurse dying—*dying, my dears*—in the midst of some *amusing* activity. Well, nursey was a bit of a pill-popper, maybe he had a heart condition, I mean, who knows, maybe death was the only way to avoid a statutory rape charge, but still … Dorian remembers the lightheadedness that came over him then, images of his own last minutes with Paul draining the blood from his head. What had they, Paul and this nurse, been doing—*exactly* what had they been doing—when he died? And, oh yes, the one about Paul's father, no, *step*father, dying under some peculiar circumstances, around the time that Paul vanished, *most peculiar, my dears.* Dorian remembers the old queen's exit line: *There was something dangerous about Paul, don't you know. It was part of his* allure.

Dorian lifts his eyes from the crossword to the big prairie sky and lets the late morning sun warm his face. With eyes closed, sound amplifies. Tree leaves rustle, somewhere a lawnmower begins its assault on the peace of the day, startled birds crack the sky, but it's all background. Foreground, here on the porch, is taken up with salvos of clacketty-clacketty-clack, like impatient fingernails on a tabletop. It's Mark tapping at his phone. Texting, no doubt. Mark likes to text.

Dorian lowers his head a little. Enough to unpeel his eyelids and peer at Mark through the scrim of his eyelashes. He observes the cupid's-bow lips of his quite kissable mouth bending into a—what? conspiratorial?—smile, the laugh lines around his eyes easing into a jolly crinkle. Ah, a private joke, a secret world.

A cloud appears—a real cloud, passing over the sun and shading the patio, but a metaphorical one passes over Dorian's heart, too. He feels a pang. *I know what follows, the autumn wind.* What's that? Some plangent little tune of years past. Did he sing it in some show? Can't remember. He reaches for a pack of cigarettes tucked behind the French press.

Mark has radar for such movements. "Are you going to smoke?"

"It's *my* house, sweetheart." Dorian peels back the foil. "Who are you texting with such diligence?"

"My resident, about a patient who's been admitted." Mark keeps his eyes on the tiny screen. He is lying. Dorian can tell. His pang sharpens. Mark is *not* an actor.

"Can't you leave it alone for two minutes?"

"No."

"Then what's the little problem?" Dorian flicks his Bic, decides to push a little at Mark's story.

"A suicide attempt. But the patient's just a big borderline."

Another borderline personality disorder. How they abound. At least in Mark's world. Folk with poor self-image, with feelings of emptiness, the self-harmers and substance abusers—all reduced to an entry in the *Diagnostic and Statistical Manual of Mental Disorders*, holy writ.

At times, earlier in their relationship, when Mark was in the full flush of his psychiatric residency, Dorian slipped in a question or two about Paul, presenting him as a friend from the olden days, otherwise named, whereabouts unknown. Did it matter what darkish facet Dix and others had turned to catch the light? For Dorian, no. He can't forget the adrenalin of those hours and days. A man gets inside you and fills your head and doesn't leave. But Mark' s diagnosis was swift, reductive:

Antisocial. Antisocial personality disorder. What you laypeople call a sociopath.

Dorian hates this. A boy he knew and loved reduced to a character in an airport thriller, the sort whose backstory includes a childhood spent pulling wings off butterflies and strangling puppies. But there is something else.

There is a fact, not a theory, about Paul Godwin. Dorian gleaned it some time later, after Dixie-May returned from Palm Beach in the spring of 1998. The two of them were at the COC's production of *The Rape of Lucretia*. It was intermission and for some reason Dix—something about the opera's impulsive prince, Tarquinius?—started talking about Paul, as she had begun to do more and more. It was Paul's impetuous nature she took as her subject that evening, as Dorian handed her the glass of champagne he'd fetched from the bar.

"My mistake, perhaps," she said leaning toward him to be heard in the crowded lobby, "was to tell him too young how his father died."

"Your first husband? How—"

"From complications of Huntington's."

Dorian must have looked blank. Dix explained:

"Rapid onset. He died when he was thirty-seven. Took his life. Paul was four, Peter two. It's a horrible, horrible disease. I kept it from the boys, but by the time Paul was thirteen, fourteen, I thought ..." A frown puckered her lips. "Well, I had to tell him. What if he ... what if he got some girl pregnant? Abortions weren't easily had in those days. But as it happened, his sexual orientation saved us from that ... at least until ..."

It dawned on Dorian: this is why Dix was chair of the Neurological Health Charities Ontario. But there was something else about the disease that was more horrible, which was eluding Dorian, though he realized it was passed genetically. Dix seemed to intuit his ignorance:

"Your heirs have a fifty-fifty chance of having it, too. They had no genetic tests in those days. Peter has been tested since. He's fine. His kids, my grandchildren, are fine."

A kind of wondering horror washed over Dorian. *Why did you marry a man with such distorted genes? Why did you have a child with him? Why did you have* two *children*?

Again, Dix seemed to anticipate him. "We rolled the dice, William and I. I was young, ten years younger—twenty-one when I married. I thought I could face anything, and he showed no signs then. And before you ask, Peter was not planned."

"When you told your son, your elder son"—He couldn't bear to say Paul's name—"what? ... how? ..."

"At our place at Muskoka. I don't know why I picked the moment I did. I didn't plan it. Rorie—my second husband, you remember?—had taken Peter to town to see a dentist, an emergency, a broken tooth, and Paul and I were left sitting on our dock. I suppose worry over Peter made me think about ... health. Anyway, I told Paul. He said very little. He was being stoic—little men, you know. But I knew he was shocked. It *is* shocking."

"And frightening."

"And frightening, yes. And you know what teenagers can be like—so unpredictable. I date his ... wild behaviour from the day I told him."

"Let's just go," Dorian says to Paul. They are well north of the others now, along the empty beach. "Back to the city."

"Why?"

"You know. My grandparents are still away. The house is empty..."

"I like it here. Your friends are cool. Except Alan."

"But they're always *around*."

"So?"

"You *know*. And what about going to L.A.?"

"Lots of time yet."

"I'd like to be gone before they get home from the lake."

"You've said. You don't want to tell them our plans. A couple more days. I like the weather here. Nice and dry. Summers are so fucking muggy in Toronto. Alanna's not going to blab. And I'm not interested in Lydia."

"She's interested in you."

"We've been through this. Nothing happened out there in the water. Don't sulk."

"I'm not sulking."

"You are. Come here." Paul reaches for Dorian, but Dorian jerks away. Paul renews the effort, lunging at him this time, and soon they are figures grappling on an empty beach, under a high sun in an unclouded sky, damp blooming along skin and running down backs, Dorian conscious in a new way of Paul's vitality and cunning as he finds Paul's legs snaking with his and they fall together in a writhing heap on a grassy rise. Anger and disappointment dissolve.

Dorian will recall this scene many times in the coming years. He's thinking about it right now, on his rented porch, in Winnipeg Beach, studying Mark absorbed in his little iDoodad. He will make use of it from time to time in those moments, with someone whose early attraction disappoints or when lovemaking grows tedious or awkward or he just wants to bloody finish. But its aftermath he will always block from memory. It is this:

When they finally slid apart onto the sandy grass in a slick of sweat, energy drained, blue sky filling their eyes, Dorian felt all Abou Ben Adhem-y, a deep dream of peace passing over him (even if he was fully awake). He was at one with the universe and filled with a growing sense of destiny. From that moment on—he was so sure—he knew exactly how his life would go. His cup ranneth over and so forth. The ring, the peace ring, which Lydia had brought back with her from San Francisco from her visit in the Summer of Love, had slipped past his knuckle. He pushed it back down his finger, twisting it around his damp skin, watching the sun glint along the silver, pleased with its beauty and general grooviness. An idea hatched in him. It was a sweet idea. He felt a bubble of delight and laughter swell in his chest. He would make penance—well, in another way, a more enduring, endearing way than their coupling moments past. He slipped the ring off his finger—it shot off as though greased with butter, falling onto his discarded swim trunks—and took Paul's left hand in his.

"Peace, man," he said, retrieving the ring and slipping it down Paul's third finger. "Keep it this time."

# 19

Lydia drifts from one mural to the next along the cement breakwater of Gimli's pier, oncoming couples and families and children weaving around her like schools of fish. She flicks a glance at the flaking frescoes on the sun-bleached wall from time to time, but mainly—sunglasses her shield—she searches the faces of men who appear to be on the cusp of middle age—the fathers of budding teenagers, the husbands of seasoned women, solitary figures. They weave around her, tanned or bearded, thickening or thin. It's a habit: Once it was the faces of boys, then teenagers, then young men, that drew her attention, but time has eliminated those categories. With every scan, she wonders, hopes, dreads, that an arrangement of eyes and nose and mouth and chin will resolve into a semblance so familiar she will know instantly this is the boy she gave away. Matthew. A few times, in other towns or cities, a face has sent her heart crashing to her shoes, but, no, it wasn't. It never is. The coincidence would be outlandish. And it would never be more outlandish than in this small place on the fringe of the world.

She has stopped this hot afternoon to drop off a second set of keys to Eadon Lodge and a cheque for the lawn care people with Carol Guttormson, who arranged to meet her at her office, though it is Sunday. She's packed, her luggage is in the trunk, the car is in the crowded lot across from the old movie house. She's kept no souvenir—well, except perhaps for the keys—and, by chance, the paper she found in the cavity of *Dead Men Tell No Tales,* which she slipped into her bag. As she distracts herself on the pier waiting for Carol to return to her office—Lydia found a Post-it saying BACK IN HALF AN HOUR stuck to the office's front door—she checks her bag again to ensure the keys are there. Her fingers brush the paper. She plucks it out and unfolds it.

25-15-21 18-5
~~9-13~~ 8-9-4-9-14-7 21-14-4-5-18 20-8-5 12-9-20-19 20-18-5-5

She counts it out on her fingers, discreetly, so she doesn't appear deranged to passers-by. 9-13 is I'M. So 25-15-21 is ... YOU. Lydia shrugs, carries on. 18-5 is ... RE. So the first word is YOU'RE. The rest comes quickly, an echo of those moments with Dorian forty years earlier. YOU'RE HIDING UNDER THE LITS TREE.

Makes little sense. Lydia looks again at the quavery lettering above the childish, though firmer, hand. Some manifestation of Bibs's wandering mind in later years. The thought comes to her with a pang, and with guilt for her absences in those years before his death. Here, on the pier, she is tempted to let the paper slip away in the breeze, the way his ashes floated away that winter day in Assiniboine Park, but something stays her hand: It's the don't-be-a-litterbug campaign of her childhood. It holds her in its grip. She can never drop anything in the street.

Lydia passes the last of the murals, glimpsing with a shudder what looks like an image of a bison skull, and turns to make her way back into the town, to Carol's office. It's nearly one o'clock. She's anxious to get the necessaries over with now. Get out of here. Get out of town. All the sunny families around her this sunny holiday afternoon cast her solitude into unhappy perspective and from it, looking toward the town, she has the disturbing experience of finding her surroundings suddenly alien, like turning in the street and seeing the face of an old friend altered by unwise surgery. This is not the Gimli pier of her youth, then a simple wooden barricade off which boys dived into the water. And that big generic hotel at pier's end—what was once in that spot? A fish store? And what opposite? She strains to remember. She can't remember. There is a band shell now where something—what?—used to be. She passes it now, notes a batch of skinny boys setting up their instruments, and from the other side, from the hotel patio, catches a snatch of conversation. A murder, apparently, in the town, last night.

Ah, so that's why police tape—god help us—was twitching in the breeze along the street near the real estate office. A cloud passes over the sun and the First and Centre intersection suddenly drains of colour. Her eyes travel to two stark figures up the street. Something about the gait of one of them strokes her memory. She strains to glimpse the face, but a hat and sunglasses—and the jostling crowd—obscures. She feels the weight of premonition.

"That woman knows you."

"I'm famous."

"You're not that famous, Dorian," Mark murmurs.

"More famous than you." Dorian doesn't look up from the book he plucked from a table in Tergesen's General Store. He's certain this annex of the store, with its tin ceiling and wooden floors, was once a drugstore, the kind with a soda fountain. He can practically smell the pills and gumballs and cherry Coke, he thinks, though perhaps it's his tricksy memory at play. He and Paul stepped in here for ice cream on their one foray into town that August, to do, at the girls' command, the shopping. Paul had with him the camera he had "liberated" from the beach.

"I'm not kidding, Dorian." Mark's voice again, intruding on his reverie.

Dorian hears a warning tone. "Not kidding what?"

"That woman. Looking at you. She doesn't want your autograph."

Dorian's eyes are still on the book, though he feels a frisson, a presentiment. Some mad fan, a psycho? "How can you tell?"

"I'm a psychiatrist."

Dorian sighs. Mark's trump card. "All right. Where is she then?"

Mark pretends to study his phone. "Look over by that rack of greeting cards. To your right."

With studied nonchalance Dorian lifts his head from the book and glances in the prescribed direction.

And there is a shutter click of recognition.

It isn't the darkness of her eyes or their roundness that's like a blow to the gut; it's no physical attribute. It's their knowingness. You could say—and Dorian thinks this in that very moment—that her eyes burrow to his very soul. And he hesitates. He should let his face light up and go to her immediately, but something akin to stage fright possesses him—much like that episode when he was briefly cast in *Rope*—and honestly he just wants to run, race down the wings, through the stage door, out into the air and breathe. But he can't. The theatre is full and his entrance is nigh.

"Dorian," he can hear her say through the tourist chatter. Her voice is as instantly recognizable as her eyes, her tone absent that counterfeit interrogatory of friends meeting after a lifetime's absence (*Dorian?*). She might as well have returned from stepping from the room only a moment ago. He crosses the few yards between the book table and the card stand, engulfed with feelings he can't peel apart—guilt, dread, attraction—and takes her in his arms. Her hair, surmounted by sunglasses, he notes, is silver grey. His hair, below the Panama, she notes, is snow white. Lydia is the first to disengage, lest her telltale beating heart give her away, planting a chaste kiss on his cheek in a perfunctory way that belies the strain pulling at her muscles. He looks the same—slim and handsome. She looks the same—slim and beautiful. Somehow they have navigated life unaltered, their prime prolonged, or perhaps they are too blinded by memory and apprehension to see what anyone else, including Mark, would see—bloom gone from rose, brow scored with line, lips thinned with time.

What to say? They look at each other in a kind of shock. They are in a public place. *What to say?* The usual opening gambits—*Fancy meeting you here. Long time, no see. How have you been?*—are ludicrous. As is, *what are you doing here*? Each has a good idea what the other is doing here.

"I'm sorry about your mother." Dorian takes the lead. "I saw the notice in the paper. Perhaps I should have called."

"I didn't call you when your mother died."

"How would you have known?"

"Briony. She keeps me abreast."

"Of course. Briony. When I was in town four or five years ago for *Night of the Iguana,* she met me backstage and mentioned Bibs had died. Funny she never suggests coffee or dinner."

"Do you? Suggest it, I mean."

"Well … no." Dorian smiles. She is as astute as ever. "Anyway, Bibs. Alzheimer's. I'm sorry."

"*We're* at the cliff's edge now, Dorian," she says, echoing Briony's remark at her mother's funeral.

"So we are." The expression seems fraught with extra texture. He looks more closely into her eyes, which he can see are careworn, tentative, and feels suddenly sad for the years they might have stayed in touch, might have visited, might have remained in each other's lives. They'd once loved each other with adolescent intensity; their lives might have evolved into a cozy friendship, but for the events of another August long ago. Now he searches her eyes, as she searches his. Both know what lies between them. He doesn't want to plunge into the past, he still wants to run from this, but the terrible day has come, as somehow, however much they denied it, they knew it would.

"The cottage," he says. "You've inherited the cottage."

"Yes." Lydia holds his gaze, conscious now of a younger man who has stepped forward and is hovering expectantly. Her eyes flick to his—they are large and green, she notes—then back to Dorian, who says:

"My friend, Mark—Mark Nelligan. He's visiting from Vancouver. Mark, this is Lydia Eadon. We went to school together.

"In the olden days," Dorian continues as Mark and Lydia shake hands. "Before you were born. Mark is a psychiatrist," he adds. "The black arts, voodoo."

"At Vancouver General," Mark says, ignoring Dorian's familiar jibes, studying the space between the two old school chums, the vibration, the tension, the menu of clues.

"That must be interesting work," Lydia murmurs.

Mark senses Dorian and his friend's impatience with him—restive mom and dad with naughty adult plans of their own and he's not surprised—though a little disappointed—when Dorian gives him a tight smile and a suggestion:

"I think Lydia and I would like to take a little walk down memory lane. You might find it a tad boring." To Mark's impassive expression, he adds, "Would you be hurt if I asked you to meet us back here in ..." Dorian looks to Lydia for affirmation "... an hour or so?"

And now they are alone together, Dorian and Lydia. Their hesitation on Tergesen's steps is momentary. As if of one mind, they move against the beach-bound current on Centre Street toward some unknown, unremembered destination, a handsome couple in late middle age, husband and wife, possibly—some passersby think—dressed almost alike, rich black below, crisp white above.

"How long have you two been together?" Lydia asks, dropping her sunglasses over her eyes.

"Mark and I? About seven years."

"And how is it?"

"Oh, doomed."

"Really? Are you sure?"

"Gay years are like dog years. Seven is a lifetime."

Lydia flicks him a glance he can't see. "Where did you two meet?"

"At a Sondheim performance, *Merrily We Roll Along*. In Vancouver. But enough about me. You? Briony told me you—"

"Ray and I have been together for nearly twenty-five years."

"Is he here with you?"

"No. He went to Japan about a week before my mother died. His daughter ... our daughter, Erin, is leaving her marriage there and she's in the middle of a nasty child custody battle. She has an eight-year-old she wants to bring back to the States. So Ray's there helping her. It didn't make sense for him to fly all the way here, then fly back to Japan."

"I'm sorry." The third time he's said that, Dorian realizes with a flush as they cross the street, darting amid the traffic affording them a momentary break in the conversation. "I mean, I'm sorry he can't be with you." He's not sure he's being merely polite or if Lydia's presence is plucking at his guilt and shame for the terrible act that stained their lives. There's so much they never said to each other then.

"Perhaps just as well," Lydia says in a tone not lost on him.

"I thought I might hear from you after your father died. I assumed your mother would want to sell the cottage. Didn't she always hate it?"

"She changed her mind. I don't know why. It was odd. Anyway, it was a reprieve."

"Then what—"

"I'm selling it, Dorian. I—"

"You can't. Oh, Lydia, you can't sell Eadon Lodge."

"Dorian, I have to. I need the money.

"Everybody needs money.

"I need the money urgently."

"Urgently? Bibs must have—"

"Bibs gave most of his money to charity when he died, to—I forget, a society for the disabled. He left enough for my mother to live on—and the house. But you've read the news, you know what's happened to the economy. That, plus my mother's renovating mania, has reduced the capital considerably. At the same time, I—we, Ray and I—have to *buy* the house we've been renting for decades. With the money from the property here we'll have just enough and not be slaves to a mortgage—at our ages. Do you have any notion of San Francisco real estate prices?"

"Move to an apartment somewhere."

"We can't. Erin and Misaki are coming to live with us while Erin goes back to school. But the point, Dorian, is: how would I explain to my husband why—*exactly* why—I'd sacrifice our home for the sake of a piece of property in Canada that we'll never come to visit?"

"Lydia ..." Dorian feels perspiration begin to bloom along his skin. The day is hot. They are passing the old movie theatre on a street that has no shade. "You *cannot* sell that cottage, that property. You know what could happen. I've seen what's changed up there."

"You've been to Eadon Lodge?" Lydia lifts her sunglasses, looks sharply at Dorian.

"No, but I've seen it from the lake. We were shooting some boating scenes a few weeks ago out on the water. Development is closing in on Eadon Lodge from both sides. Anyone who buys it isn't going to keep that little cottage long."

"I've told the realtor—"

"You've already seen a realtor?"

"Yes, I've spent this weekend readying the cottage for sale. I have to drop off the keys—"

"Oh, god. And what did she say?"

"What's important is what I said to her: I'm only interested in a buyer who wants to keep the cottage as is."

"And how likely is that?"

"I don't know."

"Once it belongs to someone else they could can do what they like. There's no law to stop them, Lydia. They'll knock it down and dig..." He stops himself, swallows hard.

"Maybe they'd miss that spot."

"You're clinging at straws, Lydia."

"Then even if... Could they connect him—"

"Paul?"

"—to us?"

"Lydia, who are you playing devil's advocate with? Me or yourself? Briony, Alanna, Alan—they were all there that week."

"They're our friends."

"They would perjure themselves? Alan? *Alan*? And even if they did—and why they would after a gap of forty years I don't know—there's people here who might remember. Paul and I got an ice cream at Tergesen's. We—"

"No one would remember Paul from that, Dorian. A lifetime's passed."

"The guy who delivered the earth and sod that afternoon. He came into the cottage. He'd remember. He was our age. He could still be around somewhere.

They pass in front of the old public school where an old swing set is still in place under a shading tree.

"Let's sit a minute," she says.

Dorian follows her, pulling a pack of cigarettes from his shirt pocket. "And what about that old guy, Elvis? Remember Elvis? After the gun went off? He was a jerk."

The scene lies before them with the force of memory. It was early evening, the light through the trees striping the lawn. Briony was cutting potatoes in the kitchen with an unexplained air of grievance, which Lydia thought then had something to do with the troublesomeness of making home-made french fries, though no one had asked her to make them. Lydia, herself, was cutting up vegetables for a salad, wishing everyone except Paul would just go away. Alanna was lying on one of the couches over the wall in the living room, not helping, an electric fan caressing her body, drinking a gin and tonic, delicate nose twitching as smoke from hot coals outside wafted through the screens. Alan was cooking—barbequing. Man's work. He was strutting around the grill and fussing with the coals to ready them to sear the hamburgers made from the ground beef Dorian and Paul had fetched in town the day before. Dorian remembers himself and Paul curled like commas into old Adirondack chairs on the lawn, drinking beer, observing Alan in all his glorious self-importance. He was the worker, a proletarian. They were louche, decadent, bourgeois. He had coldshouldered them that afternoon on the beach when they returned after a long spell with a bucket of shells. Paul had proffered Alan a shell, suggesting it as a sort of portcullis for the sand castle he was sculpting.

"Nice ring," he'd sneered, glancing at Paul's fingers as he took the shell. The girls were out of earshot, in the lake with the inflatable raft, nymphs shrieking in the waves. Dorian glanced warily at Alan for signs of some new knowledge. Alan had hard eyes. But Dorian could tell nothing.

"Peace, man," Paul replied, V-ing his fingers.

"Where did you get it?"

"My cousin here gave it to me."

"He's been wearing that thing for ages."

"So?"

Alan shrugged, turned back to his handiwork. He placed Paul's shell aside.

*Asshole,* Paul mouthed to Dorian.

That evening, as Alan kept a whip hand on the coals, Paul rose from his chair and went into the cottage to fetch two more beers. Lydia remembers herself next to Briony slicing tomatoes on a cutting board on the counter, shifting slightly so Paul could swing the fridge door open, thrilling to the brush of his ass against hers. She remembers the clatter of the bottles along the refrigerator shelf, the pop of bottle tops, her mind concentrated on cutting vegetables with such a dull knife, then the gush of water running in the bathroom. Dorian remembers Paul exiting the cottage, one of his hands gripping both beers by their necks, the other gripping ... something by *their* necks, something plastic and dripping. Water pistols.

"I saw them earlier tucked up in a space over the kitchen door," he murmured to Dorian, grinning, though Dorian didn't need the grin to get the message. Paul sat. They each took a pistol. They aimed at Alan. He was not amused. He batted at the spray like an angry bear at swarming wasps before registering the source. There followed the predictable bellowing *fuck-you*-laced invective as Dorian and Paul blasted him with needle-fine jets of water. Alan ran to get out of the way. Dorian and Paul jumped from their chairs and chased him over the lawn. Lydia remembers looking up to the kitchen window to see sprinting shadows and the towel-laden clothesline in sudden motion, sensing Briony beside her startled and uneasy, recalling herself strangely electrified. She remembers hearing above the raucous laughter someone crashing through the front door and tearing across the floor, followed by an unfamiliar metallic rattling in the living room and Alanna saying sleepily, "Alan, what are you doing?" And then someone—Alan, apparently—crashing out the door again and roaring maleness renewed, sharper, more taunting this time.

And then, the blast—like a crack of thunder sundering the air. Lydia's head snapping to the window, her cutting her finger.

Damp bathing suits and towels collapsing to the lawn, strands of the severed clothesline silvering in the setting sun. And a piercing, shattering scream.

"That Elvis guy wasn't a jerk," Lydia says to Dorian. "If he had been, he would have gone to the police."

"He saw Paul."

"Barely. And he wasn't *old*. He was old*er*. If he had been our parents' age, he would have made a fuss. He probably wasn't even ten years older than we were."

"Which means he could still be alive."

Lydia remembers the frozen moment that followed the scream, her mind racing to attach cause to effect. She remembers the couch's sharp rasp in the next room, the tea towel dropping from Briony's hand, the knife dropping from hers, her cut finger frothing blood—her scrambling through the screen door and down the steps and onto the darkening lawn, the others on her heels. She remembers Paul, fallen on a beach towel, clutching his left shoulder with his right hand, blood running between his fingers and pooling blackly on the pale cotton, his face contorted, Dorian's face captured in a shaft of sun, pale as the cotton—a prefiguring, she reflected much later, of a horror to come, and Alan chanting like a mad monk, "I didn't know it was loaded, I didn't know it was loaded."

And, improbably, before this tableau of shock and incredulity could break apart, a large black hound, like something out of hell, burst out of the gloom, trailing a leash, trailing a thickset man with slicked-back hair—suddenly an adult among the children. Lydia remembers Briony bursting into a wet sob, herself battling disbelief: a green pistol lay at Paul's side; Dorian's limp hand held its twin. Plastic guns. Plastic, *impossible*. And then she understood. She saw the dark shape of the shotgun fallen to Alan's side on the grass, heard the stranger say, "What the hell is going on?" as he bent to pull the excited dog away and reattach the leash, pushing the animal away, toward Alanna, who robotically gripped its collar.

Dorian remembers the man shifting to his knees to examine Paul. With the evening well advanced, the light low, his face leaned in, seemed almost to touch Paul's. "Are you all right?" he asked, and as Paul strained his reply through gritted teeth—"It's nothing. We were just horsing around"—he shifted his judgmental gaze to the rest of them standing in a contrite row and continued, "With a loaded shotgun? Are you crazy? Where is it? Give that to me!"

The tone of his voice broke the spell. Alanna, one hand clutching still the dog's collar, bent for the weapon and passed it over. Briony reached down for another of the fallen towels and moved to apply it to Paul's shoulder, while the stranger, who seemed to know what he was doing, opened the chamber, directed it to the light and peered in. "Single barrel," he grunted, snapped the gun back together, and turned to Alan, who was now trembling uncontrollably. "If your aim had been four inches to the right, he'd be dead."

"I didn't know it was loaded!" Alan's voice cracked.

"Jesus, I'm *fine*," Paul insisted, struggling against Briony to rise, grabbing the towel from her and pushing it against his shoulder where the shot had ripped through the T-shirt sleeve.

"We have a first aid kit in the cottage," Lydia said to the stranger, adding as if it added weight, "my father's a doctor."

"You shouldn't have this lying around," the man bristled at her.

"It's sat in a rack on the wall all my life. I've never seen anyone take it down, ever, my whole life."

"You could press charges," the man turned to Paul.

"Why don't you fuck off?" Paul snapped and moved unsteadily toward the cottage, Briony trailing behind. Perhaps the setting sun's crimson rays were amplification, but Elvis's face—Dorian recalls this vividly—blazed, his eyes seethed with contempt. He could see what this man—solid, clean-cut, tidily dressed, only a few years older (as Lydia correctly said) but somehow a generation removed—saw: a bunch of stupid, stoned, and irresponsible hippies—the usual litany of complaint of the day.

Elvis left. Lydia remembers escorting him and his dog off the property, using all her youthful charm, thanking him for his concern and assuring him that it was the most freakish of accidents, that no one was seriously damaged, that she was certain there was no ammunition in the cottage, that it was boys being boys—anything that came into her head—so that he would not contact the police, so that word would never reach her father. Her manner seemed to pacify him and then she couldn't quite get rid of him. His parents had a cottage at Loney Beach, he told her. He had been taking a long walk with Bruno, the dog, which suggested to Lydia an episode of family discord. She noticed the hand holding the dog's lead bore no ring. He was regarding her with a certain intensity. Her manner, she realized, was being mistaken for flirtation (licking her cut finger didn't help) and two evenings later, in the hours after the event that would divide her life, and Dorian's, into before and after, she feared that he would make a sudden reappearance.

# 20

"What would you have done if your mother had decided to sell the cottage after your father died?" Dorian asks Lydia in a low voice. They've moved to a pub down the street, surprisingly devoid of patrons on this hot afternoon.

"If I couldn't change her mind, I would have bought it." Lydia folds her sunglasses and slips them into her bag. "Real estate prices were lower in the late '90s. It seems there wasn't a real jump in prices here until a few years ago. For years, Ray and I were living in essentially a rent-controlled house. No real money worries ... how life changes in an instant."

The server manifests himself in Viking glory before Dorian can respond, uncertain if her last words alluded to their shared wrongdoing. *How life changes in an instant.* He is young, tall, blond, and built—yes, a Viking, but it's the horned plastic helmet he's wearing, an assertion of this Icelandic festival the town is in the middle of, that does the trick.

"'Martha? Rubbing alcohol for you?'" The line from *Who's Afraid of Virginia Woolf* lands unbidden on Dorian's lips. He had the LP recording of the Broadway production in high school and played it over and over.

"'Never mix, never worry!'" The rejoinder floods Lydia's memory and she is her teenaged self again, after school, smelling the new paint on Dorian's bedroom walls, camping George and Martha, and wondering if Dorian will make a move. She feels her face crumple, helpless to stop an unexpected, wrenching sob.

"Lydia, what is it?" Dorian puts his hand over hers.

"I'll have a martini," she rasps to the waiter.

"Perrier," Dorian orders and the waiter bustles off. "Lydia, what—?"

"Ray makes me a martini every evening after work."

"... you're missing him."

"That and ..."

"Everything?"

"Everything."

Dorian takes her hand in his, lifts it, kisses it. He says what he's sure is a lie: "It's going to be all right."

"I'm frightened, Dorian."

"You think I'm not?"

"I'm old—"

"You're not."

"—too old for this." Lydia lets go her hand, fumbles in her bag, lifts a Kleenex. The waiter returns—unhelmeted—and places tiny mats and their drinks on the table with the kind of studied gravity of an extra in a play.

Dorian watches her dab at her eyes, feels the weight of the moment. "I'm an alcoholic, did you know?" he says, turning from the departing waiter to his Perrier.

"I know."

"Briony?"

"She got one of your Twelve-Step letters."

"In which I apologize for all my manifold sins."

"I didn't get one."

"I didn't know where to find you."

Lydia examines the mascara streaks on the Kleenex with distaste, pockets the thing. "I'm not sure that's true."

"Women marry, change their names—"

"Briony married, changed her name. I married. I didn't change mine."

"Would a letter have been sufficient?"

"I don't know, Dorian. I really don't. It's not like you've *not* crossed my thoughts over the years." Lydia sniffs, fumbles into her bag again. "But I try to think of times ... you know, before ..."

Dorian watches her lift something from her bag, not another Kleenex, but a tiny bottle—hand sanitizer. She opens it, splashes gel on her hands. There's compulsion in this. He senses it. He knows the feeling. He can smell the alcohol wafting from the sanitizer and the alcohol wafting from her glass and the aroma affects him powerfully. He has a sudden yearning to grab the martini glass and gulp down its contents, order another and another and another until memory is obliterated.

"I'm editing a book about the sixties at the moment," Lydia continues, recovered a little, replacing the bottle in her bag.

"Yes?" Dorian frowns, puzzled.

"I work for a small press in Berkeley. Briony probably told you. The book isn't very good."

"Then why are you publishing it?"

"Corruption?"

"I don't understand."

"We were bought last year by a Silicon Valley billionaire. Obie Mouret. Ever heard of him?"

"Not something I follow."

"He collects antiques, small presses being one of them. He's relatively harmless—I think, never met the man—but he installed as publisher this creature with a degree from some MBA mill out east. She knows nothing of publishing, nothing of the audience for our books."

"Which is?"

"Progressive, radical, intelligent, well-educated. She's ignorant in most things, but she's conniving and ambitious. Rumour is her child—she's unpartnered—was fathered by a donation from Mouret."

"You mean, he's gay."

Lydia nods and lifts her glass. "Do you mind my having a drink?"

"No."

Lydia welcomes the first sip of gin sting her tongue. "Her first name is Melony. Spelled as in 'Crenshaw.'"

"Her parents were hippies?"

"Or fruit lovers. However, behind her back, the staff call her 'Cuntella.'"

"You, too?"

"Sometimes."

"Lydia, I'm shocked."

Lydia permits a small smile. "She wants us all gone so she can replace us with her own minions. So she sets us challenges. For me, it is to get this sixties book into quick production for next spring, for the fortieth anniversary of 1969. The book is mostly press clippings cobbled together. The writer is a friend of hers, someone with vague academic credentials and little authority on the subject—that's the corruption. Our titles are typically peer-reviewed. Not this one. His thesis," Lydia swirls the olive around the glass with the toothpick, "if you can call it a thesis, is that 1969 was the last utopian year of the last utopian decade of the utopian twentieth century."

Dorian regards her as she lifts the olive and lets the drips fall back into her glass. "It might not be a thesis, but as an observation, it's not completely off the mark," he says, regarding the gin-soaked olive hungrily. "Why—"

"Am I telling you this?" Lydia returns the olive to the glass. "Do you remember that nonsense story from late '69 about Paul McCartney having died and been replaced by a look-alike? 'He blew his mind out in a car'? A wreath around his guitar on the Sgt. Pepper cover? The *Abbey Road* cover with Paul supposedly dressed as a gravedigger?"

"Yes."

"The writer uses the end of the sunny Beatles as emblematic as that year's descent into darkness—the Manson murders, Altamont, and so on. His title for the book—and it's not a working title, it's too late now—is ..." Lydia pauses and quickly consumes the olive. She flicks Dorian a bleak glance. "The title is 'Paul is Dead.' There's a subtitle to be devised, but 'Paul is Dead' is on the footer of every page of the manuscript. I can't escape it. Paul is dead, Paul is dead, Paul is dead."

"No exit."

"Sartre?"

"What? Oh, the play? *No Exit*? I hadn't thought of that. I mean ... we can't escape it, can we? But the characters in Sartre's play couldn't escape the hell they were in, either, could they. Could they? Didn't we study it in O'Dell's class?"

"I thought they thought if they confessed to their..."

"Crimes?" Dorian lowers his voice, leans in, smells again the seductive juniper in Lydia's gin. "They did, they do, confess, but it makes no difference." If only he could have a cigarette in a restaurant. "You've never ... told anyone, have you? Let it slip?"

"I've wanted to, but no." Lydia thinks about those first months living in San Francisco, the misery of her self-imposed purdah in the apartment in the dark winter when Helen's kindness and concern almost—*almost*—brought her to the brink of telling all. "You?"

"No."

"Not even under the influence?" Lydia taps the side of her martini glass.

"No."

"Doesn't drink loosen the tongue?"

"Only for the casual drinker. Why? Did you think that I would?"

"I don't know, Dorian. You virtually disappeared that fall and then you were—"

"Hospitalized. Just before Christmas. I had what Mark would call an 'acute episode of post-traumatic stress disorder.' What you and I would call a nervous breakdown."

"I know. I think everyone knew."

"None of my old friends visited."

"My father did."

"I remember. Your father didn't exactly have a bedside manner."

"He was a surgeon. Even he admitted they were all bastards, not that Bibs was really..."

"Your father was a hard case, Lydia. I couldn't figure out why he was visiting me. I never thought he liked me. Actually, I can't recall him saying very much." Dorian runs his finger around the rim of his glass. "Did he ever say anything to you ... afterwards?"

There is a second or two in which Lydia thinks she will tell him: She will tell Dorian she had a baby. She will tell him she was the one of the unlucky less than one percent who get pregnant with an IUD. She will tell him her father could calculate with the best of them, that he reckoned her pregnancy to August, to Eadon Lodge, where only two boys (he thought) were in residence and one of them tethered to a woman he would marry a year later. She will tell Dorian her father visited him on the psych ward to inspect this boy that simple elimination told him got his little girl into trouble. She will tell him Bibs reported nothing beyond the fact of his visit; she read the adjudication in his face as he read the fear and shame in hers. But something restrains her. She cannot open this door, not now. There is too much else.

"You knew my father," she replies. "A man of few words and I can't remember what they were anyway. But I do remember being ... worried you might say something to the psychiatrist."

"No." Dorian frowns, repeats the word. "*No.*"

"I had panic attacks that year. I found I couldn't sit in the front row of the lecture hall, but if I sat at the back somehow it was worse. The backs of everyone's heads would—"

"Remind you of the back of Paul's?"

"Perhaps. It was as if I could see their squashy brains."

"Lydia ..."

"It only stopped when I moved away. You moved away, too."

"I couldn't imagine living here. I had a friend—you remember Blair Connon, who was in *And No Birds Sing*?—he'd enrolled at York University's theatre program. Somehow, miraculously, I got in, too. Took six years to complete a three-year course, but ..."

"You were married."

"Yes. Why ... ?"

"Oh, just—"

"Seemed like a good idea at the time." Dorian doesn't know why he's explaining. It was the seventies. It was a confusing period. The marriage was lavender. She was a lesbian.

"Do you have any money?"

"You mean, beyond paying for these drinks?"

"Yes, serious money, wealth."

"What does that have to do with being married?"

"Nothing, I suppose. I was just thinking about sources of money—divorce settlements being one."

"Well, not in my case. Lydia, I'm an actor—a *Canadian* actor—a grafter. Blair gave up and went into real estate."

"Your grandparents were rich. They were Old Money. We were the *arrivistes*. My grandfather was a railway worker. Yours was a grain family. You must have inherited."

"My grandparents died thirty years ago." Dorian has an inkling of where this conversation is going, but it's too late to backpedal. "Why are you asking?"

"Buy Eadon Lodge."

"Good god, no."

"But then the risk—you know what I mean—would be gone."

"But, Lydia, I have no money, not that kind of money."

"Are you sure?"

"Sure. You remember my grandfather, old Scots Presbyterian tightwad that he was. Do you really think he'd have his descendants not know the value of hard work? The Winnipeg Foundation got the lion's share. I got a little, enough to pay back my student loans, with a little left over. That's it."

"How much left over?"

"Enough for a small down payment on a house in Toronto."

"You own a house."

"I *co*-own a house. My ex-wife and I still own it together. I lived in it for a time, but now we rent it out. It provides the only regular revenue I have."

"You could sell your share to your ex-wife."

"She hasn't got a lot of money. She writes fiction—*Canadian* fiction, does a little TV. I doubt she'd want to saddle herself with another mortgage to buy my half."

"Then sell your half to someone else."

"Jesus, Lydia."

Dorian can sense her desperation—it matches his own—and silence holds them prisoner a moment. Each imagines the peril in selling Eadon Lodge to a stranger, even to an enthusiast for the quaint and idiosyncratic. Once you've sold a property, you've lost control over it—and then what follows? Lydia imagines the knock on the door, the dreaded phone call; she has never, foolishly, taken American citizenship. Would that protect her deportation, prosecution, punishment? *How she has pushed Eadon Lodge from her mind all these years.* Dorian imagines the *auto-da-fé,* the public burning, but more: the woman across from him with furrowed brow and pinched mouth not Lydia, but Dix pushed to the front of the crowd, to the seat of judgment. But comes another thought, this one more promising. He pushes his chair back. It scrapes along the floor. He says, "I have another idea."

# 21

Dorian and Lydia glance at the yellow police tape flashing in the sun and wordlessly pass on. Silence has been their companion since leaving the pub where Lydia fell in with Dorian's idea—leapt on it, if truth be told. Dorian's less sanguine about success, wondering if he's deluding himself, deluding her, but he's always felt the guiltier, the one responsible, the initiator.

*Why did you ever bring him here?* Lydia had groaned that terrible evening, her stricken features flamed and distorted in the last rays of the sun as Dorian placed Paul's body in its purple shroud onto the grass. And Dorian had no answer, because there was no answer and because there was no way to change anything and because he was in such shock that no words could slip past his knotted tongue.

"I have to tell you," Lydia said at the pub as each dug in pocket or purse for money to settle the bill, "that I did once, years ago, when the Internet was introduced, look to see if there was any record, any mention, any *thing* about Paul Godwin. I could hardly breathe, my heart was beating so, but I could find nothing."

"That's because..." Dorian snatched the bill slip from her. "Paul introduced himself to us using his middle name as his last. His full name was Paul Godwin Radcliff."

"How do you know that? *Dorian?*"

"*Shhh!*" He didn't want to say, but had to: he told her about his friendship with Dixie-May Lang. "It became unbearable, finally—and that's part of the reason I relocated to Vancouver. I seemed to awaken something in her about her long-lost son, some vain hope that he was alive somewhere. Good god, Lydia, I've sat through all those conversations, all those dinners, and parties all the while knowing

Paul's fate. It was agony. And, of course, I couldn't bear for her to know now. To know that I know and have known all along."

"Jesus."

"He had a true story, he had a backstory, he had a mother."

"But so much was ... fiction."

"It was the sixties, Lydia. He was young, it was fun, it was the fashion to appear *déclassé*, to affect being proletarian, to show you weren't some spoiled upper-class kid. What does it matter what he said about himself? What does it matter what *kind* of person he was? What does it matter what he did when he was alive? He's *dead*."

Dorian and Lydia pass a building of noticeable ill-proportion—a squat combination of fake half-Tudor timbering and a mansard roof. Dorian's calming himself with a cigarette. He squints at what appears to be a hand-lettered sign next to the door through a plume of smoke. GIMLI HOTEL.

"Is this," he says to Lydia with wonder, recalling Alanna's finickiness, "where Alan and Alanna went the day after?"

He doesn't have to say to Lydia the day after what. The day after Alan shot Paul in the arm is what. Late the next morning Alan and Alanna packed up the tent and departed Eadon Lodge. For good, back to Winnipeg, thought Dorian, who was absent in the town with Briony buying a new clothesline, and good riddance, until two days later he awoke in Lydia's bed, previous evening's horror crashing through his head, to hear Alan's braying voice outside the cottage walls, his offer to help fill the old outhouse hole.

"They went to the Viking, the motel by the highway," Lydia says. "I think it was mostly old fishermen and farmers who came here."

"Why didn't they just go back to the city? Why did they check into a hotel in Gimli?"

"Can't you guess?"

Dorian grunts. "Of course—sex."

"In our day, our parents didn't let us do it under their roofs, did they? Alanna and Alan didn't come up to Eadon Lodge for the beachfront. Besides, the atmosphere at the cottage took a turn after Alan shot Paul."

"If only he had never taken that shotgun off the wall. And it was *loaded*. How long had that shot been in the gun? Amazing it worked."

"If only Paul had never filled those water pistols. Dorian, we can go on like this forever—an unending chain of regret."

"Then why did Alan come back that next morning?"

"I didn't know you knew."

Dorian shrugs, looks up the street. "Where the hell is Mark?"

"Alan was ... chastened, I'm guessing." Lydia glances at her watch; they're late for Mark. "In the circumstances, he was gracious, don't you think? Paul."

"Possibly."

"He could have gone to the police. The RCMP has a detachment here. He probably should have gone to the hospital. Instead, he took it out on that man who appeared with the dog."

"Elvis."

"Perhaps your friend's gone inside the store."

"I'll go and see." Dorian drops his cigarette butt on the pavement.

Lydia frowns. "Dorian..." she begins, reaching for his arm, "You two are common-law, yes? So you're entitled—"

"I know what you're going to say," Dorian interrupts, the touch of her hand reminding him strangely of their last night together. "We have a contract, Mark and I. His parents insisted on it before giving him the house in Vancouver. They don't much care for me." He affects a grin. "I've gone out of my way to charm their tight little asses off when they visit. I'm too old and too ... impecunious for their precious spawn, and the old-Winnipeg-money Grant name cuts no ice in London, Ontario. So, no, it's all his. I pay rent."

"Will you know your way to Eadon Lodge?"

"I travel there in my nightmares, Mrs. Peel."

Dorian is acting cheerful, like a parent on a child's first day at school. Mark is the child.

"You'll like it," he says as they fold themselves into Dorian's rented Lexus turned furnace in the heat. "Eadon Lodge has a sort of private beach."

"I was hoping to be on the public beach," Mark says, as Dorian starts the car and sets the air conditioning to high. "Might be some eye candy."

"Don't be grumpy, sweetheart."

"I'm not being grumpy."

"It's a family beach, not Wreck Beach. You're not going to see hot men parading their wares up and down the sand here." Dorian realizes he's sounding a tad testy and he needs to keep Mark sweet. He affects a theatrical chuckle: "How about I strip down and show you my wares?"

"I've seen them plenty." Mark glances past Dorian toward the Gimli Theatre marquee. *The Dark Knight*. He saw it last month with Hugh, a first date. "Besides, what would your friend think?"

"Lydia?" Concentrating on a turn, he says something he immediately regrets: "She's seen me naked."

Silence descends for a Gimli street length or two and soon they are over a small bridge into Loney Beach. Dorian has gone this route in black and twisted dreams, but today it's a pleasant green tunnel, the road marshalled with cottages, some old, small, and quaint—relics of times past—others big and ostentatious—not that he's really paying close attention. He's much more aware of a growing anxiety, a prickling along his skin, a stone in his stomach as he retraces this route to a place he never expected to see again in his lifetime.

"You mean," Mark says after a pause, interrupting his thoughts, "she's the one you slept with at grad, in high school."

"What?"

"Lydia. Your last remark."

"Yup."

A lie, the same lie he told Paul. The deed was *attempted* graduation night, the culmination of years of flawed yearnings and false expectations, a whole mishmash of delusions that culminated in such an awkward choreography that, frankly, Dorian would rather not revisit.

Improbably—after that humiliating experience—the deed, so-called, was done at Eadon Lodge. On that last night, their terrible task finished, after they burned Paul's few effects in the old oil drum where days earlier they had toasted marshmallows over the flames of the wood from the razed outhouse, Lydia pushed his mud-streaked, aching body into the shower—the white-upright-coffin shower that Marion insisted Bibs install in the new indoor bathroom—and stepped in herself, catching him before he collapsed into a fetal ball along the soapy floor. The warm water, Lydia's ministrations, accepted helplessly, let loose a tidal flow of hot grief. He howled, howled like an abandoned dog. Dorian remembers it now, painfully, remembers that first wet burst of tears, feeling as if his face would rip apart, and wished he didn't remember—wished Mark had never asked his question. As Lydia cleaned him and held him, his salty tears mixing with snot, all of it running down his face as the water streamed from above, he found himself erect and in a moment pushing into her with the unconscious hunger of an animal. Weeping and fucking, fucking and weeping: Dorian remembers it like a sick yesterday. And later, Lydia wrapping him in cotton sheet, how like a shroud, and placing him in her bed where he collapsed into a deep sleep that he would never again have.

And now Dorian catches his first glimpse of Eadon Lodge—a flash of white through a scrim of green, wrought by a glint of sunlight. His heartbeat quickens and it's just enough to take his attention from his driving. The gravel road ends abruptly and the car bounces on a hummocky belt of grass, corduroyed by ancient embedded tire tracks. The road this far north was a mud track forty years ago—Dorian's certain that's true—but the crude parking lot has undergone no improvement. And here they are, as they were forty years ago—he gasps to see them again—Goliath's molars (as named by Bibs in a rare flight of fancy)—three great flat Tyndall-stone boulders that demarcated the border of the once-isolated Eadon property.

Dorian steps from the air conditioning to the moist grassy heat of the afternoon. He glances back down the road to the new properties.

The last, on the beach side, one he must have glimpsed during the water shoot the other week, has a FOR SALE sign. He remembers nothing there but forest forty years ago. And forest on the other side. Forest, forest, forest, bisected by a crude track. He jerks around to glimpse Mark past the roof of the Lexus. The air pixilates suddenly. He is falling, fainting. He grips the edge of the open door and takes a ragged breath.

"Dorian?" He can hear an edge of anxiety in Mark's voice. "Are you all right?"

"Vertigo." Dorian struggles to sound assured. "I'm fine."

He's not. The rocks, the trees, the air, the aroma, everything is suddenly synesthetic—the air colours, the plants speak, the rocks smell—and he is filled with unspeakable dread. He is once again with Paul, parked on this very spot, under these very trees on a very hot August afternoon. He is once again looking at Paul over the roof of the Volkswagen, brimming with lust and excitement and apprehension. He is once again on the brink of adventure.

"Just give me a minute," he says to Mark, who has moved to open the trunk and is fetching his bag with his swimsuit and towel.

"Do you want your stuff, Dorian?" Mark lowers the trunk lid. "Dorian? Are you sure you're okay."

"I am fucking fine. Shut up. Yes, get me my bag."

He's better. He just had a moment, that's all—a wobble, a wonky bit, though Mark takes his arm and says with a snicker, "C'mon, old man" and Dorian snaps, "Watch it!" They proceed past the molars down a path beaten through a curtain of trees onto a patch of sunlit lawn, and there, shimmering in the muggy air, as though seen through a camera lens smeared with Vaseline, is Eadon Lodge.

# 22

Dorian lights another cigarette and drags deeply. He can't bear to go into the cottage just yet.

"Not much has changed," he remarks to Lydia, exhaling a feather of smoke. Aimless conversation. Mark is within earshot, though squinting at his iPhone in in a patch of shade. They are gathered on the front lawn. Still.

"The yard's changed," Lydia says. "Some of the big trees are gone. A windstorm in the eighties, I think. Many of these are new, fast-growing ash or willow. You'll have to take a look behind the cottage." She telegraphs him a warning glance.

"Later, perhaps," Dorian returns the glance knowingly and addresses Mark. "Are you going for a swim?"

"Yes." Mark draws the word out sulkily.

"Then," he murmurs, glancing again at the cottage, at the screen door so ably, so fatally, oiled all those years ago by Alan, "I guess we should go in and change. Are you ... joining us?" he adds to Lydia.

She shakes her head as if the idea were abhorrent. It is abhorrent. Reliving the jolly old trek to the beach? Please, no.

"Lydia can give us a quick tour first," Dorian says to Mark, looking for a place to toss his half-finished cigarette and girding his loins. "Eadon Lodge is ... unique."

"I'm selling it," Lydia says to Mark as she leads the way to the steps.

"Oh?" Mark says.

"I live in California—"

"Dorian was saying."

"—so it doesn't make sense to hold on to it."

"What a shame. My parents have a cabin at Grand Bend, on Lake Huron. I'd hate for them to sell it."

Dorian's seen pictures of the "cabin." It's as grand as the shore it's on. A grand cabin at Grand Bend. Fashionable, loveable, inheritable. Who could ask for anything more?

The screen door opens much less noiselessly now, but it's not important now. He steps in behind Lydia and Mark—steps in as he had, behind Paul, on that August day all those years ago. *Christ Jesus.* His eyes rove the dining room's boxcar space. Nothing has changed: the faded oriental rug, the linoleum-topped table, the mint-green chairs. It might be the very same air, the very same dust motes, the very same Pinesol. His eyes go to the wall. There's his father's name and date. And, pencilled below, there's his own. But Paul's signature has vanished. He runs his fingers along the paint. Yes, he can feel a faint indentation, reverse Braille.

Lydia and Mark have stepped through the open double doors into the living room. He can hear her giving him the potted history of the cottage that he and Paul had received: grandfather had it built it in nineteen-blah-blah by Icelandic fishermen blah blah blah. The dining room is sunny but the living room lies in cool shadow. Always it was in cool shadow, but who among them, other than Briony, was ever awake early enough to witness the room in morning light?

Dorian prepares to step into that cool shadow when a sudden, never forgotten, but never replicated sound shoots ice water down his veins. There is no sound like it. There is no sound like the to-and-fro, to-and-fro of wooden rockers weighing on linoleum—not wood, *linoleum*: scrunchy, squishy, squeaky. Mark or Lydia has set one of the rocking chairs in motion. Surely not Lydia. She must remember Paul collapsing into that rocker, remember the scrunchy, squishy, squeaky sound that eclipsed the dying music from the gramophone.

Lydia remembers very well, but, oblivious, Mark had perched himself on the wide arm of the grandfather rocker—the very arm on which Paul perched that night—and is absently rocking the chair with his feet. He is looking around like a polite tourist as Lydia describes the provenance of this or that artifact. She can tell he's not intrigued.

"Dorian?" she says, and he can hear the urgency in her voice.

Dorian could use the toilet, though he's not desperate. Draining the lizard would buy some time, but no corner of Eadon Lodge, including the bathroom, is free of memory. He takes a deep breath.

"Isn't it marvellous?" he enthuses, sweeping in, as if from the wings, Vera Charles in Bermuda shorts. Mark is looking out through the sliding windows, past the screen, to the lake. Lydia is standing by the library table. Dorian stops, his eyes drawn helplessly upward.

The electrolier is gone.

Dorian suppresses a gasp, sees the warning in Lydia's eyes. He continues: "It really is a great space. Roomy but somehow cozy. I'd forgotten how quirky it is. Oh, look at the old stove! So great in the evenings, wasn't it, Lydia? And that old desk! What do you think, Mark?"

"Yeah, it's sort of cool."

"And all those books. I think book-lined shelves really make a room."

Mark flicks him a puzzled glance and rises to examine the books. The rocker rocks. Dorian's soul shrivels. "Anybody actually read these?"

"My grandfather did," Lydia answers Mark's question.

"I don't recognize a single author ... or title."

"*Sic transit gloria,*" Dorian says.

"Is there somewhere I can change?" Mark asks.

"One of the bedrooms." Lydia points. Two closed doors stand side by side, framed on the right by the Victrola and on the left by the sideboard. Dorian's eyes go to the shotgun above.

"Take the door on the left," he directs Mark.

"What's behind the one on the right?"

"A scary ghost."

Dorian can't think why he directed Mark to the second bedroom, Briony's room, as he thinks of it. Something to do with that memory in the car? Of Lydia and him swaddled like cried-out babies on that old iron bedstead in the first bedroom after that terrible night?

Dorian never subscribed to the hippie mystic-crystal-revelation-and-the-mind's-true-liberation bilge that Briony did—transcendental meditation and the *I Ching* and astral travel and all that. But he senses the presence of a fourth in this place. There *is* a ghost. Paul has slipped past the double doors. Dorian whiffs salty sunbaked skin and a whisper of patchouli, feels a hand feathertouch the small of his back. Without thinking he lets his own hand travel back to greet another's warm flesh, but of course there's nothing there. He looks at Lydia. Behind door No. 2 is a progression of undressing noises.

"The lake seems high." Dorian says, groping for some camouflaging conversation. "I don't remember it that way from ... before."

"It must be higher, yes. Wait till you see the beach here. There's a lot less of it. I can't think what will happen if there's ever a big storm on the lake."

"Are you joining me?" Mark's muffled voice comes over the half-wall.

"Where?"

"On the beach, of course."

"You go down. You know where it is."

"Yes, it borders that large wet thing. A lake is it?"

"I'll join you in a minute. What do you think of the bedroom?"

Mark doesn't respond. He exits in board shorts and flip-flops with a towel over his arm. All set for a day at the beach. He pushes the Ray-bans down his nose. "Well, are you coming?"

"In a minute. Give me a minute. Have you got a blanket?"

"Damn, one's in the car. Got the keys, Dorian?"

"Wait." Lydia steps to the living room's corner closet containing the linens of decades and pulls out a grey wool blanket, pilfered from the railway her grandfather worked for. "Use this."

Together Lydia and Dorian watch the younger man flip-flop to the screen door, his figure silhouetted in the frame. Dorian thinks of his younger self going out that door, towel and blanket in hand, innocent.

"The squeak's returned," Dorian remarks.

"*Tempus fugit.*"

Dorian's eyes go once again to the shadowy cottage rafters, the array of slats that are the building's skeleton, to a small cluster of exposed wires at the centre. Lydia eyes follow. He doesn't have to ask the question. She supplies the answer:

"I cut it down yesterday. I couldn't bear to look at it."

"What did you do with it?"

"I dragged it into the lake." Lydia shivers at the absurdity. She was mad to do it. "I hope your friend doesn't step on it."

Mark steps on it. Actually, when Dorian makes his way to the beach, he sees Mark bent over in the lake, bottom raised, back muscles flanged, straining at something below the water's surface. It isn't immediately evident what he is doing.

Mark waited a while for Dorian on the strip of beach. Tried reading off his phone. Gave up because of sun glare and settled on the scratchy old blanket, resigning himself to the silence broken only, after a while, by the sound of his own pale Vancouver-y flesh sizzling in the tanning oil he'd slathered on. He moved to the water.

Fuck, it was cold, penis-shrivellingly cold. He looked around, arms hugging his goose-pimpled chest, and pushed tentatively into the featureless lake under the featureless sky, a thin green shimmer in the east the seam. He peered. *Land or mirage? Would the line vanish on approach?* For a stark second, Mark sensed the agoraphobe's terror. He turned quickly—to the yellow button in the blue sky, to the white cottage in its foliage frame, to Dorian, not yet in swimsuit, emerging through the screen door, with Lydia, walking, walking, walking, yes, but turning away, around the cottage, to—what direction is that?—north.

What, he thought, are they doing now? It's been a peculiar afternoon. "Seen a ghost" is the phrase quick to mind to describe the two old friends meeting at Tergesen's. Mark watched with wonder the miraculous ebb tide of blood in his lover's face, the actorly self-possession falter. He watched, too, the advancing woman, rigid with something suppressed. Since, there's been crackling tension and elusive conversation. Dorian and Lydia have been cat-on-a-hot-tin-roof-y, mommy-and-daddy-have-a-secret-y. *Son, sit down. Your mother and I are getting a divorce.* Mark scooped a little water onto his shoulder and flinched as the cold streamed down his torso. Lydia: A hint of obsessive-compulsive personality disorder there? That cottage so orderly? Her appearance so immaculate? Maybe. Mark held his nose and plunged his torso into the water. He rocketed out with a gasp and a yowl. The gasp was for the cold. The yowl was for something sharper.

The electrolier tilts on the lip of wet sand, surreally out of place, like one of those melting watches in that Dali landscape. He shifts on the blanket he's sharing with Mark to banish sight of the thing but he can still see the deep grooves Mark made dragging it up the beach. He readjusts his body again, closes his eyes.

No damage to Mark's feet. Damage, more, to his sensibilities: *Where the fuck did* that *come from?*

Dorian reaches for his bag, for his cigarettes. Mark deciphers the sound and motion. Supine, face shrouded in sunglasses, he appears to address the sky: "You seem to be smoking more these days."

"Consider the alternative."

"Then smoke over there." Mark waves his arm vaguely.

"The breeze is blowing off the lake. Away from you." Dorian flicks his lighter, draws the smoke into his lungs, glances at the sludgy brown lake he was filming on weeks earlier, notices Mark's hand crawl across his boyish chest.

"Should I get my nipples pierced, do you think?"

"I think you should get plates put in your lips. That's what all the A-list faggots are doing this year. I read it in *The Advocate*."

"'Total war'?"

"'Total.'"

"Did you do *Virginia Woolf* lines with her?"

"Lydia? Oh, yes. She was my Martha. You're my Martha now."

"Well, aren't you sweet." Mark listens to Dorian take another long drag. "Is there something on your mind?"

"Not really ... well, okay." Dorian pulls one out of a hat. "I was just thinking about a parasailing scene Ethan and I have to do next week."

"Ethan ... ?

"Elias. The star of *Morningstar Cove*."

"Is he the hot one, the blond? Who wants you to be his daddy?"

"That's your little fantasy. He's the star of the show."

"Are *you* parasailing?"

"Does this amuse you?"

"Have you been a good boy while you've been here?"

The question comes almost but not quite, given the daddy thing, out of the blue. "Of course," Dorian lies. He visited the baths in Winnipeg one weekend. "You?"

"Likewise," Mark lies and mourns the lost opportunity—and his feeble courage: This might have been the moment to begin a discussion of their future together, though it's not as if he'd rehearsed introductory remarks.

And yet, at this very moment, as Dorian gazes over the lake, on this beach, on this very spot where, long ago, he spent ten transformative days, he is seized by domestic yearning, that Mark should be the last and only. It's all so clear; it's not too late. He'd done it before, but the longest, his marriage to Rachel, was born of expediency, of madness, of ambition, of drink, of drugs, of everything false, and there was never any question of being ruled by fidelity.

Or is he being driven again by expediency? He pushes the thought away, runs his hand over Mark's arm, feeling the soft hairs. "It's pleasant here," he says. "The sun. The heat."

"Hardly Cabo."

"Well … you wouldn't want to be in Cabo in the summer, would you?"

"No, I suppose not … though there'd be endless blue sky at Cabo. Not like Vancouver summers sometimes."

"Endless blue sky here."

"That lake, though. Freezing!"

"As opposed to what? Kits Beach?"

"It's kind of brown."

"Lake Winnipeg? Well, it's sort of a … a bile duct that strains all the river water around here before it flows north, toward the ocean."

"Bile duct—that's an attractive image."

"I thought you'd like it, you being a doctor."

"I'm not a doctor who deals with bile ducts."

This isn't going well. Dorian lifts his hand from Mark's arm and shifts on the blanket, finding himself again with a jolting view of the electrolier on the beach. *Planet of the Apes,* the final scene: that Statue of Liberty crown poking from the sand. He saw the movie at the old 72nd Street Playhouse, late June 1968—anything to get out of New York's brutal heat. *You maniacs! You blew it up. Goddamn you all to hell!* Wondrous. Horrifying. Charleton Heston confronts the terrible truth of the past.

Dorian raises himself on his elbows, butts the cigarette in the sand out of Mark's sight. "Lydia's selling the cottage."

"So she said."

"Let's buy it."

There's a pause, a beat. Sound—water lapping, gulls crying—fills the void, and when Mark's voice intrudes, it's—not unpredictably—bemused:

"This place?"

"It's quaint."

"It should be curated."

"Lydia said there's been some attempt to declare Eadon Lodge historic."

"Why would you be interested in a cottage *here*?"

"What we've been talking about—the sun, the heat, the blue sky."

"But—" Objections fire along Mark's synapses. He rises on his elbows and pushes his sunglasses to his forehead. "You're not interested in this part of the world." He studies Dorian's profile for some clue. Finds none. "I know you were born here, but you've never had anything nice to say about it."

"I've come in the winter a time or three for a role in a play. You don't want to be here in the winter, if you can help it. But the summers are different."

"I can't take two months off."

"Neither can I."

"Then what's the point?"

"Well, we could have a few weeks here in the summer, and then rent it out."

"Rent *that* out? Who would rent it?"

"All kinds. Lots of people want an authentic cottage experience—screen doors, wood stoves, that kind of thing."

"I think people would rather rent a cottage with a dishwasher. You're from the olden times, Dorian. Besides, what?—how many weeks a year could you rent it out? It's not winterized—ten weeks of rental income? It doesn't make sense. What's she asking for it?

"Low six figures-ish. Cheap compared to B.C. prices."

"Yeah, but still ..." Mark frowns. "And what's with the 'let's'? Let *us*? How much would you put in?

"I'm not sure, really."

"You mean you want *me* to buy it?"

"I didn't say that."

"Then what do you mean?"

"Never mind. It was just a thought, a whim, a mere bagatelle."

"Come on, Dorian. What's going on?"

"Lydia needs a quick sale, that's all. I thought I might be useful."

"You know, the two of you are acting just plain weird. And that ugly lamp or whatever it is over there: You can't tell me she didn't toss it in the lake. In my profession, we refer to that kind of behaviour as 'crazy.'"

"Do you? Well, I have no idea how that would have got into the lake. I doubt a woman could 'toss' it in anyway."

"It's not that heavy. And if you look farther down the beach you can see the remains of gouges in the sand where someone dragged something into the water—recently."

Dorian doesn't care to revisit the electrolier. He sighs and says:

"Look, I was just wanting to help out an old friend."

"By making a six-figure land purchase? That's some old friend. If you're that devoted to her, then you buy it—borrow the money, take out a mortgage ... a second mortgage. You've got that house in Toronto."

"Rachel owns half of it."

"Then borrow against your half, I don't know. You must have some money. You came from some wealth, didn't you?"

Dorian's not having this conversation twice in one afternoon. "I guess I've been a grasshopper, you virtuous little ant. It's a fable," he responds to Mark's puzzled expression. "Never mind."

Dorian plays out the first of two possible endings to this exchange: He appeals to Mark, entreats him. *Please will you do one thing for me. I'll get the money back to you somehow. No, I can't tell you why. You'll have to trust me. But it's vitally important.*

Mark drop his sunglasses and settles back onto the blanket. Dorian looks down at him, seeing his own funhouse reflection in the lenses. The virtuous little ant remark was a mistake. Mark hasn't a trace of real cruelty. He's just sensible. And that makes sense. He thinks about Lydia's entreaty: he could, he must, somehow (*how?*) raise the dough, buy Eadon Lodge himself, and force himself to do something that will plunge him past the edge of horror. Then, and only then, he can pass Eadon Lodge on to someone else.

"I guess," he says to Mark, feigning petulance, "Lydia will just have to find a buyer."

*And I,* he thinks with dread as Mark grunts his assent, *will have to find a shovel.*

# 23

Lydia's fingers knead the ground beef, but her eyes remain on the lawn past the kitchen window, fixed on the split clothesline, now two pale and flaccid snakes on the grass. She barely notices the southern sky darkening into thundercloud towers. The meat is refrigerator-cold, gelatinous, disgusting in its squishiness, and despite the Worcester sauce and onion, stinking of carnage. To look down at the bowl—past her bandaged finger—is to look at raw flesh, pinky-red as a wound, Paul's wound. Her gorge rises. She suppresses it. What else can she do?

She's not hungry. Her stomach's in a knot. And why wouldn't it be? But for chance, she would be staring out the window into the aftermath of a scene of real carnage, a darkening yard filled with serious men, police ... and more police, waves of them. One future ended, one future ruined, four futures blighted. The brutal final scene of *Bonnie and Clyde,* seen at the Capitol last January with Ross on what would be their second-last date flits through her mind. She had to close her eyes and press her face into his shoulder.

Bibs flits through her mind, too. How will he react, if he finds out? He mustn't find out.

They fall back to their earlier tasks, some of them, as if preparing the meal or having a nice drink can send them back to an hour before. Alan is returned to the coals in the barbeque, a beer in hand, which he is swiftly downing. He and Alanna are having a low conversation that is only a murmur to Lydia's left ear. (*Treachery?*) Another conversation drifts into her right ear, though the words are clearer. Briony, who has cleaned and bandaged Paul's upper shoulder, is insisting he remain shrouded inside a Hudson's Bay blanket she pulled out of the corner cupboard. For the shock. Lydia removes her hands from the cold goop and leans back to see past the door frame into the dining room to Paul in a chair. The blanket is a rich purple. He looks like a caped young warrior king enthroned. He catches her eye and smiles the smile of one tolerating the ministrations of a body servant. He knows she is a princess cast into the kitchen by some evil spell and she knows, despite hands chilled by cold meat, that she could better minster than Briony. She wishes all of them would go away, back to the city, and leave her alone, with Paul. She didn't want all these people here in the first place—which isn't true, but Lydia is moving swiftly away from a denial of feelings, several of them.

Lydia briefly wonders where Dorian is. He's slipped off to the beach, where he is weeping helplessly.

Paul flashes the peace sign. Alan receives the gesture gracelessly. They are not eating indoors at the dining room table, as they have been doing, mostly at Briony's insistence. They're scattered on chairs of various sorts—Adirondack, folding, chaise lounge—on the front lawn or, in Paul's case, on the cottage front steps, which has the odd effect of placing him facing the others, like an actor on a stage. The evening seems suddenly dying: long accordion streaks of shadow and light play over the grass. At some distance to the southwest, which only Paul can see, a ribbon of lightning flares from massing clouds; a rumble of thunder follows, but the others pay it scant attention. Between bites of hamburger, Briony is blitherblathering about Gestalt therapy, which she only faintly understands. *Let's work through it!* is the distillate. But the others, shattered still by the near shattering of their young lives, crave the therapy silence affords—or at least desultory elephant-in-the-room-disguising chitchat: *Finished that Nabokov novel yet? So, half a million turned up at Woodstock, wow.* Life*'s done a spread on Sharon Tate's murder. Saw it in the drugstore.* But below the brittle iceberg tip, some are planning their exodus. Some are thinking how they will keep news of the episode from their parents, whom they might flippantly refer to by their first names but who still loom large like punitive superegos. Alan, who is on his fifth beer now and simmering with humiliation and anger over the near end of a bright future and new, dark one begun, tells Briony to shut up.

"Is this the kind of *crap* you're going to feed your clients when you graduate?" he says

This is when Paul raises his left hand and parts his fingers. A glint of sunlight catches the ring, itself stamped with the symbol of peace. Lydia is intrigued that he, who came so close to being tragedy's victim, should appear the least troubled. In that same glint of sun, she notes his crooked smile and a flash—what is it? glee? delight?—in his baby blacks, and she feels pulled toward it, wants to bask in its radiance.

"And you can fuck off, too." Alan's face darkens. "Back to wherever you came from."

"That would be Toronto, Alan," Paul says smoothly, swaying a little, like a toked-up boy at a love-in. "If you're ever in town, look me up."

"I'll pass."

"Hey, man, be cool. It was a water pistol. I'm not mad that you tried to kill me."

"I didn't try to fucking *kill* you."

"Ah, but what would Sigmund say?"

"Freud? There are no accidents? That's bullshit. I did not know that gun was loaded."

"You didn't know that gun was not *not* loaded."

"Fuck off." Alan points his mayonnaisey knife at Paul. "There are accidents. What our dog does on the kitchen floor is an accident."

"I thought you were a determinist? Aren't Marxists determinists? Isn't history—"

"Freud didn't say humans weren't exposed to chance. You think a sperm meeting an egg is predetermined?"

Paul doesn't stop his swaying. "Look, man, something may look like an accident, but if you were able to unravel all the threads, to trace back through all the moments leading to an event, you would see how inevitable it all was."

"Then you must have a death wish." Alan barks. "All of life's little fucking moments have brought you here ... to *die*.

"Or you have a death wish against me."

The gainsaying continues. Lydia, barely touching the food on her plate, wearies of it, blocks the words, attunes to the tone—Alan aggrieved and aggressive, Paul cool and just-fucking-with-you-man, but not without counter-aggression. Hornlocking. Male conversation. These baritone rumblings are the very air of the student lounge at University College when she passes through to another class. One more year of this sophomoric nonsense and she is on her way to her own perfect future—a good grad school in Toronto or Vancouver, maybe even the States. She would like to tell the boys to shut up. *Can we have some peace?* She dreads a fight. *Could there possibly be one, after what's happened?* Alan is gripping his dinner knife threateningly, isn't he? The atmosphere seems to crackle with new tension. Or perhaps it's the electricity in the approaching storm. Lydia's eyes pass to the leaves on the ash in sudden rustle, the willow branches in sudden animation. She feels cool air now brushing her back through the slats in the chair. Her nostrils detect ozone atoms, sharp and fresh and clean. She is conscious, for the first time, that the thunder is not distant. They will have to herd into the cottage before very long. She does not want this.

And she is lucky. Or perhaps it is no accident. All the intertwined causal threads of the universe, however remote in origin, large in number and complex in interaction have knotted together to give them leave to finish their meals at the very moment the rain, hard and cold, crashes down. And do they rush into the cottage? No. As if by unspoken agreement, they splay: Alan and Alanna race for their tent, Paul and Dorian for the Petit Trianon, Lydia and Briony for the cottage, where they will remain until the morning. Dishes and glasses litter lawn and chair arm, receptacles for fat rain drops, pools for birds and dragonflies.

Only later did Paul and Alan's argument—the no-accidents, the death-wish—return to Lydia, seeping into thoughts already transformed by horror's long half-life. Did it affect Dorian? In retrospect, did he find their clashing words as premonitory as she? She didn't ask him. She never had the chance. She could ask him now. He's standing right in front of her, on the lawn at Eadon Lodge where thirty-nine years earlier they sat before the rain came, back from the beach, where he left Mark to continue sunbathing. But she won't ask. Good god, meaning-of-life sophomorics are as long gone as warming your bum on the radiators at University College. It's the stuff of youth. And perhaps old age. She is not there yet. She is middle-; late middle- and life in the middle, as someone once told her, is a practical task. Mark, though he doesn't know it, has narrowed their options. But the option Dorian presents to her is the stuff of nightmares.

"No," she tells Dorian. "No," she says again. "You can't. It's terrifying. You can't."

"Can you think of another option? Whether I buy it and flip it or someone else buys it, it has to be done."

"The real estate agent will find the right buyer."

"Who? Who, Lydia? Who will want this old cottage? You've seen the building development around—"

"Come around to the back lawn," Lydia interrupts him. "If you think you can bear it. Can you?" she asks, noting him hesitate. "It's hard, Dorian. This is hard. It seems unimaginable we're here ... now ... doing this."

"It wasn't my idea then."

"*Dorian ...?*"

"I'm sorry. That was unfair. I lost my wits that night."

They round the west side of the cottage, the bedroom side where, Lydia remembers, she listened to Alan slamming his car door and his footfalls that last morning. Lydia was around this side once, only once, with Carol Guttormson, the real estate agent, on the requisite tour of the property. She was transfixed by the transformation time had wrought.

"There." Lydia points toward the northwest corner of the property.

"Oh." The word comes out like a little whimpering sigh. Dorian sees what Lydia saw and, for a moment, the sigh connotes relief. This pit of his worst memories, of his worst nightmares, has vanished. This cursed plot is no longer trampled grass and muddy scars. It is a tangle of scrub and shrub and trees he can't identify—ash? willow?—rising to the sky, scintillating in afternoon sun, as benign and picturesque and vaguely English as anything in a city park.

"Do you see?" Lydia asks.

Dorian sees. Relief passes to disbelief. He realizes what he has proposed to Lydia is as staggering in labour as it is in imagination. And then a cloud, one of few this peerless summer day, crowds the sun and casts Eadon Lodge into shade and he is thrust back to that calamitous night like a cross-cut in a film. He is peering into the abyss of a black and stinking hole and to his surprise he is blinded by tears.

# 24

Dorian gags. His stomach lurches. Acid soars to sear his throat and only the force of what's left of his will keeps a torrent of spew from splashing on the grass. He has already pissed himself, but his mind barely registers it. It seems one minute he was naked, the next partly clothed, the next with wet running down his leg to pool on the living room linoleum. But Lydia had neither seen nor heard. She was backed into the sideboard, screaming.

Now they are outside, lifting the plywood barrier off the privy pit, releasing the filthy reek of a dozen summers, suppressing their heaving guts. The plywood sheet is awkward, heavy. They stagger over the grass and upend it against a pine. The evening is drawing in. The eastern sky is nearly black, the surround of bushes and trees merging into a mass of grey-purple, the colour—in the dying light—the same as the blanket rolled and tied on the lawn.

Tears stream down Dorian's face, though he isn't howling as before. That remedy he's exhausted. But he can no more stop the flow than he can stop the rain from falling. He puts the crook of his arm to his nose to wipe the snot and it blocks, mercifully, the wafting stink. He and Lydia return to the pit edge, stare down. There is blackness. It is bottomless, an abyss.

Dorian feels his legs buckling. If they are to do this terrible thing, they must do it soon. Now. Too much time has gone by. If they change their minds now, how would they explain to others the time passed, the body moved, the opened pit—on top of everything else? A groan rises from his chest and a word forms on his lips:

*No.*

It was Lydia who recovered first some sensibility, some capacity for reason, some ability to speak. It *was* her idea. Burying him.

There was already a grave dug—the old bog pit.

How long do they stare into the hole? Not long, but long enough for the western sky to purple, the leaves to blacken, the moon to climb above the lake, the cottage to fall into silhouette and its windows wax gold. When Dorian carried Paul in his blanket-shroud out the cottage and down the steps, lurching, crazed with fright and grief, Lydia followed with one of the gas lanterns. Now it sends flickering shadows along the grass and in that moment Dorian sees movement within the blanket, an awakening, a struggle to be free. *He's alive.* He falls to his knees and sets his scrabbling, shaking hands to working the knots of clothesline binding the blanket, weeping, and grunting Paul's name.

But Lydia is beside him, pulling at his hands, her eyes blinded now in tears, unmoored by his panic. "Stop it, Dorian. Stop it! He's dead. Paul's dead!"

This time Dorian's "no" is not silent. He howls the word into the silent night and collapses onto the blanket.

It is Lydia who retches.

Dorian strains to lift Paul's body, to rise with it, to deliver him—it—into the grave, in some valedictory fashion—god knows what he's thinking—but his strength, or perhaps his will, is sapped. He pushes his sweat-slicked forearms under the blanket. The grass is cool, the floppy weight of the blanket still—god, how can this be?—still warm, still limp. Struggling, he collapses again on the shrouded body, his head pitching toward the black gap, and he screams. Lydia pulls him back. Dorian falls on the grass, his back pierced with pain, and looks at, but does not see, the indifferent sky. He struggles to his feet. Wordlessly, gasping, he and Lydia each take an end of the blanket, but it offers poor purchase and slips from their damp fingers. They try again. And again. And then, possessed by this terrible reckless task, all thought of elsewise vanished, they surrender to an indignity: they fall on their knees and roll the thing, like a log, over the grass and tip it past the hole's soft edge, where it seems to suspend in air for split second, a purple roll, before disappearing into the void. No sound like what follows will ever intrude on their lives again, but it will seep into their dreams. Not quite a thud, not quite a plop, the *je ne sais quoi* of an unstoppable mass meeting an immovable surface defies their powers to describe it, ever, even to themselves—and never to others.

It's the sound of no going back.

The acid bile now runs out of Dorian—it can't be stopped—a torrent pouring from his gut into the grave, burning a hole in the back of his throat. He collapses on the verge, groaning. Lydia weaves her way to the Petit Trianon where she knows her father keeps shovels among the gardening tools. The summer evening deepens into darkness, and they, weakened by dread, horror, exhaustion, spend the hours filling the pit with the soil left by Dirt Guy.

"That's the same shovel," Dorian says, astonished and horrified. "But where's the other one?"

"Dorian, you can't do this." Lydia wipes the line of perspiration along her hairline. The late afternoon simmers. The airless storage room of the Petit Trianon blazes. She hates being sweaty. The small space, crammed with lawnmower and weed whacker, old paint cans, old garden hose, plywood sheets to cover the cottage windows in winter, cobwebs, stinks of gasoline. A cloud of flies zips past her face.

"You could bring another shovel from the city. Or I could buy one up here."

"But you would need a pick, or something, wouldn't you? ... An axe? A chainsaw? The trees ... it's not an easy job." *God, is she falling in with this plan*? Yes, reopening the grave, exhuming the body—she can barely countenance the words—could resolve their ... she can't think of a potent word ... their *predicament*, their *plight*, their *crisis*. But it's unimaginable—the doing of it. Oh, she can *imagine* it: the rhythm of the blade in and out and in and out of the earth—the *scrape*, the *scrape*—the *thunk* when the shovel hits something other than soil, the glimpse of blanket, rotted, faded, the smell of corruption, the ... She watches Dorian root through the old tools. She fills with a horror so deep, her legs turn to jelly, the air before her eyes fizzes. She grips the doorframe to steady herself. A sliver of wood pierces her palm, but she barely feels it. Kitchen gloves. He would have to wear kitchen gloves. There's a pink pair in the kitchen. A hazmat suit. Where would you buy a hazmat suit?

"No," she says again, struggling to speak, her voice coming to her from far away. "No, you can't do this. It's impossible."

"Have you got a better idea?" Dorian turns to her. She sees a mania in his blue eyes. The same stare as when he shaved his head in high school, when he dressed as a flasher that awful Halloween, when he dragged her into roles in *Death in Life* and *And No Birds Sing*. And, in truth, Dorian feels like he is snapping. He would love a drink.

"But the ... remains, Dorian. What about the remains?"

"The lake."

"How?"

"We have boats on the *Morningstar Cove* set."

"But ... this property, Eadon Lodge—it's not as isolated as it once was. There's only one empty property south of this one. People walk by all the time."

"Cover of darkness, Mrs. Peel."

"What about your friend?"

"Mark? He leaves Friday. There's no filming next weekend."

"You're saying you'll do this next weekend."

"*We*'ll do this. I can't do it alone."

Lydia struggles for consciousness. I have six days—to change his mind, to change my mind, to sell, to refuse to sell, to abandon buying the Lincoln Street house, to confess to Ray, to Erin, to Misaki, to...

Only a drawl behind her head brings her back to bracing reality.

"And what is it"—Mark's voice intrudes—"you can't do alone?"

# 25

Dorian and Briony are together in Dorian's Beetle rattling south through Loney Beach toward town, Briony with shopping list in hand. She has groceries to get at Tip Top, bread and buns to get at Central Bakery, and a new clothesline to get at Golko's Hardware, to replace the one severed by the shotgun. She feels faintly irritable, tired—signs she recognizes as portent of a migraine, the curse that heralds the curse. Magically, at thirteen, when menses and migraines arrived in tandem, she thought that if she were very very good in all things, at home, at school, at church, she could stave off the headaches. Now she tries to think of the debilitating headaches as less her cross to bear and more a manifestation of the first of the Buddha's Four Noble Truths: life is suffering. She'd give a thought to the last three Noble Truths and the Eightfold Path, but the prodrome has an insidious way of lifting the hatch to thoughts less than pure of desire, hate, and delusion—which will keep her lashed to the karmic wheel.

For instance: Lydia suggested to her—to *her,* not to Dorian—that they take their time in town, and Briony, who had a glimmer as to why, asked why nevertheless, bringing the cool and confident Lydia to a rare blush, a secret smile, and no reply—and Briony to a not-so-rare blush, a thin smile, and an averted glance to the shopping list.

Briony will do her bright-starred friend's bidding, but now, in the car, she gives herself over to thoughts less charitable—to finding some excuse to force Dorian to turn the car back to the cottage, to catch Lydia and Paul *in flagrante delicto.* Her jealousy sits like a stone in her stomach.

As for Dorian, he's mostly annoyed at being Briony's chauffeur. Couldn't she have taken Lydia's car to town on her own? What's he needed for? Maybe if Paul had come along ... but he said he'd cut the grass or maybe get a start on filling in that old outhouse hole.

Dorian has the radio cranked up. "Get Back" is funking along, Paul McCartney's voice admonishing someone—Jojo—to get back to where he once belonged. Dorian would like to get back, get back, get back—to the city. If he is going on this wild adventure to California with Paul—and he is, absolutely—he wants to pack and be well down the road before Dey and Nan's return from Coney Island and their inevitable attempt to stop him. And yet Paul seems inclined to linger. I love the sun here, he said this morning, stretching himself on the bed and shooting him a teasing smile. There's sun in California, Dorian pointed out, weakening. My arm's still sore, Paul countered, yet pulling Dorian closer with that same arm. And it's copasetic now that Alan's fucked off—with Alanna. Somehow, despite the lovemaking, executed with quiet finesse given the Petit Trianon's thin walls, Dorian feels, as he barrels down the road, that something is sort of Hamletingly out of joint, but he hasn't time for much more thought because, annoyingly, Briony has turned the radio down. Still, she has to raise her voice above the air gusting through the open window:

"I think they want us out of the cottage."

"What?" Dorian says.

"Your cousin and Lydia."

"Why?"

"Why do you think, Dorian?"

Dorian makes a dismissive noise as they make their way to the Gimli Theatre where Lydia suggested they scope out the coming attractions. And yet Briony has planted the proverbial seed of doubt: Lydia, freshly showered, in the Chinese dragon dressing gown of her mother's, scribbling out a grocery list at the dining room table, saying to him, "your turn," as if he hasn't been contributing financially to the holiday, which he hasn't, and "take Briony," as in, you males don't know how to shop properly. Paul, staying behind, a convert—suddenly?—to good works: He offered to cut the grass now the sun has burned off yesterday's rain.

No.

No, no. It's not possible.

Yes, he's noted Lydia's glances Paul's way. Covetous? Is that what they are? But, no, Paul's a new element in their midst. Why wouldn't the others appraise him? Yes, Paul's flirted with Lydia—the dancing the other night, the horseplay during the skinny-dip. But, no, he knows Paul's nature. It's the same as his own.

And yet Lydia is beautiful. And Paul is wild.

No. It's bullshit.

He pulls up by the theatre—a small-town affair. Glass cases out front contain posters of the current and coming attractions. *Easy Rider* is playing at seven and nine.

"Looks cool," he says, glancing past Briony's shoulder.

"It's about two guys who go across the States on motorcycles. I read a review in the *Trib*."

"Really?" He notes Peter Fonda's name. Never heard of Dennis Hopper.

"They die at the end."

"Thanks a lot, Briony. Now you've wrecked it."

"I hate it when people die violently at the end."

"Good god. *Romeo and Juliet, Hamlet*—"

"You and Paul go, then. It doesn't look very nice."

Dorian puts his car in gear, hops out, and lifts a brochure from the wooden box next to the front door. He presents it to Briony.

"This is for what's on in September, idiot," she says. "We won't be here."

Dorian is a little startled at the unBrionylike vehemence.

"It's very white."

"So?" Dorian glances over Briony's shoulder at the package in her hand. They're in Golko's Hardware. The place smells of sawdust and new plastic.

"The old clotheslines had gone grey. They do. Bibs will know this is new."

"Why would he care?"

Briony shrugs. "Dr. Eadon is sort of ... peculiar, don't you think?"

"He's not a barrel of laughs. But, Jesus, Briony, it's only a clothesline. It's not an heirloom. Is Lydia actually worried about this?"

"I guess she's wondering how she's going to explain needing a new one."

"It's old! It wore out!" Dorian is growing impatient. He wants to get back, get back, get back to the cottage. "I don't know why you didn't just reknot it or something."

"Tried. Didn't you hear the squeaks from the pulley this morning?"

"No."

"Well, it was too short. What do you think? Fifty feet? A hundred feet? Two hundred feet?"

"Fifty?"

"It has to wrap around twice, remember."

"A hundred then."

"Maybe two, just in case."

"Fine, two. It's cheap." He glances at the covering of the tightly looped line. Eighty-nine cents. "We can use what's left over to hang cats with."

"Dorian!"

On the way to the till Briony fumbles in her bag and pulls out a dollar bill. "I'm not sure why I'm paying for this."

"Didn't Lydia give you some money for it? It's her family's cottage. Anyway, Alan's the one who should pay for new one. He shot ..." Dorian lowers his voice as they pass some other customers. "... he shot the old one down."

"Your cousin started it."

"Not that again."

"*Do* you think there are no accidents?"

"I think accidents are ordained by the universe for our education."

"Do you?" Briony turns to him, her freckled face glowing.

"Don't be ridiculous."

Dorian can't stop his heart tripping in his chest as he and Briony approach the cottage. The seed Briony planted earlier has germinated into an unfamiliar anxiety and he would much prefer to tiptoe down the crude path through the trees from the car park, but tiptoeing's best on a carpet of wool, not a carpet of leaves, and not only is Briony scrunching the grocery bag she's clutching to her chest, she's nattering on about something she heard on the radio like a women determined to keep bears at bay. He's barely listening to her. His eyes rove the side of the cottage for flashes of movement by the window, for the sound of scurry and rush: door closing, feet padding, taps running, but the cottage squats in the high sun of early afternoon, the only movement an insipid puff of smoke rising from the chimney, the last gasp of the morning fire, the only sound, besides chatty Briony, that of geese. Dorian looks up to the chevron in the sky. It's heading south, damn. Autumn is coming. He and Paul must get going. Dorian's eyes descend to the lawn. No evidence of grass cut. His heart thuds. Paul was to cut the grass.

As they step into to the kitchen, Briony calls in a too-loud voice, "we're baaaaack."

Dorian drops his bag on the counter, steps into the dining room, and takes a quick glance through the open double doors into the shadowy living room, the wall opposite thinly lit by a small curtained window. He looks left, where he sees a portion of the first bedroom, Lydia's bedroom, where the cover, the purple HBC blanket is drawn up, the bed made.

"Lydia?" Briony calls again, dropping her bags next to Dorian's. She notes his body language, his stockstillness.

They both strain to listen. A page snaps loudly, like a rebuke. "I'm reading," comes a vexed voice on the other side of the wall.

Dorian glances at Briony, who returns a wan smile.

"The bakery was already out of cinnamon buns," she calls. "I got some vineterta."

"What about bread?" Lydia calls back.

"We got the Icelandic brown kind."

"Good."

Dorian abandons his grocery bag for the living room. He sniffs the air for some telltale aroma, but only the morning smell of wood ash lingers.

He peers through the gloom to the tiny pool of light cast over the couch by a lamp on a wall shelf. He sees Lydia stretched out, her hair a crown of light, a halo, her face barricaded by a book—which she doesn't lower, though she must, Dorian thinks, sense his presence. Truly gripped by its content? His eyes roam the room. All cats are grey in the dark.

"Yes?" Lydia says after a moment, lowering the book. The pages shine in the light, but, backlit, Lydia's face falls into shadow.

"I thought Paul was going to cut the grass?"

"The mower wouldn't start. Apparently."

"Oh ... Do you want me to look at it? The mower?"

"Doesn't your grandfather use a lawn service?"

"Yes, but..."

"Then, Dorian, what do you know about lawnmowers?"

"Not much, I guess."

Lydia returns the book to face barricade. Dorian detected no artifice in her voice. His spirit lifts.

"Still on that Nabokov?"

"Nearly finished."

"Where is Paul, by the way?"

"At the beach, I think."

"Then I guess I'll join him."

"Did you get the clothesline?"

"Yes."

"Would you mind putting it up first? I'd like to wash a few things."

"Oh." The bloody towels from the shooting, he thinks. "All right."

"And there's still that pit to fill, remember. The earth's been there a few days."

Lydia puts on her Marion voice—bossy, wifey, naggy. She doesn't mean it, but she means it, and that's okay. All is well. While Briony unpacks the groceries, Dorian puts up the new clothesline. It's easy. He whistles while he works.

Dorian looks back on that afternoon—Saturday, August 30, 1969—as the last in his life of undiluted joy. It's a lousy thing to think, and he doesn't think it often, especially since he's sworn off the sauce, but when he does, he's riven by a yearning nostalgia

And this Sunday, August 3, 2008, it returns unbidden—the memory of it, triggered by some mnemonic, the soft air, the sunshine, the blue sky, the waves as he and Mark take their leave of Lydia and Eadon Lodge, and perhaps it's that grief slipping past the mask that makes Mark pause and ask him suspiciously, "Are you all right?" as they pass down the path to the car. "What is it you can't do alone?" Mark asked a little earlier at the Petit Trianon. "Wash a cat," he'd replied.

Briony made sandwiches, but she turned down taking hers to the beach, as had grown the habit. Dorian might have picked up on the clues: he knew, as their circle of friends did, that Briony suffered migraines, but he was too filled with anticipation to notice what Briony's earlier prickliness presaged. She said she'd rather stay in the cottage and have her lunch; her "Celtic skin" had had too much sun already. Lydia called from the living room, where she hadn't budged from the couch, that she would do the same. She, too, had had too much sun.

Groovy, said Dorian's inner voice. We will be alone together, Paul and *moi*, on a crescent of golden sand under a golden sun. And when he walks down the path through the arbour gate to the beach, the purloined camera in hand, he is overtaken suddenly, unexpectedly, by a surge of ... *what's Briony's word? Maharishi Mahesh Yogi's word? Bliss?* ... yes, *bliss*. This is bliss. It must be. It's like a new sun being born in his abdomen (*solar* plexus!) sending its radiance fluorescing along his nerves, up through his limbs to blaze in his head. Like a string crescendo, twenty-four bars, *I'd love to turn you on*. It's unaccountable, this feeling. It's animal, in its way. Not exactly lust. A little lust. *Turn you on*. More like some universal well-being, a gift bestowed on him in this moment by some smiling god. *Turn you on*. A sign that all will be well and all will be well.

And all *will* be well. They will head back to the city tomorrow to begin their California adventure and the rest of their lives. Paul will agree. They will be turned on to the world and the world, of course—how could it not?—will turn on to them.

Dorian sees first the purple blanket like a magic carpet on the sand. On it is a towel, suntan oil, sunglasses, a coil of the old clothesline, and an unopened book. He twists his head to see the spine. *Dead Men Tell No Tales* by E.W Hornung. He smiles. The book isn't for reading. He looks up: Paul is standing hip deep in the water, gazing out toward the pencil-line mirage of the far opposite shore, under a canopy sky so blue it is almost dizzying. He sees the dark hair curling down the nape of his neck, the slim, taut V of his tanned back disappearing into the band of his pale swimsuit. But, no, that's no swimsuit covering the mounds of his buttocks, he realizes with a surge of delight. Paul is naked, at the beach, in the afternoon. But where is his suit?

Dorian drops their lunch, the camera, and his own towel on the blanket. Shucks his T-shirt. His swimsuit too? In a minute. He sits down, ignoring the hard sand beneath the old blanket, and lets his eyes photocapture the perfection of the moment, the lake calm, Paul motionless, time stilled.

Soon Paul will turn and see him on the blanket. He will wave and gesture for Dorian to join him and Dorian will, eagerly, the calm waters breaking into ripples around him. He will remove his swimsuit. They will horseplay like a couple of innocent boys until the lakewater's cold becomes too much to endure and drives them onto the searing sand, first Dorian, who will snatch up the camera and take a picture. They will fall onto the blanket. Paul will open *Dead Men Tell No Tales* where his swimsuit, next to the dope, will fall out.

And the world will fall away.

# 26

"I came back to Winnipeg for the first time in 1978 when Nan died," Dorian says to Lydia. "It was the first funeral I'd ever attended, strange to say. I was what? Twenty-nine? The committal was awful. I didn't realize 'committal' meant 'burial'. I suppose I'd blinded myself to the facts. Thank god there was a toilet in the little church.

"But what I remember most is waking up the next morning to find Dey chopping down the apple tree in the backyard, one my grandmother loved. He was in a complete fury, face red, swinging away at that beautiful tree."

He is telling Lydia bits of this story as they sit in a the old Adirondack chairs at Eadon Lodge under the shade of another tree—an ancient spruce—awaiting a verdict that will direct their morning, if not the remainder of their lives. Watching his aged grandfather savage the tree, watching the leafy crown topple onto the lawn to a sickening rustle, drove home to him the awful power of grief, and how he was forced to repress his own.

He's not sure why he's telling Lydia this stuff. Nerves? Partially. He's mired in dread. He's been off his game at *Morningstar Cove* much of the week, garbling lines, forgetting others, missing cues. It's the weekend now, the week after the Icelandic Festival. Mark returned to Vancouver the day before. Lydia spent the week in Winnipeg. The Oxford Street house sold quickly, for a little over asking price, the new owners taking possession September 1. Dorian has a chainsaw next to his chair. He bought it at a Home Hardware along the highway south of town.

"I remember that tree," Lydia murmurs, leaning forward to lift a bottle of Purell from her bag on the grass. "Your grandparents stood us there for grad pictures."

"I'd forgotten." Dorian hasn't really forgotten. The foolish, drunken, failed attempt to make love to her. He watches Lydia squirt the gel on her hands and rub them with ritual movement. She is as mired in dread as he, he can tell. Her sunglasses may be her shield, but he sees her eyes, dark against dark, darting toward the cottage again and again. A real estate agent is inside, with, it seems, a good prospect—if that's what her thumbs-up gesture means.

Lydia *is* mired in dread. She's managed, barely, to distract herself during the week in last acts of dismantling her childhood home, but here, now, at Eadon Lodge, she can't ignore the acid drip drip drip on the stone in the pit of her stomach as her eyes dart to Dorian's chainsaw. Carol Guttormson's presence may be nothing more than a reprieve and soon she and Dorian will be mired in a task so ghastly, so unbelievable, she has to remember to breathe.

It's in the hinterland between wakefulness and sleep that her mind slides helplessly to the details of exhumation, a clinical word she clings to, prefers to "digging up the body." She knows there will be horror—sharp and nasty horror—and she tries not to dwell on detail, but questions howl in her head: What happens to an uncoffined body buried four decades? Bare bones and skull with rictus grin? A mummy with stretched and leathery skin? Something in between, spilling worms, swarming beetles? What about the soil? Will that make a difference? Paul was buried in topsoil, trucked in, not in whatever soil lies next to this glacial lake. What do forty prairie winters do to something six feet under? As sleep overtakes her, she imagines the rasp of the shovel blade along the soil, the denser tone when it strikes ... touching it, lifting it ... the smell, god, what will it smell like ...

Dorian has a tarp in the trunk of his car. He showed it to her. He has gloves, he has boots. He's bought that chainsaw. He is prepared. They've talked on the phone this week, each call an intrusion into her hard-won equanimity. She is letting him take the lead, as she took the lead that fateful night. She, in either denial or hopefulness, has brought no heavy-duty work clothes with her from the city—but then she brought no heavy-duty work clothes with her from San Francisco. Why would she? She is dressed as if for a summer's outing, shorts, a casual top—the strappy sandals are truly a mistake. You're going to have to go into town and get something to wear, Dorian told her, his mouth a grim line.

"Your grandfather chopping down the apple tree has an Old Testament resonance."

Dorian lifts an eyebrow. "Adam and Eve? Expulsion from paradise? Well, English was your major."

"Why did you bring it up?"

"I think I was thinking more that my grandfather, in a eccentric, repressed Scots way, could at least give expression to his grief at the loss of someone he loved. I knew why he was doing what he was doing."

"And you couldn't ... over Paul."

"How could I?"

"I suppose you did ... in a way."

"In a way, in an unhealthy way, but let's not go into it. Those cottage walls," Dorian gestures with his cigarette, "are pretty thin."

Something like silence envelops them a moment. A bird caws. Leaves rustle. Carol and whoever she's with—a youngish man; they were introduced—in the cottage make muffled noises. The walls *are* thin. Dorian tosses his cigarette butt into a bush and reaches in his pocket for the pack. There is no peace in the silence.

"I don't remember you smoking that much in college."

"I took it up more when I quit drinking. I had to do something with my hands." Dorian begins the ritual—strike match, light ciggie, release satisfying first plume of smoke. "Christ," he says tossing the match to the grass, on another train of thought, "we were naïve. So fucking naïve. Sometimes I read magazine articles or hear commentaries on TV about those years, the sixties and all the radical this and radical that and I think, what are they talking about? Do you remember that party scene we were in in *And No Birds Sing*? It's 1968. We—the guys—are wearing suits, to a party, like our dads. And our hair, barely past short back and sides. It might have been 1958 or 1948.

"Briony was the most naïve of us all. If she hadn't caught us at it, then maybe—"

"Caught you at what?"

"Briony caught Paul and me with my tongue in his mouth." Dorian glances at Lydia. "You mean she never told you? That day, you know, the day she and I went into town to buy groceries and a new clothesline? After we got back, you and she had lunch here, at the cottage, while Paul and I were at the beach by ourselves. When we came back, she—or you—had put all the towels and things that had fallen on the ground the night before back on the new clothesline, and so, thinking no one could see us hidden, we started fooling around—kissing. Briony saw us—inadvertently photographed us, actually. She was completely shocked. Can you imagine? In those days you could be completely shocked. Anyway, that's why she insisted on going back to the city."

"She said she had a migraine."

"She said. Maybe one was on the way, but was she in the throes of it? You couldn't have thought so, otherwise why did you let her take the Greyhound?"

"Impatience, I suppose.. I wanted to get back here. I sensed the migraine was more excuse than anything, it's true. But I didn't care."

"You wanted to come back here and go to bed with Paul."

"Yes."

"Again."

"Yes."

"And how was he?"

"Dorian, does it matter? It's been forty years."

"I'm curious."

"It was fine."

"I bet it was more than fine."

"All right. It was more than fine."

"Mrs. Peel, really, after that lunkhead Ross Whatsisname you went out with for eons, I'll bet it was mind blowing, as we used to say in the olden days." Dorian twists his head. "Jesus mothering Christ, how long does it take to assess 600 square feet of ancient cottage?"

Lydia follows his eyes. She and Dorian arrived at Eadon Lodge almost simultaneously to find Carol Guttormson and her client, a rather short, chubby man with scruffy holiday beard wearing cargo shorts and a T-shirt with Crime Wave emblazoned on it. Second visit, Carol mouthed to Lydia, introducing him as Jonathan Black. He peered at Dorian as if he had seen him somewhere before and askance at the machine in Dorian's hand.

"We thought we'd clear some of the overgrowth," Lydia said.

"Oh, don't do that," Jonathan responded.

A hopeful sign? Lydia thought so, said so to Dorian, but after Carol and the Boy Wonder disappeared into the cottage, he glass-half-emptied Lydia: A buyer—any buyer—could still flip it or sell off part of the acre it sat on or ...

But Lydia isn't this moment thinking of the urgency of shucking Eadon Lodge. She's thinking of Paul, once so alive. Yes, submitting to him in bed was mind blowing. He exuded sex in a way she hadn't known before—in the way he breathed, in the gaze of his eyes and the parting of his lips. She'd been often turned off by physical stuff with boys, putting up with this or that, tying to overlook some clumsy manoeuvre. Ross had been eager in a taurine sort of way, but unimaginative, she finding only counterfeit satisfaction in his satisfaction—something she didn't realize until Paul devoured her body in that very bed in the first bedroom in that cottage over there and carried her over the cliff edge of desire. She realized, even then, even in her naiveté, that his charm carried with it a whiff of something more dangerous. He was the Gothic lead, the antihero, the bad boy. Her first of that species. Her last, after what was to follow.

"Was he your first?" she asks Dorian.

"Was who my first what?"

"What do you think I mean?"

Dorian takes a drag of his cigarette. "First love. Is that what you mean?"

"No, but it will do. You said something about love when I dropped you off from that horrible Halloween party I had. Do you remember? 'I loved him,' you said. Briony was a bit fixated on the past tense—love*d*."

"Was she. Funny old Briony. When you think about it, so much turned on her naiveté. She had never seen two men be ... *intimate* before."

"Dorian, *I* had never seen two men be intimate before. And what an introduction I had."

"If I thought an apology would help, I'd give one."

"Besides, I think Briony was partly jealous ... and confused... Do you know, 'I loved him' were the last words I heard you say until we met at Tergesen's last week?"

"I did. Love him, I mean. Strange—now, it's only the memory of feelings I have, not the feelings. But my memory is ... what? What cliché can I use? Where's rewrite when you need it? A door opening? A blinding light on something that had been half in shadow? That's *Streetcar,* by the way. It's the charisma of first love, which can never come again, right? It doesn't matter what flaws you realize later, what half-truths you learn later."

"Half-truths?"

"I've told you I know his mother and ... well, let's just say he was more of a reckless teenager than you or I. His mother worried she'd told him too early how his father had died and that's maybe why he was so ... impetuous."

"I don't understand."

"Paul was three or four when his father died early of Huntington's, so there's a fifty percent chance that he ... Lydia?"

Lydia feels the blood draining from her face. Or had a groan escaped her throat? Was it a groan that stopped Dorian, that set him staring at her with fierce consternation? Will she tell him now, *now,* that she had a child, who might be his, but—*oh god in heaven*—who might not be? Who might be out in the world, somewhere, near middle-age, perhaps with children of his own, unaware of a harrowing genetic legacy, perhaps experiencing the first insidious symptoms? She can't stand this. How much longer can she hoard *this* secret? She opens her mouth to speak, but no words come forth. She strains. But she is saved—or thwarted—not by a bell, but by music. Dorian jerks his head toward the cottage.

"What is that ... that accordion sound?"

Lydia finds words. She replies weakly, "I guess they're trying out the Victrola."

"It's ... oh, Christ, Lydia, it's 'True Love.' Cole Porter's," he adds to her puzzled frown. "From *High Society*. Bing. Grace." And, more furiously, when her frown deepens: "We were playing it ... that night ... has nobody changed the record in *forty years*?"

"I'll get them to stop."

"Never mind. It's stopped."

"You mean, that was what was playing when—"

"Yes. *Yes*. You don't remember? And it's still on that turntable."

"Coincidence, surely ..." Lydia remembers now the faint strains of accordion as she approached the cottage that evening, the song ending as it began, the record almost over by the time she slipped into the cottage. The choice of song to accompany what she saw seems to her now grotesque.

"... although," she continues, the moment for confession lost, grateful now for the distraction, "my father rarely put on a record here. I don't know why. He played records all the time at home." She regards Dorian picking at the paint on the chair. "Bibs was funny about the cottage. I'm not sure he ever enjoyed a minute here. I wonder why he didn't just get rid of it after my grandfather died. If only he had."

Dorian's fervent wish, too. He's beginning to doubt his resolve. Executing what he's planned all week in the cool of his rented cottage at Winnipeg Beach seems like madness now, like some scene out of a 'B' movie. He will cut the few skinny poplars, slash the few shrubby bushes, as soon as the Boy Wonder and Carol have gone. Then there's stumps to dig out—or around. The spade is in the Petit Trianon. So is an axe. The chainsaw might prove useful in this, too. All this he can do in the afternoon and early evening—hopefully, though he has no real idea. He's not assured he knows what he's doing.

And then ...

And then, at some hour, this evening, before the sun sets, he will fetch the motorboat he rented from its mooring at Gimli Harbour and bring around to the beach at the cottage. Shouldn't be difficult. The lake is calm. Lydia will hold a lamp on the shore to guide the way.

And then ...

And then, the digging will begin in earnest. Darkness will set in. The moon will only be half-full this August 9, not almost full like the day they buried Paul. Dorian takes a calming drag on his cigarette, but it doesn't work. His guts recoil. Like Lydia's, his imagination runs riot through the miasma of slime and sucking earth and filthy air, through the hours of exhausting labour—he is, god, what? fifty-nine years old—to find ... what? Some iteration of a cadaver like a thing in an anatomy class? God, let there be clean pure bone. Let there be no hint of the flesh that once cushioned the bones. And please, let the ring be there, the peace ring. But, oh god, it will be encircling not flesh but bone. He feels his gorge rise.

And then, the wrapping of the remains, in the tarp. Tying it. Tying it with weights, stones. (He has some in the back of the rental.) Then to the boat and the water where under cover of darkness they will ... He takes a last drag on this last cigarette and flings it away. The morning is growing hot, but there's a haze in the air—grain dust from nearby farms—hints of autumn. Shadows are tinged orange. It might be August 1969.

"It was you who told me how my father really died."

"Did I? Oh, yes, I remember now. I'm sorry."

"You know, then," Dorian says, "that my father killed himself after leaving this place, this cottage."

"Yes, I think I knew that. How do you know?"

"The juxtaposition of dates. He signed the wall in there July 12, 1952. His obituary dates his death to the same day."

"Ah, yes, I remember you thinking it bad luck to sign the wall at the end of your visit, so you signed it on arrival."

"Why *then*? ... I think I know the reason, though," Dorian amends. He glances at Lydia. There's an alertness in her eyes. "You know? You've always known."

"Not always, no. But something my father once said ... about you, when we were around fourteen—it puzzled me at the time."

"Me? What ... ?"

"A cliché—the apple doesn't fall far from the tree. It was only years later that I understood what he was suggesting."

"I got the truth out of my mother before she died. Still, even then, after all those years, she didn't want to talk about it ... but she didn't deny it ... so, your father knew ... or suspected."

"They were in the war together, weren't they? And medical school. Close quarters."

"You're not suggesting ... ?"

"My father?"

Dorian looks at her slyly. "He seemed like a man with a secret to me."

"Not *that* sort of secret, Dorian. He was simply a man of his times—they were all sort of stoical, uncommunicative, weren't they? The fathers? It was the war that did it."

"I haven't the faintest idea what my father was like. As I say, my grandparents, my mother never mentioned him. My father had no brothers or sisters to ask. I should have asked your father what my father was like, but your father always seemed so ... intimidating. And I guess I never really thought to ask, wouldn't know how to frame a question. And would he have told me the truth?"

"I don't know, I really don't." Lydia glances toward the cottage's front door. Carol is pushing it open. She can see her face, but can't read it. *What will be Mr. Black's verdict?* "We'll never know. Life's not like a novel where you can have some narrative voice intrude with the bare facts. If it were a play or film you were in, what do you think happened here, with your father, that summer?"

Dorian's eyes follow Lydia's glance. He itches for another cigarette. "I think ... maybe your father had learned something, knew something, and told my father. Warned him? Something that would have ... what? Ruined him? He was a doctor, a GP. He worked with children."

"If you were gay in 1952 you lived a hidden life."

"Was it so different seventeen years later, Lydia?"

# 27

The books sold Jonathan Black on Eadon Lodge. That's what Jonathan said to Ívar Guttormson when he invited his colleague to see his new acquisition one afternoon on the Labour Day weekend.

"Off-road reading," Jonathan explained his literary project in front of the cottage's rows of marshalled book spines. "Or extreme reading."

Ívar stroked his beard, which was much fuller than Jonathan's, and snowy white. He grunted noncommittally. He was aware of the conceit, which was enjoying a certain vogue in literary circles, particularly in the U.S. The notion was to read through some author's oeuvre—usually within the frame of a year's time—and produce an amusing and not completely uncritical recounting of your armchair voyage.

But was it a good idea for young Jonathan Black, PhD, English department sessional lecturer, eager (*though was he?*) for a footing on the tenure track? Ívar thought not—not that he gave much of a damn anymore, being on the cusp of well-earned retirement himself and looking forward to leaving the tedious internecine struggles behind. Jonathan made do teaching three undergraduate courses a year, at ten thousand a pop. How was he affording this cottage, dilapidated as it was? There was a rumour he gambled—and with some success. Or might the cash have come from a divorce settlement? Jonathan was splitting (*had split?*) from his wife, a fetching little thing, who directed some human rights institute the University of Winnipeg was cashing in on. In Ívar's day, few men benefitted financially from divorce. How well he knew: He was paying two ex-wives alimony—half the reason he was still doling out moonshine to dunderheaded undergraduates at age sixty-eight.

Ívar peered at some of the authors' names on the faded spines, none of them immediately recognizable, proof—as if proof were needed—that obscure schlubbiness was the destiny of most writers. The road to immortality lay in placement on a university syllabus. None of these books looked like they'd seen the back end of a syllabus in generations.

"Perhaps you'll revive some long-lost classic," he said to Jonathan, not believing it for a minute.

"Well, it'll be fun at least," Jonathan grinned.

*Ah, fun.* There was something too earnest, eager, gauche—what was his granddaughter's word? *geeky*? about Jonathan. Fun, reading all these old old books? In a year? He made a swift tally of the total: five hundred—six? And where would he find the time to more than skim half of them?

Jonathan noted the roving eyes. "I'm going to pick a shelf at random. I'm not doing all of them. There are 512 books. I counted."

Even a shelf's worth seemed tortuous. Ívar smiled at his colleague. Jonathan was young, energetic. They all had websites these days, these kids. They blogged. Performed at poetry slams. Wrote comic books they called "graphic novels" and (the horror!) self-published them—or "tweeted" them, for all he knew. Lots of balls in the air, irons in the fire, gigs cobbled together. They had to. And maybe that was just fine. Things change. Life goes on. Tra la la. Who knew? Perhaps Jonathan's project ("A Year of Reading Crap" was Ívar's working title) would be a winner and bring lustre of some sort to the department. Or perhaps Jonathan had no desire for tenure anyway.

Ívar was eager to leave. A host of friends and acolytes was waiting for him at his summer home where he and Maya, wife #3, were hosting a little end-of-summer soiree. He probably should have invited Jonathan—still could, but, oh, somehow the boy didn't fit. He was an oddball, even by English department standards. He took a last sip of the *brennivín* Jonathan had thoughtfully provided and, as he exited through the screen door, gave him a piece of advice whose wisdom would become apparent four weeks later:

"You really need to do something about that old spruce in the yard."

Jonathan removes a carton of cream from the GE Monitor-Top fridge, glancing again at the antique warranty on the kitchen wall behind, void now these last seventy years. Wow! He loves the fridge. He loves the Victrola in the living room and the Quebec heater and the iron bedstead—all the stuff in his new possession. Eadon Lodge is so awesome. It's like Dylan Thomas's boat house or Roald Dahl's gypsy house or Vita Sackville-West's writing tower. But that microwave sitting on the old kitchen wood stove is getting the heave-ho. He flicks open the carton's spout. Did Dylan or Roald or Vita have a microwave? *Duh, no.* Jonathan pours the cream into his coffee (okay, the coffeemaker stays; how else do you make coffee?) and looks out the window to the fallen leaves rolling and twisting across the faded grass and to the denuded aspen bent against a wind that has been rising all afternoon. The leaves are audible in their turmoil—a lovely autumnal rustle. The spruce tree branches, too. They creak. Off to the east—he can make this out if he twists his head—the October sky appears as a grey blanket spreading low over the lake. Jonathan feels a funny little frisson. He recognizes it: he's nine, at his grandmother's in Fort Frances, on the veranda, playing Trivial Pursuit with his cousins as the rain thunders on the roof. But he's inside, where no danger intrudes, warm, safe, and dry. How cozy is Eadon Lodge? It's *awesomely* cozy. A log fire is crackling in the living room right now. Parchment lampshades cast a mellow glow. He has a fridge full of prepared food, for his own private little Thanksgiving picnic. (Maybe keeping the microwave isn't such a bad idea after all.) He will read, write, think, maybe watch a film on his laptop (okay, another concession to modernity), then pack up a shelf of books into boxes. These he will take to the city for winter reading, for his off-road project, which he could tell Ívar didn't think highly of. He's looking forward to the coming storm, anticipating the contrast between the comfort of the cozy little cottage and the turbulence of the evening—just like at Grandma's. He's not worried. Eadon Lodge has stood for eighty years.

This cottage property is the most expensive of his whimsies—more expensive than the Porsche 911 Turbo he bought when he was in grad school at Queen's. *That* riveted everyone's attention, including

Sara's, who probably wouldn't have paid attention to him in any other circumstances. He sold the Porsche after a few weeks. He only bought it for babe-magnet purposes and after a few weeks needed the cash. Jonathan plays poker.

Played. He *played* poker, first, in tournaments when he was an undergrad at the University of Waterloo, then, when he was in graduate school, online as well. It was a roller coaster, man. Cloud nine. Rock bottom. Big paydays. Horrendous downswings. But he learned mucho. Became a Zen master of his emotions. He did not cease from mental fight, nor did his cards sleep in his hand in those crazy days. All that and completing his master's thesis, too! But, in the end, playing poker for a living felt neither productive nor constructive. Sara helped him see the soullessness. So he banked his winnings, which are so nicely and sufficiently income-producing that he can tell the tenure committee to stick it up their collective ass, if it suits him. Unfortunately, money can play an ugly stepsister in divorce. Sara's said she doesn't want anything, wants the split to be amicable, and he's inclined to trust her. She, unlike he, comes from money. Her daddy's rich. Sara is Daddy's girl, but Daddy has a ruthless streak.

Jonathan returns to the living room, sets his coffee on the old pedestal desk, and goes to stuff another log into the Quebec stove. The fire within crackles satisfyingly when he raises the metal lid, sparks fly and vanish into the air. Eadon Lodge will be his perfect summer base for uninterrupted writing and thinking: no Internet here, no TV, no phone—well, no landline. The only thing he'll change is the cottage's name. The carved sign over the door—Eadon Lodge—will go. He will have another one done—Black Lodge. It's so perfect. After all, one of his many projects is examining "Northern Gothic" as a mode of national allegory in Canadian writing and "Black Lodge" seems, well, sort of northern Gothic-ish, no? Jonathan glances at the long shadows cast by the lamps. *So* Gothic! Well, in the most obvious sort of way. It's mid-afternoon but outside the dark blanket is drawing tighter over the sky. A few steps past the old Shaker rocking chair to the living room window confirms it. The leaves and trees continue their macabre dance.

And he can hear the waves hurling themselves against the shore. And he, inside, so cozy.

He sits in one of the armchairs at the desk, sips coffee, remembering he mentioned his northern Gothic interests to the woman he bought the cottage from—Lydia? ... Lydia ... Eadon. Eadon Lodge. *Duh.* He recalls the glance she gave him, though he can't find a word to describe it. Penetrating? Haunted? Bit Gothic, really. She seemed more interested in his long-range plans for the cottage than in his academic pursuits, though she worked for some sort of quasi-academic publisher in California. He assured her that he had no intention of changing a thing in the cottage. The ... er ... unique nature of Eadon Lodge was its attraction to him—and he meant it: Weeks earlier, he had seen Guy Maddin's surreal documentary *My Winnipeg* and yearned with every acolytish bone in his body to make his own *My Cottage*. Besides, if he wanted any old second home at a beach, he could have purchased any of dozens on offer. "Fear not," he said to her in his best superhero bass, bowing ludicrously, "I shall treasure this cottage as you and your family have treasured it, lo these many years." She managed a smile at this bit of theatre, though the smile didn't rise to her eyes. Her companion—who the heck was he? her husband? his face, so familiar—merely shot him a single lifted eyebrow.

Despite the caffeine from the coffee, despite the tumult outside, despite the tasks ahead, Jonathan feels heavy-lidded. Why not a short inaugural nap on the couch, lumpy thing that it is? He imagines the old couch, lumpy or no, being as comfortable this afternoon as his childhood bed. There's one of those lovely Hudson's Bay blankets in the corner cupboard. He'll fetch it. He will dream afternoon dreams.

Jonathan awakes to cold air pouring along his cheeks. A louvred window across the room, improperly fastened, he guesses, groggily, has flown open. Was there a crash? Did he hear a crash? He struggles out of the blanket and pads across the room to shut the window, lifting his cellphone from the desk to check the time. Barely an hour he's been asleep? Maybe. The wind sieved by the screen is uncommonly strong—

and, now, almost howling. He stares out to an agitated tracery of tree boughs, flailing shadows in light more late evening than late afternoon, startled at the weather's increased vehemence. He pushes the louvres back into the frame, but now the covering curtain jerks and billows. Shit! There *was* a crash. The window glass shattered against the edge of the bookshelf. Shards glitter along the couch. The fire from the heater will not subjugate this cold.

Jonathan's an academic with hands as pudgy as yoghurt, but he's not a complete boob, having grown up on a farm near Hanover, Ontario. Among the inventory, stored in the sleeping cottage, are plywood sheets—left over from some renovation, though he can't think what. He can use one to cover the broken window. Hammer and nails are in an old trunk here, in the cottage. Easy peasy. He can do this. He drops another couple of logs into the Quebec stove, fetches his jacket, moves through the chilly kitchen to the door, pushes through, and steps into a blast of wind and barrage of leaves whirling around his body like a host of frenzied sparrows. He catches his breath, or, rather, a gust of chilled air races to plug his nose and throat. The scene before him is transfixing. A wild cacophony of heaving, groaning tree branches plays counterpoint to wind rising from howl to screech to shriek, and over there, the roar of waves pounding the shore. It is thrilling. Not even a branch, ripped from a nearby tree, thudding at his feet, keeps Jonathan from stumbling, head bent, toward the beach. He steps over it, the window task forgotten, hugging his jacket against the flailing leaves, passing through the gate to the grassy rise over the sand. *Lash me to the mast, boys! This is epic stuff!*

But there is no sand. No beach. No shore. The water crashes along the verge at his feet, sending a mist of spray along his exposed skin. Stunned, he gazes at the heaving lake waters, great grey ridges, wide grey chasms, thrashing and churning, violently restless, exploding with spume. Now exhilarated—the scene is electric—he shouts, "Let Jove fly with his thunderbolts!" but his ears strain to hear his own voice against the roar and shriek. His eyes travel to the sky, barely a shade lighter than the roiling lake, here and there delivering a sickly light to silver the massive coils of water. Jonathan attunes himself to it all, eyes roving the land, the lake, the sky, so that he can later call up each detail of this ominous, Boschian scene. He takes deep breaths of the air, intoxicated by the ozone. It is amazing that anything can withstand this assault of wind and water.

And yet, with that thought, it strikes him that this tumult may be only a beginning. Where are the Jovian thunderbolts? Where is the rain? Coming. Soon. And with more force. He can sense it, with a sudden and visceral acuity. He turns, glimpses Eadon Lodge with its windows glowing port holes, riding the storm like a ship, and races toward it, through the gate and back into the yard, heart pounding. The shed is unlocked—he unlocked it earlier looking for a better broom—and he finds the plywood sheets, stacked neatly by size. He grabs a small one in front. But outside, in the gale, the board flails and thrashes like a sail in his hands, sending him careening across a lawn strewn now with frail branches and tree twigs, threatening to tear away from his grip. As he nears the cottage steps, a jagged flash of lightning renders the sky white, thunder crashes like a barrage around his ears, and a wall of rain descends out of the darkness, drumming onto the board, onto his head and jacket.

But he is inside now. He shakes off the drops, whisks the board through to the living room, scrambles for hammer and nails from the old trunk in the bedroom. Rain pounds on the roof, pours through the broken window, drenching the curtain, the wind behind setting magazines and papers skittering across the floor. Jonathan jerks the couch below the window aside and sets the plywood over the window, balancing the bottom on his knee as he grapples with hammer and nail. Loud as the punctuation of metal on metal is, it is nothing to the screeching intensity of the wind and rain attacking the cottage walls, which creak and groan under the assault. Shaken now, Jonathan glances at the tension rod that bolsters the sides of the cottage to see that it's holding, and misdirects his hammer. He howls as the hammer smashes into his thumb. The plywood swings dangerously on its hinge of a single nail, striking a bookshelf, sending a row of books tumbling to the floor and onto the glass-sharded couch. Somewhere else—from the dining room—comes the sound of more shattering glass—one of the old gas lamps, he is sure, but covering this window is his imperative. The cottage will be restored to coziness soon, but is it shaking? Or is he shaking? He removes his bruised thumb from his mouth and quickly completes the window covering. He could abandon the cottage, run for cover to the car, away from the canopy of demented trees, and considers this as he gathers up some of the fallen books—they're from the chosen shelf for his project.

And then he stops, his ears alerted to a new, low, terrible moaning and his mind races over the landscape outside. He has a sudden vision of that old spruce tree a few metres from the bathroom window listing and keeling, its ancient roots straining against the anchoring earth, but to no avail. Surrendering to the gale, it plunges horrifyingly, tearing through the roof and collapsing the cottage like a house of cards. And it's as though Jonathan Black is possessed of strange foresight, for a moment later, as he hastily throws *Dead Men Tell No Tales* into the cardboard box, a great ripping sound like no other that afternoon—or ever—rends the air. Jonathan sustains five seconds of absolute paralyzing terror, his mouth open in a silent scream, before a weight too brutal to imagine sends his insubstantial body through the splintering wooden floor and the stove explodes into a spree of liberated flame.

# 28

Dorian frowns up at the airport TV screen, at the bobblehead reading the news. *Shut up,* he mouths.

He returns to the script on his knees and tries to concentrate. It's Patrick Hamilton's *Rope*. Again. Charmaine, his agent, is unaware of the ... *incident* the last time he was associated with a production of this play. That was in 1981. The Toronto Free Theatre. Guy Sprung directing. Him in the role of the callow undergraduate, Granillo. No one then—as far as anyone knew—had mounted *Rope* on stage since Christ was a pup. Written in 1929, a half-century later it couldn't even be branded a chestnut, so far had it fallen from the repertoire, but Sprung has seen the 1948 Hitchcock film version in a repertory cinema in New York and thought he could make it "relevant," as the saying went in those days, setting it post–Vietnam War rather than post–First World War. Now there seems to be a new vogue for it. The Old Vic is mounting it in London. Dorian is reading it for A.C.T. in San Francisco, for the 2009–2010 season. With Iraq war overtones, no doubt.

Dorian's eyes drift off the page—not because he is remembering the *incident*—but because he can sense a set of eyes on him. It's a not-unfamiliar sensation. As he said mockingly to Mark in Tergesen's store in August, *I'm famous*. With some reluctance he looks up and gets a jolt.

It's Dix. He drops the script onto the empty seat opposite.

"Darling, how good to see you." He rises and hugs her, with air kiss, feels the bony lightness of her under his hands. "What are you doing here?"

"I'm going to Calgary. My granddaughter's getting married next weekend."

Peter's daughter, of course. It doesn't need to be said. Dix has only one child, living.

"How nice ... but October?"

"Yes, it *is* hurried, but it's not what you think. Something to do with work and travel arrangements to Hong Kong."

"Is Peter with you?"

"No, he and his wife will come on their own, in time for the rehearsal." Dix replies, to Dorian's relief. Peter took him aside at a party once in Toronto and warned him away from his mother. "Did I know you were going to be in Toronto?"

"No, sorry, Dix. I was only in for the weekend, sort of last minute. A wedding, speaking of weddings. An old friend of mine and his partner decided on the spur of the moment to marry at Thanksgiving. So here I am. Or, there I was."

"Well, I'm sorry to have missed you."

"Me, too," Dorian lies. In the years since he moved to Vancouver, he has returned to Toronto on any number of occasions, for work or play. Only if he's certain Dix would learn of his presence—cast in a play, for instance—does he get in touch.

In fact, Dix knows there are times Dorian's been in Toronto and hasn't called. She is even better connected than he thinks, and though he may be an accomplished actor, the twitch between his eyebrows, the way he held her gaze too firmly, tells her the "me, too" is a bit of a fib. Why? Who knows? Friendships falter. And polite fictions are the unguent of civilization.

"Did your summer go well? I haven't heard from you. That series filmed in Manitoba ... ?"

"*Morningstar Cove.* It went well enough. Hardly the role of a lifetime, but it pays the bills. It's renewed. I'll be filming there again next summer."

"When will it be on TV?"

"It already is. Started last month on Global in Canada. ABC Family, if you get it from the States."

In fact, Dorian's invitation to read for *Rope* is a consequence of the American broadcast of *Morningstar Cove. Rope*'s director's daughter is, predictably, besotted by the blond hunk star of the show, but the director's eyes passed to Dorian who, he thought, had the demeanour for the role of Sir Johnstone Kentley, the father of the play's young victim. It's not a lead role, but, what the hell, it's six weeks in San Francisco. He's looking forward to seeing Lydia under happier circumstances.

"I'll look out for it," Dix says.

"I'm not sure *Morningstar Cove* would be your cup of tea."

"What's your next project then? Is that a script I see? Exciting. Something here in Toronto?"

"San Francisco. A play."

"Oh, how interesting. May I? I won't lose your place." Dix bends to retrieve the script before he can say yea or nay. He'd rather the latter.

"*Rope*." Dix reads the title, frowns a little. "I've seen this."

"The Hitchcock film."

"No. Well, yes, I've seen the Hitchcock version. I think. But I know I've seen it on stage."

"Really?"

"Oh, long ago. Late forties."

"Which is when the film came out."

"This was in London." Dix hands him back the script. "William—my first husband—and I had flown there for some business thing. It was my very first flight, propellers, you know, refuelling at Gander, quite the adventure in those days—not like this." Dix flicks a glance through the window at the ranks of jets on the tarmac. "I remember it—May, 1949. But I remember the play because the next morning, I experienced another first—morning sickness. How funny."

"Funny how?"

"I was thinking about Paul—my son, you know—before I saw you." She studies his face. "You realize that I was carrying—"

"Mmm."

"Anyway, I ran into someone a little earlier whose son was in school with Paul, so it put him into my mind."

Dorian cocks his head sympathetically, says nothing.

"Forty years, next year," Dix continues, handing him back his script. "Hard to believe. Did I ever tell you I took up private investigation again?"

"Again? No. I remember something about a detective possibly tracing him to ... Barrie, was it?" Dorian knows perfectly well it was Barrie. It plagues him, this tracing. It's like watching floodwaters advance. "We were eating at Pastis, when you told me. This was years ago."

"That investigator seemed to have his limits. I thought I'd try again. This one managed to trace him to Wawa."

"Oh, god, Wawa. I think it was the black hole of hitchhiking in those days. Once there, you couldn't get out. Great lineups along the highway..."

"Did you—?"

"No, no." Dorian realizes he's been unguarded. What he knew of Wawa's reputation he knew from Paul. "Getting out of Wawa was part of the lore of the day."

"Some former truck driver remembers dropping him there, so there's no doubt he was moving west. To Vancouver? Where did young people want to go in those days? You're thinking this is futile. I can read it in your face."

Dix is reading Dorian's face incorrectly. He may have composed his face for empathy, but the mask is ready to slip.

"I don't think it's futile," he lies humbly, twisting the script in his hands.

"I'm going to be eighty-two in November, Dorian. I've accepted that Paul's likely not alive. But before *I* die I would like to know what happened to him." Some indefinable emotion flickers in her face. Some old Orange Ontario grit, he thinks, and he's not wrong. She adds, "A good friend of mine's granddaughter is an editor at *Chatelaine*. She thinks it would make a good story. I should have thought of such a thing years ago."

"Good idea," Dorian responds with false bravado. Here is danger, here is ruin: *Chatelaine*'s circulation is vast. Someone will turn the page: "A Mother's 40-Year Search," a picture spread, a number to call. Yes, why didn't she think of this before? Why did he and Lydia never think of this possibility? Because they didn't know Who. He. Was.

"Peter doesn't think it's a good idea." Dix's eyes flick to the nearby TV screen.

"Well," Dorian forces a grin, "fuck him."

Dix affects shock at the language, smiles, contemplates him a moment like he was a wayward child. "Dorian, dear, do have a good flight. You will tell me when *Rope* opens in San Francisco, won't you? I might fly down."

"Of course. Be in touch soon."

An air kiss and she is gone, wheeling her carry-on down to a gate a little farther on. He watches, as if to make sure she is safe, but really to let himself decompress. He sits, returns to the script.

And now he doesn't want the part of the father. Doesn't want to do the play at all. He thought he could do it the last time. Then, he'd read the script. There was the table read. The blocking rehearsal. All was well. But next came full rehearsal. Act I, scene I, and he is holding the rope in his hand, the rope that will strangle the boy. His hand trembles, his mouth goes dry, and not simply words but sound vanishes from his lips, for that afternoon, that week, that fortnight. He lost the part. "Conversion disorder," Mark once said, though in reference to a patient repressing her witnessing of her child's murder: anxiety is "converted" into a physical symptom, blindness in the woman's case.

Mark didn't come with Dorian to Toronto to attend the wedding and not because he was on call at the hospital over the Thanksgiving weekend or suchlike. He wouldn't have come anyway. Mark and Dorian are parting ways. The thin edge of the wedge thickened with the conversation about buying Eadon Lodge and, Dorian learned soon after he returned to Vancouver at the beginning of September to find Mark skittish and withdrawn, he had met someone else. Presentiment prepares no one for shattering fact: Dorian's not yet out of the house, they are in the "being civilized" stage, but the unanchoring has plunged him into something like grief. He craves a drink.

An announcement. Dorian half listens to the beginning. The plane taking them to Vancouver has arrived. Finally. He looks up, sees it taxiing through grey mist outside the window, glances left to see Dix in her departure lounge, one hand on the upright handle of her case, other hand on hip, studying the TV screen. He peers at the one nearest him, and at ones further down the rank. The newscast is the same. He catches some prettily coifed creature droning on about something, but it is the crawler along the bottom of the screen that catches his eye in the few seconds before the next news item: Three dead in Manitoba storm.

He thinks nothing of it.

# 29

There's always some busker—musician, magician, whatever—in the pavilion or the plaza, someone to brush past, someone to ignore. Today, it's a guitarist picking out something flamenco-y, singing—very sweetly—something familiar, the words manifesting as the BART's long escalator takes her from shadow to light. *A love like ours could never die.* She is Eurydice emerging into the upper world. She is being fanciful. The guitarist—blue eyes, long blond hair tied in a braid, Obama T-shirt ("HOPE")—picks her from the crowd, gazes like a lover right at her, right into her eyes. *Orpheus, don't look at me*: A little scream in her head. She *is* being fanciful. He casts her a radiant smile. *As long as I have you near me,* he continues, and it works: Lydia reaches in her purse and pulls out a five. She is flushed with rare well-being, a strange sensation unconnected, she thinks, to anything about this day, the last day of October. The weather, perhaps? The Bay area has had a string of uncommonly fine days. Good news? Dorian is coming to San Francisco for a role in a play. Happiness on the home front? The Lincoln Way home is hers and Ray's, the bank is happy. Erin and Misaki arrived last week from Japan, with Ray. His long absence has been hard to bear.

The Campanile begins to ring. It will ring nine times over downtown Berkeley. Lydia doesn't need to look at her watch. She is going to be late. She is almost never late—never being late being part of her nature. She feels a tiny stab of anxiety. Some of that lucky feeling begins to fray. Ray's lovemaking, a train delay at Embarcadero, has made her late, but that's no excuse. She has a 9:15 meeting with Cuntella to finalize some details for the spring 2009 catalogue and the walk to Countervail Press's office on Addison takes all fifteen. She reaches for her cellphone, unlocking it from its imprisoning baggie. She will call Manson, her associate editor, to say she's on her way. She flips open the phone and sees from the display that Ray has left a message. A second stab of anxiety. Ray is a man of routine and discipline, sequestered with his art like a hermit unless jonesing for coffee takes him to the kitchen. He calls in the morning only if there's an emergency.

An hour is spent in Cuntella's office not reviewing the spring catalogue, but with the rest of staff listening to her chalk-on-blackboard voice, looking at designs for a new logo for the press. Lydia spends it numbed by dread. Ray's message, picked up as she walked down Addison, was voiced in a mix of curiosity and concern: *Honey, someone's called from Canada and wants to talk to you. A Mountie. She wouldn't tell me what it's about, but she gave me a number for you to call…*

Lydia recognized the prefix. It was the same as Carol Guttormson's—642. Back in her own office she awakens her iMac from sleep. The computer faces away from the hallway.

Lydia's fingers hover over her keyboard. Why would the RCMP be reaching out all the way to San Francisco? Surely Briony would have got in touch if something … Or Dorian. Dorian certainly, if it were dire.

When Lydia types "Gimli" into Google and clicks on the news tab, her eyes alight on headlines with "storm" and "deaths" in them, and feels a flutter in the pit of her stomach. But the stories are nearly three weeks old. How can anything in them pertain to her? Again, Briony—surely she would have phoned or emailed if … Or Dorian? Perhaps not Dorian. In Vancouver, stories about Manitoba would be inconsequential. In the United States of America, Gimli and its travails—windstorm, deaths—would pass unnoticed.

Yes, a windstorm—she clicks on a CBC entry—the great Lake Winnipeg whipped into a late-season tornado, waves surging, trees on shore uprooted, shorelines vanished, a path of destruction—more devastating than the one in 1988. The storm of the century, says a subhead, though the century is only eight years old. A lead photo of downed trees over a road. And news of death. Three deaths—an elderly man caught on the lake in his sailboat, a middle-aged woman (a former mayor) driving blinded by rain into a ditch, and young man in a cottage fire. The names are unrecognizable, but for one.

Lydia's heart contracts with pity over the details. Jonathan Black was young and vital, with, as they say, everything to live for, and he died harrowingly. But horror follows. Eadon Lodge and its grounds and its secrets are unchampioned, unguarded, unsafe. But worse: Her eyes fall on a certain picture—one of a slide show of ten of the regional havoc—and her breath leaves her body. It's Eadon Lodge, she is certain, but there is no lodge, not any more. There's only a charred absence, a bed of cinder in a Breugal landscape, unrecognizable. It's the tiny shadow—picture centre—of the eccentric crown of the Monitor-Top fridge, somehow triumphing over the fire's devastation, that registers the truth. Her eyes swim over the cutline: tree toppled ... cottage collapsed ... wood stove ... tinderbox ...

She can't bear it. She turns back to the home page. But there is worse still. A subhead for a related story, emblazoned red, captures her attention. Three words and the floor seems to fall away, as if in a nightmare. She could—should—scream, weep, but she is frozen into inaction. And she must look ghostly because Manson slips into the frame of the door at that moment, coffee in hand, armed for a bitchy little debrief on the stupid logo. His smirk falters as the words to the venerable question escape his lips:

"Are you okay?"

Lydia sees Manson as if at a distance, a blur in blue and grey. She answers mechanically, "I'm fine."

"You don't look fine."

Lydia marshals some inner resolve. Her hands, trembling over the keyboard, fall to her lap to form a tight damp ball—a gesture, she realizes, that makes her look like she's hiding something. She hates bluffing Manson. He's her work-husband, she tells Ray, who finds this funny, though she no more confides everything to Manson than she does to Ray. She must look ghastly, saucer-eyed, *something!*, for Manson leans away, when she says, again, with vehemence:

"I'm fine, Manson, really. Just give me a few moments to deal with something here and I'll come to your office. I've something to ask you about ..." Her first impulse, bad impulse, is to say "Paul is Dead," now at the proof stage, but can't release the words. "... one of the upcoming projects, okay?"

"Okay." Manson's tone mixes uncertainty and disappointment.

"And would you mind closing the door?"

She clocks his startled response and proffers a reassuring smile, which collapses with the click of the latch. Her eyes dart back to her screen.

"STORM UNCOVERS BONES"

*Jesus.*

It can't be.

Her mind begins rationalizing, backtracking, denying. The storm, she read earlier, encompassed a sizable area. Though the epicentre was Gimli, communities to the north and south were affected. Who knew what lay beneath the earth there?

The link. She has not clicked on the link. She must click on the link. She stares at the three words in contrasting blue type.

She cannot not click on the link.

She takes a breath, clicks, and the world stops.

> Posted: Oct 18, 2008 5:17 PM CT Last Updated: Oct 18, 2008 7:46 PM CT
>
> RCMP say emergency crews working north of Gimli Wednesday in the wake of Thanksgiving Day's windstorm have discovered human bones.
>
> Gimli RCMP spokesperson Sgt. Tori Sinclair said the bones seem to be old but how long they have been in place has yet to be determined. The bones have been sent to the medical examiner's office and have been confirmed as human.

The RCMP officers are now working with the examiner's office to try and identify the person.

It doesn't matter that it's brief, that it's little more than a headline amplified. It's the words *north of Gimli* that chill her. She can't delude herself. She knows why Canadian police are contacting her.

Lydia tried calming herself by scrubbing the phone with Purell before punching in the numbers, thinking she could wait and make the call from home, but she doesn't want Ray to hear, to see her in this anxious state. How will she explain any of this to him, anyway? She pushes this from her mind. She concentrates on sounding like a law-abiding citizen, surprised to be contacted by the police, but, of course, only too happy to cooperate.

She is speaking with the very sergeant in the news story, Tori Sinclair, who explains that Lydia's number was given to her by Carol Guttormson, at Interlake Real Estate, as the previous owner of a property north of Loney Beach.

"If that's Eadon Lodge, then, yes, I was owner ... briefly," Lydia says, trying to match the sergeant's flat and measured tones. "My mother died in the early summer and so I inherited it."

"She owned it for how long?"

"Well, I suppose technically the cottage was my father's. He died in 1998, so my mother had it alone for ten years. But it was built by my grandfather—my father's father—in the 1920s."

"When did your grandfather die?"

"Not long after I was born—in 1950, I believe. I was born in '49." Lydia frowns slightly. Her heart, thrashing in her chest, eases a little. Interest in the cottage's ownership is not what she's expected. "May I ask—"

"We had a big storm here at Thanksgiving. There was a lot of destruction in the area. Your cottage—your former cottage—was destroyed—"

"Oh, no."

"—and the new owner killed."

"Good god." She knows this, but hearing it voiced shocks her. "How—"

"A tree took the cottage down. Mr. … Black was inside at the time. There was also a fire."

"A fire? Oh, my god. How awful. His poor family …" And now she anticipates a new line of questioning. She can feel her pulse racing. "But I don't see how I can … ?"

"Ma'am, the storm turned up some human remains on your former property."

"Oh?"

"The pathologist has established that the bones belong to that of a male between seventeen and twenty-one years of age."

Lydia wants to faint, to put her head in her hands and weep. The only saving grace is that Sgt. Sinclair cannot see her, cannot read the distress in her face. Only the timbre of her voice can hint of deceit. She strains to keep the breath in her lungs from ratcheting and says the first thing that comes to her mind:

"How odd. Could it be an Indian burial ground?"

"No, ma'am." The measured tone is suddenly censorious. "There is no evidence this is a First Nations burial site."

"I see. Of course."

"According to the pathology report, the body has lain in the ground for more than sixty years, but less than eighty."

"*What?*" The mathematics are wrong, simply wrong. Can forensics be this imprecise, this off the mark, this inept?

Sergeant Sinclair repeats her last comment, adding, "This puts the burial within the time-frame of your family's ownership."

"But … I'm not yet sixty myself, Sergeant. I wasn't alive at the time. I don't know how I can help you." She wants to laugh. This is insane. *What of the remnants of the HBC blanket?* But she can't ask those questions. Doesn't dare ask. "If you're thinking this has something to do with my family, I don't know how."

"Ma'am, we're treating this as an unsolved murder."

"An unsolved—"

"Did any member of your family possess a firearm?"

"A firearm?" Lydia repeats dully. The word confuses her. She thinks of Americans and their mania for weaponry. Her family—her birth family—is *Canadian*. "No."

"The barrel and receiver of a shotgun were found among the remains of the cottage fire."

"Oh ... well, yes, there was a old shotgun at Eadon Lodge," Lydia begins, wonderingly, "hanging on one of the walls. It was an ... ornament. I never saw it taken down in my life." A lie. Alan Rayner racing across the lawn in the fading light flits through her mind. "It was my grandfather's. I think he and my father would sometimes go duck hunting nearby in the Netley marshes before the war. How does this—"

"Shot was found near the remains."

"Shot?"

"Gunshot."

Lydia is stunned to silence. Had *shot* remained in Paul's body? Is this the damning evidence? But Alan only grazed Paul. Briony ministered to his shoulder with mercurochrome and a bandage. There can't have been shot left in Paul's arm. Could there have been? Wouldn't he have been in too much pain to ... Lydia banishes her last image of the living Paul. She thinks: how serious the police are being about this. Shot pellets are small, she knows that. They must have sieved the soil.

"Ms Eadon?"

"Yes, sorry. I ... I don't know what I can tell you. Sixty years ago, you say? Or seventy or eighty?"

"I realize this is difficult for you. Can you tell me if you know stories of ... conflict in your family or among your family and their friends?"

Lydia looks wildly about her office as if the Countervail titles and the reference books and the myriad magazines held the secret. "I don't know. I have no idea. I know so little. Our family was small, at least on my father's side. There was only my father and his father. My grandmother died in childbirth."

"I see."

"Not giving birth to my father, I should add. My father had a younger brother. He was ... mentally challenged and died young. My grandmother's sister came from Ontario to take care of the boys and was their surrogate mother for a number of years, but I'm not sure what became of her. Long gone, in any case."

Lydia suddenly remembers Helen's story of her grandfather and his sister-in-law, Aunt May, as she was called, arguing at Bibs and Marion's wedding. "I have a feeling," she adds, "that she and my grandfather didn't get along. But I don't think that's much help to you and that's about all I can think of. My father spoke little of his family. He was of that generation, you know, the generation that went through the Depression and the war. They were stoics."

"Family friends?"

"Who would come to the cottage in those days? I have no idea. The cottage was really used so little, mostly a few weeks in August each year, some weekends. My father would go down from time to time just to cut the lawn. He was a surgeon, always busy, took few holidays."

"And you?"

"Me? When I sold the property in the summer it was the first time I had been back in nearly forty years."

"I see. Well, thank you, you've been very—"

"Sergeant," Lydia interrupts, contrives to make her voice light, "out of curiosity, would you know what happens to the property now?"

"No."

"Who Mr. Black's heirs might be ... ?

"No, I'm afraid I don't."

"It's just that he seemed to sort of fall in love with the cottage. It's all very sad. I suppose with winter setting in up there, little will be done with the property."

"Not likely, no. It's starting to snow here now, actually. Snow on Halloween. You're lucky to live in California."

"Yes, I suppose I am." Lydia glances at the sunny street outside her window, imagining white blanketing the black remains of the cottage.

Only one thing could take her back to Manitoba and that she pushes from her mind.

"Anyway, Ms Eadon—"

"Just one more question, if you don't mind." Lydia hesitates. *Will she tempt the sergeant to suspicion?* She frames it this way: "I can't help wondering ... I mean, all those summers of my childhood not knowing, I suppose, that I was treading on someone's grave. Where was it exactly? It would be nice to know."

"I can answer that." Lydia listens to another rustle of paper. "The remains were found, let's see ... in the southeast part of the property. Does that help?"

Lydia lies: "Yes. Yes, it does."

# 30

"Fuck."

"What happened?"

"I cut myself."

Lydia sucks in her breath sharply. "Are you all right? Can I get you a bandage?"

"No. It's no biggie." Ray turns, his left index finger stuffed in his mouth.

Ray is at the kitchen counter making their ritual pre-dinner martinis—not with olives, but with a twist. The lemon tree in their back garden produces small orangey-yellow fruit, slightly sweet and intensely aromatic.

"The vegetable peeler?"

Ray nods, pulls his finger out to speak. "I've never done that before. With a peeler, I mean."

Lydia feels sudden damp film her skin. Shock, she recognizes—and *that* is shocking. *Why?* And the answer comes when the words—Briony's, on a Halloween long ago, slip from her lips. "Run your finger under the cold water."

"Are *you* all right?" Ray says, a frown forming along his lips, before turning to the taps. "Cuntella being a bitch?"

"Oh ... the usual. She's been obsessing about a new company logo."

"And ... ?"

"Looks like clip art."

"What?"

"Clip art!" Lydia raises her voice above the water's hammering. She gazes at Ray's back in its Hawaiian print. In truth, she's feeling a little faint—nauseated, in fact, though she ate little lunch.

"You know," Ray turns back to her. "Maybe I'd better have a bandage … or it'll be pink martinis for you and me, baby."

She can feel Ray's eyes on her as she fetches the bandage from the junk drawer too neatly organized to warrant the name. She begins to unpeel its paper sheath.

"*Are* you all right?" he asks again.

"Oh … long day, long week." She wraps the bandage around her husband's upright finger. "You did get stuff for Halloween, yes?"

Ray grunts in assent. "Say, what about Dudley Do-Right? … or Dorothy Do-Right, I guess it was."

"Who?

"The call this morning. From Canada." He cocks an eyebrow and drops his voice for a stentorian announcement: "From the Royal Canadian Mounted Police." He finds the idea of Canada faintly comical. He subscribes to all the clichés: beavers, toboggans, and maple syrup. He draws them on cards. "Are you helping them get their man? They always get their man, you know."

"No." Lydia laughs lightly and turns to deposit the bandage wrapping in the trash, glancing at the unsettling Edward Gorey wall calendar over the towel rack. She's rehearsed something for Ray. "Eadon Lodge, it seems, is no more. There was a big storm in Gimli earlier in the month. A tree fell on it and that was that."

"Oh, honey. I'm so sorry. Are you … I mean, you weren't really attached to the place, were you?"

"God no." *God no.*

"Its sale made all the difference to affording *this* place. Still … kind of too bad." Ray turns back to the cutting board and the lemon. "And the Mounties phoned to tell you this? Amazing. I mean, that cabin wasn't even yours anymore."

"I guess they thought it was a courtesy."

"Wow." Ray also subscribes to the notion that Canadians are unusually polite and courteous. "I can't imagine our cops doing something like that. Poor guy that bought the place. Hope he had it insured." He hands her the stemmed glass, the lemon peel curled inside the bowl reminding Lydia—suddenly, for no reason—of a tiny fetus. "*Kanpai!* Here's to the week that was."

Lydia sets her glass on the counter next to a box of Misaki's crayons. She's going to be sick.

Ray teaches a class in freehand drawing Saturday mornings at Fort Mason. He leaves Lydia lying in bed. He brought her breakfast, still concerned over last evening's episode of sickness. Something she ate, she said. A shrimp salad at lunch, must have been off. A fiction, Ray believes. Accumulated stress—her mother's death, packing up a house and an old life, purchasing this house, money worries, work worries—I mean, *bang!* Little wonder Lyds threw it all up—though she's never done that before.

Lydia doesn't much like breakfast in bed. Crumbs, the chance of slopped coffee, spilled juice. But she suffers it gladly on her birthday and at Mother's Day because it gives Ray pleasure. She sets the tray aside, grimaces at the barely touched coddled egg, now cooling and jelling, hardening into repulsiveness. She has no appetite. She would like to be alone, but she isn't, and that's all right in this instance. Misaki has crawled into bed beside her, fallen asleep over a book, the warmth of her little body and the gentle susurration of her breathing a welcome comfort. Lydia stares out the window at the fickle San Francisco sky, clear and blue yesterday, overcast today. Her thoughts unspool.

Her champion is dead. Young Jonathan Black was to protect and preserve the cottage, its property and chattels from here to her own dying breath. She'd felt assured by his enthusiasm, by his declaration that he would never, ever, in a thousand years, build one of those vulgar second homes. She remembers the day later in August, after the paperwork was complete, meeting Dorian for the last time in Winnipeg Beach, on the set of *Morningstar Cove,* where they were shooting a scene inside a restaurant, the street strewn with cables, the set sealed from view by a wall of cameras and technicians.

"Is it done?" he murmured, after she'd picked her way past gaffers and gofers and, led by a PA alerted to her coming, found him hunched over a video monitor wedged among plant pots and tables with, she presumed, members of the production team.

"Yes. Well ... at least postponed."

"That'll have to do, I guess." Dorian ushered her away to an unpeopled corner and whispered. "Even with that guy buying it, I would still liked to have cleared that—"

"You say that now, Dorian. But could you? Could you really have borne the horror of it? The *remains*?"

"Shhh."

"And the chance of your being—"

"Our being."

"—caught in the act was just too fraught. Clearing bush, yes. Excavating a hole, no."

She remembers Dorian, in the terrible dad jeans of his costume, pushing a hand through his abundance of white hair, looking suddenly old and careworn, and feeling her heart begin to break.

"Did you get your money back on the chainsaw?" She couldn't think what else to say. This was a farewell—the sort they should have had in their youth, at an airport or a train station, each going on to glory, speaking fine words and good cheer. Who knew when they would meet again? She could see the mist in his eyes matching her own.

"I haven't returned it yet." He put his arms around her and said into her ear, "Do you really trust that kid not to flip the cottage?"

"Is there any going back?"

He released her, regarded her with sorrow. "Is there *ever* any going back?"

Did Jonathan Black have a will? Did he have heirs? Lydia wonders this as Misaki stirs next to her. He was separated—not divorced—from his wife, no kids, the real estate agent had told her. If he died intestate, wouldn't his wife inherit ... everything? something? despite the breakdown in their marriage? Lydia considers retrieving her laptop to look at Black's obituary in the online *Winnipeg Free Press* to pluck out the wife's name, but is there any point? Eadon Lodge is no longer hers to bargain over. She thinks of phoning Briony, who might know something about Eadon Lodge's fate. But if Briony knew something, surely she would have phoned her already, yes? Lydia decides not to phone her. Arousing Briony's curiosity might not be a good thing.

Dorian. She will phone Dorian, though. Another one apparently oblivious to this new tilt in the earth's axis.

But what about the bones? These *bones,* for heaven's sake, found in the southeast of the property, not the northwest. Is it possible the sergeant had the map, the paperwork, the drawing, the computer image, whatever, of the property upside down, northwest becoming southeast? That must be it, and yet Lydia refuses to subscribe to the notion that women are somehow direction-challenged. Nor did the sergeant sound like some bored functionary.

Can, then, buried remains shift over time? Not that distance. Impossible.

Can the pathologist be so off the mark? The age of the remains between sixty and eighty years? *Sixty and eighty?*

And there is the shot. The fire-scarred remains of a shotgun.

A death, by shotgun, sometime between—what?—1928 and 1948.

Lydia hears Erin stir in the bedroom across the hall. Her eyes rove her own bedroom, glancing over the potted yucca cane grown now to six feet, the Victorian wicker chair she'd had restored when she lived with Helen all those years ago, the white cork board artfully displaying fifty sets of earrings she no longer wears but loves anyway, the tidy vanity table with two framed photographs, the Beljik rug she bought at Palayan's with Ray when they first moved in together. All so at peace. And now this intrusion.

That there is a body, another buried body (it *must* be another) at Eadon Lodge seems preposterous, a punchline of a feeble joke, a cruel taunt from some prankster god.

A violent death, an unmarked grave, yet a generation—at least—earlier. What could have happened?

It is spring. It is evening. The property is isolated. There is a young man with … someone. One of them has a shotgun, a different shotgun than the one at Eadon Lodge. There is an argument, a gun is raised …

It is summer. It is night. The property is isolated. A drifter tries to break into a cottage that looks unoccupied. Her grandfather is slumbering. He wakes, snatches the gun off the wall …

It is fall. It is morning. The property is isolated. Some gang of thugs arrives with the squealer who betrayed them …

What else can it be? The property is no potter's field, no native burial ground. Lydia plucks unthinkingly at the edge of the bedspread, her eyes once again roving the room, though this time registering little. *What can it be?* Her attention falls for a moment on the photographs on the vanity; their silver frames somehow catch a valiant ray of November sun slipped past the cloud barricade. The oldest: her wedding day, she and Ray, at City Hall, she in a tailored suit, the wide shoulders now regrettable. The newest, from her parents' bedroom: Bibs and Marion, their wedding day, smiling in the open door of a Buick, Bibs in a dark suit spattered with confetti, Marion clutching the marriage licence. Unbidden, an old anecdote spins to the surface of thought: Helen's, about Bibs and Marion's wedding reception, some unpleasantness between her grandfather and his sister-in-law, May, the woman who raised Bibs and Lits, then vanished from their lives. Uncle Lits, who died so young, an absence at the wedding, a presence only in a photograph. In the 1930s, you could die of influenza, and Lits probably wasn't a strong boy. She recalls seeking his grave in that churchyard in Narborough in the late '80s, failing, and Bibs, so furious at her attempt, though perhaps in his incipient dementia he was merely confused.

Lydia's head falls against the pillow. She's feeling mentally exhausted, on the verge of surrendering—gratefully—to slumber, but just as the balm of sleep comes over her, a new and terrible thought jolts her awake. She pushes it away. It will not go. Memories crowding her mind now, she slides from bed, careful not to wake Misaki, barely conscious of her movements, and pads across the rug to the window overlooking the back garden. She sees not the lemon tree which produced the garnish for last night's martini; she sees the old spruces in Eadon Lodge's yard, the childish cryptogram in that old novel, her father at Eadon Lodge: moody, taciturn, restless, slipping into town to have a drink at the hotel, her mother frazzled and exasperated. Bibs resisted alteration to the cottage, surrendering to some novelty only when Marion turned virago. Nostalgia? A refusal to spend good money, child-of-the-Depression that he was? And Marion: all those years petitioning him to buy a summer home at Lake of the Woods or Falcon Lake or Wasagaming—somewhere pretty and prominent, where her smart friends gathered. Then, after his death, her conversion to Eadon Lodge. Despite her age, she could have sold it, bought a new place, and, inveterate renovator to her death, gone giddy redecorating. What changed her mind?

And now, with a clarity that leaves her gasping, she sees that Bibs didn't cherish the cottage. He hated it. It was no haven. It was hell. A hell he had to endure. And, like his daughter decades later, he didn't dare sell it to anyone he couldn't trust to leave it be.

But would she ever know for certain?

It's the Sunday morning the weekend before Christmas and Ray is running his hand along Lydia's lovely back. How many accumulated hours of their marriage has he spent in bed stroking Lydia's body? Who's counting? This morning, however, as his hand moves up and over the smooth surface toward her breasts, he startled by an unfamiliar sensation along his fingertips. Her ribs feel ... well, they feel different, more defined.

Lydia is half *not* in slumber. She senses the shift in Ray's gentle motions, his fingers now firmer, more exploratory, like her doctor's at Kaiser Permanente when she went for her general check-up. Dr. Chen didn't register any particular change in Lydia's appearance. How could she? She sees forty patients a day, and Lydia perhaps twice a year. But she did notice a weight loss on her chart. Stress, Lydia said, before Dr. Chen could even think about ordering a raft of tests. She says nothing to Ray.

Ray says nothing to her. He locks his qualm away. Women always seem to be dieting, anyway, and perhaps Lydia is, too—though he suspects stress. She has been wan, more preoccupied than usual these last weeks. He is alert to her work situation, of course, the skirmishes with Cuntella. He is the cheerful vessel into which she pours her disgust when she returns home from Berkeley every evening. This year they'll have a winter holiday. Mexico. Hawaii. Get her out of the office. Get some sun on her bones.

It's true: Countervail Press's work atmosphere is progressing from noxious to toxic as Cuntella insinuates herself into its every function. Her fixations—or perhaps Obie Mouret's, hard to know—seem to ride herd over every editorial decision. Manson left last week. His partner, an HR manager with Chipotle, was transferred to Denver, but Cuntella's assigning him to a hagiographic treatment of Ronald Reagan's foreign policy was the last straw anyway. Manson, god love him, told Her Highness, whose adipose bottom happened to be squeezed into leather riding pants that day, to fuck herself and the horse she came in on. He stormed out. She had him photoshopped out of the annual report's "Countervail Press Team" picture spread.

Losing her work-husband, her ally, is foreground trouble—almost, if truth be told, a useful distraction, a practical task to be solved: the hiring of a replacement. What thrums in the background, hums along her taut nerves, is the ruin of an ancient cottage fifteen hundred miles away, a blackened spectre covered now in the snow that began falling at Halloween. She has heard nothing from the RCMP. Sgt. Sinclair has not phoned again. The little fillip of press attention paid to the uncovered bones seems to have vanished in a world in thrall to novelty. Is this a good thing? Is this a bad thing? If silence can be sinister, then the silence from north of the 49th parallel is just that. Briony phoned Advent Sunday, but her news, sad, was of Ted's decline. Lydia commiserated, made no mention of the Thanksgiving storm. She talked with Dorian in Vancouver who, unremarkably, had heard nothing of the weather event in Manitoba. "Bad news, Mrs. Peel," he said tonelessly, though she could hear his ragged breath. "Very bad news."

It's the snow, the snow that smothers that Arctic country, bringing a halt to everything. Nothing will be resume until the frozen lake and frozen land crawl out from under the dead hand of winter. Meanwhile, she eats less. She picks her way through Christmas dinner with Helen and Joe and the girls. She picks, too, at the skin along her thumbs, leaving them raw and bruised. Erin notices. She and Ray trade notes. She's covering everything in the fridge now—even the jars and bottles—with Saran Wrap. She had Ray wave, rather than blow, his birthday candles out, and her tidying up after Misaki is compulsive. It'll be paper seats on the toilet next.

The garage is on the ground floor of Lydia and Ray's house, the living quarters are above—classically San Franciscan. But neither has a car, so the garage is a dank repository of the detritus of modern life. Not for long. Months of to-ing and fro-ing with the city bureaucracy over permits and plans mean the renovation can begin at the end of the month. Erin is eager for a place of her own, but Ray knows his daughter and granddaughter are unlikely to be tenants forever. The flat will eventually be a revenue generator, much needed with their 401Ks severely compromised and some sort of retirement sooner than later for at least one of them. Lydia eyes the clutter over the top of the box of Christmas decorations she's returning to one of the shelves, which will need emptying in advance of the builders. The joy of having Erin and Misaki in the house for the holidays has strained their pocketbooks, as it often does anyway, which makes Lydia even more desperate to find a way to raise money without arousing Ray's notice. It's impossible. If she went to him, she could more explain why she needs a six-figure sum than she could argue for *not* selling Eadon Lodge last summer. That would be confession.

It's January 6, a Tuesday, the end of the annual twelve-day Christmas break Countervail Press takes. The temperature is fifty-five degrees and the sky in the Outer Sunset is patched with grey cloud. It's pleasant with a light jacket. In Manitoba, the weather is bitterly cold, several degrees below zero Fahrenheit. Unpleasant even in a parka. Lydia knows this.

Like some glazed-eyed porn addict, she finds herself drawn to her computer screen, sending her search engine on the lookout for news of bones and bodies and cops in the north, and finds only the plummeting temperatures.

Her eyes fall on her thumbs as she pushes the box of decorations onto the low shelf. The skin is like torn apple skins where she's chewed. She's begun picking at the skin along her feet, too, and they are now two walls of diseased flesh. No one but Ray sees that. This activity is new. She's never done this before. It's like she's some sort of neurotic teenage girl cutting herself. She knows this but can't seem to stop herself. Only when Ray gently takes her hand and pushes it away from her feet does she stop. For a few minutes. Helen wonders, but does not enquire, if she isn't experiencing a kind of delayed grief for the child she gave away all those years ago. *Is it possible?* Sometimes she can't imagine anything worse than going to your grave wondering where your baby is. The rest of them—Ray, Erin, assorted colleagues—blame it on the tension at the office, mad crazy Cuntella, she of the batshit stare and clown makeup and leather pants driving Lydia to breakdown. She lets them think this is true. It's convenient.

She glances at the adjacent box, one of several, marked with felt pen, her own elegant printing, and an inelegant description: *Oxford Street Stuff*. Papers and photo albums and oddities never sorted. Is now the time? Why not? Ray is working in his home office at the back of the house and with the odds and sods of the holiday season cleared up, she's at loose ends. The box is sealed with packing tape, but Lydia takes a battered screwdriver from Ray's work bench and tears open the seal. An aroma of must and dust rises to her nostrils, but something else, too, some tincture of the Oxford Street house, a powerful conjuring of beeswax polish and fresh paint that sets off a wave of unaccountable sadness, her eyes misting as she pulls back the box's flaps. A Freemason's apron is on top, covering Bibs's framed medical degrees, his eyeglasses, his wallet, a purple felt Crown Royal bag filled with old coins, a wooden box with his watch, rings, and cufflinks.

She digs a little deeper—many of the things are from her father's den. She finds again the stationery letterheaded WINNIPEG GENERAL HOSPITAL with the crude bird's-eye of Eadon Lodge and the "X" that so alarmed her she'd put it away, as she'd put it from her mind all these months. Her heart judders a moment, but now she sees the X marks a spot not to the north of the cottage, where Paul was buried, but to the south, roughly the location of the tree downed in that Thanksgiving storm, roughly where Bibs had originally wanted his ashes scattered. She releases a held breath. Perhaps that's all this drawing ever was, a prompt to his heirs from a senescent man.

Really, why is she holding on to these things? Deal with them now, or put it all back in the box and let the dust gather? She lifts the case Helen plucked from the back of the cupboard in Bibs's den. Is it a briefcase? It looks almost like an old-fashioned suitcase a child might have, it's so small. Of course, it's as locked as it was in Winnipeg, key missing. She considers the screwdriver. The case is worth nothing, has no utility, holds no sentiment. She wedges the tip of the screwdriver under one snap and pulls sharply. It doesn't give easily, but after several yanks and a bash with a hammer, it unlatches with a meaty *thunk*. The second snap gives way with more ease, and the lid is freed.

It *is* a briefcase.

From inside, Lydia lifts to the grey light of the garage a beaded metal chain with a couple of steel disks attached, one red, one green, with Bibs's name and number embossed, what appear to be two silver war medals—one with George VI on one side, another with marching figures depicted—a bronze star with "The Italy Star" embossed on it, epaulettes likely taken from a uniform, a small well-thumbed book—a service and pay book, the cover says—and a silver cigarette case.

And the soft bed on which those items rest?—letters, lots of letters.

# 31

"*Rope* came up on TV once, years ago. In the seventies. I was living with Helen, my cousin, then. The opening scene was enough. I couldn't watch it."

"So no comps for you, Mrs. Peel."

"Thanks, but no, Dorian." Lydia's eyes move unwillingly to the artwork on the museum wall, one of Peter Max's, colours so Popsicle-vivid, her queasiness grows. "I don't know how you can bear to be *in* it."

"I play one of the guests, an older man. I'm not onstage until the second act. So I'm not part of that opening scene." Dorian says nothing about his own fraught introduction to *Rope* in the early eighties. "What have you done to your hand? Eczema?"

"No." Lydia glances at her thumb. Her face—it shocked Dorian a little when she pulled off her rain scarf in the lobby—is drawn, skinny Minnie-ish. At least the bubblegum pinkness off the painting plumps it up a bit. "Just anxiety—response to. Everyone thinks it's work related. I haven't asked how you are. How are you?"

"Fine."

"You look fine."

"Do I? Smell my breath."

"I noticed it when you hugged me earlier."

Dorian notes the worry and pity in her expression. "I've had a drink—"

"I guessed."

"—or two."

"You *seem* okay," Lydia says, but reconsiders her assessment. Yes, he is a bit florid, a bit bouncy on his feet. On the phone two days before, he sounded scatty, as if untroubled by the reversal that bound them together anew, but now, she thinks, yes, he'd likely had a drink then.

They agreed to meet in Golden Gate Park at the de Young Museum. It's a short walk for her and a stroll to the park on a Sunday afternoon is nothing that would rouse Ray's curiosity. Dorian came by cab. He could make no sense of Lydia's Muni directions from Union Square.

His eyes travel to a blazing silkscreen of the word LOVE with some vacant flower-sprite creature. He peers at the adjacent tag. *Love, 1968,* it says, no surprise. It's part of an exhibit, *Peter Max and the Summer of Love.* "I was never a falling-down drunk, Mrs. Peel. Just my own little way—sometimes—of dealing with anxiety."

"When did this start?"

"After your phone call last fall. About the ... little holocaust at Eadon Lodge."

"I couldn't *not* tell you, Dorian."

"I know."

"How's ... Mark handling it? The drink—"

"Mark? There is no Mark. We've split. Gone our separate ways." Dorian waves a hand, as if the relationship had been a mere whimsy.

"I am sorry. He seemed very .... Why?"

"He's twenty years younger than me, Mrs. Peel. The young should be with the young. Or the middle-aged with the middle-aged. Or something."

"I'm not sure age is that important."

Dorian shrugs. "It had run its course anyway."

"I'm very sorry."

"So you've said. Don't be."

"Then where are you living?"

"With friends in Vancouver, temporarily. Lot of couch surfing in my line of work." Dorian purses his lips as they step down the gallery. "So with Mark out of the picture, there's no money from that source."

"There wasn't the first time."

"No. I think that my hinting we buy Eadon Lodge was the beginning of the end. Or, perhaps, the end of the beginning of the end. Whatever.

Never mind. The point is ..." Dorian loses his train of thought as he takes in another Max: It's a silkscreen of an enormous blue peace symbol attended by a flock of doves.

"The point is ... ?" Lydia prompts, glancing at the tag, the wording on which is as redundant as half the others. "Oh! Remember that souvenir I brought back with me when I was visiting my cousin here that summer of '67? That ring? Everybody wanted to try it on. Have you still got it?"

"You don't remember?" Dorian feels himself wobble, clutches her arm. "Lydia, the peace ring is with Paul."

Lydia turns to stare. "You mean ..."

"He was wearing it. I gave it to him to wear. It's *on* him."

"But ... why didn't you take it *off* him?"

"It was dark when we—"

"I ... Dorian, *everyone*—all our friends—will remember that ring."

"My point then, Mrs. Peel—what are we going to do?"

"As I've said on the phone, we have to get the property back."

"But your suggestion is—"

"To buy it. To buy it back."

"We're exactly where we were last summer," Dorian hisses, glancing at a docent leading a tour group in their direction. "And like last summer, neither of us has the money. But the question is—is it even for sale? I've looked online. Nothing. Will it ever be for sale? Whatsis—"

"Black, Jonathan Black."

"—Black's heirs may want to keep it, develop it! Who knows? Isn't there a wife?"

"Estranged wife, according to the real estate agent last summer. But there was no mention of a wife in the obituary."

"*Very* estranged, then. Divorced? Maybe. Who would his heirs be? He's young. I'll bet he had no will. Did you have a will in your thirties? He probably died intestate and everything will go to ... who? The wife?"

"I think it depends whether they're divorced or not."

"His parents, then."

"And do you think his parents are going to want to keep a property on which their son died?"

"Why don't you ..." Dorian begins, pulling Lydia away from the clutch of people now gathered around *Peace, 1967*, "... contact your realtor friend in Gimli and see what you can find out?"

"I don't dare, Dorian. She's probably on the same ... curling team as that RCMP woman. It's a small town. They talk. There's that other body, remember ... ?

"A police investigation could put everything in limbo. It could be months before they can—"

"She'd wonder why I'm so interested in a property I was once so happy to get rid of."

"I need a drink."

"No, Dorian ..."

"I said a drink, Mrs. Peel. That could mean simply a nice cup of tea."

Lydia gazes over the de Young's sculpture garden—Henry Moores and a couple of Pop Art apples. The mid-March weather is pleasant, somewhere in the mid-sixties, she guesses, opening her jacket a little. They're sitting at the museum's outdoor patio, Dorian fiddling with something in his shoulder bag. From a distance comes the sound of a brass band in the park's bandshell.

"No smoking here." Lydia guesses Dorian's intent.

"No smoking everywhere." Dorian reaches instead for his wineglass. "Have you heard anything more from the RCMP about the body—the *other* body?"

"No." It's not true. She's had a couple of calls. Winter snows have not completely obliterated the enquiry, which has moved to some investigative unit in Winnipeg. Family history seems to intrigue the inspector assigned the case. Lydia was able to dissemble. What can she say about the world before she was born? She can only repeat what little she knows of her family's history. Are there no dental records? she asked Inspector Dolak at the criminal investigation division of the RCMP in Winnipeg. No matching missing persons reports from the 1930s? None that they can find, he said. Lydia wanted to ask the inspector, as she'd earlier asked Sgt. Sinclair, after seventy years can it really matter? There's no one to arrest now. But she didn't ask. Dolak's answer, she knew, would be the same as Sinclair's.

Seventy? It might as well be forty.

Dorian cradles the wineglass. "At least we know who it isn't. You *are* sure?"

"Absolutely sure. I asked both the sergeant and the inspector about the body's location. It's impossible it's Paul."

"It's impossible there should be another body on that acre of land."

Lydia lifts her teacup and looks over its rim at Dorian bathed in the pearly park light. The memory comes, unprompted, of him crumpled in the shower at Eadon Lodge, oblivious to the hammering water, of her stepping from her own filthy, sweaty clothes to join him, struggle to lift him, begin the ministrations that would end—insane it seems now—in bed.

"Not impossible."

"How not impossible?"

"I think ... I think it's Lits."

"Lits is who?"

"My uncle. My father's brother. You remember. Bibs and Lits. My father had a younger brother—his Irish twin, so-called—who died young."

"That's right, I remember the story now. He was ... mentally challenged or something." Dorian lifts his wineglass, hesitates. He sees something unravelling in her expression and realization dawns. "And he was buried at Eadon Lodge? But ... why? Is such a thing even kosher? I don't remember a marker. I thought ... wait, wasn't he buried in England? How do I know that?"

"Because I must have told you once."

"So—"

"There was shot found among the bones, I told you that on the phone earlier."

"Yes, but—"

"It had to be my father. Or my grandfather."

"Who *shot* him? His own brother? His own son?" Dorian drops the glass. Wine splashes on the table. He studies Lydia's face. "Shot him, your uncle? Lydia, why would you think that?"

"It's horrible thinking it, I don't like thinking it, but ..."

"But?"

"But ... I found some letters among my father's things after Christmas—war letters—some between my father and my grandfather and a few from my father's aunt—my grandmother's sister, May, a spinster who came from Ontario to take care of the boys after their mother died."

"Yes..."

"In one my father describes an Italian boy—simple, my father writes."

"Simple?"

"What we used to call 'mentally retarded.' Intellectually disabled. Like Lits. The boy was killed by sniper fire. This is at Ortona. Your father would have been there, too," Lydia continues, but Dorian, unschooled in his father's war, shrugs. "My father wrote"—and Lydia remembers the words assaulting her as if they had been styled in boldface—"'I thought of Lits and how he died.'"

"That's it?"

"Isn't that enough?"

"No. Maybe just seeing some poor kid die reminded him of his brother."

"'*How*' he died, Dorian. '*How*.'"

"Okay, then, by gun. But *why*?"

"An accident. That must be it. Anything else is too horrible."

"Why wouldn't they report it?"

"Why didn't we?"

Dorian blinks. "We thought our lives would be ruined."

"And they—my father, my grandfather—must have had the same thought. Imagine the consequences of a criminal conviction—"

"I have, I do, Lydia."

"—my father, already motherless, would become fatherless. Medical school was my father's ambition. His future would have been destroyed."

"How would they get away with it?"

"How have *we* gotten away with what *we* did?"

That stops Dorian. He gazes off toward the apple sculptures. *Luck?* Which is running out. "But … England … ?

"This is the point. Lits isn't buried in England. I'm certain. In the eighties, I went to my grandfather's birthplace in Norfolk, which he and my father and my uncle visited before the war, where Lits is supposed to have died of influenza, but there's no gravestone, no record."

"But that doesn't mean—"

"Eadon Lodge is isolated—*was* isolated. We know that. And the trip to England gave them a way to explain Lits's absence." Lydia raises the teacup to her lips. "I always thought my father nostalgic about the cottage. But he wasn't. He was safeguarding it. Why did he never sell it? My mother disliked the place. They could have afforded a cottage where your grandparents had theirs. And then my mother keeping the place after Bibs died. Why? In his dementia, he probably said something, told her enough for her to understand she needed to hold on to the property. And—*and*, Dorian—there was that shotgun on the wall at Eadon Lodge …" Lydia pauses. The tea is growing cold. A thought intrudes. "I wonder …"

"You wonder … ?"

"… why there was shot in the gun when Alan pulled it off the wall that time."

"I don't understand."

"Elvis muttered that the gun was single-barrel. Not something I ever noticed."

"So?"

"I can't imagine the gun was ever used again after what happened to Lits. The barrel should have been empty."

Dorian frowns. "What? You mean … someone reloaded it later."

"Can ammunition still work if it's sat in a gun for decades?"

"You mean Paul, don't you? Loaded it ... as a prank. Where would he get the shells?"

"There were some in the old desk."

Something passes between them: dismay at the callow stupidity of youth, including their own.

"Let's not think about that, Mrs. Peel. We can't know. We'll never know. Just like we can't know, never know, about your uncle."

"We might, if they ask me for a DNA test."

"A DNA ... how—?"

"They can. From teeth and bone."

"Well, so what? So what if poor old Uncle Lits was buried at Eadon Lodge? So what if it's anybody? You're not responsible for something that happened before you were born."

"You don't control a secret, Dorian. A secret controls you. A secret controlled my father. I'm sure this is the secret. And for the last forty years a secret has controlled me ... and you."

# 32

It's late now.

Dorian doesn't hear Paul emerge from the bedroom despite the door's protesting hinge because he's busy crumpling sheets of newspaper into balls and stuffing them into the wood stove. An evening chill has crept into the cottage interior. Dorian feels the linoleum floor cool against his soles, the air cool around his exposed skin. In the bedroom, afterwards, sated, as their slippy bodies dried, he noticed Paul's skin, the scoop of his stomach, turning gooseflesh and suggested a fire. He pauses now to swipe at a sticky trail along his own goosefleshed thigh with a sheet of the newsprint and it's in that moment he senses someone behind him.

"How did you get loose?" Dorian asks, turning to see Paul shimmering in a black, silky kimono emblazoned with golden dragons, the old clothesline in one hand.

"You're no boy scout."

"And you are?"

"Well"—Paul turns the robe's collar up around his neck with his other hand—"I know how to tie a knot."

"You could have got loose while we were—"

"I could have, yes, but you know ..."

This is all so new to Dorian, so free: the iron bedstead a playpen, the old clothesline a lariat, Paul a sexy starfish, splayed, vulnerable, submissive—for once. What would his censorious grandfather say, if he knew, if he had a hint, of what he was doing with this wild child, the two of them, now, with Lydia and Briony miles away, released to fashion their world their way? He watches the flames race down through the stove's cavity, flinches at the sudden roar of paper and kindling and wood catching fire all at once. He quickly covers the stove with its lid, steps back, glances away. He's ravenous. The pot does that. Across the room, on the library table, there's the remains of a vineterta, but he lingers by the stove. The warmth of the fire is delicious along his naked torso.

"Where did you find the robe?" he asks Paul, who has gone to lift the Victrola's lid.

"In the closet in the bedroom."

"It's Marion's," he murmurs, though he doesn't like to imagine Lydia's mother in such a slinky thing.

Paul's back is turned to him now. The robe is too small for his frame, the hem too high, the sleeves too short. Cinched across his slim waist, it throttles the dragon slithering up the silk and ripples with the rhythm of Paul's shoulder muscles as he winds the gramophone. The needle hits the shellac with a crackle and a hiss and the plaintive lilt of an accordion passes from the machine's primitive speaker. Dorian watches Paul lift his arms, watches the back of the robe loosen, sees the dragon freed, then fold and fall to the floor with a silky rustle to offer up a gift—a serpentine line of heedless beauty that dazes and arouses Dorian: bronzed back dipping, pale bottom swelling, taut thighs arcing, limned in a green-gold phosphorescence wrought by the filter of the bedroom screen.

Paul swivels, one hand on hip, his torso in a sleek *contrapposto* to the stance of his feet, and beckons with the other, the invitation clear. Dorian has never danced with a man before. How ... wondrous and strange and defiant. But who will lead? Paul negotiates the confusion of limbs and Dorian finds himself in democratic embrace, no leaders, no followers, as they move to the music over the cool linoleum in no particular pattern. They are the same height, dark and light, one's cheek against the other's. Dorian gazes at the pink shell of Paul's ear, how exquisite. Paul murmurs into his: "Are we okay?"

They weren't okay.

Briony's urgent need to leave for the city, to palliate the headache apparently swelling in her poor little head, stirred the waters in a new way: maybe all of them should pack up and leave—now, together?

But the afternoon was too far gone to tidy the accumulated mess of ten days living at the cottage. (And that outhouse hole still wasn't filled and sodded over!) Unvoiced was reluctance to quit their summer idyll, however much the cooler mornings and hazier sunlight signalled autumn and back-to-school. Dorian was eager to get on to California before Dey and Nan resumed their lives in the city, but he wanted Lydia to leave him and Paul alone in this little bit of heaven, if even for one extra day.

Lydia wanted Dorian to leave her and Paul alone. She suggested coolly that *he* drive Briony back to the city in his Beetle. He flashed on something hooded in her expression and the suspicions Briony kindled earlier in the day flamed. She's *your* friend, he hissed. It's *my* cottage, she hissed back. As if she had overheard, Briony made it clear she expected Lydia to drive her. A flurry of packing, of tracking down missing items, of trips to the trunk of Bibs's car, the last with Paul and Lydia carrying Briony's father's Coleman cooler down the path, through the curtain of trees, Briony turning back to fetch one last thing from the cottage, almost as if she'd planned to forget this one last thing, so she would have Dorian to herself for a minute. In that minute, on the front steps, she, the Reverend Telfer's little girl, turned to him, her expression hard and mean in a way Dorian had never seen in her before and her saying in language he had never heard from her before, "she really is balling him, you know. I gave you a big fat hint in the car earlier. What do you think this afternoon's trip into town was all about? Getting him away from you, *cousin* Dorian."

So Lydia is driving Briony back. She'll stay in the city overnight. That's the plan. The nights are drawing in. She doesn't want to drive in the dark. She'll return to Eadon Lodge in the morning. Dorian won, would have Paul to himself, but Briony's words turned his gut to gall. The effect must have shown on his face, for Briony's lips twitched in a bitter smile before she swept off to the waiting car. A few moments passed, an engine started, tires hit gravel, and Paul returned, emerging from the light in the trees, smiling as if at some private joke. The sight of him seared Dorian with passions never before entwined, dimly recognized—jealousy, confusion, loss and treachery, desire. Paul joined him on the step, teased him with his smile, reached to unzip his fly. Dorian swatted his hand away.

Paul's eyes widened. "What's the matter? Hey, we've got this whole cabin to ourselves for the night."

"You balled Lydia."

"Says who?"

"Briony."

Dorian watched Paul's expression shift, the eyes take on a supplicating shine. "She came on to me. What could I do?"

*Nothing*? The word screamed in Dorian's skull. He was helpless to stop his face crumpling and a sissy tear spurt from his eyes. A swift turning, a blind thrashing into the cottage, into the bathroom, the heavy door slamming shut behind him, the door locking, the surge of mortification for reacting so girlishly. And then Paul's voice on the other side of the door:

"Look, man, I'm sorry. It just happened. Haven't you ever ... ?"

"No."

"I thought you said you and Lydia—"

"No!"

"It didn't mean anything. Hey, we're going to L.A. together—tomorrow, after Lydia gets back. Promise. Come on, Dorian. Look, I'm really sorry..."

Door knob rattling.

"Dorian, come on ..." And then, softly, as if Paul had bent to speak into the keyhole, which he had. "Love you."

Years later he would ponder the absence of the personal pronoun, but then the few—the two—words startled him. They were magic. Only his mother and his grandmother spoke them, and only before he passed into his sulky teens. He looked at himself in the mirror over the sink, and despite the room's gloom with the window blind drawn, he could see the flush beneath his sunbaked skin.

"You can punish me. I know a way."

Dorian didn't understand those words and didn't care. He opened the door.

"We're okay," Dorian murmurs now, pulling Paul closer. The record ends—too soon—in a sequence of scratches. A 78's limit is about three minutes. Dorian reaches over to return the needle to the beginning. They start again. A moth, feathery and dusky, floats over the gas lamps, as if made languid by the warmth. The sun, low in the sky now, filters through the curtain of trees, through the bedroom screens, to brush the floor on which they turn and turn as languidly as the moth. The record ends. They begin again. Dorian is conscious of his erection pressing into Paul's hip, of Paul's into his. He begins to kiss his way down his lover's neck down his torso, the goal apparent to them both. But, as the song ends again, Paul pulls him up and kisses him and says, "I know something else we can do."

# 33

Briony is the last to board the Greyhound and she doesn't wave to Lydia, though Lydia raises her hand in half-hearted way. After a minute, the door closes with a pneumatic hiss and the bus pulls away from Dorothy's Café, headed for who knows how many stops before it reaches downtown Winnipeg.

"How are you going to get home from the bus station?" Lydia asked when they turned off Highway 9, following the Greyhound into Winnipeg Beach.

"Cab, I suppose."

"You could phone your father."

"It'll be late."

"Are you sure you really want to take the bus?"

Lydia offered her one last chance in the rites of politeness. Briony really didn't want to take the bus into the city. Lydia really didn't want to drive her. Briony's migraine was incipient, not crippling. Lydia knew Briony's migraine was incipient, not crippling. And yet they continued the seesaw of lies from their first sighting of the Greyhound as it turned out of Gimli ahead of them onto Highway 9.

"But your head..."

"I'll be fine, Lydia, really I will."

Lydia returns to the car and jams her key into the Buick's ignition, annoyance and elation contending. She's thank-god *relieved* to be shucked of Briony, who's spent the last couple of days all Mother-Superior, lips pressed as if she had sucked something bitter, culminating in her grumpiness over agreeing to take Dorian away to town to leave her free to have some time alone with Paul. Yes, she's sorry Dorian didn't show up with Blair Connon, sorry he showed up with his cousin instead, but she can't help it if men find her more attractive. Perhaps if Briony were less Earth Mother, less frumpy, she might stand half a chance. And Briony so tense and tight in the car as if she were about to explode with god knows what. Lydia turns the car back onto Highway 9 out of Winnipeg Beach, to head north again, return to Eadon Lodge.

*Now we are three.* And there's no more reason for this adolescent sneakiness. Briony is departed, as have Alanna and Alan. No avid ear on the other side of the partition wall. She has the cottage all to herself. Dorian can damn well lump it and stay in the Petit Trianon. Why should he care if his cousin shares her bed? The two of them will be gone on their California adventure before long anyway, if that ever comes to pass.

She rolls down the window, lets her hair blow free, speeds through Sandy Hook, a ragtag trail of old cottages between Winnipeg Beach and Gimli, ignores the speed limit sign, glances at a beautiful boy in swim trunks heading for an evening swim, glances at her watch. The Tip Top should still be open. She'll buy some pickerel for supper, yes. There's still the wine that Alanna brought and Paul will have some weed—yes. She imagines another languorous evening swim, yes. Somehow Dorian will not be present—just she and Paul will be on the beach as day turns night and the moon rises over the lake, a golden orb magnified in the humid air.

Only afterwards—long afterwards—when she allowed her mind to touch on the events of that evening did she recognize she had been visited by premonitions of disaster. Stepping out of the car by Goliath's molars with the bag of groceries, for instance. Why, in that moment, did the silence send a shiver down her back? The evening was still, yes, but sound was not truly absent: leaves stirred, a bird cawed, some small animal rustled in the undergrowth. Yet something stopped her from letting the weight of the car door fall into the frame with that rich, heavy *chunk* her father had found so satisfying; she let metal kiss metal instead, as if not to wake a sleeping baby. Perhaps—she thought this later—the absence of human sounds was the source of her disquiet.

Six people together punctuated the world with noise. But two? No screen door slammed, no voice rose in laughter or argument, no drain flushed, no glass clinked, no radio played. Or did she hesitate, grocery bag gripped to her chest, because the phalanx of trees between car park and cottage seemed to loom before her like a dark forest in a fairy tale? No, nonsense, nothing occult there. The effect was wrought by a low band of black cloud—she had noted it in gaps driving along the Loney Beach road—shielding the sun in its descent to the horizon. And yet, for a moment, she felt as if she were in a film, in those moments before the axe falls, the trapdoor opens, the ceiling collapses.

When she brooded on this later, she wondered, if she had been more susceptible to atmospheres, more intuitive, the way Briony was (or at least thought she was), would she have bided her time, turned back, retraced her route to town for a few hours? If she had, how utterly different her life would have become.

But now Lydia pushes groundless fears from her mind as she steps through the curtain of trees. They're irrational, a chance encounter, she thinks, drawing on her Victorian Identities course, with the pathetic fallacy. She would have leaves dancing, flowers nodding and rocks brooding next, for heaven's sake.

She doesn't see the sun reappear below the band of cloud. Her back's to it. But her heart lifts at the effect. Light moves with arrow speed through the trees, gilding the leaves, bursting against the far cottage wall and blazing it. Everywhere is veiled in gold, the air, the trees, the grass. And—maybe the pathetic fallacy isn't so bankrupt—life responds: Leaves dance in a sudden burst of breeze, the hollyhocks nod, the rocks ... well, the rocks remain impassive, but Lydia's sense of the ominous eases.

She rounds onto the front lawn, where shadows cut deep streaks into the golden lawn. Now she hears strains of music. Someone has the Victrola on. She sees through the dining room window a glimmer of light from deep in the cottage interior. Someone has the electrolier on. She smells wood smoke. The boys have started a fire in the Quebec stove. There is life, and life is good. She mounts the front steps.

The scratchy record continues as Lydia lets the screen door close behind her. She places the bag of groceries on the dining room table, noting the double doors to the living room are closed. Puzzled, but not perturbed, she moves to open them. They are almost always propped open by a pair of old flatirons, closed only on cool evenings to contain the heat of a fire in the stove (and it isn't that cool this evening). The doors are wooden, but the top panel of each is glass, warped through some cheap manufacture, and light, low and mellow, trickles though them. Dorian and Paul have lit the gas lamps. Through the glass, she can see one of the lamps flickering on a stand by the far wall, dappling the room with shadow. The boys are there, they must be, though they are being oddly quiet.

Before turning the doorknob, Lydia angles her head to look deeper into the room. She should be able to see straight to the bank of east windows. She doesn't. Something blocks the view. She sees, but she can't take it in. Can't take it in. Her mind can make no sense of what's before her eyes. Paul is suspended in the air, back to her, hovering, victorious over gravity, a naked angel yet wingless, and he's giving ... a benediction? to someone ... someone ... who? ... Dorian? She glimpses an outline of another figure (who else could it be?) kneeling—can he possibly be kneeling?—in the rocking chair. But it's the electrolier shimmering like a crown above Paul's head that now draws her gaze, upwards from the fantastical vision to ... she can't take it in. She takes it in. It's ... an apparatus. The fantastical vanishes and horror crashes over her in heart-pounding waves. She cries out. She must have cried out. Later, she can't remember her screams splitting the air, her throwing open the doors, tearing across the floor. It all seems a mad succession of sight and sound, terrifying then, terrifying in memory: the door crashing against the sideboard, the rocking chair squeaking frantically, a weight descending before her eyes, a gargled grunt, a strangled cry, a soft snapping, a shriek—and, suddenly, Dorian, mouth gaping in a rictus of terror, eyes staring in a blaze of disbelief.

Can he be dying? How to account for the air turning white around him? He must be dying. Dorian feels himself founder, his legs buckle, his stomach heave, though some primal resolve keeps his bowels from loosening and fouling the floor. Lydia he sees as if through the small end of a telescope. What is she doing here? Why is her mouth opening and closing? Why can't he hear her?

Lydia vanishes.

She is beside him with a knife. He feels her force as she pushes past him, and it is that force, auras touching, that sweeps away the fizzy stars and sends him hurtling back to the sharp-edged world. Someone's legs are kicking frantically near his face. A horrible gurgling sounds from above. And Lydia is scrambling on the rocking chair, failing, screaming, screaming, screaming—he can hear her now—"Help me! Help me cut him down!" He stares up, past the heaving chest to the freakish crown slicing shadows in Paul's scarlet face, along the distended eyes, on to the arms flailing, falling, flailing. The full horror tears into this consciousness. He pulls Lydia off the chair, yanks the top rail around for Paul's feet to perch—as they had when they began—but the chair is heavy, unwieldy, Paul's feet now jerking feebly, toes slipping past the berth. "The ladder!" Why didn't he think of it? Sobbing now, sick with fright, Dorian stumbles across the room to the stepladder leaning against the corner clothes closet, drags it, thrashes at its bloody fucking unwieldiness, Lydia shaking, chanting, *ohgod ohgod ohgod ohgod*. "You!" he gestures vaguely toward the ladder and somehow Lydia understands as he scrambles back onto the rocking chair, finds a balance, and grasps Paul by his thighs, heaving the weight of him into the air, loosening his neck, *oh, god, please god,* from the noose. Lydia—Dorian can hear her crash up the metal steps, hear her keening now, sense her flailing at the clothesline above Paul's head, *oh, god, oh Christ,* and he knows the knife is blunt, know it's one of those fucking crap old knives from the kitchen, *oh Jesus, hurry, hurry, hurry*. The weight of Paul is awful. A wet sob rips from his throat. The weight of him was wonderful.

And suddenly, as if in a dream, Paul careens toward him, send them both flying off the chair and onto the cold, unforgiving linoleum.

"*Wake up, wake up,* please *wake up.*" Dorian's eyes and nose run and leave their wet on the face waxen in the electrolier's light. He presses his lips back on Paul's, willing that they not be cooling, not be motionless, as he forces the breath of life into his lover's throat. He knows nothing of proper mouth-to-mouth resuscitation. None of them do. None of them learned. None of them were offered lessons. Lydia tried the kiss of life, too. But she saw, where Dorian didn't, that it was too late. It was too late even as she sawed and sawed and hacked at the rope.

"He's gone," she intones, feeling a great weariness come over her. She looks at the curve of Dorian's back as he's bent over Paul's body, the buttons of his spine straining the skin. "Dorian." She bends to brush his shoulder and repeats, "he's gone."

A hellish groan corrodes his throat. His face falls from Paul's lips to his bruised neck, pressing against its waning warmth, his body wracked now with sobs. Lydia looks away, as if to allow private grief, looks up, at the ugly electrolier, around, at the gas lamps casting their shadows over the tables and chairs and books and pictures, back up to the frayed remains of rope hanging from the support beam, to the remains of rope loosely encircling a—what is it? an old tea towel?—around Paul's neck. She is dry-eyed. It is shock. She senses this. She knows some convulsion of emotion will seize her, senses its inexorable advance. But not yet, not yet.

"Dorian, *Dorian.*" She is pulling at his shoulder now. He is pushing himself on top of Paul's body, is already pressed chest to chest. "Dorian, *please.* Don't!"

After a minute, Dorian drops his head, as if in supplication, then raises himself, peels himself from Paul's flesh, turns his eyes from Paul's to Lydia's as he pushes himself to his feet, takes in her dazed stare. His jaws move, but nothing comes out. Together, as if their heads were pulled by invisible wires, they turn to look at this incomprehensible *other,* so frail and vulnerable and a word they can barely think, much less say: dead. The bird, expired only days ago in this very room, its glassy eyes staring, flits through Lydia's mind. But Dorian jerks away suddenly. Lydia sees panic swell his eyes. He thrashes from the room. A door bangs open. Lydia hears the agonizing retch, the splash in the toilet, the ghastly groans.

And now here she is, abandoned to this. This horror. She has never seen a ... (and now she must admit the word) ... *dead* ... body before. It horrifies her, confounds her: how can the difference from a sleeping body be so acute? He looks ... dead. He is dead. Paul is dead. She turns her head away, her body trembles, her thoughts roil. Outside, shadows have nearly engulfed the trees and she more clearly sees the room—and her staring self—reflected darkly in the window glass.

*What do they do now?*

Dorian staggers back into the living room, glancing against the door, a fistful of tissues pressed to his mouth. He gapes at Lydia and at the fallen Paul as if he had come upon a wholly novel and astounding scene. Lydia takes in his full presence. She is Eve. She has eaten of the apple. She looks away. "Put some clothes on," she says, her first words of instruction in what will be a terrifying night. Dorian looks down at himself. He is Adam. He burns with mortification. He retreats to the second bedroom, returns in a moment in T-shirt and shorts, Paul's, Lydia sees but doesn't query. It's dark in there, he's lost his mind. She has more urgent questions.

"What were you *doing*? I don't understand."

"We ..." Dorian grips the edge of the sideboard to steady himself. Nausea attacks his stomach anew. "I don't know, I don't know..."

"Was he ... were you ... were you helping him to ... *kill* himself?"

"No, no. It was a ... game."

Lydia's eyes run to the ceiling, to the stub end of the rope disappearing into the darkness of the rafters. "A game ... ?"

"It doesn't matter. It doesn't matter." Dorian can't stand. He sinks down again the wall between the two bedrooms, covers his face. The early evening courses through his mind—Paul's laughing command he absent himself to the Petit Trianon for a time, his own return to the cottage to find the noose in place, his own wondering questions, Paul's tempting invitation, the allure, the transgression, the danger, the dope, the wine, the loss of fear, being out of control and not caring, the why-not. His life had been channelled by fear of what he wanted, of what he desired, by fear of punishment, of ostracization, of obliteration. He'd released himself from his safe place and now, and now .... He can't bear to tell Lydia what they were doing.

But Lydia has an inkling. Such a thing was beyond her wildest imaginings a few moments ago, but now she finds herself in a new and stark world of strange appetites. She is struck by another thought: "But he's your *cousin*."

Dorian groans. He can hear the disgust in her voice. He pulls his hand down his face, rocks his head back and forth. "He's not my cousin."

"What?"

"He's not my cousin. I picked him up hitchhiking coming back from Mom and Bob's."

"Why did you say..."

"I don't know... I didn't want anybody to think I ... we ..."

"Oh, God, Dorian."

Lydia collapses onto the couch. *What do they do now?* She thinks of her parents, of their reaction to this ... to this ... she can't find a word. *Catastrophe*? *Abomination*? Of their shock, horror, embarrassment ... anger. She can't bear to think of her father's anger. How a track of fear threaded through their young lives; fear of parents, of teachers, of authority, of getting into trouble, of getting caught out, of being punished. She recalls the fear she and Ross had when they broke the key. That was only a *key*. A key to this ramshackle cottage. The shame is unbearable. She's ruined. They're ruined. Their parents' lives are ruined.

*What do they do now?* What is the protocol? One of them drives to the RCMP station in Gimli. What will they say? But there is no alternate story they can concoct. Paul didn't just die. Young men don't just *die*. Unless they're in Vietnam or in a car crash or jump off a building high on acid. And the way Paul died is so appalling, so shocking, so *sick*. How will they explain it? Her eyes move helplessly to the body, to Paul's beautiful body. It commands the room. She sees the bruising peeking above the thin towel along the neck. Her heart, fluttering less these last moments, leaps again and begins a new pounding at the scene that would follow. She imagines the face of authority, the questions, the skepticism, the disgust. Can't this go away? Can we run this film backwards? We can't.

"We have to get the police," she says at last.

"No."

"Dorian."

"*No!*"

"What choice is there?"

"No. We can't. We just ... can't. Dey ... Nan ... my mother. How..."

"And what about *his* mother? Oh, god, I can't stand it. Get up and get a blanket from the cupboard. We have to cover him. And his eyes are open."

"Please shut them," Dorian whimpers, struggling to his feet. He pulls a purple blanket from the pile. *Oh, not that one,* Lydia thinks. The others blankets, ill-piled, tumble to the cupboard floor.

"You shut them."

"Please." The blanket slips from Dorian's hand to fall at Paul's feet. "Oh, god ... I can't believe it."

"Close his eyes, Dorian. Do it."

"Oh god," Dorian says again, sinking to his knees, reaching for Paul's eyes, recoiling from the soft-hard of the sclera along his fingertips. Averting his glance, he presses the lids closed. His stomach lurches.

"And now the blanket." It doesn't matter which one it is. "Cover him. Cover his face at least."

Dorian obeys, staggers back, hits the library table. The gas light shudders, throwing spikey shadows over the room, over the shrouded shape on the floor.

"If he's not your cousin, then who is his family? Who *is* his mother?"

"I don't know. Not really. Some people in Toronto. He told us, remember? A mother, his father's d— ... gone. He has a stepfather. Oh, god, oh god." The horror shoots along his nerves and he sinks again to his knees.

"If only he'd gone to the Maritimes," Lydia intones hollowly. "Why didn't he go to the Maritimes? I forget."

"Changed his mind at the last minute." Dorian struggles to stop his voice slipping into a keening. "I don't know, what does it matter?"

Lydia lets this seep into her mind. She lets it rest there where it begins to work like a yeast. "So ..." she says slowly, staring across the room at Dorian, at him in pathetic huddle, his face grotesque, red and puffy, now burrowing into folded arms. She is revolted. She is filled with pity. She wants to flee. She cannot leave him. Their lives are over. Their lives cannot be over.

"So ..." she begins again, "his parents didn't know he came west ..."

"No."

"... no one knows he came this way."

"A few truck drivers on the Trans-Canada, maybe."

"And he didn't call home from your grandparents'."

"No." Dorian's arms muffle his voice.

"No?"

"Yes, no."

"Are you sure?"

"Yes, we never left the house."

"And he never used one of the payphones in Gimli."

"No." Dorian lifts his head, his eyes pleading. "We were only in town once. Lydia, what diff—? Paul is *dead*. What are we going to do, what are we going do? Please, *please*, tell me what we're going to do."

The blackbird once again flies into Lydia's imagination, only this time with a force greater than those in dreams.

# 34

Some on the *Morningstar Cove* set notice a difference in Dorian Grant from the summer before—a deeper webbing in the skin below his eyes, the whites of which look like parchment sometimes, a droop in his jawline—as if he had aged more than one winter. (Rumour has it he turns sixty this year, though Wikipedia says fifty-seven.) His smile is at times watery, his glance preoccupied, his hair, when he arrived in Winnipeg Beach to resume shooting *Morningstar Cove,* brittle, flat black from a bad dye job, which had to be restored to its natural white. Roberta Schreiber, the director of photography, a veteran of the trade, has seen it all, and she would say Dorian Grant has been enjoying a drink or two—which is his business—but if it creeps into his work then it isn't. And it is creeping into his work. He is less well prepared, flubs a line more often than before, and is, at turns, short with the crew. Truth is, he's becoming less of a pleasure to work with.

More truth: Dorian feels hollowed out. His nerves are raw. He wonders at times if he isn't going batty. Sara Hindle, his old Toronto pal who plays his silver-set love interest, knows he's drinking secretly though he accepts only Pellegrino in her company.

Perhaps, he thinks, not for the first time, as he cleans off his makeup, he shouldn't have signed on again for this fakakta kiddie show. No one forced him. (Well, except his pugnacious agent, Charmaine, with her eyes on the money.) His character could have been written out of the series. But he felt his choice was again Hobson's. He had to come back here, to this navel of his little world. The almighty Internet has failed him—and Lydia—and there is something he is desperate to know. He couldn't bear another month of waiting.

It's Dorian's first day off from filming, a grey Saturday morning in early June, punctuated by half-hearted spurts of rain that make dust craters on the sidewalk next to the real estate agent's on Centre Street and dance on the baseball cap pulled low over his forehead.

He doesn't remove his sunglasses to read the for-sale notices in the window, though he'd have an easier job reading the print if he did. He's more recognizable in this town now, what with *Morningstar Cove* having run a course on TV. Every once in a while—in San Francisco, in Vancouver, in an airport, in a restaurant—indifferent eyes will pass over his and brighten in vague recognition. He doesn't *not* take pleasure in such encounters. He isn't oblivious to his own narcissism. But for once in his acting career he actively seeks the anonymity of dark dead glass barricading the windows of his soul. He thinks about Dirt Guy and Elvis, who crossed their path at Eadon Lodge all those years ago and now, more urgently than last summer, he wonders—paranoid as it is—if they're still around town, able to see the boy in the man if they glimpse him, and connect him to the past.

He lights a cigarette, cupping his hand against the splats of rain, and looks from one notice to another, anxious to find, dreading to find, the one that will advertise the former Eadon Lodge property's availability. He will buy it. He will remortgage his half of his Toronto house. This he has agreed with Lydia. Then, at his leisure, by stealth—somehow—he will do what he was prepared to do last summer in haste and madness—excavate the property and remove all evidence—then put it back on the market.

But these notices don't, any more than the Internet listings, declare Eadon Lodge for sale. His focus shifts to his own reflection in the tinted window glass. He sees his mouth a thin thing, turned down in a Beaker frown, and runs his hand involuntarily along an incipient crease running from nostril to jaw. The bottom half of his face looks haggard. He affects a smile and peers through the glass. He notes people in the office, though the tinting obscures their features. He hesitates. He has the rest of his cigarette to decide. Carol Guttormson will surely recognize him, sunglasses or no. He doesn't want to deal with her. What if the property *isn't* on the market? Will she store his query in her mind like a squirrel with a nut? But as he waits a middle-aged woman pushes out through the door. Glimpsing past her, he sees inside a lone male in a yellow polo shirt, young, buzz-cut, barely more than a boy. He flicks the butt to the sidewalk and steps in. He keeps his sunglasses on. He is, he says casually, interested in properties north of Loney Beach.

The boy smiles with practised delight and trips off a few listings.

"I heard there might be one where there'd been a fire or something last fall."

He's met with an accordion forehead, quickly smoothed by enlightenment. "Oh, I know—where they found the body."

"Body?" Dorian goes cold.

"Some guy from way back."

*Way back?* To someone this child's age Princess Diana's wedding is way back, Watergate is way back, the moon landing is way back.

"When did they find this body?" Dorian's grateful for the sunglasses, grateful for his training in voice control.

"Last fall."

*That* body. Christ, Dorian thinks, I need a drink.

*That* body isn't important. Lydia has heard no more from investigators about *that* body, though he knows, for she's told him, that *that* body feels like a straw and her back the camel's. He's worried about her. She sounds awful on the phone.

"A fire *and* a body," Dorian says wishing, for Lydia's sake, he could pursue local gossip. "That's something. It must be going cheap, then."

"No one's made a listing with us."

"Someone else?"

"We're really the only game in town." His fingers fly around his keyboard. "And it's not on multiple listings."

"Just a whim."

"I can ask my colleague when she comes in, Mr. ... ?"

"Really, it's nothing." A peek over this sunglasses, a smile, and he's gone.

Dorian lights another cigarette and strolls down past the old hotel to Tergesen's. He can't think where he might glean some information about the fate of the Eadon Lodge property. The bakery? The hotel? The library? The museum? He can't go to the RCMP, of course. A bell tinkles above his head like a zazen announcement as he pushes through the door into the store redolent of cloth and leather and old wood—but with none of the crowd present when he and Mark visited last year. The jammed racks of summer clothes hold no interest for him. He heads to the book annex at the back. There you can loiter, strike up a conversation. And Dorian does, though he has to lift his sunglasses and reveals himself. His interlocutor is an older woman, round of frame, round of face, whose welcoming smile from behind the sales desk doesn't quite reach her eyes, which are discerning, a merchant's. He affects interest in some local titles on a nearby table. *The Beauty and Treachery of Lake Winnipeg* is the subtitle of one of them.

"I hear you had some treachery here last fall," he says, turning the cover to the woman.

She lowers her glasses, glances past the rims, one eyebrow rises. "The publisher'll need to do an update."

"That bad?"

"Pretty bad. A lot of damage, a lot of trees down, roofs gone, boats sunk."

"And some deaths, I understand."

"Three."

"Terrible. I think I heard one of them was a tree falling on a cottage and killing the owner."

The woman nods, bends her head to a pile of books on her desk that need new pricing labels affixed. She finds the customer insincere, and she knows who he is, one of the *Morningstar Cove* actors; her granddaughter is devoted to the series. "He'd only just bought the place, too."

"What a shame. But there was something about another body..."

"You mean the former mayor. Her car crashed into—"

"No, I meant a body, long buried, uncovered—"

"Yes, yes." She has much to do and is feeling impatient, finding the customer curiously pointed in his questions. "Found on the same property where the tree killed the young man. It's a bit of a mystery, really."

"They don't know who it is?"

"Not that I know of. It's seventy years ago or more, the burial. There's not many left around here who can remember those days—at least clearly."

"The investigation's ongoing..."

"I suppose," the woman says noncommittally. Yes, it is ongoing. She was talking with Sergeant Sinclair only the other day, telling her about her father-in-law, who lives down the street at the Betel home and has, at age ninety-one, a mind as clear as the bell over the store's front door. Baldur says there was always something queer about the Eadon family that owned the property for years and years. The old man had two sons—Baldur used to knock around with them a bit when they were boys. One of the sons was *þroskaheftan*, could be violent and got hard to handle when he got older. And then, one summer before the war, there was only one son, the smart one, what was his name? Malcolm. "Bibs," they called him.

"Odd, the two deaths," Dorian remarks.

"Well, seventy years apart."

Dorian flips through book, affects nonchalance. "The property must be haunted. I wonder who will buy it?

"The old Eadon property? I don't know."

"Not for sale?"

"I haven't heard." She has too heard. It's not for sale. It's sold. Or, rather, the owner, the heir of that young University of Manitoba lecturer who died, has made some private arrangement with her own family disposing of the property, with some redevelopment plans already approved by the rural municipal council. The woman behind the desk is amused to thwart her interrogator. Like many townsfolk, she endures the presence of tourists for the sake of commerce. "If you're interested in it, you might check with the real estate office down the street."

Dorian give his head a sharp shake to the negative. "This book looks interesting. I think I'll get it."

The woman's smile snaps to the midpoint of her face. "I hope you enjoy it. The cash desk is in the next room."

Dorian retraces his route down the June-green tunnel through Loney Beach that he travelled with Mark the year before, the route he travelled with Paul forty years before, in that rattle-trap Volkswagen, stripped to the waist, stubble on their chins, Paul's dope in his backpack, Dey's gin in his, Top 40 on the tinny radio, looking for adventure. His rental car, a boring Chrysler that smells of new fake leather, purrs along in air-conditioned splendour, though the temperature doesn't warrant it. The Sirius satellite radio, which, irritatingly, he can't figure out how to adjust, plays a tune faintly recognizable—what is it?—a baroque instrumental of something Beatle-y. The words trickle into his head: *There are places I remember all my life, da da da da ... some are dead and some are living...* No thanks. No fucking soundtrack, please. Thank god the radio's on/off button holds no mysteries.

His heart is beating faster. He hates this, hates that his fear and trepidation intensify with every mile. How insane is it to return—this year—to the scene of the ... of the ... (he shuns the c-word) ... anyway? This is *insane*. If there's no indication of the Eadon property's fate in town, why would there be here? Maybe a sign, a notice ... a clue? He feels uncannily like he's slipped into a dreamscape, a variation of the one that's beset him for years, of travelling down this very road, more often—and inexplicably—in blinding winter white, toward a nameless, unpeopled doom—while wraithlike figures press against him. They are not—he knows this instinctively, the way you do in dreams—Lydia or Briony or Alanna or Alan, or even Paul. They are the bit players—Dirt Guy, Elvis, Band-Aid Girl—gathered like some malevolent bon voyage party.

Dorian parks. The three-stone barrier is there, eternal. He gets out of the car. No notice, no sign. At least here. He hesitates. He should turn back. He can't help himself: He finds himself drawn forward inexorably, much as he is in the dream. This is *insane, insane*. He walks the path, pushes past new-minted leaves, luminously green in the morning's pearly light, conscious of his own quickening breath, his footfalls, his keys jangling. Already absence is presence: the view through the crosshatch of branches is of distant trees, not of white cottage wall. He slaps back a branch and, suddenly, he is on a blasted heath—of fire-blackened tree trunks, of fire-blackened grass, of fire-blackened waste. He pushes his sunglasses to his forehead. The magnitude of the destruction stuns him. Eadon Lodge itself has vanished, reduced to ash spilling over the scorched cement pad, only the stark outlines of old fridge and old cook stove—triumphant over all—suggesting the life once lived in this place. Utterly unnerving is the fallen fir, a brutal thing, slashing the open space as if an enraged giant had thrown down his stave. Its trunk is charred and pitted, a few branch stubs pierce the air like withered arms, a maze of exposed roots clings to a clot of soil ripped from the anchoring earth. It killed someone and, in way, resurrected someone else. A strip of blue and white ribbon droops off a root end in the motionless air, a relic of last fall's police presence, Dorian realizes. Yes, the opened grave is *here,* at this southwest corner, not over *there,* at the northeast, past the shell of the Petit Trianon. This is only confirmation; it is no relief. His eyes linger on that distant corner. New grass pushes through fire-blackened patches, some trees are singed, but they are intact. Paul's resting place is intact.

He takes out another cigarette, lights it with a shaky hand (*god, his nerves are taut*) but doesn't let go the match, though he might wish for another fire, an even fiercer conflagration this time, an explosion of flame that would turn six feet of earth to ash and blow it sky high. He wishes his mind wouldn't travel back to that fateful night, but it does.

"*What?*"

"You heard me."

Dorian heard her. He can't believe it. He stuffs his hands over his ears. He won't hear it. He can't stand up. He can't sit. He wants only to lie down, curled next to Paul, next to the shrouded shape that is Paul ... was Paul. "No," he says, pauses to draw breath, draw out the word. "*Noooo!*"

"Then we have to go to the police, Dorian. What else is there to do? We can't leave him here."

Dorian looks wildly around the room. He can't think. He can't think. Lydia can think for him. But her tone is suddenly furious:

"This is your fault. This has nothing to do with me."

"Oh, don't." Dorian whimpers. Her words sting. "Please don't." He looks at her. A world outside this nightmare intrudes. He gasps, "Briony! Where ... ?"

"On the bus. She decided to take the bus."

"You weren't supposed to come back until the morning."

Lydia flings her hair back over her shoulder. "Are you suggesting ... ?"

"No ... I don't know. No."

And yet Lydia feels a sickening stab of culpability. If—always the *ifs* that will haunt her all her life—she had taken Briony to the city as she had said she would, as they thought she was going to, she would have been none the wiser. She would know nothing of this. Nothing as bizarre, as shameful, as shocking as this ... this, whatever they were doing. And Paul would be alive. Of course, he would be alive.

Silence imprisons them. A visitor, a ghost perhaps, would see two figures hunched, heads bowed, praying perhaps, though one is sobbing to sear the soul. A visitor would hear the dying fire crackle, gas lamps hissing, the old fridge rattle in the next room, a bird outside caw harshly. He would wonder at the mantled shape on the floor, clearly human. He might wait for one of them to speak, or he might not have the patience, as it's a while before one of them does. It's Dorian, his voice hoarse, breaking, beaten:

"Where then?"

"We have a place already. We don't have to dig."

"I don't under—?"

"Where the outhouse was."

Dorian lifts feverish eyes to hers. "Oh, no. No!"

"It has to be filled anyway. I promised my father it would be."

"I can't do it. I can't. It's ... unimaginable. It's a ... Lydia, it's a ... I can't put him there. I can't put someone ... oh, god, someone I loved down there." Fresh tears spill over Dorian's lids. "I loved him, don't you see?"

Lydia stiffens. Moments ago Dorian and Paul were cousins, second cousins, blood. Moments ago she anticipated Paul being in bed with her. Moments ago, her world stood right-side up. "You've known him for all of ten days.

"I don't care. That doesn't matter. How long should it take?"

"That didn't look like love to me."

"What would you know?"

"What would *I* know? What would *I* know? More than you, you ..."

"You ... ? You what? Say it."

Lydia's control breaks. Hot tears sting her eyes. She can't stop them coursing down her face, can't stop her strangled scream: "You *pervert!*"

The word snaps the air between them, then rips through Dorian's gut like a burning lance. Sticks and stones may break his bones, but words have never hurt him—because the words, *those words,* have never before been said to his face.

"Oh, god, I can't believe this," Lydia puts her head in her hands, tries to gulp back tears. "I can't believe what's happened. I can't believe I'm sitting here and ... *he*'s there, d—." She severs the word, lowers her hands. She wants to hurt Dorian, hurt him badly, with all the hurt and rage at her command. "Do you know how your father died? Do you have any idea?"

"What ... ? My father? What's that got—"

"He hanged himself."

"What?"

"You heard me. He *hanged* himself."

"He died in a car accident."

"No, he didn't."

"How do you know?"

"My father told me. People have been keeping the truth from you for twenty years!"

"I don't believe it. Why are you saying this? Why are you telling me this?"

"I don't know. *I don't know!* Because you were doing *this*, playing this ... *game!*" Lydia jerks her arm toward the ceiling.

"Oh, god ... why did—"

"I don't know *why*. I just *know*!"

Dorian looks at Lydia through bleary eyes, her face a blotchy shapeless arrangement of pink and white. He'll remember this day, this hour, these minutes as the very nadir of his existence, an expulsion from paradise, the end—cruelly, fantastically—of their long and safe and privileged childhood. Their lives have unravelled. He wipes the snot from his face, the wet from his eyes, Lydia's features come into focus: the eyes staring wide, the mouth twisted, her whole face burning with what looks to him to be anger or terror.

Silence descends between them once again. The wood in the stove crackles, but with less intensity; the cottage is cooling—both could feel it—the light from the west—both could see through the bedroom screen—almost vanished. The clock on the library table—Lydia, nearest, can hear it—ticks with relentless measure.

"Not that hole." Dorian's words arrive as a tired sigh. "I can't put him there."

"What do you think would happen if we dug a fresh grave?"

"Don't say 'grave.'"

"What would happen?"

"I don't know... someone would notice?"

"Someone would *see*, Dorian. My father would. The broken grass, the mound of earth..."

"They'll come looking for him."

"Who?"

"His parents, the police..."

"Not here."

"But ... Briony, Alanna..."

"Paul left, went back to hitchhiking."

"I was going with him."

"You changed your mind."

And it was decided. They were terrorized, naughty children, defaulting to a child's actions: to deny, to cover up, to lie. Dorian remembers them beginning the task in a silent rhythm, as if they had rehearsed it in their adolescent dreams, somehow suppressing the horror of fashioning the Coronation blanket into a proper shroud, a purple package tied with bits of the offending clothesline, of lifting him—oh, god, the dead weight, the jelly lifelessness. He lifted him, Dorian did, carrying him, *Pietà*, pushing through the screen door, stumbling through darkness, followed by Lydia with one of the gas lamps, a ghostly procession to the Stygian hole at the far reaches of the property, sinking to his knees next it and then, only then, emitting a low keening that would not, could not stop, until finally the fateful, irrevocable step—the ignominious rolling of the body into the pit. And the sound, the sickening thud as body in motion meets immovable object.

Shuddering at the memory, Dorian doesn't hear the footfalls behind him, nor the jangling of dog tags on a collar, nor the pronounced throat clearing until the man with the dog is before him and he's looking into old eyes rimmed with suspicion and disapproval. Dorian starts, stumbling against one of the fallen fir's blackened roots. The sunglasses bang onto his nose.

"Are you staying in the area?" the man asks, reaching to pat his dog, a black Labrador.

"No." Dorian brushes his shirt sleeve, annoyed. The shirt is white, streaked now.

"Just visiting then."

"Yes."

"We've had a number of visitors come here."

"Oh, yes?"

"Kids, scavengers—"

"Scavengers?"

"Attracts a certain type, this kind of thing does. Amazing what people will take. Sinks. An old toilet." There's an insinuation in the man's tone, and Dorian bristles with distaste for this officious asshole. He's seen the neighbourhood watch signs along the way in. He affects the cold drawl he used in a play or two: "I knew the family that owned this. I came here once as a teenager." As he says this, his eyes travel with the scorn of his comparative youth to the older man's cheeks with their broken veins, the sunken eyes, the wattled throat. He catches his breath, rues his declaration. The man's censorious regard is the trigger: This is the guy who appeared among them when Alan's shotgun blast grazed Paul. It's Elvis, hair subsided to a monk's tonsure. He sends his eyes to the dog. *Christ!* Same breed.

"I just thought I'd come see," Dorian softens his tone. "I ... heard what happened."

The man grunts, continues to study him as if unmollified but—and thank god, Dorian thinks—the sunglasses and baseball cap lend him the anonymity of a tourist.

"Well, I like to keep an eye out," the man says.

"Are you working for the owners, then, in some capacity?"

"No."

"Ah, well, I was sort of wondering what will come of this. Funny it hasn't been cleared."

There's something slick about this guy, the man thinks. The linen shirt, that expensive car, something shiny (*moisturizer?*) about his face, what he can see below the sunglasses. What's he really doing here? Most of the other rubberneckers he's known, cottagers from way back, have places at Loney Beach; a few Winnipeggers have happened by to gape, these days including Filipinos or East Indians. This property, he's pretty sure, will be cleared before too long. He's seen folk—other out-of-towners—coming and going, and his councillor mentioned that some development scheme has passed the bureaucratic hurdles of the municipal council. So if this guy is some rival developer—well, tits up, buddy, too late. He's had a cottage here for nearly fifty years, been walking his dog up here for nearly fifty years, seen the number of cottages explode, big buggers too—not really cottages, but second homes, and he expects whatever's built here will be as big and brazen.

When the man fails to reply, Dorian continues, "Is it on the market? I don't see any signs."

"Are you interested in buying?"

"No. Just ... curious. Nice beachfront ... as I recall."

"Less of it after last fall's storm."

"Is it for sale?"

The man enjoys playing this guy. There's something familiar about him, too—something about his eyes before the sunglasses dropped over them—but he can't put his finger on it, some wisp of an unhappy memory of long ago. "Beats me," he replies, smiling. "Check with the real estate office in town. They're sure to know."

# 35

Her cell rings as Lydia exits the flower shop on Irving. It's Dorian. She recognizes the number. She doesn't answer. She would have a flicker of dread—or, possibly, if it were another day, even yesterday, a flicker of hope—but she already knows what he has to report. It's been a day for phone calls, and she doesn't like to talk on the phone in the street.

She watches the fog beginning its progress up the street from the ocean. Fool her: she should have put on the quilted jacket when she exited the house, but she was too anxious to leave. When the fog rolls over her the temperature will drop ten degrees in an instant. She's skin and bone these days, they say—and she overhears—down to a size four, the envy of her book club, though the six of them say nothing to her about her chewed thumbs, her dull eyes and dull hair. They know she's anxious about her job—they chitchat more than discuss literature—but is there something else? Is it Ray? Her marriage? That can't be. It's Ray who sent them the invitations to Lydia's birthday party this evening, through the mail, no less. The Big Six-Oh! in a lovely script only an artist like Ray would fashion. Maybe Lydia's just anxious about turning sixty.

Lydia's given precious little thought to the milestone birthday, politely acceding to Ray's plans for a big party, graciously giving in to its inevitability. It's that other (possible) inevitability that's been consuming her thoughts, never more so than today. She shivers, and it's not in anticipation of the blanket of fog creeping toward her. She shifts the cone of freesias in her hand and pockets the phone after glancing at its screen. Dorian has left a message.

Helen's call first. Busy, buoyant Helen, who is bringing the cake for the party. Did Lydia know, she asked as she about to ring off, that a *body* had been found on the grounds at Eadon Lodge? One of the Winnipeg Clifford cousins who had somehow put two and two together and mentioned it in a letter. *Oh, Jesus Christ, fresh hell.* Lydia fought to control her breathing, jerked the phone away so Helen wouldn't hear. Somehow, Helen continued, a bunch of bones popped out of its grave last fall during that big storm they had up there. She thought she was being entertaining and wondered a little at the dead air on the other end. *Really? I had no idea,* Lydia managed to croak when she recovered her sensibilities. *How odd.*

And now Ray will wonder if that's why the RCMP contacted her last fall. It wasn't Canadian politeness, it was police procedure. And Helen, of course, will not keep mum—not that Lydia could ask her to. She will make it her party piece. Lydia has yet to concoct what she will say to Ray, not knowing that he already knows, has done his own Googling.

Lydia glances at the window of Ouroboros Fine Used Books as she passes. Amid the display, visible by its glaring use of Psychedelia typeface, is that sow's ear—*Paul is Dead*: *The Twilight of the Sixties and Utopia's End* by Brander Milne, Cuntella's little friend. Published in early March, now, at the end of June, it's already slouching toward oblivion. The reviews are dismal, the sales worse—as she knew they would be—but Cuntella is scapegoating her for her failure to fashion a silk purse. How many drafts of a resignation letter has Lydia devised? Many. But many days she keeps a level head only by the routine of work: up, out, BART, some office chatter, nose into manuscript, out, BART, home, dinner, bed. She walks on, feeling the air chilling, though the bank of fog remains a distance away. *Paul is Dead*? The least of her worries. Paul is dead? Another matter entirely.

A milestone birthday brings the well-wishers out of the woodwork. But Inspector Dolak could hardly have been aware that this Saturday was her birthday. Or could he have? Now here she is submitting to the simmering paranoia that infects her adopted country. She remembers a mini-bout of this sensation in the seventies when she was, briefly, a proofreader for *Ramparts* in its FBI-targeted twilight. The same sensation revisits her today: an almost occult sense of being watched. Crazy, yes? She's had no communication with the Canadian police since Sergeant Sinclair's call last fall and here they phone on a Saturday, a *Saturday*—to unsettle her, to goad her? She had imagined the Case of the Mysterious Bones had gone cold after all these months, but not so. Inspector Dolak's weekend is taken up with it, apparently, though something about his tone suggested he thought investigating the provenance of bones buried seven decades a pain in the neck. He apologized, though, for the Force's not getting back to her sooner and asked: Would Lydia submit to a DNA test? This is what she feared, this is what she told Dorian might happen. She affected nonchalance. (*I can't imagine what it will prove, but if you like ...*) Was there a choice? What fresh hell—speaking of fresh hells—would refusal bring?

And yet that fills her with nothing like the foreboding Briony's innocent phone call has wrought.

Lydia walks along Irving, passing Citibank and Walgreen's, glimpsing the brooding fog, so much damper in the Sunset, draw nearer, almost craving the cloak it will be. The Outer Sunset, her home for a quarter-century, is foggy, windy, mostly flat—not tourist San Francisco, a sober place, an acquired taste. She can see the Pacific Ocean when she steps out her door, feels as far away as you can get in North America. She has a sense, however irrational, that she may never walk this way again.

Briony's phone calls stir her guilt, always. Briony's the good friend who stays in touch. Lydia wishes she wouldn't, wishes the connection would wither and die, so the past she represents would no longer flame into life. So she pushes Briony out of mind from day to day, from year to year, but she can't now. Not this minute. She expected Briony's condolences and curiosity at Eadon Lodge's destruction months and months ago, at least in their phone conversation last Christmas. She learned then of Ted's decline. Now, today, she's learned Ted's MS has worsened precipitously. He's been choking on his food, he's been growing delusional, violent, she's been battling the Home Care bureaucracy. Ted went into a nursing home this month. Briony's matter-of-fact, hardened in some ways to the terrible chaos of life—hers, her children's, her husband's, her clients'. Lydia made all the right remarks, all of them anodyne, for what could she do for Briony? And all the while she wanted to twist the conversation to her own desperate urgency: what have you heard, what do you know, about the cottage? How can that property's fate be so sealed? Briony chattered away: Imagine us being sixty. Who'd think we'd be as old as our parents? Don't trust anyone under thirty, ha ha! Hope you have a wonderful day! Have a great party! Oh, and I forgot to mention—Eadon Lodge: I was sorry to hear it burned down. Last fall, Briony added in a tone that suggested Lydia should have got in touch with *her* over this incident. Oddly, Briony seemed to know nothing about the old bones raised to the sky, or at least she didn't mention it to Lydia.

But Briony did learn something about the property. It's from whom she learned it, and the details she imparted, that sent Lydia hurrying out the door—jacketless. Briony ran into Alanna just the other day. At an Italian grocery, each shopping for the same take-out lasagna. Hadn't seen her in years, though Briony's always surreptitiously kept up with the doings of the Roth-Rayners, their wealth, their success, their Crescentwood home, their Lake of the Woods cottage, their Warhols, their terrible, troubled son. And their lovely, accomplished daughter, who has some big job at the University of Winnipeg and who, like her mother, it seems, married someone not quite suitable in the parental eye, but unlike her mother, was on the verge of divorcing him when the marriage was severed another way, rather spectacularly.

"I suppose it's ironic who owns Eadon Lodge now," Briony said.

And Lydia agreed, her voice catching, her hand shaking, the phone dropping.

And now Dorian is calling again. She feels the vibration in her pocket more than hears the tinny ring against the ambient noise along Irving. The fog is nearly upon her, its wispy tendrils snaking along the sidewalk, veiling the store fronts, shrouding the cars. It all seems a little too Gothic in the circumstances, she thinks, adjusting the cone of flowers and reaching into her pocket.

Dorian refrains from the preliminaries. He doesn't remember it's her birthday.

"Lydia, there's heavy equipment at Eadon Lodge. We were filming on the lake yesterday and I could see them moving into place. I finally found out today who the property passed to. It's worse than we could ever imagine."

Lydia welcomes the cool damp as it wraps around her. She feels borne along by it, as she would by a river's current. "I know, Dorian. I already know."

# 36

Alan would happily cut short this visit, wishes he could find an excuse to leave, but enduring his host's company is, in this instance, the price of doing business.

Stuart McFadyen, his business partner in this Gimli property development deal, is tolerable company, man to man, man among men, as they have been this morning at the Sandy Hook golf course with a few of his local cronies. And he's tolerable at larger social events, fundraising dinners and the like, where he presents himself as expansive and charming. But at this couples getaway at the McFadyens' Pelican Beach house he's shown an unpleasant facet of his personality—talking down to his wife as if she were a stupid little girl. And Mariëlle is a senator, no less, appointed in the last round of prime ministerial honours. Stuart was the local party bagman for years, but it was his *wife* who got the honour. Prime ministerial humour? Prime ministerial oversight? Or did the prime minister's eye rove past Stuart's Humpty-Dumpty proportions to rest on Mariëlle's svelte form and decide the Red Chamber was in better need of decoration than another old toad? Is this why Stuart is such a boor around his wife?

But there's more: Alan has fallen in love with her, with a violent and unexpected jolt.

Some time later, after the contrived fancy-meeting-you-heres and the fumbled grope at the Gallery Ball in which she will shrink from him, her body contracting in a way that signalled her disgust, he'll recognize it as infatuation, born of some little acknowledged absence in his life. But at this moment, this Friday in July, the yearning, the adolescent cry, *I want more,* feels intensely like the real thing, a euphoria rising from somewhere in the gut and racing along his veins. This bolt out of the blue, so unexpected so late in life, is why he's delaying returning to Stuart's. He stopped to pick up another case of beer from the motel along the highway. He told Stuart he would do so when they were leaving the golf course. But at the back of his mind was a detour to the property they're jointly developing, the old Eadon place. It's crazy, but it's the only goddamn place he could think of for a little privacy, to have a think, to indulge these feelings of lost control. If he's too much more in Mariëlle's orbit, Alanna will twig to the gravitational pull, and he can't have that—not yet. So it isn't nostalgia sending him up the road through Loney Beach .

His memories of those days forty years ago at Alanna's friend's summer cottage run through his thoughts like disjointed scenes in a barely remembered film. None are particularly vivid. What stands out? Deliriously plowing Alanna over and over and over in a tent until he almost lost consciousness? That stands out. Laying sod over that shithouse hole? That stands out, too, mostly because whatshisname ... Dorian and that so-called "cousin" of his didn't lift a goddamn hand to help. Wait, not true, he has one vivid memory. Has he been repressing it? Jesus, there was a time when he had nightmares about it. He nearly killed that guy, that "cousin," with a loaded fucking shotgun. *That* stands out. If he'd had better aim, if that guy—*Paul, was it?*—had veered another way, god knows what his life would be like now.

Alan glances into the rear-view mirror and sees for a moment his eyes, the lids drooping a bit, the laugh-lines clearly visible, but not bad, not bad. He lifts his hand from the steering wheel and brushes it through his hair, which is still thick. His jawline shows a hint of incipient sag, but only a hint, and when he smiles he still has that boyishness Alanna once told him first attracted her. He's a damned sight more attractive than Stuart, whose hair, vanished well below the crown, is worn hippyishly long, whose face is as pale and freckled as Puffed Wheat, whose paunch hangs over his belt like a melting pumpkin.

*I love you, Mariëlle.* The words, rehearsed, run through his head. He says the words out loud, flicks a glance in the rear-view mirror, reddens. He's not a blusher.

He and Alanna live much like siblings these days—the dwindling in ardour and frequency a mystery almost untraceable. When did they last have sex? (Passover, if you can believe it.) He wonders about the ebbing for other guys his age, but he really hasn't got any close buddies any more, guys he might consider broaching the subject with over a few beers. The men he knows now—he acknowledges this dolefully—are all colleagues, employees, business partners, bullshitters—like the great son-of-a-bitch Stuart McFadyen, who roared off ahead of him on the highway as Alan turned into the motel parking lot. His boyhood pals? Vanished. His university comrades? They were never friends, only soldiers in a revolution that never came to pass. He became a nonperson to them when he betrayed the great working class to join his capitalist-stooge father-in-law's construction business.

Alan's mind switches, helplessly, to Mariëlle's slimness, her elegance, her aloof grace, and compares them—unfairly, he knows—to Alanna's, whose backside has swelled like a summer cloud, whose complexion has turned sallow, whose manner has become severe. Unfair, because Mariëlle is more than a decade younger. Unfair, because Mariëlle hasn't had the marrow sucked out of her by a child gone off the rails by addiction. Unfair, because Mariëlle, a successful businesswoman, is not a vapid shopaholic like the wives of many of his colleagues. Will he ever have her? He senses she senses his ardour. She avoids his glance. He feels humbled and speechless in her presence. He'll never have her. Should he dare try to have her? Almost alone among his associates, he has been uxorious. But when his father-in-law brought him into the business, made him crown prince in place of his dead son, he extracted this promise: no whores, no girlfriends, no fucking around behind my daughter's back, for Alanna was the apple of his eye and the crown of his labours. And Alan swore fealty because Berko Roth was a fierce old bugger and because he saved him from a life of idiocy and because he loved Alanna. Still loves her. In his way.

Alan stops at the building site. Three big rocks once barricaded the property to traffic. He remembers that. Alanna nearly dinged one of them parking her Mustang on their arrival. They're gone now, of course, removed to allow heavy machinery access. He lifts his eyes through the windshield to the middle distance. A few healthy trees remain, retained to lend eye-appeal to the development. They form a paling, and Alan can detect the sunshine flash of an excavator in motion. It's almost noon. The machine's operator should be knocking off soon for lunch.

Alan steps out of the car into the July heat to the tortured shriek and grind of machinery that's so been the soundtrack to his working life it might as well be Muzak. He notes the old footpath to the cottage vanished, a broad rutted swath of ruined grass marked with the trails of caterpillar treads in its place—no surprise. How else is heavy equipment to move on site? He's expecting no surprises, anyway. When he bought this property from his late son-in-law's estate, he sent one of his project managers to inspect it with Stuart. He didn't need to. He already knew it well. And he wouldn't bother now, but for finding an excuse to cool his jets.

*Mariëlle.*

Alan glimpses what should be the contractor's shack—and must be—but it's too ... nice. He realizes it's the old sleeping cottage, tool shed, outbuilding thing, saved by chance from last fall's storm and fire. Dorian gave it some silly French name. Dorian he can remember. He's popped up on TV in this or that, and once Alanna dragged him to the theatre where Dorian was in one of its forgettable productions. Briony he wouldn't recognize if he passed her in the street, he's sure. Nor Lydia, probably. Alanna keeps up with these people intermittently—well, at least the women. He never thinks about them, couldn't care less about them, really. Forty years ago, he dismissed them as privileged little South End twats, spawn of the enemy class, card-carrying members of the bourgeoisie, and so on and so on, with their private language and high school familiarity and daddies who bought them cars. (Even if he was going out with one whose daddy bought her a car.)

The excavator grinds on, its metal teeth scraping the ground, peeling off thick layers of earth, lifting into the air, into a waiting truck bed. Alan, watching, finds the rhythm soothing. He is reminded of himself, aged five, watching the workmen pave the street in front of his house in Windsor Park. He remembers the primal smell of the caked gumbo earth and wet cement, which got into this blood because construction for him was never some default summer job—he sought it out, hungry to display his aptitude, his young body, his new working-class sensibility. He imagines himself again, on that excavator, conjoined to the thrusting of the boom and the spiking of the arm as it tears into the moist soil, imagines himself fucking Mariëlle deliriously.

The old Eadon property, former Black property now, is an expanding no-man's-land, vegetation blasted, concrete pad smashed up, earth gouged, all reminders of the cottage and its genteel world vanished. Alan recalls Eadon Lodge a white box shimmering in sunshine, the interior an arrangement of shadowy rooms, that high ceiling disappearing into gloom and cobwebs. He paid only passing attention to the great storm that crashed through the place at Thanksgiving last, unaware that his daughter's estranged husband had even bought lakeshore property until she blew into his and Alanna's in tears with the news. Sara is the apple of his eye and the crown of his labours, and he tolerated his son-in-law the way Berko had tolerated him, ready when the boy was ready to put away childish things. Berko lost his son in a freakish ballooning accident in Turkey. Alan was losing (had already lost? It doesn't bear thinking about) his son to meth, somewhere in Montreal.

The excavator stops in its movements, its engine switched to idle. Alan glances at his watch. Not yet noon. He arches an eyebrow at the operator in the cab who, though his eyes are wreathed in sunglasses, shows no sign he knows he's being observed. Alan gets it. He pulled this kind of shit, too, when he was young, to stick to the boss. But the operator doesn't spring from the cab, lunch pail in hand, smiling at release. He's lifted himself, awkwardly, from the seat as if transfixed by something in the excavator's bucket. He removes his eyewear, leans closer to the window. Then he switches the machine off, the hush of a summer day rushing in to take its place.

Puzzled, though not concerned, Alan watches the worker—young, fit, as he himself once was—scramble from the cab and hop heavy-booted to the ground. As he does, he glimpses Alan at his post by an old elm that weathered the storm—Alan all duded up in stripy polo shirt and pressed shorts, fresh from the golf course shower and an air-conditioned car. The young man seems to freeze, his body language projecting wariness. Alan can't read his facial expression at this distance, but something in the young man's stance draws him from his post.

"This is private property," he says, as if he had been taught to say it.

"I'm one of its developers, Alan Rayner."

"Oh ... shit, sorry."

"Is something going on?" He's reading now the uneasiness in the guy's small dark eyes. Possibly part Aboriginal, Alan guesses. The braid's a clue.

The guy gestures toward the bucket. At first Alan sees nothing of note amid the clay and stone. And then he does.

"Oh, Christ."

Alan knows, without knowing how he knows, that the mud-caked bones are not those of some animal. He himself has been with work crews when they inadvertently exhumed the bones of a dog or a bison when he worked construction those summers in the late sixties. He knows *that* is a human femur and *that* is a pelvic girdle and *that* is the rounded hollow of an eye of a human skull. Yet irritation overcomes repugnance. The bones exhumed by last Thanksgiving's storm contributed, at police insistence, to this spring's start date delay. Now, fuck, here we go again. This property is cursed. Construction will halt, an investigation will begin. Bloody winter will set in before construction can resume and they've already pre-sold three units with a scheduled June 2010 opening.

The young man beside him is expressionless, quiet, unmoving, as if awaiting instruction. With the excavator stopped, all that can be heard is the chatter of birds and the shush of waves lapping the shore. Alan thinks. He knows the right thing to do. But the right thing doesn't prevail in this business. He looks again at the slimy mess of bones poking from the blanket of dirt, notices a shred of cloth of some nature, faded purple, adhering to the femur, moves around to look into the cavity in the earth last gouged by the excavator's savage teeth and sees, yes, what must be more human remains. A fat beetle of some nature scurries over the remains. Alan's gorge rises. He looks up quickly, past the man, around the property, toward the shack.

"Are you the only one here?"

The man averts his eyes. "Ben had to go into town."

Uh huh. Ben's fucked off somewhere until the truck's filled. Sleeping on the beach or having a swim. These rural characters are such slackers. But, in this instance, that's okay. He puts his hand in his pocket and fingers the winnings from their side bet at golf, a wad of Stuart's fifties. That, plus what he already has, amounts to about seven hundred dollars. He studies the man's expression. So hard to read, these guys. Will he take the money? Would Alan have, forty years ago? Yes, he thinks, he would have: it would have been subversive, in the style of the day.

And he can appeal to the practicalities: if work is halted, this guy could be out of a job—or at least inconvenienced.

"Look," he says, "here's the deal. If we report this, work will stop, and for Christ knows how long. We don't know who this ... guy ... woman ... person might be ..." He glances at the man for a discernible reaction. There is none, but at least their eyes meet now. "It might be best if we just, you know, find another spot for him ... it. It'll mean a little extra work for you, but I can pay you some overtime right now. Okay? What's your name, by the way?"

"Noskye."

"Noskye," Alan repeats, smiling conspiratorially, wiggling his hand in his right pocket. "How would that be? Would that be okay?"

Noskye triangulates the bucket's contents, Alan's face, Alan's pocket. "Okay."

Alan glances again into the bucket. A flicker of doubt slows the hand that will leave the pocket, that will shake the hand, that will seal the deal. Those bones were some mother's son. Or daughter. But they were uncoffined (surely), they've been buried a long time, long before a cottage was ever here (surely), the grave unmarked, unvisited. This is no desecration. Alan is rationalizing, backtracking a bit. If this is some native burial site, ol' Noskye here isn't raising an objection. He extends his hand. His hand is met.

"Okay, then."

Alan's learned to love the dance of deal-making, however small. He's pleased with himself. He shifts back a little to let Noskye climb back up into the cab and as he does a glint of something metallic, caught in a ray of sunshine, teases the corner of his eye. He peers into the bucket, *what the hell is it?* Sees nothing, then he does. He holds up a warning hand to Noskye not to fire up the excavator and, revolted, brushes his fingers along the soil, gingerly past what looks like a finger bone, to pluck up the shiny tiny thing. He swipes off some of the gluey muck with his thumb, frowns at the exposed surface, at the distinctive markings. He's puzzled, but not at the markings' meaning. At something else. He rummages through flickering memory, *what the hell is it?* Recalls nothing.

Then he does.

# 37

"Something came for you this morning, by the way."

"What is it?"

"Well, how should I know, Dorian?"

Charmaine gives her client a vexed glance as she turns to her desk to root through the mail for the envelope. They're in her Yaletown office, standing by the window that overlooks the street. Really, she thinks, he's not looking his best, though, granted, the light streaming in this September 22 morning isn't flattering—to anyone over forty. It's been a couple of weeks since *Morningstar Cove* wrapped up and Dorian's been back in town, staying with friends in Maple Ridge. Too bad about Mark. He was a sort of a steadying influence. *Anyway, put the colour back in your hair, Dorian, for fuck's sake. You look like the old fart you played in the series.* She doesn't say this, of course, though she is worried about him—in her professional capacity: She had reports back from the *MC* set that a certain sparkle seemed absent in his performance. Fortunately—in a way—the series is wrapped forevermore. No third season. Therefore, no word that Dorian's character would be written out—drowned before the opening episode or something. It's a grafter's life, acting. A casting director called her the day before, seeking actors for the old Robert Young role for a pilot of an ABC reboot of *Marcus Welby, M.D.*, and her first—well, third—thought went to Dorian Grant, but, observing the slight tremor in his hand, she's giving him fourth thought. Early Parkinson's? Or is it the drinking? She's knows he used to be a bit fond of the bottle back in the '80s, '90s in Toronto. The DP at *Morningstar Cove* (an old high school friend, oddly enough) said she thought he might be hitting the sauce. But, like, whatever: it's never seriously compromised his craft. Lots of actors are big boozers: Richard

Burton, William Holden, Errol Flynn, Oliver Reed. Of course, they're all dead. *Were* big boozers. *Were.*

With Charmaine's back turned, Dorian's eyes go again to the pair of moose's antlers painted white high on the wall above her desk. *New?* Maybe they're the whimsy in the corporate-cliché monochrome Charmaine's going for, but to him they look like wings hacked from an angel's back. Clarence Odbody's wings, maybe, the ones he earned in *It's a Wonderful Life* for showing George Bailey the positive effect he had on other people's lives. *Who tore them off? And why?* They remind Dorian more of the antlers on the walls of Eadon Lodge, but he won't think about that now, he's tired of thinking about that. His nerves have been fraying for months. He's backed off calling Lydia. Hasn't told her that Dix's "mother's-agony" story is squeezed between recipes in the new issue of *Chatelaine.* Lydia's backed off calling him.

He takes the envelope from Charmaine's hand. His hand quivers, he notes with dismay. Since he's been back on the West Coast, "resting," as they say in the trade, he's been resting with a glass of vodka and peach cider never too far from reach. Michael and Lauren, whose basement flat he's renting, join him in the daily debauch, as they, too, are "resting," there being a bit of slowdown in Hollywood North, what with the Canadian dollar so strong these days. He's had a little eye-opener for breakfast, won't need another drink till late afternoon, so he's T'd up for this little strategy meeting with Charmaine. He needs to work. He's only himself on stage, on set, on camera.

The envelope is small, padded, the label neatly typed, addressed to him C/O KWUSEN TALENT MANAGEMENT INC., 1236 HOMER STREET, VANCOUVER, B.C. It's light, too. With a little lump inside. No return address. *Meh.* Dorian prepares to pocket it in his jacket.

"You're not going to open it?"

"I suppose I could. Would it give you pleasure, Charmaine, if I did?"

"Yes. Yes, it would. It might be like opening a box of Cracker Jack. There's something hard in there. I felt it when it arrived. Remember Cracker Jack with the little prize inside?"

"I'm as old as you are, darling."

"Not quite and fuck you." Charmaine pushes her ropes of ruby beads higher up the crepe of her neck as Dorian tears the top open. He reaches in, but his fingers are too big, the package too tight, to grasp the object slide to the bottom. He turns the envelope and shakes it over his hand. He feels something slight strike his palm.

"What is it?" Charmaine looks over the tops of her ruby frames at his hand. "Oh, it's a ring. How lovely! Mark changed his mind? Dorian ... ?"

Dorian stares at the silver band in his hand, strangled for words. A tremor tears along his flesh and the band tumbles to the carpet. Charmaine casts him an exasperated glance and bends awkwardly to pick it up.

"Oh! It's got peace symbols on it. How quaint." She examines it, slides it down a couple of fingers of her left hand in succession. It fits her fourth. She da-da-da-das the opening notes of Mendelssohn's wedding march. But Dorian has gone paler than one of her old clients when she told him Disney was dropping his contract over kiddie-porn rumours. Her smile falters. "Dorian ... darling, what is it?"

"It's nothing."

The faltering smile turns full frown. "Is there a note?" She sees his other hand still clutching the envelope.

"No note."

"I don't understand. Is someone returning it to you? Is the ring yours?"

"Is the ring mine?" Dorian hears his voice echo as if from a thousand miles away. "I couldn't possibly say."

# 38

It's a day for letters and happenstance.

Lydia is the only person in the house alert to the metallic rattle of the mailbox lid opening and closing, and her impulse—almost Pavlovian, born of solitary freelance days before Countervail Press and marriage when the post crowned the day—is to get up and go down to see what the world has fetched up to the door.

She's nearest the street, at the table in the dining room, coffee, a plate of orange slices, her new iPhone, her *Chicago Manual of Style* and laptop arrayed in front of her. Ray is sequestered at the back of the house, in his office overlooking the garden. Erin was up and out early, to class at Hastings Law School. Misaki is in her third week at Jefferson Scott Key elementary. Lydia walked her there a couple of hours earlier, watching her skip along and sing, glad that the disruptions to her life had not affected her, at least on the outside. The two of them ("the girls") are living now in the garage conversion, completed last month. Finally. Lydia loves them dearly, but a mother-and-child's messiness can strain her nerves. A whiff of new lumber and plaster and paint lingers still. Lydia can detect it beneath the perfume of the freesias on the sideboard, transporting her—but briefly—to Oxford Street and the redolence of her mother's renovations.

Also laid out on the table before her is a manuscript of selected writings in Milton critical studies, which she's editing for University of California Press. Lydia left Countervail in mid-July, a month after her birthday. She'd been there twenty-five years, the last eleven as editor-in-chief. She'd turned sixty. If she retired then, there'd be a nice symmetry to it, which was part of Ray's argument. You'll be much happier and healthier away from Cuntella, he insisted. And he's right. She has been lifted from the anxiety and despondency that's haunted her for a year, though not having to endure Cuntella's braying voice and absurd demands day in, day out, is less the reason than Ray supposes.

It's three months since she learned from Briony and Dorian that Eadon Lodge had fallen into the hands of Alan Rayner and his property development company and she's expected every day for the sky to blacken but, as days passed to weeks to months and the sky clung to blue, she crept from her slough of despair and began to imagine that, somehow, she and Dorian had been granted a boon from a god—Milton's very God, maybe—to whom she long ago lost allegiance. Even the attention given to Lits's bones—and they had to be Lits's; she had the cheek swab; the genetic connection was confirmed—failed to undo her, despite fifteen Warholian minutes of Winnipeg media interest.

Lydia eats the last slice of orange. Stickiness adheres to her fingers and stickiness is intolerable. She pushes back her chair, rises, and pushes through the swing door to the kitchen, with the plate, to remove the ick.

She told Ray about the bones—Lits's. She told him late that afternoon of her birthday, in this kitchen, by the refectory table, as he pumped a balloon inflator, before Helen and Joe and other friends arrived. She wept as she told him about the bones unearthed by the storm, about the RCMP request for a DNA sample, about her horror and shame, which had begun to overwhelm her, and which she understood—but did not say—was nothing more than a release for horror and shame too rooted to expose. And Ray, as usual, was wonderful—understanding and puzzled and relieved, all at once. This, too, he thought, is what's been gnawing at my wife's mind, as she has been gnawing at her own flesh. And he laughed as he dropped the balloon inflator and held her in his arms, because what else could you do but laugh? It happened so long ago and it had nothing to do with them and he didn't believe in that sins-of-the-father thing anyway.

Lydia washes her hands and takes a fresh towel from the rack under the wall calendar to dry her hands, averting her eyes, as she's done since January, from the calendar's upper part, from the artwork. For Ray it observes the work of German illustrator Heinz Edelmann.

For most everyone else, it observes the Beatles' animated musical, *Yellow Submarine,* a film she has never seen, never wants to see. Ray told her when he tacked the calendar up (because he remembers that collegiate madness forty years ago, too) that the eponymous song supplied another "clue." According to the nutty conspiracy theorists, in the nautical voice section of the "Yellow Submarine" John Lennon says, "Paul is dead, dead man, dead man." Ray offered to put the CD on. No, thanks, Lydia shuddered then, shudders now. Three more months and the noxious reminder can come off the wall. Ray's already bought 2010's—twelve months of Arthur Rackham's illustrations.

Much better.

Lydia's eyes land on the calendar's lower part, however. It's September 22. "Autumn begins" the text box informs her. A British calendar, though she'd already gathered that from the absence of text boxes for Presidents' Day and Memorial Day. Here, in the U.S., autumn is called "fall." "Fall begins." The thought resonates, not pleasantly. She reflects on the manuscript she is editing. Milton describes another kind of fall.

Enough of that.

She turns back to the dining room, recalls suddenly the mail, the tiny treat of her freelance days, and turns instead to the stairs. The smell of new construction grows more intense as she descends to the door, but the air outside, when she pushes open the door, is sweet and cool, the last of the morning fog burned away. The green border of Golden Gate Park across the street shimmering in the sunshine draws first notice. But something nearer catches the corner of her eye—a sweet little dumpling of a bird lifeless on the tiles. Did it hit the window above? She didn't hear it. Her heart contracts with pity, but a kind of dread follows swiftly. She can't bury it. *God, no.* She can't touch it. She can't bear it. A dead bird holds an old memory; Briony thought it a portent all those years ago at Eadon Lodge. She'll interrupt Ray. He won't mind.

Quickly, as if the dead thing might come alive, she lifts the mailbox lid on its rusty hinges, reaches in, pulls out a bundle, and shuts the door behind her. Relieved now, she glances at the top item, her copy of the *New Yorker,* and as she climbs back up the stairs fingers through the rest—the flyers, a Lands' End catalogue, the Amex and PG&E bills, something official looking with a Japanese stamp for Erin, a realtor's brochure. Her eyes fall on a handwritten return address on a letter peeking from behind a Chinese take-out menu. She stops. She's reached the landing now. She pulls the envelope out. It's addressed to her in a hand that reminds her vaguely of her father's, strong, cursive, masculine. Puzzled, she pivots the letter a little, because the writer has placed the return address along the short side.

Matthew Rafiel, she reads, returning to the dining room and dropping the rest of the post on the table. And the address—in Palo Alto, not far. She fingers the envelope, feels the first twitch of unease. The paper is heavy, linen-based, stark white against her raw pink thumb, still healing from protracted gnawing. She tilts the envelope to the window light. The sheen of the ink suggests a fountain pen. The postage, ninety-five cents, reflects its weight. The letter is hefty. It's plump.

It's important.

But it's the first name that stirs her consciousness and loosens her memory, focusing her vague anxiety into an admixture of dread and excitement. Did she write her chosen name, "Matthew," down on some form at the hospital all those years ago? Did Helen mention it to the social worker, to a nurse? Was it somehow conveyed to the young childless couple that left with her baby? Or did they simply pluck it from the air, as she did, only to learn later it was one of the most popular names for newborns of the day?

It doesn't matter. It doesn't matter

Her heart is tripping now. She can't quell it. She's had dreams and nightmares and fantasies about this moment for forty years and yet never in her waking hours has she known what she will do, how she will act, how she will *re*act. The spectre of Huntington's disease has intruded on her thoughts since Dorian's disclosure. Should *she* begin a search for her lost son? But what could she do for him? What difference would it make? On this, she's powerless.

She turns the envelope over, runs a trembling finger over the sealed flap, brushes the thin seam which lies between her and certainty, between her and doom, between her and joy. Her heart pounds in her chest as if some small animal were trapped inside. What should she do? She's frozen in indecision. She wants to cry, but she can't, not now. She needs a private hour, two, three. And when will she next get those? When Erin and Misaki are visiting Erin's mother in San Mateo this weekend. When Ray's teaching his Saturday class at Fort Mason. And—*oh, god*—she can hear him in the kitchen, pottering around, pouring a last cup of coffee, cutting some piece of fruit. *What if he comes in?* The bird! The bird on the tiles outside. It's the poor dead bird that is upsetting her, that is making her pale and weepy.

And he is coming in. Ray is coming in. He is near the door.

And her phone is ringing.

She shoves the envelope quickly under her style guide. Her eyes dart to the screen.

It's Dorian.

# ACKNOWLEDGMENTS

Paul is dead, but as of September, 2018, the following are not, and for their assistance in various ways, I am most grateful: Neila Benson, Lorne Bunyan, David Carr, Dean Cooke, Karen Haughian, Michael Phillips, Lesley Sisler, Paige Sisley, Lewis St. George Stubbs, David Stackiw, John Whiteway, and Snolaug Whiteway.

The author gratefully acknowledges the assistance of the Manitoba Arts Council and the Winnipeg Arts Council.